# *the*
# yadayada
## *Prayer Group*
# GETS CAUGHT

# *the* yadayada *Prayer Group* GETS CAUGHT

*a Novel*

## neta jackson

INTEGRITY®
PUBLISHERS
*Nashville*

*Jac*

THE YADA YADA PRAYER GROUP GETS CAUGHT

Published by Integrity Publishers, a Division of Integrity Media, Inc.,
660 Bakers Bridge Ave., Franklin, TN 37067.

HELPING PEOPLE WORLDWIDE EXPERIENCE *the* MANIFEST PRESENCE *of* GOD.

Published in association with the literary agency of Alive Communications, Inc., 7680 Goddard Street, Suite 200, Colorado Springs, CO 80920.

Scripture quotations are taken from the following: The Holy Bible, New International Version. Copyright © 1973, 1978, 1984, International Bible Society. Used by permission of Zondervan Bible Publishers. The Holy Bible, New Living Translation®. Copyright © 1996. Used by permission of Tyndale House Publishers, Inc., Wheaton, Illinois 60189. All rights reserved. The New King James Version®. Copyright © 1982 by Thomas Nelson, Inc., Publishers. Used by permission. All rights reserved.

This novel is a work of fiction. Any references to real events, businesses, organizations, and locales are intended only to give the fiction a sense of reality and authenticity. Any resemblance to actual persons, living or dead, is entirely coincidental.

Cover design: Brand Navigation, LLC I Mark Mickel I www.brandnavigation.com
Cover Photo: Steve Gardner I Pixelworks Studio I www.shootpw.com
Interior design: Inside Out Design & Typesetting

*Library of Congress Cataloging-in-Publication Data*
Jackson, Neta.
The yada yada prayer group gets caught / by Neta Jackson.
   p.  cm.
Summary: "The Yada Yada girls get caught in the lies we all tend to believe about ourselves, God, each other, and life"—Provided by publisher.

ISBN-13: 9-781-59145-361-1
ISBN-10: 1-59145-361-5 (tradepaper)

1. Women—Illinois—Fiction.  2. Female friendship—Fiction.  3. Christian women—Fiction.  4. Chicago (Ill.)—Fiction.  5. Prayer groups—Fiction.
I. Title.
PS3560.A2415Y333   2006
813'.54—dc22

2006017104

*Printed in the United States of America*
06 07 08 09 10 VG 9 8 7 6 5 4 3 2

*To my own precious grandchildren,*

*Havah Noelle and Liam Isaac,*

*God's gift of life and laughter*

# Prologue

WEDNESDAY, JULY 2, 2003
11 A.M.—DOWNTOWN CHICAGO, ILLINOIS

*I*t might not be a champagne-colored Lexus, but Chanda George was having a hard time containing the bubbles of happiness threatening to uncork right there in the backseat of the North Suburban Yellow Taxi. *Ooo, Lord, Lord. Thank You, Jesus.* It felt good to climb into a car and say, "Take me to dis address, mon," then sit back and let the cabbie drive her around, as if she were a pop star. She'd had it up to *here* with city buses and commuter trains—her only transportation since she'd arrived from Jamaica ten years ago with a green card and a toddler on her hip. Standing at bus stops and on el platforms in Chicago's bitter winters with two, then three babies clinging to her skirts had defined her existence for the past decade. Single mom. Working poor. Tired.

Never again. She was going to call a cab whenever she wanted.

Maybe even a limo. Till she got that Lexus with the leather seats, anyway. Wouldn't be long now.

A giggle escaped. She'd won *again*. Not the lottery this time. But that nice man on the telephone told her she'd been "specially selected" to receive one of four major prizes. *Mm-hm. Dis mama be one lucky woman*, she thought. *Can feel it in mi baby finger*. She smoothed out the wrinkles in the silk print skirt hugging her thighs. Then she frowned and sucked her teeth. *Nah, nah. Don' you be takin' all de credit, Chanda George. God's favor be what it is. Smilin' down on you like—*

"Mama!" A tug on the sleeve of her silk print blouse jerked her back to the stale interior of the yellow cab, the smell of ancient cigarettes clinging to the upholstery. "Mama! Which prize you gonna get?" Her twelve-year-old chafed at the tie around his shirt collar, which was rapidly turning damp in the July heat. "Hope you get that red SUV. It's got a TV in the back an' a DVD player!"

"You hush, Thomas." She pronounced it To-*mas*, the way they called her daddy back in Kingston. "What we need dat big truck for! Mi take cash—or maybe dat free vacation to Hawaii. You like dat, now, eh?" The taxi slowed and Chanda glanced out the window. "Oh. Must be we here now. Tuck your shirt back in, mister."

The taxi double-parked, making traffic pull around them. Chanda looked at the red digits on the meter: $16.05. She fished a twenty out of her bulky purse and handed it over the seat. "Keep de change."

Thomas was already out the door and onto the sidewalk. Chanda struggled out of the backseat, tugging at her slip and the silk print skirt, which threatened to hike up the back of her legs. She took in the building with shaded eyes. She'd expected one of the big downtown hotels—maybe even the press, taking pictures of "the lucky two-time winner" for the evening news. But the building was low-slung, plain, brick. Big green plants inside the doors. Downtown, but not the Loop.

No TV news vans lurking about.

But a cheerful printed sign taped to the double-glass doors said VACATION GETAWAYS—MAKE YOUR DREAMS COME TRUE. GLASS SLIPPER VACATIONS. WELCOME, PRIZE WINNERS! Chanda smiled and licked her lips. Shrugging her heavy bag over her shoulder, she grabbed Thomas with one hand and pulled open one of the doors with the other.

Didn't matter if Glass Slipper Vacations handed her the prize money in a posh hotel or in a born-again warehouse. She'd won, hadn't she?

This was her lucky day.

## 2 P.M.—CORNERSTONE MUSIC FESTIVAL, BUSHNELL, ILLINOIS

Garbage detail. *Gross.*

Muttering under his breath, fourteen-year-old Chris Hickman pulled a full bag out of a can, tied it off, dragged it to the side of the service road, and shook out a clean plastic garbage bag. At least garbage pickup was one notch up from cleaning the showers yesterday. Now, *that* was nasty.

Still, once he put in his four hours each day with the work crew of kids from Uptown Community Church, he was free to hang out listening to the music fest bands. He'd counted a dozen music stages on the Cornerstone grounds, some of them starting at noon and going until midnight. The bands on the main stage each night really rocked—Relient K, Rez Band, a bunch of others—even with their Jesus-this, Jesus-that lyrics. Sound jacked up to damage decibels. Hands waving, bodies swaying. People diving off the stage. And they weren't even stoned!

Chris grasped the neck of his green volunteer T-shirt and mopped the sweat off his face, glad that Cornerstone was a hundred miles from Chicago. It wouldn't go down with his homies back on the bricks if they saw him wearing the wrong colors. He was still a "shorty," a new recruit to the Disciples. Hadn't proved himself yet.

Ducking into the next tent, a booth selling all kinds of Jesus T-shirts, Chris looked around for the trash can. But his eyes snapped to a guy with a spiky Mohawk on one side of the tent airbrushing caricatures onto shirts. Chris sidled over to watch. A white girl with tiny rings in her nose and her lip and a stud in her tongue posed for her caricature. "Make it say, 'I love Jesus.'" She grinned. "That'll freak out my parents."

Chris watched the caricature take shape. Not bad. But he could do better. *Had* done better, though he usually had the wall of a building to work with. But the airbrush didn't look that different from using a can of spray paint. "Can I try?" he blurted.

The guy with the Mohawk looked up and frowned. He tipped his head at Chris's green Cornerstone T-shirt. "You a volunteer? They send you over to help?"

"Uh, yeah. I'm a volunteer."

"You got any experience? How old are you, anyway?"

Chris thought of all the el underpasses he'd decorated. "Yeah.

Lots of experience. A bit different, but I can do this." He ignored the question about his age.

The Mohawk guy handed the girl her T-shirt and took her twenty-dollar bill. "I dunno. Can't afford to mess up any shirts." He glanced up as a young guy, maybe twenty or so, bypassed the ready-made T-shirts and headed their way. "Need help, buddy?"

"Hope so." College kid. Clean-cut. "I'd like a T-shirt with a picture of Jesus walking on the water, you know, during the storm, and beckoning to Peter. With the words, 'Come to Me.'"

"Look, man, we don't really do—"

"I can do it."

Mohawk guy and college kid both stared at Chris.

"I can do it. Let me try." Chris licked his lips. Could he do it? He knew that story from Sunday school. Once he saw a picture in a Bible storybook. But the picture had been drawn from Peter's point of view looking at Jesus. Something about it didn't set right to Chris. He'd love to turn it around.

The college kid grinned. "Why not? Let him try."

Mohawk guy shrugged. "It's your money. If he messes up a shirt, somebody's gotta pay for it."

A white T-shirt was stretched on an easel. Chris tried out the airbrushes for a minute or two on some butcher paper, getting the feel for the colors, then set to work. A quiver of excitement expanded in his gut until his insides felt giddy. All he could think about was the picture taking shape on the material in front of him. The back of Jesus in the foreground, gnarly hair whipping in the wind, waves splashing about His feet, one hand reaching out toward a floundering boat in the background . . .

Chris glanced furtively at the college kid, who slouched easily in the chair the girl had vacated. The figure in the boat took shape, leaning out over the choppy water, hand outstretched, longing in his face.

A shadow fell over Chris's shoulder as he started in on the lettering: *Come to Me.* Mohawk guy sucked in his breath. "Well, I'll be damned."

"What?" The college kid got up. He came around and looked at the drawing on the shirt. "Why . . . that's me stepping out of the boat." He swallowed. "Wow."

"There you are!" Chris jumped when he heard the familiar voice. "We've been looking all over for you, Hickman." Josh Baxter entered the tent, followed by José Enriques and Pete Spencer. All in Cornerstone green. The garbage crew from Uptown Community. "Come on, man. We've got work to do."

"Just a minute." Mohawk guy held up a hand. "I could use this kid."

"On his own time, then. We've got a ton of garbage to pick up. *Now*, Hickman."

"Wait up. You draw this, *amigo*?" José Enriques, fifteen, peered at the T-shirt on the easel. "That's *good*, man—OK, OK, Baxter. We're comin'."

Chris flushed at the praise as they climbed into the waiting service cart, piled high with plastic garbage bags. José was all right. Latinos were *the enemy* back on the bricks. But that was there. This was now. And he'd just tagged the best piece of his life.

## 3 A.M.—CHICAGO'S SOUTH SIDE

The toddler screamed on her hip, his nose running, but the young woman holding him with one arm didn't even try to soothe him as she hit the speed dial on her cordless. *Please, Mom, pick it up . . . please, please . . .*

"Rochelle!" A male voice yelled from the bedroom. "Can't you make that kid shut up? I'm trying to get some sleep here."

"Shh, shh," she whispered to the little boy. Sure, her husband was trying to get some sleep—after coming in at two. With no explanation. He was the one who woke up the baby, turning on the lights, yelling at her, telling her not to mess in his business when she asked where he'd been. *Oh, please, Mama . . .*

But the answering machine on the other end kicked in. *"Hello. We can't take your call right now—"*

She clicked the Off button. She couldn't leave a message on their answering machine. They might return the call, and Dexter might answer the phone. *No, no. She'd just have to go up there. But what if her mom wasn't home? She couldn't just wait out on the street, not with the baby—not at night. Not in this heat.*

"Who you callin' this time of night, woman?" His voice was so close, so heavy with threat, that Rochelle jumped, dropping the phone. The toddler in her arms only screamed louder.

"I . . . I, uh—"

Her husband was wearing only his boxers, his body hard and lean from working out at the gym. They made a handsome couple, everybody said. And when he started putting on those muscles, her girlfriends really crowed. *"Oh, girl, that man is so fine" . . . "You better watch out, some ho gonna steal him" . . . "You ever don't want him, throw him to me!"*

Slowly, deliberately, Dexter picked up the phone and punched a button, peering at the LED readout. "Your mother." Sarcasm dripped off the words. "Now, girl, what you gonna go call your mother for this time of night?"

He stepped closer. In her face. She felt his hand reach behind her and take hold of her hair—the long, thick fall of kinky curls every beauty shop in town envied—pulling her head back, back until her throat stretched upward and she was staring into his cold, narrow eyes. She could feel his strength. Pain shot up the back of her head from his tight grip on her hair. Fear dried out her mouth as one thought pulsed in her brain: *With one snap, he could break my neck.*

The toddler stopped screaming, as if mesmerized by the tension between his parents. In the sudden silence, Rochelle, frozen in his grip, heard Dexter's voice next to her ear. Low. Menacing. "Don't you be thinking about leaving me, Rochelle. Or taking my baby. Or you gonna regret the day you step out of this house."

# 1

*J*'d been married to the guy for twenty years, and he still didn't get it. Crowds. I hated big crowds. He knew that. So why was he asking me again?

"You go," I said, climbing up the short, wobbly stepladder and pouring birdseed into the feeder dangling from one corner of the garage roof. "Stuff yourself. Have a blast. Just"—I backed down the three steps on the miniladder—"take the cell phone and let me know when you're on the way home." I stuck the stepladder into the garage and headed for the back porch of our two-flat.

"Aw, c'mon, Jodi." Denny sounded like a teenager who'd just been told he couldn't have the car keys. "The Taste is no fun going alone. And there's only two more days. I'd take Amanda and Josh if they were here, but they're blasting their eardrums out at Cornerstone," he grumbled. "They were gone last summer too. I haven't been to the Taste in two years!"

I glanced at him sharply. Yeah, the kids had been gone this time last summer—on that mission trip to Mexico. But that wasn't the reason Denny had missed the Taste of Chicago last year. I'd just gotten out of the hospital after getting banged up in a car accident and the Fourth of July slid right past us unnoticed, like the Energizer Bunny on Mute. But if Denny didn't remember, I sure wasn't going to bring it up.

"You don't have to go by yourself." I was doggedly cheerful. The prospect of a long, quiet summer evening at home alone was sounding more and more appealing by the second. No kids, no husband even, who, God love him, was still *male* and took up a large portion of the house and my psyche. A girl needed a break now and then. "Call one of your friends. Take Ben Garfield. He's probably driving Ruth crazy anyway. She'll kiss your feet for getting him out of the house."

I flopped down on the porch swing and reclaimed my plastic tumbler of iced tea, sweating in a puddle where I'd set it near Willie Wonka's inert body. The rhythmic rise and fall of the chocolate-haired rib cage assured me the old dog was still with us.

I raised the iced tea to my lips, vaguely thinking it'd been fuller than this when I set it down—and over the rim saw Denny still standing in front of me, hands stuffed into the pockets of his jeans, shoulders hunched like one of Peter Pan's lost boys. "What?"

"I don't want to go with Ben. I want to go with you."

I rolled my eyes. *Cheater! Villain!* My visions of solitude, peace and quiet, that Ernest Gaines novel I was dying to read with only our dear deaf dog and a good fan for company evaporated as quickly as spit on a hot iron.

Denny Baxter knew exactly how to shoot his arrow into my Achilles heel.

"You really want me to go?"

"Yes."

I sighed. "All right. But, mister, you owe me one."

The dimples on either side of Denny's mouth creased into irresistible parentheses. "Hey, it's going to be fun! We need some time together while the kids are gone—not talking about serious stuff or anything, you know, just having a good time. Pick your poison! Jerk chicken . . . ribs slathered in barbecue sauce . . . Italian ice . . . that Totally Turtle Cheesecake at Eli's . . ." My husband's eyes closed in anticipatory bliss of sampling the city's finest eateries, whose yearly ten-day culinary extravaganza on Chicago's lakefront always culminated on July Fourth weekend. "And we can watch the fireworks tonight from Buckingham Fountain," he added.

That was tempting. Chicago always did a big show on Independence Eve. I'd heard that the fireworks were coordinated with a fantastic light show at the city's signature fountain along with a live concert by the Grant Park Symphony. And Denny had a point about "just having fun." The past two months had taken a huge toll on us—emotionally for sure, but physically and spiritually too. Some good things had happened, like Josh's graduation from high school and that awesome celebration we'd had last Sunday morning when our church and New Morning Christian met together in their new space in the Howard Street shopping center. But the recent hate group incidents on Northwestern University's campus, the so-called free speech rally that had just been a cover-up for spewing hate and fear, and the cowardly attack that had left our friend Mark Smith in a coma for two weeks—*that* had been tough. Tough on Nony and Mark's family, tough on the Baxter family, tough on the whole Yada Yada Prayer Group.

Though, I had to admit, we did learn a thing or two about "get-

3

ting tough" spiritually. All of us had felt helpless and angry at the twisted attitudes and sheer evil behind that attack on Mark. But we discovered prayer was a spiritual weapon we could wield with abandon. Praise too. That was a new reality for me, but it made sense. As Avis pointed out at one of our Yada Yada prayer meetings, the devil can't do his rotten work too well in an atmosphere filled with praise and worship for his main Adversary.

I chugged the rest of my iced tea. "OK, so when do you want to leave? Parking's going to be a nightmare." I'd heard the Taste drew thousands of hungry palates. I shuddered. Didn't want to think about it. Threading through waves of sweaty flesh. Trying to ignore all the bouncy boobs in skimpy tank tops. Dreading the inevitable visit to the rows of Porta-Potties . . .

Denny pulled open the back screen door, a droll grin still lurking on his face. "Soon as we can get ready. Don't have to worry about parking if we take CTA." The screen door slammed behind him.

"What are you smirking about?" I yelled after him.

The screen door cracked open, and he poked his head out. "Didn't want to tell you, but since you asked." His dimples deepened wickedly. "Willie Wonka slurped up the top third of your iced tea while you were feeding the birds. In case you wondered."

The screen door slammed again as I let the plastic tumbler fly.

I'D FINISHED REFILLING A COUPLE OF WATER BOTTLES and adding them to the sunscreen, sunglasses, and windbreaker in my backpack when I heard someone at the back screen door. "Hey, Jodi."

I looked up. "Hi, Becky! And who's that cutie hiding behind you? Andy Wallace! I see you!"

Our upstairs neighbor—well, the long-term "guest" of our upstairs neighbor—stood at the back door, still sporting her new haircut and color, a rich brunette with auburn highlights swinging chin length in front of her ears and short and feathered in the back, courtesy of Adele's Hair and Nails. Behind her, a tousled head of dark curls peeked out from behind his mother's skin-tight jeans. Little Andy giggled.

"Come on in, you guys." I held open the screen door. "Denny and I are leaving in a few minutes—kids away, parents play, know what I mean? But I didn't know Andy was coming to visit this weekend. Is he staying for the holiday?" I felt like I was babbling, but I often felt like that around Becky, trying to fill in the gaps of awkward conversation.

"Uh, that's kinda why I came down." Becky cleared her throat. "Didn't mean to eavesdrop, but with the heat an' all, I had all the windows open upstairs, an' I heard you an' Denny talkin' 'bout goin' to see the fireworks downtown. And, uh, I, uh . . ." Becky cleared her throat again. I tensed. Was she going to ask if she could go with us? But she knew better than that! She was on house arrest for another four months, and that electronic monitor thing she wore strapped to her ankle would alert the authorities quicker than Instant Messaging if she left the premises. ". . . uh, was wonderin' if you guys would mind takin' Little Andy with you." Her left hand fell gently on the little boy's head as she drew him even closer to her side. "He ain't never seen no fireworks before."

A dozen thoughts tumbled around in my brain as I searched for an answer. Becky Wallace had come a long way since she'd first appeared at our *front* door last summer with a ten-inch butcher knife, desperate for money to spring a heroin fix. *Huh.* God sure had a weird sense of humor. The woman who'd robbed and terrorized our whole Yada Yada Prayer Group that night was now standing at my back door like any other mom, talking about fireworks and the Fourth of July.

Well, like any other mom who'd taken a detour through drug rehab and prison.

I stalled. Dragging a three-year-old along wasn't exactly what Denny had in mind when he said the two of us needed to just have fun. "Uh, did you ask Stu?" Leslie Stuart, Yada Yada's fix-everybody social worker, rented the apartment upstairs and had taken Becky in as a housemate when she'd been paroled. "She'd probably love to take Andy to the Evanston fireworks tomorrow night—they're closer than the ones downtown. Evanston does the Fourth up big, too, with a parade and everything. Might be more fun for Andy."

"Nah. That ain't gonna happen. Stu said she's goin' to some family reunion or somethin' tomorrow. Leavin' first thing in the morning. I'd take Andy if I could." Becky looked at the monitor on her ankle and shrugged. "But if it's too much trouble . . ."

I stared. Stu going to a family *reunion*? In the entire year-plus I'd known Stu, she'd only mentioned her parents once and had never visited them as far as I knew. I wasn't even sure they lived in the Chicago area any more. In fact, Stu acted as if she and her parents weren't exactly on speaking terms, though who rejected whom wasn't clear either.

"Uh, well . . ." I felt caught between Andy's big eyes, peering at me hopefully from behind his mother's leg, and my husband's expectations. Taking Andy could be kind of fun—except for the extra trips to the Porta-Potties. "Tell you what. Let me talk it over with Denny. Give me ten minutes, OK?"

WE TOOK ANDY.

When I told him my dilemma, Denny rolled his eyes and muttered something that would probably earn an R-rating from Pastor Clark. But we both finally agreed that Becky didn't have many options when it came to doing things with Andy. House arrest was house arrest. And we still had two more days until our kids came home from the Cornerstone Music Festival to get some one-on-one time together. A holiday weekend at that.

I threw in some antibacterial handwipes for those trips to the Porta-Potties and packed raisins and granola bars in case "curry goat" and "jerk chicken" weren't on Andy's list of What Three-Year-Olds Eat. And once Denny shifted gears from twosome to threesome, he took Andy under his wing as we hustled to catch the Red Line.

"Hey, hey, we gotta run, Little Guy, and catch that train!"

"My name ain't Little Guy. It's *Andy*."

"What? Candy? Whoever heard of a boy named Candy?"

Squeals of laughter. "Not Candy. *Andy!*"

"Whatever you say, Little Guy."

On the el train, Andy crawled up on Denny's lap and the two of them pressed their noses to the window as the train snaked up-close and personal along the backsides of brick apartment buildings. They made quite a pair. Denny, short brown hair with sexy flecks of gray running through it, looking every inch the athletic coach he was at West Rogers High School. And Little Andy, his skin a milky brown, highlighting his mixed parentage. Definitely "hot chocolate with whipped cream," as Becky Wallace liked to say.

"Hey, Little Guy. See the flower boxes on those windows? That building is so close! Look, here they come! Should I pick some for Miss Jodi? Huh? Huh? . . . Oh, too late. We were going too fast."

"Aw. You can't pick dose flowers, Big Guy. The window ain't open!" Curly Top dissolved into giggles.

We transferred to the Brown Line at Belmont, which took us around Chicago's Loop—the heart of downtown—and got off at State and Van Buren, at which point it was only a three-block walk to Grant Park and the lakefront. I trailed along with the backpack as Andy pulled Denny forward, excited to get to "the Paste." OK, if Denny was going to ride herd on Andy, maybe this wouldn't be so bad after all.

We bought a roll of food tickets at one of the ticket booths and wandered down the long line of eateries lining Columbus Drive, which was blocked off to traffic. Reggio's Pizza . . . Vee-Vee's African Cuisine . . . Sweet Baby Ray's . . . Taqueria Los Comales . . . Jamaica Jerk . . . "Oh, babe," Denny said, licking his lips. "This is almost better than . . ." He waggled his eyebrows at me, knowingly.

I punched his arm. "Ow," he complained. "I said *almost*."

Andy was more interested in the popcorn vendor and the ice cream cart jingling its way between the long rows of eateries. I said yes to the popcorn and no to the ice cream, while Denny ordered a prime rib quesadilla for himself at the Grill on the Alley, and a grilled lime chicken chopped salad for me. He looked so funny with salsa dripping off his chin that I started to laugh. "You're a pig, you know that, Denny Baxter?"

Denny stuffed another bite of quesadilla in his mouth, unapologetic. "No rules, no manners, just food heaven," he deadpanned—though with his mouth full, it came out *no ruves, no mannerves, juf foo' heav'n.* I just rolled my eyes at him and tackled my lime chicken salad with a plastic fork.

"OK, next pit stop," he said, licking off his fingers. "But maybe we better get Andy something first. Whatchu want, Little Guy?" He looked this way and that, then looked straight at me. "Jodi, where's Andy?"

"Andy? I thought you . . ." I spun around in a circle. Nothing but bodies in front of, in back of, on all sides of me. Big bodies. Skinny bodies. Babies in strollers. Towheaded wailers dragged along by the hand.

But no Andy.

# 2

*I* gasped for breath, my insides flopping about like a fish stranded on the beach. *He can't be lost! He was here just a second ago.* "Andy?" I yelled, adding my voice to Denny's. "Andy!" But in the babble of languages, rowdy laughter, and music thrumming all around me, I knew it was useless.

Denny grabbed my arm. "You stay here, where he saw us last. I'll look."

"Wait!" I yelled after Denny's back, but in moments, I lost sight of him, swallowed up by the crowd.

"That's stupid," I muttered. "How does he know Andy went *that* way?" I took a few steps in the opposite direction, squinting down the endless rows of vendors and booths. But all I could see was a swarm of T-shirts, strollers, and baseball caps.

The reality of the situation sank to the bottom of my stomach like a heavy stone with my emotions tied to it. *Oh God, Oh God, Oh God . . .* Tears threatened my vision. I wiped them away angrily. *God! This can't be happening! He isn't even our own kid! Becky trusted us with him! I can't go home and tell her, "Andy's gone. We lost him. Sorry."*

I danced impatiently on my toes. I should go looking *now*, not stay here! How far could a kid get in two minutes? He's only three. Unless—

Panic rose in my throat. What if somebody snatched him? Lured him away with promises of ice cream or kittens or—

I started to run. "Andy?" I screamed. "Andy!" Trying to avoid a double stroller, I plowed into a man with a large paunch, both hands balancing paper boats of noodle-something. "Watch it, lady," he growled, holding the food high.

"S-sorry. I . . . my little boy, he's . . ." I stumbled away.

"Lost kid?" the man called after me. "Notify security, lady. Orange vests."

*Security . . . orange vests . . .*

I whirled this way and that. No orange vests. "Oh God, Oh God," I moaned.

*Jodi! Stop!* The Voice in my head snatched me up short. *Go back. Stay where you were, or Denny will waste time looking for you too.*

I knew I wasn't thinking straight. I wanted to keep running, yelling, doing *something* to find Andy. But, yes, I needed to go back. Denny was right. I should stay at the last place we'd seen Andy— the last place he'd seen us.

I took a deep breath and willed my feet to go back. The Grill's placard, listing its menu items, came back into view. I searched the two lines waiting at the booth, hoping against hope that Andy would be standing there, crying, wondering where we'd gone.

But . . . still no Andy. No Denny either.

I wanted to bawl. But instead, I sniffled my cries into a prayer.

*Jesus, I need You bad. Please help us find Andy. Please, Jesus! Protect him. Send all those warrior angels to guard his life, his safety—for Becky's sake. And for mine. I can't . . . I can't lose another mother's child . . .*

Suddenly, clear as day, I knew the devil was just waiting to accuse me, to drag me down, fill me with fear. But fear wasn't going to help. This wasn't about me or the car accident last summer or that other mother's kid. This was just about finding Andy.

*Think, Jodi. Think like a three-year-old. Where would you wander off to? Where would you want to go?*

I glanced around, not in panic this time but taking in my surroundings. The crowds of people seemed to shrink into the background as I tried to see what Andy might see. Like the ice cream cart we'd seen earlier, propelled by the back end of a bicycle. Or the balloon man over there making—

Balloon animals.

I don't remember whether I ran or walked or flew the hundred feet to where a middle-aged man in a black hat, a huge drooping moustache, and striped suspenders was twisting long sausage balloons into all sorts of critters for the admiring crew of children clustered around him. "Make a g'raff!" shouted a little boy's voice, a voice with a giggle. "A *purple* g'raff!"

I gulped relief like life-giving air.

Andy.

THE THREE OF US—Andy, me, and the purple balloon giraffe— were standing in front of the Grill on the Alley when Denny hustled up with a female security guard in an orange vest. Denny's face lit up when he saw Andy, shot a funny glance at me, then offered a sheepish shrug at the security guard. "Guess the lost is found. Sorry."

The guard waved a hand and walked on. "That's how we like it to turn out."

Denny squatted down to Andy's level. "Hey, Little Guy! You scared the heck outta me! I couldn't find you."

"See my g'raff?" Andy waggled the purple balloon in Denny's face. "His name is Purple Guy. He's hungry."

Denny's grin wobbled. "Yeah. Me too." He straightened up. "Bet I know what he wants."

"Pizza!"

Personally, I was hoping we could head back, avoid any more big crowds, forget the fireworks, just focus on getting home in one piece. But, according to Andy, Purple Guy *needed* a slice of pizza. And he *needed* to see fireworks.

So we stayed. We even found a great place to sit on the low wall running along both sides of Buckingham Fountain, mesmerized as the water bounced and sprayed, lit up with brilliant, ever-changing shades of rainbow hues. But wouldn't you know it, Andy fell asleep before the first rockets shot into the air over Lake Michigan; he didn't even wake up when the ones with big booms shot brilliant white lights in all directions. Just stirred from time to time, snuggling deeper under Denny's protective arm.

Denny slipped his other arm around my shoulder and pulled me close. "Kinda takes you back, doesn't it?" he murmured between booms and falling twinkles above our heads, his eyes fixed on Andy's face, angelic in sleep. "Maybe we—"

"Denny!" I pulled away from him, aghast. "Maybe we nothing! We're over forty!"

"So? Look at Ruth Garfield. She's pregnant, and she's almost fifty."

"*Denny!* Be serious. You know getting pregnant at her age is a big risk. All sorts of things could go wrong."

Three big booms went off in a row, followed by brilliant corkscrews of light in red, white, and blue. Andy stirred. Denny sighed. "Yeah, I know. But maybe we shouldn't have stopped at two. Three kids. Or four. That'd be nice." He shifted Andy's weight, brushing back the curls from the boy's sweaty forehead.

I giggled. "Yeah, but I guarantee they wouldn't be cute three-year-olds at this point. They'd all be *teenagers*. And we've already got two of those."

But Denny's musings left me unsettled. Ruth Garfield. Forty-nine going on fifty and *pregnant*. Hoo boy. After several miscarriages and a foster daughter who'd been reclaimed by the natural mother, Ruth had seemed resigned to childlessness. Which was fine by her husband, Ben, who was at least ten years her senior and looking forward to retirement. Then Ruth had missed several Yada Yada meetings the past couple of months. *"Not to worry,"* she'd said, waving off our concern. *"What's a little stomach upset?"*

Some stomach upset.

The doctor told her she was almost three months. Due around Christmas.

Ben had blown a cork. Acted as if Ruth had gone behind his back or something. Pushing her to get an abortion before something went terribly wrong . . .

The finale burst into the sky over Lake Michigan, booms and whistles and *wheees* raining stars down on the hundreds of boats out on the water, their running lights aglow. "Hey, Little Guy.

Look." Denny shook Andy awake. The little boy sat up, blinked, then clapped his hands in wonder.

I watched Becky's child, wondering about the child growing in Ruth's body. Boy? Girl? Healthy? What *were* the risks for a pregnancy at fifty?

The sky hushed. Sulfur smoke drifted lazily downwind. Boats set a course toward their harbors. Denny hefted Andy onto his hip, and we headed back toward the el station, carried along by the crowd.

I *really* needed to call Ruth and find out what was happening. Like tomorrow.

HOLIDAY OR NO HOLIDAY, Willie Wonka nosed me out of bed the next morning with his usual urgency. "Why don't you pick on Denny?" I grumbled as I let the dog out the back door. But the dog and I both knew no amount of cold-nosing would wake up the Slumbering Sack. Wonka scrambled down the porch steps and headed for the far back corner of our postage-stamp yard to do his business.

I started the coffee. *Huh. Wonka's probably God's Secret Service agent in disguise, assigned to me personally, to get me up before everybody else in the household for some one-on-One with my Maker.* And I had to admit, these early morning prayer times had become more . . . more *indispensable*, especially since I'd started feeling the strange burning inside me to pray, and keep praying, for "that girl"—didn't know her name—I'd seen at the hate group rally at Northwestern. The one I strongly suspected had later turned informer on the thugs who'd beaten up Mark Smith.

15

Maybe she'd done that as a result of my prayers! I hadn't said that to anybody, though. I mean, who did I think I was, anyway? Nobody thought of Jodi Baxter as a mighty prayer warrior—myself included. But I still felt excited. God was listening! God was shaking things up, wasn't He?

I grabbed a cup as the coffeemaker gurgled its last gasps. *But why doesn't that urgency to pray for her go away?* The girl still came to my mind first thing every morning, her face—late teens, eyes wary, defenses up yet vulnerable—etched in my memory.

I poured myself that first, wonderful cup when I heard footsteps tripping down the outside stairs from the second-floor apartment. I poked my head out the back door. "Stu!"

Leslie Stuart stopped, startled, a leather saddlebag-purse slung over one shoulder. "Oh. Hi, Jodi. Didn't think anyone else would be up this early on a holiday." Her long honey-blonde hair was freshly tinted, one side tucked behind her ear. She wore khaki slacks, a white blouse, and a sporty denim jacket. Smashing, really.

"Becky said you're going to a family reunion. You didn't tell me! *What* family reunion?" Not that Stu had to tell me everything. But this was big news!

Stu jiggled impatiently. "Yeah, I know. I . . . Actually, Jodi, I could use your prayers. Yada Yada's too. Got this invitation from one of my cousins to a family reunion. Wasn't sure I was going to go. You know, after . . ." Her voice trailed off.

Yes, I knew. After finding herself pregnant, abandoned by the father, embarrassed and afraid to admit it to her ultraconservative family. So Stu had just dropped out. Got an abortion. Got a new life—new job, new suburb, new friends. Until earlier this year, that is, when she'd stopped running from her past, from God, from the forgiveness and unconditional love she needed so badly.

"Hey, it's OK." I stepped out onto the porch. "I know, you didn't make the decision until yesterday." She grinned sheepishly. *Bingo.* "Will you see your parents? Where do they live?"

"Indianapolis. Don't know for sure if they'll be at the reunion. I hope so. I think." She sniffed the steam rising from my mug of coffee. "Got any more of that in a travel mug? Can't believe I haven't had any coffee yet. See? I'm a wreck already!"

Had to admit, I enjoyed seeing Stu get flustered. She had a habit of getting *me* all flummoxed by her keen ability to do everything right and be one step ahead of me. But I gave her a big hug, took two minutes to pray with her, and sent her off with Denny's travel mug of fresh coffee.

"Oh God," I murmured as Stu's silver Celica zoomed out of the alley. "Open the arms of her family. Make this a *real* reunion." Then I added, "Thank You, Jesus!" As Florida Hickman always said at Yada Yada, might as well start the thanksgiving early, since we *know* God's gonna come through. Somehow.

Florida . . . I wondered what the Hickman family was doing for the Fourth of July. Fourteen-year-old Chris was at the Cornerstone Music Festival with Josh and Amanda and the Uptown youth group. *That* in itself was probably a real holiday for Flo. She was so worried about her eldest son hanging out on the streets too much. She and her husband, Carl, wanted to move from their old neighborhood to get Chris away from bad influences, to get Carl closer to his job working for Peter Douglass . . .

Peter and Avis. I knew *they* were out of town. Drove to Ohio to visit Avis's oldest daughter and the twins. Delores Enriques had to work. Ditto Yo-Yo. Edesa Reyes, Lord help her, was at Cornerstone—Josh's idea to invite the attractive college student from Honduras to help him chaperone the younger teens. Chanda . . . she'd said something about winning a free vacation to Hawaii. *Huh.* What was *that* all about? After winning the Illinois lottery, why did Chanda George, of all people, need to get a free anything?

My mind sorted through the rest of my Yada Yada sisters as I stripped sheets off beds, started a load of laundry, and unloaded the dishwasher, stalling for time until I could reasonably call Ruth Garfield. Maybe go visit. She and Ben never went out of town. Real homebodies, those two. But maybe they should have. Taken a cruise. Gone to Hawaii or something. If they were going to have a *baby*—at their age—they'd both be ready for a retirement home by the time the kid left for college.

*Sheesh.*

I waited until ten o'clock to dial the Garfields' number. Ben answered. "Yeah, she's here. Fanning herself like a geisha doll. I tell ya, Jodi . . ." He didn't tell me, just yelled, "Ruth! Pick it up!"

An extension picked up. Ben's line went dead. "Ruth? It's Jodi. Am I calling too early?"

"Early, smearly. You're fine, Jodi. It's Mr. Grumpy who got up on the wrong side of the bed. I'm pregnant. I'm up and dressed. What more does he expect?"

I stifled a laugh. "I was wondering . . . what are you doing today? Can I come over to see you? Take you out for coffee or something?"

"Coffee! Ugh." Ruth made a retching noise on the other end of the line. "Even the word makes me want to throw up. That's how I knew I was pregnant in the first place. Coffee I love. But that was then. This is now. Tea I'll take. And . . ." She hesitated. When she spoke again, she had lowered her voice. "I could use the company, Jodi. Ben took me to the doctor yesterday. Doc gave the usual song and dance about all the risks of a pregnancy 'at your age.' Risks, schmisks. I told him this baby is a miracle! What do I care about risks? But Ben—he thinks I'm dead and in the casket already. All that's left to do is pick the color of the flowers. Nuts he's driving me!"

From the background I heard Ben yell, "I heard that!"

Ruth never missed a beat. "Sure. Come on over, Jodi. We'll have a grand time."

I hung up the phone gingerly. Wasn't so sure about that.

# 3

*A*n hour at the Garfields left me as edgy as a Mexican jumping bean. The tension between Ben and Ruth had crackled through the house like a loose livewire. I couldn't be sure if it was simply fondness disguised as bickering, or if one of them was about to blow a gasket. I wanted to debrief with Denny when I got home but found a note instead saying he'd gone up to Evanston Hospital to visit Mark Smith. *Rats.* I wished we'd coordinated our "holiday" better. I hadn't seen Mark (or Nony for that matter) since last Sunday, when a Medicar had showed up at New Morning Christian Church's new home in the Howard Street shopping center.

New Morning (Mark and Nony's church) had been renting space from Uptown Community (our church) while they searched for a new place to worship. The vicious attack on Mark by members of a white supremacist group had forced our two churches—one mostly white, the other mostly black, sharing the same space—to ask some hard questions: Were we going to let the actions of this hate group fan the embers of distrust and division between us? Or would we seize the opportunity to show the world—no, show *ourselves*—that God's love and unity were more powerful than Satan's lies?

Heady stuff. Of course, none of us knew where this line of thinking would actually take us. But last Sunday, New Morning had invited Uptown to a joint celebration of God's provision in the large unfinished storefront they'd found. New shopping center. Great location for outreach. Adding to the jubilation had been the startling headlines that same morning: an unnamed "female member" of the Coalition for White Pride and Preservation had fingered those responsible for the attack on Professor Mark Smith. An arrest was "imminent." I wanted to keep shouting, "Hallelujah!"

And then the Medicar had showed up, with a beaming Mark Smith in a wheelchair, still swaddled in bandages from the beating that nearly cost him his life. Didn't know how Nony talked the doctors into letting Mark out of the hospital for a few hours. But when Nonyameko Sisulu-Smith had wheeled her husband through the double-glass doors—well, that's when the celebration of God's goodness really rattled all those plate-glass windows. Probably rattled all the shopkeepers trying to do business in the shopping center that morning too.

I'd really meant to get up to the hospital this past week to see Mark and Nony, but just getting the teenagers off to Cornerstone fried all my good intentions. Hadn't even had time to do more than catch the headlines about the arrest of two men identified as White Pride members. But Denny had good news when he got back from the hospital a couple of hours later. "Nony says Mark can come home sometime next week. It's just . . ." He leaned against the kitchen counter, sweat beading his forehead, sipping the glass of lemonade I handed him. The temperature was hiking up to the high eighties for the weekend. *Huh. Wouldn't want to be camping at Cornerstone in heat like this. Poor kids.*

I realized Denny hadn't finished his sentence. "Just what? That's good, isn't it?"

"Sure. It's just . . ." He sighed. "They've got a long way to go. Mark needs a lot of rehabilitation after that head injury. He gets confused. Can't remember stuff. Can't tie his shoes. And he needs surgery on that damaged eye. He might . . . lose it. The sight in that eye, I mean. He's definitely not going to be able to teach this fall."

"Oh, Denny." Sadness welled up for my friends. Hadn't Nony and Mark been through enough already? Then my sad turned to mad. God had done a mighty thing when Mark came out of that coma. Why did there have to be so many nasty loose ends?

I blew out my frustration. "It's going to be a long haul for Ruth and Ben too." I hefted the pitcher of lemonade. "Want some more?" I refilled our glasses, and we wandered out to the back porch, hoping to catch a breeze. But the elms hovering overhead hung limp and still.

Denny grunted as he settled on the porch steps. "She tell you any more about what the doctor is saying?"

"Uh-huh. Guess the big scary possibility is a Down syndrome baby. A one-in-thirty chance, something like that. Or another miscarriage—though she's past the three-month mark now. Ruth considers *that* the miracle. To her, God is giving her the child she never had. Nothing else seems to matter."

"And Ben?"

I snorted. "Oh, he's a big help. Keeps coming up with all these statistics off the Internet about higher risk of death for pregnant women over forty. Or developing diabetes. Or the baby having low birth weight, stuff like that."

"He's scared, Jodi. For all his bluster, Ben loves Ruth."

"Yeah, well, he sure has a funny way of showing it. He's making her miserable. Nagging her to death about going to Planned Parenthood or a women's health center. She won't hear of it, says they're just abortion mills. Frankly, I think he just doesn't want the bother of becoming a daddy at age sixty."

Denny grunted again but said nothing for several minutes. Then, "Hey. Where's Andy? Is he still here? I've got something for him."

"I think he's watching videos. I heard the TV upstairs."

Denny rummaged in the pockets of his cargo shorts. He pulled out a skinny box. Sparklers.

"Denny! Where'd you get those? Illinois doesn't sell fireworks!"

The dimples in his cheeks appeared. "Yeah, but the guy with his coat of many pockets hanging around the el station does."

ANDY AND DENNY HAD A SQUEALING GOOD TIME with the sparklers in our backyard when it got dark. I fired up the charcoal grill and invited Becky and Andy to eat with us on the back porch, just hanging out and working our way through grilled lemon chicken, early corn on the cob, and root beer floats. In the distance, we could hear *boom boom boom* from nearby suburbs shooting off their own Fourth of July fireworks.

I was glad Denny got the sparklers. This was a boring weekend for Andy to visit his mom, with Josh and Amanda gone, and Stu too—though I heard her Celica pull into the garage late Saturday night. At least she and Becky were able to take Andy to church on Sunday morning. Becky had gotten permission from her parole officer to attend weekly services once Pastor Clark wrote a letter on her behalf on church letterhead. When we got to church, Carla Hickman, age nine, was swooning over Andy like a doting little mama. For a girl with two big brothers, here was a little boy who didn't boss her around or tell her to get lost. And cute to boot.

Uptown's worship service that Sunday didn't quite measure up to last week's double celebration, what with two of our best worship leaders gone—Avis visiting her grandkids and Rick Reilly chaperoning our youth at Cornerstone. But even with several families away for the holiday, the upstairs room we used for worship was nearly full. *And* stifling hot, even with fans in the windows.

Florida tracked me down right after the benediction. "You heard from the kids, Jodi? They still gettin' back tomorrow? Both Carl and I gotta work. You think you could see Chris get home? Don' want him hangin' out *anywhere* till we got us an understandin' what's goin' down and what's *not* goin' down till school starts—Carla! You put that baby down 'fore you drop him on his head!" Without waiting for any answers, Florida hustled after Carla, who was trying to carry Andy like a baby doll in spite of the little boy's indignant protests.

I tried to grab Stu and ask about her family reunion, but she just sidled off. "Can't talk now. Tell you later. It was . . ." She waggled her hand in a so-so motion before disappearing down the stairs and out the door.

I stared after her flowing blonde hair and red beret. "Don't you go getting all distant on me again, Leslie Stuart," I muttered at her back.

Denny and I tried to make the most of our last day *sans* teenagers. We drove up to the hospital to visit Mark after church, then took a bike ride along the lakefront. I was pooped by the time the bike path ended at the north end of Northwestern University's Evanston campus—and then we had to turn around and go the same distance to get home. By the time we hung the bikes in the garage, I could've fallen into bed and slept around the clock, even if it was only suppertime. But Denny ordered Chinese, which we ate in the living room with three fans blowing on us while we watched two of our favorite Bogart movies back to back: *Casablanca* and *The African Queen.*

And then it was Monday. And the kids came back.

AT FIVE P.M., Uptown Community's fifteen-passenger van double-parked in front of the church—a two-story storefront on Morse Avenue that had been remodeled twenty years ago into office and classroom space on the first floor, and a kitchen and large, all-purpose room that served as a "sanctuary" on the second floor. Rick Reilly's Suburban pulled up behind the van, and sleepy-eyed teenagers tumbled out of the two vehicles. Amanda climbed out of the van clutching her pillow and her threadbare Snoopy dog. Couldn't believe she took that worn-out stuffed animal! A grin tickled my insides. She might be almost sixteen, but a little girl still lurked in that womanly body.

And then José Enriques climbed out right behind her, carrying Amanda's backpack. My inside grin faded. The girl-woman—and her first serious boyfriend—was taking over the child faster than I was ready for.

I reached for my daughter and gave her a big hug. "Mm. Missed you, kiddo."

"Hi, Mom. Hi, Dad. How's Wonka?" Amanda's voice was muffled by her dad's bear hug.

"He's been missing you, pumpkin. Slept in your room every night. Tried to get up on your bed, but no way was I going to actually *lift* him up there."

"Aw. You should've, Dad. José! Did you hear that? Wonka missed me so much he tried to sleep in my bed."

José, who'd been lurking two steps behind Amanda, grinned widely, as if relieved to be included. "*Buenos dios, Señora* Baxter. *Señor* Baxter."

"Hi yourself, José," Denny said. "How'd you like Cornerstone? You need a ride home?"

"Aw, that's OK, *Señor* Baxter. I can take the el." José's grin widened. "Cornerstone was *magnifico!*—except they need more Latino bands."

"Well, hang on a moment. I think we're supposed to take Chris Hickman home and that's halfway there. Might as well take you. Where's Chris?"

While Denny was offering taxi service, I looked around for Josh, then saw him unstrapping the large tarp on top of the van covering luggage and camping gear. Pete Spencer was helping him, handing down duffle bags to outstretched hands. Did Pete need a ride home too? Yo-Yo hadn't said anything. Ben Garfield usually chauffeured Yo-Yo's brothers when they needed a ride somewhere—Oh.

A large, pearly green Buick pulled up and double-parked across the street. The driver's window rolled down. "Pete!" bellowed Ben. "Get in the car! I can't find a parking space within three dang blocks—" The rest of Ben's bossiness was mercifully cut off by the automatic window rolling back up. I grinned. Ben and Ruth Garfield, bless 'em, had taken Yo-Yo and her half brothers under their wings a few years back, though Ben sometimes acted as if he was being forced to swallow worms.

Pete rolled his eyes and pulled out his own bag. "Sorry I can't stay to help," he called to Rick Reilly, Uptown's youth group leader. "My ride's here."

Rick slapped him on the shoulder and waved him off.

*Wow. Thank You, Jesus,* I thought. *Only You know the effect this Christian music festival had on all these kids. And Pete . . .* I frowned. He was a nice enough kid, but basically a likeable pagan, giving Yo-Yo, his sister-guardian, a big headache recently. Pete was seventeen. Going to be a junior. Thought he was too old to have to obey the house rules, like curfew and telling her where he was going. Yo-Yo herself had been a Christian less than a year—and only baptized two months ago. It wasn't as if Pete had a lot of Christian training coming up.

And then there was Chris Hickman. At least *his* mom was an out-and-out, in-your-face believer, trying to raise her kids up right. Florida would tell you in a minute that she was "six years saved and six years sober!" Her husband, Carl, too—though he was a lot quieter about it. But those early years when their family was in disarray had to have been disaster on the kids. DCFS took the kids away. That's what really shook Florida sober. Even then, it took her five years to find Carla, her "baby." Only got her back a year ago.

"Hey, Mom. Dad—catch." Josh, eighteen and newly graduated, tossed his duffle bag at his dad. "Take this home for me, will ya? I gotta run some kids home."

"Not so fast!" I protested. "Welcome home, you." I gave him a hug.

He grinned and hugged back, looking more like our "normal" Josh now that he had quit shaving his head. His sandy hair had grown out about an inch. Needed a trim over the ears, but still—

*Wait a minute.* Was that a *tattoo* peeking out beneath the sleeve of his T-shirt? "Josh!" I grabbed his arm. "What's this?"

Josh pulled his arm loose. "Nothing much," he called over his shoulder, trotting off. "Tell you later. Mr. Reilly! Who are the kids who need a ride?"

Later? I wanted to see it now! A tattoo? A forever design needle-pricked into my son's skin that would *never* wash off? *My* kid? I thought sending Josh and Amanda to Cornerstone would be safe! It was a *Christian* music festival, for heaven's sake!

"Jodi?" Denny interrupted my inner muttering. "Have you seen Chris? I can't find him."

I did a quick glance around. "Uh, no. Ask Rick. Or Josh. They had to bring him home in one of the vans."

We trailed after Josh, who was talking to the youth group leader. "Either of you know where Chris Hickman is? We're supposed to see that he gets home."

"Oh. Didn't know that." Rick Reilly pulled on the brim of his Cubs cap. "He was riding with me in the Suburban, took off just as soon as we got here. Said he was taking the el home."

I eyed Denny. *Oh, brother.* Florida was going to be as mad as a bee with its stinger in backward.

# 4

Chris, I learned later, didn't get home until midnight. I called Florida right away to let her know we'd failed to hook up with him, but I had to leave the message on their answering machine. She called me back around seven, fuming. "That boy gonna be grounded for the rest of his natural life!—which ain't gonna be long if I get my hands on him. I *tol'* that boy he was s'posed to go straight home an' wait. Lord, help me!"

Guess I should've asked Flo to call me when Chris got home, just to be sure he got there safely, but I was a bit distracted by all the dirty laundry and the huge appetites Amanda and Josh brought home from Cornerstone. Not to mention the tattoo etched permanently into Josh's right arm.

"OK, show me." I held up my hand like a traffic cop when he came through the back door after dropping off José and the other kids who needed a ride home.

"Chill, Mom." Josh snitched a handful of grapes I was about to toss into a fruit salad. "I'm eighteen. A high school grad. I don't need permission to get a tattoo."

"I didn't say you did." OK, I'd been thinking it. "Just . . . show me."

He popped another grape in his mouth, gave me that amused smile he reserved for his maternal parent, and pulled up the left sleeve of his T-shirt. I squinted at the deep blue-green calligraphy etched into the bulge of his left arm. Looked like an "N," a "T" linked to the "N" with a circle, and a jazzy "W." *N . . . circle/T . . . W . . .*

I gave up. "I don't get it."

He grinned. "That's the whole point. You don't get it. You ask me what it means. I tell you NOTW—stands for 'Not of This World.' If you're a kid on the street who's clueless, I tell you that I'm *in* the world, but not *of* it—you know, a conversation starter to talk about Jesus."

"Oh." I resisted rolling my eyes. "Couldn't you have just bought a T-shirt?"

"Mom! That's wimpy. You wear it a few days, toss it in the dirty clothes, and put on a Bulls shirt or something. They challenged us at Cornerstone to lay our bodies on the line one hundred percent for Jesus—like He did for us." He pulled down his sleeve. "What's a few needle pricks compared to Jesus getting pierced by railroad spikes and the pointed end of a spear?"

I was having a hard time making the connection between Jesus laying down His life for us and Josh getting a permanent tattoo, but I bit my tongue. At least he didn't put something stupid on his body like *Born to Booze* or *Josh Loves Edesa*. In fact, I had to admit I was touched by his all-out faith. Not that I wanted to encourage any more tattoos!

I swatted his hand as he tried to snitch more fruit salad. "Glad you're home."

THE HOLIDAY WEEKEND FADED into Chicago history, and the summer rut took over. Denny and Josh left first thing the next morning for their jobs coaching summer sports for the Chicago Park District. Amanda slept in while I took messages from Uptown and neighborhood moms who wanted her to babysit. Most of them had figured out by now they had to get their bids in early. I was proud of Amanda's knack with children. She got raves from both kids and parents as a top-notch babysitter. *Maybe she'll be a teacher someday, Lord,* I thought, scribbling yet another message. *Like me.*

Which was why I didn't dare say it aloud. Suggesting that my daughter might follow in her mother's footsteps was a sure way to kill *that* idea.

Both Denny and I had jobs with the Chicago public schools— Denny as an assistant coach at West Rogers High, and me teaching third grade at Mary McLeod Bethune Elementary, where Avis Johnson-Douglass was the principal. I was still taking summers off, though it was getting harder and harder to make our minimal teachers' salaries stretch for an entire year. Moving into the city two years ago had put both of us at the bottom of the pay scale again— and we didn't get tenure for another year! But God had been good, so good. He had provided everything we really needed. Maybe not everything we *wanted*—a *real* vacation would be nice, somewhere exotic, just Denny and me, no kids, no dishes or laundry or dog poop—but I wasn't going to complain. "Thank You, Jesus," I breathed, hiking into the living room where CNN News was blabbing away. Another suicide bombing. The manhunt for Saddam Hussein was on. The president admitting that intelligence about weapons of mass destruction in Iraq may have been flawed . . . I clicked the TV off. There were a *lot* of things I didn't understand about the world we lived in, and sometimes it seemed like the only thing I knew to do about it was pray. Which used to seem like a cop-out to me.

But not any longer. Prayer was becoming my second language, me and God having a running conversation all day long. About Denny and the kids . . . about my sisters in Yada Yada and all the challenges they faced . . . about tensions in the world and our city . . . about the nameless girl I'd seen at the campus rally, caught up in that hate group. *Have mercy on us, Lord . . .*

I was stuffing a load of dirty whites into the washing machine in the basement of our two-flat when the phone rang yet again. "I'll get it!" Amanda yelled. *Good,* I thought. *She's up. She can answer her own phone messages.*

"Mo-om! It's for you!"

*Huh.* Wouldn't you know it. I hustled back up the stairs as fast as the rod in my left leg allowed and picked up the kitchen phone. "Hello. This is Jodi . . . Oh, hi, Nony!" *Rats!* I'd meant to call Nonyameko and ask when Mark was coming home. Another good intention that fizzled like a wet firecracker.

"Hello, Jodi. You have heard the good news? Mark is coming home tomorrow."

"That's what Denny said, Nony! I'm so glad. How can we help? That's going to be a big adjustment for you and the boys."

A brief silence met the obvious. "Yes." Her voice had lowered. Softened. "Yes, it will. But that is why I am calling. Is Denny home? I need help moving some furniture and putting up a bed in our dining room. Until Mark can manage the stairs."

"Oh, Nony." My voice choked up. Nony lived with the aftereffects of Mark's beating 24–7. How easy it was for me to put it out of my mind for hours, even days, as life went on. "Denny's not home now, but we could both come up there tonight. Is that soon enough?"

JOSH CAME WITH US THAT EVENING to help move furniture in the Sisulu-Smiths' ivy-covered brick home in north Evanston, not far from the university. I peeked into the family room where Hoshi Takahashi was playing War—the card version—with Nony's two sons, Marcus and Michael, while Josh and Denny took apart the polished oak dining room table for its trip down to the basement.

"Say hello to Mrs. Baxter," Hoshi ordered, even as she took the next hand.

"Hello, Mrs. Baxter," the two boys chorused, never once taking their eyes off the cards as they each slapped down the next one from their shrinking stacks.

Hoshi smiled smugly as she took the last two hands. "I won! Now scoot. Get ready for bed."

As the boys headed upstairs, I hugged the slender university student. "What would Nony do without you, Hoshi?"

She waved off my comment. "It is I who am blessed, Jodi," she said in her heavily accented English. "The Smiths have given me a family *and* a home. It is—how do you say it?—working out for both of us."

Hoshi had been one of Dr. Mark Smith's history students. Knowing how it felt to be an international student far from home, Nonyameko had taken the young Japanese woman under her wing, told her about Jesus, and brought her to the Chicago Women's Conference a year ago. *That's* where we had met the rest of the motley crew that became the Yada Yada Prayer Group. When Mark was attacked by members of a local White Pride group—for daring to expose their particular brand of free speech for the hate-mongering it was—Hoshi had practically moved in to help care for the boys so that Nony could spend long days and nights at the hospital.

I followed Hoshi's sleek black ponytail upstairs and peeked into the Smiths' guest room while Hoshi supervised the boys brushing their teeth. *Whoa!* What happened to the framed African prints and bold black-and-gold décor that Nony loved? The room had undergone a transformation. Pastel watercolors of Japanese countryside hung on the walls. A pale-blue-and-cream comforter matched a cream knotted rug. And at least a dozen framed family photographs sat on the dresser, the desk, the nightstand.

With Mark's long convalescence looming, it looked like the living arrangement had become permanent.

Crossing the room, I picked up a gold frame on the bedside stand with a portrait of a man and a woman, obviously Japanese, with rather flat features, straight black hair, and . . . smiling. My heart squeezed. I recognized the woman—Hoshi's mother. The man must be her father. I was surprised to see the smiles. Mrs. Takahashi certainly had never allowed even a hint of a smile when she visited the Yada Yada Prayer Group with Hoshi, nearly a year ago. In fact, the image of Mrs. Takahashi etched in my mind was her stubborn refusal to relinquish her pocketbook to a knife-wielding Becky Wallace, who—

"Yes," said Hoshi's voice behind me. "My parents." She gently took the frame from my hand and gazed at the portrait, her teardrop-shaped eyes misting. "Takuya and Asuka Takahashi. I . . . miss them very much."

I wanted to ask if she'd received a letter yet after that disastrous visit, when they'd basically disowned Hoshi for abandoning her ancestral religion, but I knew she hadn't. She would have told us. Instead, I followed her around the room as she pointed out a favorite aunt, two younger sisters, her grandmother, more aunts and uncles, a bevy of boy cousins with laughing eyes and casual good looks. "They were my playmates growing up," she said fondly.

No wonder Hoshi adored Mark and Nony's two boys.



I TOOK AN ENCHILADA CASSEROLE—Delores's recipe—over to the Sisulu-Smith household the next day, but I didn't stay long. I'd hoped to say hi to Mark, but he was asleep on the bed in the dining room, exhausted after the stressful move from the hospital. Nony told me that Pastor Joseph Cobbs and another brother from New Morning Christian Church had taken off a half day from work to pick them up and get Mark and his wheelchair and other equipment into the house. To top it off, they'd gassed up the Smith's Audi 200 sedan and taken it through a car wash.

"I didn't realize it was so dirty until they washed it," Nony said sheepishly.

I giggled. "That's what you get for having a car the color of beach sand. Doesn't look dirty even when it is."

"Champagne! The color of *champagne*, not sand." She started to laugh—the kind of laughter born of exhaustion, bordering on tears.

I gave her a squeeze. "You're going to get through this, Nony.

God's going to see you through. Look what He's done so far! Just take it a day at a time."

*Yeah, right.* "Easy for you to say, Jodi Baxter," I mumbled to myself a few minutes later, pointing our minivan toward Sheridan Road and heading south toward Howard Street, the border between Evanston and Chicago. "It's not *your* husband who still has brain trauma from getting smashed in the head with a brick."

Rain started to splatter on my windshield. I turned on the wipers. Pieces of a Bible verse I'd memorized for Sunday school years ago darted around in my head like the huge drops chased by the wipers on the windshield until it came together with a *swoosh* . . . *"If one of you says to him, 'Go, I wish you well; keep warm and well fed,' but does nothing about his physical needs, what good is it?"*

I snorted. "Are you talking to *me*, God?" I knew He was. OK, OK. I should get on the phone and call Yada Yada. Line up some meals. Sit with Mark so Nony can get out. Make sure somebody keeps the car tuned up . . .

But my spirit was troubled, even as I made mental lists and tried to think of things that would be most helpful to Nony. *For how long, Lord? How long?*

# 5

*I* sent e-mails and made phone calls for the next couple of days, trying to line up at least two or three meals each week for the Sisulu-Smith household—make that the Sisulu-Smith-*Takahashi* household—for the next month. Most of the Yada Yada sisters were eager to pitch in. But I ran into a few hitches.

"Ooo, Sista Jodee," Chanda said. "Would be glad to cook Jamaican oxtails and red beans for dem, for true. But mi movin' in less dan t'ree weeks! Mi kitchen all tore up!"

Of course. Chanda was moving into her new house! But what woman packed up her kitchen three weeks ahead of time?

"That's OK, Chanda. I understand you're busy getting packed. Uh, what day are you moving?" I seemed to remember a rash promise on the behalf of Yada Yada to help her move when the time came. Just thinking about it put my brain on overload.

"Oh, now, don't you worry about dat. I hired a mover—an' not dem college movers either. Don't want mi new neighbors tinkin' some trash moving in nex' door."

I let out a slow breath of relief. "That's great, Chanda." Chanda was doing everything first class these days—and I, for one, was grateful. It'd be hard to feel obligated to pack and move Chanda and her kids on top of giving Nony and Mark the practical help they needed.

"Oh, sure. Did I tell you, Sista Jodee, mi tinking about a vacation 'ouse? Right on de beach!"

I nearly dropped the phone. "*What?!* Chanda! You didn't buy *another* house, did you? What beach?"

"Jodee, Jodee." Chanda's tone was patronizing. "Dat not how dese tings work. Mi don't have to *buy* it. Dey call it a time-share! You be knowin' what a time-share is, don' you?"

"Vaguely." I didn't usually run with the time-share crowd.

"An' dat not all. Mi won a free vacation to Hawaii! *Free*, Sista Jodee!"

This was too much. "Uh, Chanda. I want to hear all about it. Really. But I still have a bunch of other calls to make. Later, OK? Bye!"

"Wait! Sista Jodee—" But I hung up. I'd apologize later.

Avis was the other hitch. I tried calling her at home several times that week, even tried the school office but only got the answering machine. We hadn't talked since she and Peter got back from Ohio after the Fourth. I didn't get hold of her until Saturday evening, and even then she sounded rushed. "Uh, I can't make a meal for Nony and Mark right now, Jodi. I'm sorry. Things have gotten a bit complicated here . . ."

In the background I heard a toddler screaming, throwing a tantrum.

A baby? At Avis's house? What in the—

"Jodi, got to go. I'll call you back. Or see you tomorrow at church." She hung up.

Avis didn't call back. But I did see her at church the next morning. She was at the front of Uptown's all-purpose room huddled with Pastor Clark when we Baxters clattered up the stairs with only minutes to spare. I ducked into the church kitchen with my seven-layer salad for the Second Sunday Potluck—the weather was too hot and muggy to actually *cook* anything—then scanned the room. Josh had come early to set up the soundboard, Amanda was sitting with some of the teens who'd gone to Cornerstone, and Denny had saved me a seat. Didn't see Peter Douglass. *Rats.* He'd been attending New Morning's services lately, which met in this very room Sunday afternoon. That in itself was a good reason to merge our two congregations—he and Avis wouldn't have to choose between churches.

As Avis laid her Bible on the simple wooden podium and said, "Good morning, church! Would you turn with me in your Bibles to—" I saw a young African-American woman sitting alone on the far side where Avis often sat, a squirming toddler on her lap. She looked so familiar . . .

And then I remembered. One of Avis's daughters! I'd met all three of them at Avis and Peter's wedding two months ago. Had Charette come home with them from Ohio? No, Charette had twins, a boy and a girl, a year or two older than this little one. This had to be Rochelle, who lived here in Chicago on the South Side—the one with the little boy named after Avis's first husband. *Conrad Johnson the Third.*

I tried to concentrate on the call to worship Avis was reading from the book of Isaiah. "Forget the former things; do not dwell on the past. See, I am doing a new thing!" But I kept stealing peeks at

Avis's daughter. Beautiful—like Avis. Visiting? But she hadn't come just today—at least, sounded like she and the baby were there when I called Avis last night. And where was the husband? Couldn't remember his name. But he'd been a looker, for sure. Like he'd walked out of the pages of *GQ*. He and Rochelle had seemed cozy enough at her mom's wedding; maybe he was just out of town on business or something. But why was Rochelle looking so sad? She didn't sing, though to me it was almost impossible not to get sucked into the powerful words of the first praise song . . .

*We will lift up our hands!*
*We will lift up our hearts!*
*We will lift up our eyes beyond the hills*
*To where our help comes from!*
*Our help comes from You . . .*

But Rochelle didn't lift up her hands or her eyes, not even an eyelash.

Pastor Clark based his sermon on the same Isaiah passage Avis had read. "Forget the former things. . . . See, I am doing a new thing!" He didn't say as much, but I wondered if he'd chosen this text because of the idea floated at the men's breakfast a couple of weeks ago about possibly merging with New Morning. That would certainly be a "new thing"! Still wasn't sure what I thought about it. But he did talk about the spiritual danger of always looking at the past or getting too comfortable with our present circumstances, because God was in the business of continually transforming our minds and hearts and lives to line up with His purposes.

A pretty radical message for Pastor Clark, a widower who probably could have retired several years ago and who reminded me of Mister Rogers, comfy old sweater and terrible tie to boot. Frankly, I thought he deserved to slow down, take it easy, not be talking about gearing up for "a new thing" God wanted to do.

*Nice deflection, Jodi,* said the Voice in my spirit. *Don't worry about how this applies to your pastor. How does it apply to you?*

I almost snorted. *You talkin' to me, God?* Dumb question. Of course He was. But I wasn't quite sure of the answer. Seemed like God had had me on a fast track of "new things" ever since Yada Yada came into my life.

Before the closing song, Pastor Clark reminded us that since New Morning was still using our building for worship that afternoon, they had been invited to "come early, bring a dish, and join us for our monthly potluck"—which could make a nice bridge between the two services, at least on second Sundays. It was a good idea, but as it turned out, only a handful of New Morning folks showed up for the potluck. Avis and Rochelle, I noticed, disappeared rather quickly after worship and didn't stay. Well, I'd catch Avis later today at Yada Yada.

Denny and I sat across from an older black couple, Debra and Sherman Meeks. She was a teacher like myself but taught special ed kids in another school district. Her husband seemed a good ten or fifteen years older and took frequent breaths from an inhaler. Debra said something about "we both have grandkids." A second marriage?

Denny and Sherman talked about the state of the Cubs and the White Sox—what else?—while Debra and I chatted. "I love your seven-layer salad!" Debra had a serious serving on her paper plate. "Never get this unless I go to a church potluck. I'm too lazy to make it myself." She, on the other hand, had actually cooked—a wonderful pot of "dirty rice," that spicy jumble of hamburger and rice I'd only seen on the menu of the local Dixie Kitchen. The way the teenagers were snarfing it up, she wouldn't be taking home any leftovers.

Florida, Stu, and Becky Wallace sat at another table with two single women from New Morning. The kids, on the other hand—including Florida's two youngest and Little Andy—just roamed the room in a pack, grazing as they went, sitting down, hopping up, running around, and hopefully getting fed. Somehow.

We were digging into somebody's banana cream pie when Stu came by and plopped a basket on the table. "Chair fund," she called out cheerily, unloading another basket on the next table. I peeked in the basket. A dollar and some change.

I made a face. "We may be sitting on these dreadful chairs a long time."

Debra threw back her head and laughed. "You said it, not me."

I grinned. I kinda liked this lady.

Other New Morning people started to arrive to set up for their afternoon service as we put away the last of the tables. We greeted each other with *hello–good-bye* smiles, though I hugged Debra and Sherman and said, "I'd like to come to another New Morning service sometime." I braced myself for *"Why not today?"* but I knew there was no way, not with Yada Yada meeting at my house tonight.

But all Sherman said was a gentle, "Likewise." And he winked.

Denny was quiet on the way home. "What?" I prodded.

He shrugged. "Just wondered why Pastor Cobbs and his wife from New Morning didn't come to the potluck. The people aren't going to come if the leaders don't."

# The yada yada Prayer Group Gets Caught

ACCORDING TO OUR RATHER LOOSE SCHEDULE, it was Nony's turn to host Yada Yada for our bimonthly meeting. But given the fact that Nony's house had just been turned into a convalescent home, we automatically skipped to the next name on the list: mine.

Under normal circumstances—meaning, the kids typically went to youth group Sunday evening—that usually left only Denny and Willie Wonka to hole up in the back of the house with an ancient thirteen-inch snowy TV. But the church bulletin said, "No Youth Group Tonight" since the teens had just returned from Cornerstone a few days ago. Guess Rick Reilly needed more time to recuperate.

Couldn't blame him.

I was just about to run upstairs and ask Stu if we could meet at her apartment instead, when Denny announced he was taking Amanda to a movie, and Josh said he'd be back in time for breakfast. "Just *kidding*, Mom," he said when my mouth dropped open. "I'm going to hang out at Jesus People awhile tonight. Some of the guys I met at Cornerstone invited me. Can you drop me off at the el, Dad?"

I watched my trio head for the garage. Well, that worked out. But since when did Josh's jeans look as if they'd been ripped to shreds by a grizzly bear?

The doorbell rang, and the Yada Yadas started drifting in. Delores Enriques and Edesa Reyes, who usually came by el, were the first to arrive. Delores said, "Edesa, *mi amiga*, you play hostess at the front door. I will help Jodi in the kitchen."

I opened my mouth to say I already had iced tea and pretzels in the living room, but the mother of five children firmly propelled me down the hall, through the dining room, and into the kitchen. "Jodi!" she hissed. "It is Edesa's birthday in three days. Are we doing anything for her tonight?"

"Tonight? No! I didn't know!"

She wagged her head. "*Perdóneme.* I was hoping you knew. Things are still so crazy at our house that I didn't—"

I touched her arm. "Is Ricardo still saying José has to drop out of school?"

Delores rolled her eyes. "I will be in my grave first! What did we come to this country for? So our *niños* could get a good education! José wants to go to college! And he's going to go, if I have to . . ." She made a face. "Never mind. What about Edesa?"

For a moment, my mind scrambled . . . and then I slowed down. "Next time we meet. We'll do it then. We'll have more time to do it right."

The round face brightened. "You are right, Jodi! *Sí, sí,* we must do it right. That girl, she is a jewel." She hustled back toward the growing clamor in the front room. I followed with a pitcher of ice water and paper cups. Even though Delores and Edesa came from different countries—Delores from Mexico, Edesa a "black Honduran"—the two women were more like mother and daughter. And *my* daughter was crazy about Edesa and all of Delores's children. Especially José. I sighed. What if Amanda and José got married someday? Delores and I would be—

*Whoa, Jodi. Those kids are only fifteen. OK, almost sixteen. But we are not going there.*

I counted noses in the living room. Almost everyone. Adele Skuggs . . . Ruth and Yo-Yo . . . Stu and Becky from upstairs . . . Hoshi (but not Nony, no surprise there) . . . Florida . . . Chanda . . .

Avis was the last to arrive. She looked a bit frazzled, had even forgotten her earrings—though she did have her big Bible that looked like it was ready to fall apart if she sneezed. I pulled her aside. "Avis, are you OK?" I whispered. "What's with Rochelle and the baby? Surprise visit?"

She didn't smile. "Could say that. The same day we got home from Ohio, Rochelle showed up with Conrad, saying she's frightened. Dexter's gotten verbally abusive, has threatened her physically several times. At least that's what she's saying. Dexter, on the other hand, has been calling frantically, begging her to come back, saying it's all a huge misunderstanding."

"Oh, Avis. That's got to be tough."

She nodded grimly. "Understatement. I'm really worried about Rochelle. She cries all the time. But our apartment is *not* set up for three generations. I mean, I love Conny. But he's upset too; he cries for his daddy. It's getting on Peter's nerves."

I could well imagine. Avis and Peter had only been married for two months. Ruth would be quick to point out that in Jewish culture, newlyweds were supposed to have a whole year before going to war or taking on the world.

Avis rubbed her temples, as if she had a migraine coming. "This hasn't been the best week for something like this to happen. I've had two meetings with the local school council, because the school board is threatening major budget cuts this year. But I've been so distracted, I can hardly wrap my mind around work."

"Avis! Jodi!" Ruth's voice whipped around the corner of the living room like a lariat, catching us and pulling us in. "A prayer meeting we are having or what?"

But I held on to Avis's arm for another moment. "Budget cuts? What kind of budget cuts? What are you going to have to cut?"

Avis looked at me strangely. "I . . . don't know yet, Jodi. But we do need to pray."

# 6

Something about the way Avis looked at me made me nervous. Budget cuts? Was she implying she'd have to trim the size of her staff? I trailed after her and perched on the arm of the couch as she opened her Bible to get Yada Yada started. But my mind was scanning through the teachers at Bethune Elementary. There'd been three new hires since I'd come on staff two years ago—but all three had left at the end of last year.

My heart sank. Nope. I was still the newbie. If she had to let someone go, it'd be "last hired, first fired."

*Oh God. I can't lose my job! Avis wouldn't—would she?*

I squeezed my eyes shut, trying to focus on what she was saying. "Many of us are facing major challenges right now." Avis glanced around the group. "Ruth is pregnant—"

"At *her* age." Yo-Yo snickered. Sitting on the floor in front of Ruth, she promptly got a whack on the back of her head. "Ow!"

Avis's mouth twitched and almost smiled. But she went on. "Nony, of course, is caring for Mark, who came home from the hospital this week—"

"Thank ya, *Jesus!* *Thank* ya!" Florida wagged her head. "Mm-hm."

"—but still has a long road of rehabilitation ahead."

"Have mercy, *Señor,*" Delores breathed.

I could tell Avis was struggling to stay on point. Would she mention that her own household had just doubled overnight?

But she flipped pages in her big Bible. "Before we share what's on our hearts and pray for one another, let's first line up with the Word of God. Paul's letter to the Philippians, chapter four, verse six says, 'Do not be anxious about anything, but in everything, by prayer and petition, with thanksgiving, present your requests to God. And the peace of God, which transcends all understanding, will guard your hearts and your minds in Christ Jesus.'"

Familiar words. Seemed as if I needed to come back to this particular scripture like I needed three squares a day. I took in a deep breath and let it out slowly. *OK, God, I get it. I shouldn't get uptight before I even know what's what about the budget cuts. Maybe it doesn't have anything to do with my job . . .*

*Fat chance.* Worry niggled at my prayer. *You're toast, Jodi Baxter.*

But I pressed on. *But You said we can bring our requests to You, so please, God—*

"—with thanksgiving," Avis said. "So before we bring our requests to God, let's spend a few minutes thanking Him for Who He is and for all He's done for us."

OK. So I was jumping the gun. I shifted gears and joined the litany of thanks offered there in my living room by a chorus of female voices. "You are awesome, God! We love You!" "God, You are God all by Yourself, and You all about takin' our messes and makin' things straight—hallelujah!" "Thank You, Jesus, for Chanda's new house." "Ooo, yes, Jesus! I tank You!" "Thank You,

Lord God, for all the ways You provide for us—jobs and income and food on our tables." (I snuck "jobs" in there.) "And thank You for Ruth and Ben's baby—"

*"Yes! Yes!"* followed that prayer and then silence. Large in everyone's heart was the concern, *Would this baby make it?* I peeked through my eyelashes at Ruth. She was blowing her nose into a lace-edged hankie.

"Uh, God. I'm new at this prayer stuff." Becky Wallace's eyes were squeezed shut. I guiltily shut my own. "But I wanna thank You for the sisters in this group and all the love they've poured out on me and Little Andy. I know I got a long way to go, Jesus, but thank You for bringin' me this far. And help me not to bum out on You."

Now the prayers were mixed with laughter and hallelujahs.

"Me, too, God," Yo-Yo chimed in. "But in the thanks department, I'm real glad Pete got to go to that Cornerstone gig, even if he does think they were heavy on religion. So thanks. And, if it's OK with You, I'd like some of what he got there to stick—oh." Yo-Yo looked up, stricken. "Guess I wasn't supposed to ask for anything yet."

By now we all had our eyes open. Even Avis laughed. "That's all right, Yo-Yo. Maybe it's time to bring our requests to God and each other. Who'd like to start?"

I eyed Stu. I'd really like to hear about that family reunion.

But Florida jumped in. "Hickman household sure do need your prayers. Thought Chris was gettin' the message when we grounded him. But, then, what do I find in the backpack he carry ever' time he go out? Spray paint. Jesus, help me! Don't know what to do with that boy! Police gonna catch him for sure if he's taggin'."

Delores cleared her throat. "José said he saw some drawing Chris did at Cornerstone."

Florida smacked her head. "Don't tell me that boy got himself in trouble at Cornerstone too! Mercy! He just got himself grounded another two weeks—"

"No, no," Delores protested. "A picture on a T-shirt. José said it was very good."

"*Humph.* Don't know about that. His teachers complain 'cause he doodles all over his homework, turns in a mess." Florida shook her head. "But what can I do? Can't take away his drivin' privilege 'cause we don't have no car."

Adele snorted. "The boy's only fourteen anyway."

Florida ignored her. "Still, we lookin' to move 'fore school starts, Jesus help us. We got all three kids crammed in one little bedroom. Chris sleepin' on the couch most of the time. But Carla growin' up, needs a room all by her own girl self." As Florida talked, my eyes focused on the long scar that ran down the side of her dark face. She'd never mentioned it, and I'd never asked. The scar was wide, like it hadn't been stitched properly. *Oh, Flo. What happened to you?*

"Where do you want to move?" Stu asked Florida.

"North Side if we can. We'd be closer to church, closer to Carl's work. Fact is, I wanna get Chris outta that neighborhood. Them Black Disciples runnin' over the place. And you know Chris. Lookin' up to all they swagger and gold chains. He's ripe for the pickin'." Her eyes were fierce. "But they gotta step over this mama first."

"Yeah," said Yo-Yo. "Toss Pete in there. Don't think he's runnin' with no gang, but he don't see nothin' wrong with smokin' weed, playin' around with pills an' stuff. Man! He oughta know what that stuff did to our mama. She still zoned." Yo-Yo sounded like she was going to cry. She was only twenty-three and trying to raise her two teenage half brothers. I'd cry too.

"I think maybe we should stop right here and pray for our children," Avis said. "Whether they're little or whether they're grown, all of our kids need a lot of prayer. My Rochelle needs our prayers right now too. Adele? You want to lead us out?"

*Avis! That's all you're going to say about Rochelle?*

But Adele with her sixth sense—or maybe God's gift of discernment—picked right up on Avis's half comment and plowed right into a prayer for Rochelle. "Glory, Jesus! The Bible says God loves us like a mother loves her nursing child, so we know You understand about our kids who are grown. They still break our hearts, because we can't kiss their troubles and make it all better. They're grown but they need Somebody, Lord, who will walk with them, holding their hand when we can't. So I'm praying for Rochelle now, Jesus!" Adele Skuggs, owner and chief beautician at Adele's Hair and Nails, reached deep in her spirit and her voice rose. "You know she's got that baby and that good-lookin' husband. Whatever she needs prayer about is about them too—"

*Ooo. Right on, Adele!*

"—and whatever is hurting Rochelle is hurting Avis and Peter too. So, Jesus, we ask You right now to take charge of this situation . . ."

I was breathless. Did Adele know what this was about? No, she couldn't! But before she finished, she'd prayed up and down for Chris Hickman, for Pete Spencer, and threw in most of the other Yada Yada kids for good measure.

RUTH DIDN'T LOOK PREGNANT—YET. She'd always been a bit thick in the middle, and her usual dark dresses had little shape. In fact, as I hugged her good-bye at the end of Yada Yada, I couldn't help wondering if she was mistaken. "You all right, Ruth? You didn't say much tonight."

"Puh! What's to say? I talk too much about this baby, people start to argue with me. 'You? Pregnant? A bad joke. Must be cancer. *Oy gevalt*, at your age. Poor Ben.'" She snorted. "Better to keep my mouth shut."

A car horn outside pumped three long brassy notes. "Yo-Yo!" Ruth yelled out my front door. "Tell Ben to keep his shirt on! I'm coming, I'm coming!" Then she patted me on the arm. "Thanks for asking, Jodi. You, I don't mind. And . . . we need prayer." She bit her lip. "A lot of prayer."

We hugged a long moment, and then she was gone.

Chanda was the last to leave. "Sista Jodee! Can you give me a ride home?"

"Ack! Chanda, Denny has our car." I yanked open the screen door. "Maybe the Garfields haven't left yet." But the taillights of the big Buick were already winking away. I stifled an expletive or two. Why didn't Chanda grab a ride with Adele or Avis when she had a chance?

I faced Chanda. "Sorry, Chanda. No car. Denny took Amanda to a movie."

"When dey be back?" Chanda flopped down on our couch. "Mi can wait."

It was all I could do to keep my mouth from dropping open. The nerve of this woman! I wanted to clean up after Yada Yada, then relax and read a book or something. Not babysit Chanda

George. Then I had a revelation. Stu! Stu lived upstairs. Stu had a car. I'd just run up and ask if she could—

"Wanting to talk 'bout someting, anyway." Chanda dug around in her oversize bag. "Mi hoping you and dat mon of yours know someting about dese time-share vacations." She pulled out a wad of glossy pamphlets and a business-looking folder.

I parked my Stu idea and sank down on the couch beside Chanda. *You're a selfish brat, you know that, Jodi Baxter? Money or no money, Chanda is a single mom and probably very lonely. How much time do you actually spend with her, anyway?* I took one of the folders. Hawaii beckoned.

"Now dat—" Chanda's eyes shone. "Dat's mi free vacation to Hawaii! Hawaii, Sista Jodee! Airfare, t'ree nights, two meals a day—all free! What you tink about *dat*?"

That I didn't believe it for a minute. "What's the catch?"

She looked confused. "Catch?"

"That's it? You won a free vacation? Or is there something else? You said something about time-share."

"Yes, yes, dat vacation be mine. Easy as squish big mosquito. Just go to dis reception an' listen to all dey facts about 'time-share' vacations, den pick up mi free tickets. No obligation, dey say. First time free!"

*Reception. Slow death by sales torture was more like it.*

The back screen door slammed. A moment later Amanda poked her head into the living room. "Hi, Mom. Hi, Ms. George." Then she ducked back out again.

"Hey, babe! We're home!" Denny's voice from the kitchen. Waylaid by the refrigerator, no doubt.

I smiled at Chanda. "Car's back. I can take you home now."

"No, wait." She laid a hand on my arm. "What mi wanting to ask, Sista Jodee . . . dis reception be coming up dis week. Dat's when mi get dem tickets to Hawaii. But . . ." She looked sheepish beneath her crown of stylish corkscrew curls. "Dey talk so fast, Jodee. Mi cannot understand all dey say. So mi asking, could you come with me? So mi don't miss anyting."

# 7

*I* punched my pillow and flopped over. Too hot to sleep, even with the window fan on high. Were we the last people on the planet without air-conditioning? Had to be at least eighty-five degrees and 100 percent humidity—at midnight! I glanced resentfully at Denny, bare-chested, mouth open in sleep. *Would it break the bank to get a small air conditioner for our bedroom window? Huh? What would it be—a hundred bucks?*

Fear licked at my sweat. Now wasn't the time to buy an air conditioner. Not if I was about to lose my job. "Oh, God," I moaned and flopped again. My oversize Bulls T-shirt, damp and wrinkled, wadded up around my middle.

"*Uhhnnn,* Jodi," Denny mumbled beside me. "Quit rocking the boat."

That did it. I slid out of bed, padded into the living room, where the fan in the bay window was going full blast, and pulled the recliner around until it lined up with the mechanical breeze. Maybe I could fall asleep out here. As I sprawled in the recliner,

Willie Wonka's nails clicked on the wood floor; then his cold nose touched my hand.

I scratched the top of the dog's noggin. "Sorry I got you up, Wonka." For some reason, the dog's gentle affection made my eyes puddle. *OK, God. I know it's not just the heat. I'm scared. I don't want to lose my job! I like teaching!* Didn't I? OK, so there were some months I threatened to quit every other day. No-show parents at parent-teacher conferences. Kids who spoke English as their second language and could barely read. A too-crowded classroom, where half the kids might qualify as ADHD. But overall, teaching at Bethune Elementary had been God's gift to me. Nonreaders becoming readers, late bloomers blooming, aha moments of learning. A few special children, like Hakim Porter, who had worked his way into my heart, only to have to let him go. And Avis Johnson-Douglass, the best principal a teacher could ask for. Not only a great boss, not only the worship leader at my church, not only the person who'd invited me to that Chicago Women's Conference a year ago where we met all the other Yada Yada sisters—but also one of my best friends.

Or so I thought.

*"Avis!"* Fear and frustration welled up in me, along with new tears. *"You can't do this to me!"* I meant to be yelling in my head. *Good grief.* Did I yell out loud? I sat up, held my breath, and listened, but all was quiet at the back of the house. Relieved, I sank back into the recliner.

*Good grief is right, Jodi,* said the Voice in my spirit. *Are you back in prayer kindergarten? Whatever happened to 'Do not be anxious about anything, but in everything—with thanksgiving!—present your requests to God. And the peace of God will guard your heart and your mind'? You don't even know anything for sure, but you're already high-tailing down the road of anxiety.*

55

Using my rumpled T-shirt, I wiped the tears off my face. It was true. I was working myself into a state and I didn't even have the facts. And—I swallowed—even if I did lose my job, had God brought me this far to leave me now? Somewhere in the back of my brain, I could hear the words of that processional, the one the choir at Adele's and Chanda's church had sung the Sunday Yada Yada visited.

*We've come this far by faith*
*Leaning on the Lord!*
*Trusting in His Holy Word*
*He's never failed me yet . . . I'm singing*
*Oh, o-o-o-oh, o-o-o-oh! Can't turn around*
*We've come this far by faith . . .*

GOD'S PEACE MUST HAVE PUT ME TO SLEEP because I was still in the recliner when I woke up the next morning, mere minutes before the alarm went off in our bedroom. And I did feel peaceful for most of the day after the Baxter men left for their summer jobs. After walking Willie Wonka, I put on some gospel music to help me tackle the pile of mending that filled an entire laundry basket; had to turn it off to take a phone message for Denny from West Rogers High. Even delivered iced tea to Becky Wallace, who was down on her knees in the backyard weeding the flower garden.

"We shoulda planted some tomatoes in that real sunny spot." She rocked back on her heels, wiping the sweat off her face with her arm as she took the glass of iced tea. "Maybe next spring."

Would Becky still be here next spring? Surely—

She squinted up at me. "Hey. I got some good news."

"What?" I sank down onto the grass. That's what I needed. Some good news.

"Know how I been tryin' to find some kinda job I can do at home till I get this monitor off my ankle? Telemarketing or stuffin' envelopes—somethin' like that."

I nodded. The classifieds section usually disappeared before we even picked up the newspaper from the front porch each morning. But not many work-at-home ads panned out. Some wanted money up front for the "kit" which was "guaranteed" to double or triple your investment in the first month. Others did background checks, and that was the last she heard from *them.*

"Anyway, talked to my parole officer, an' he says I can get a regular job—you know, workin' somewhere away from home. I been on house arrest almost three months with a clean record"—*Yeah,* I thought, *except for the time Stu caught you high on weed that one night*—"so all I gotta do is tell him my work schedule, figure in travel time to an' from, an' be here when I'm s'posed to." She shrugged.

"That's great, Becky! Really!" I could only imagine how stir-crazy she must be, stuck here at the Baxter/Stuart premises on Lunt Avenue. "But, how are you supposed to go out looking for a job? I mean, that usually takes a lot of running around."

"I dunno. Guess I gotta talk to the PO 'bout that part." She squinted at me again. "You got any ideas for jobs?"

*Jobs? Huh. If I did, I ought to be checking them out myself.* Almost blurted that I might be joining the ranks of the unemployed, too, but I swallowed the thought. No, no, I wasn't going to go there. "Definitely will keep my eyes and ears open, Becky." I took her empty glass, then hesitated. *"Don't be anxious about anything, but in everything with thanksgiving present your requests to God . . ."*

"Say, Beck. You wanna pray about it? Like now?"

PRAYING WITH BECKY ABOUT A JOB made me feel hopeful about mine. Maybe I was ready to graduate from prayer kindergarten and move into first grade. Just had to remember to keep giving stuff to God instead of worrying it to death, like Wonka with his nasty old rawhide bone. And it was working. Peace followed me around most of the day—that is, until Chanda called me late that afternoon to ask could I pick her up at six fifteen? The reception started at seven.

"I can't believe I agreed to take Chanda George to one of those time-share promotions!" I fussed to Denny, who got home at five o'clock and was getting ready to go for a run along the lake.

He snickered, pausing to sort through the day's mail. *"I* think it's hilarious. Seems like I remember you telling me you'd pack your bags and go home to Mother if I ever dragged you to one of those things again."

I swatted him with a potholder. "Yeah, that's because you saw it as a *cheap date.* Not to mention that you got thrown out by those two bouncers because you threatened to enlighten 'the other suckers'—the phrase you used, I believe—about the so-called free gifts we'd been offered. I was *mortified."*

"Hey. Just doing my civic duty. That car phone they promised for showing up was free all right. Just didn't work unless you bought the installation package for thirty bucks."

"I know, I know." I groaned. "But I'm not good at this sort of thing. Maybe *you* should go with Chanda, keep her from making a big mistake."

"Aw. It'll be all right. A lot of people buy time-shares these days. It's probably legit. And she's got the money. Let her enjoy." Denny planted a kiss on my forehead. "OK, I'm off. If you're gone before I get back"—he waggled his eyebrows—"have fun." He made for the back door.

"Wait!" I plucked a sticky note from the refrigerator. "You got a call from the high school. They want you to call back."

"Oh, brother. Was it the AD?" Denny and the athletic director at West Rogers High had their, um, differences.

"Nope. A woman. She just said call the high school office."

Denny digested this. He took the sticky note and studied the number, frowning. Then he shrugged. "Too late to call today. I'll call tomorrow." And he was out the door for his run.

I watched him disappear into the alley. Why would Denny get worried about a call from the high school office? My own anxiety kicked into gear again. Last summer Denny hadn't known until two weeks before school started whether he had a job or not. *Budget cuts.* But he'd kept his job as assistant coach for boys' soccer, basketball, and baseball. He'd wanted to stay with "my boys," as he called them, building on what he'd tried to develop the year before.

But now . . . was it all going up for grabs again? Along with *my* job?

CHANDA WAS DECKED OUT in a two-piece, bone-colored pantsuit—the kind with a tailored jacket worn long to midthigh. Chunky bone-and-black earrings and a matching necklace were perfect against her warm, brown skin. Only problem was, I forgot to ask what I should wear. I'd shed my shorts but had just pulled on a denim skirt and a clean white T-shirt. Even forgot my earrings.

Oh, well. This was Chanda's evening. Let her shine. Or not. I really didn't care.

I pulled into a self-pay parking lot around the corner from the address Chanda had given me right at seven o'clock. Six bucks after six. Not too bad. But I handed the ticket to Chanda to avoid any confusion about who was paying.

"Two plane tickets to Hawaii, all expenses paid, mm-hm." Chanda was floating. "Wish Dia's daddy would straighten up his sorry self. We could get married an' dis be our honeymoon—"

"Chanda! Dia's daddy is *not* going to 'straighten up' in time to use that ticket to Hawaii! Girl, don't let DeShawn mess with your head. You know better than that. Come on." I locked the minivan, and we headed out of the lot.

"You right, you right, Sista Jodee." She giggled. "Smooth as butter, 'bout as spineless." She sighed. "But dat mon one good dancer. Sure would like to see 'im do dat hula."

That struck us both funny, and we were still laughing as we followed two couples through the door of the brick building that said GLASS SLIPPER VACATIONS. A man in a dark suit held a clipboard. "Your names, please?" he asked the two couples, who seemed to be together. He checked their names off his clipboard and turned to us. "Uh . . ." He seemed momentarily flustered. "Name, please?"

"Ms. Chanda George." Chanda tilted her nose in the air, as if daring the man to find fault with that.

"George . . . George . . . ah, here we go." Smiling, he checked her name on his list. He turned to me. "And yours?"

Now I was the one flustered. He wasn't going to find *my* name on his list. I was about to squeak, *"Jodi Baxter,"* when Chanda took my arm, her nose still in the air. "Ms. Baxter be with me."

The man didn't move. "I'm sorry, Ms. George. But this reception is by invitation only."

*Oh, good grief.* I was going to spend the entire evening sitting in my car.

"Dat's right," Chanda sniffed, waving a card in his face. "An' dis invitation say to bring your spouse or partner. So we goin' in."

I nearly swallowed my tongue. My eyes bugged at Chanda, but she marched past the man, still gripping my arm. I didn't dare look at his face; I was sure he was gaping at us. When we turned a corner, following the couples ahead toward a large room full of small tables covered by white tablecloths, I hissed, "Chanda! Are you crazy? Now he thinks . . . he thinks . . ."

Chanda sniffed again. "Don' care what he tinks. You get to bring somebody. Single woman like me, dey want we to come alone. Use a lot of big fancy words. Not be fair."

"OK, it's not fair." I spoke through my teeth. "But if you come as a 'couple,' they are gonna want *both* partners to sign their legal contract! They're not dumb. What happens when they want *me* to cosign your . . ."

A young man in a suit and tie, latte-skinned but probably African-American, met us at the door of the large room. He barely looked old enough to have a driver's license. "Hello!" He extended a friendly hand, perfect teeth widening in a ready smile. "Ms. George! And you are . . .?" He shook my hand too. "My name is Michael, and I am your host this evening." He waved toward a couple of burgundy-skirted tables along the far wall. "Help yourself to the hors d'oeuvres. Drinks are complimentary, of course. I'll wait for you at table number seven over there."

Chanda made a beeline for the food, loading up her plate with shrimp kabobs, tiny rolled sandwiches cut in wheels, melon chunks, grapes, and hot croissants. A punch fountain splashed in the middle of another table, along with soft drinks and red and white wines. I grabbed a china plate. Might as well make the most of it. It was going to be a long evening.

# 8

*W*e'd been there an hour already, nibbling hors d'oeuvres, while Michael enthusiastically paged through a fat, glossy notebook of time-shares in Hawaii. He'd started with resort villas to drool over, complete with private beaches, Jacuzzis, "tastefully appointed" bedrooms, balconies overlooking the ocean, floating weeks—and elegant prices to match. Even Chanda had choked. "Forty-nine thousand dollars? For one week?"

"No, no, ma'am. One week every year for the rest of your life! You *own* that week! It's yours." Michael beamed. "Each sale I make, I earn points toward a time-share like that. Maybe I will be your neighbor."

"You do dat." Chanda started flipping vinyl pages. "You can be mi neighbor in a resort dat don't break de bank." I stifled a snicker.

"Of course. We have many beautiful resorts in a moderate price range."

My eyes glazed as he pointed out the features of time-shares that cost thirty-five thousand . . . twenty-eight thousand . . . twenty-two thousand . . .

"Excuse me," I said. "Michael, we need to use the ladies room, which is . . . ?"

He looked slightly alarmed. "Of course." He pointed to the far side of the room opposite the door we'd entered. "Right over there."

I didn't know whether to laugh or panic. They obviously didn't want us just skipping out. "Chanda!" I whispered as we each chose a separate stall. "Are you sure you want to buy a time-share you're locked into for *your whole life?* Maybe you don't want to go to Hawaii every year. Maybe you should just give up that so-called free weekend in Hawaii and buy a plane ticket. Cost you a whole lot less than those time-shares."

Chanda flushed the toilet and came out of her stall, banging the door. We met at the sinks. "Dose tickets be mine if I listen to dey sales pitch. Don't *have* to buy." She washed her hands and bumped the air dryer with her elbow. "Come on, Sista Jodee. Let's see what else dey have. De prices going down."

When we got back to our table, Michael had disappeared. Instead, a middle-aged white woman with short reddish hair and chunky earrings was waiting for us, a smile plastered on her face. "Michael is taking his break," she explained. "I'm his supervisor. Have you decided which time-share you are interested in?"

"No, no," Chanda murmured. "What be de cheapest time-share you got?"

The woman looked gravely disappointed. "Oh. Well, of course. I can show you some in the ten-thousand-dollar range. But I took you for a woman of exquisite taste. I don't think you'd be happy with something so basic."

*Oh, brother.* But I noticed Chanda preened a bit when she heard "woman of exquisite taste."

"Look." The woman leaned close to Chanda and lowered her voice. "Just between us. I am authorized to offer one person a thousand-dollar discount on any of our time-shares over twenty thousand dollars, tonight only. You are obviously someone looking for value as well as elegance. Why don't we look at some in that—"

Just then lights flashed, bells rang, whistles blew. I jumped, thinking it was a fire alarm. But all over the room, sales people rose and began clapping. A young Latino woman at table eleven stood up, sheepishly beaming. *What in the—?*

Chanda's eyes rounded. "What? What?"

Our sales lady glowed. "That is our first Glass Slipper sale tonight. She not only gets a free weekend vacation in Hawaii, but she gets *four* tickets, not just two."

Chanda glared at me. "Four! Dat should be me! Mi got t'ree kids. How I know which one to take wit just two tickets?" She whipped back to the sales lady. "What de *second* sale get?"

AS I DRAGGED UP THE BACKYARD SIDEWALK sometime after ten o'clock, I heard the creaking of the porch swing in the shadows. "Denny?"

"Hey, babe. Glad you're home. You forgot to take the cell."

I could barely see his face in the darkness. "I know. Sorry." I wearily climbed the steps and sank down onto the creaky swing beside him. "Whew. Am I glad to be home."

"I'll bet." His arm, resting on the back of the swing, slipped down around my shoulders and pulled me closer. "Next time, take the cell. In case you have a flat or something."

I snuggled. "Aw. You were worried about me." *Wait a minute.* I straightened up. "What are you doing out here? Is everything OK?" Denny was usually flipping back and forth between TV news channels at this time of night.

"Yeah. I guess." He shrugged. "Watched the nine o'clock news. They had a segment on that White Pride hate group tonight. Ran a picture of Mark—Mark before the beating, thank God. Also mug shots of the two guys they arrested. Kinda made me sick to my stomach. Decided to skip the rest of the news." He expelled a sharp breath. "Still makes me so *angry*, Jodi."

I laid a cheek on his hand resting on my shoulder. "I know." I wondered if Nony had seen it. Couldn't imagine having my pain splashed all over the news like that. The swing squeaked in the silence. I looked sideways at my husband's face, tense, dimly outlined in the glow from the pole light in our alley. "The guys they arrested—you still pretty sure one of them was the same guy who threatened Mark at that rally?"

Denny snorted. "Oh, yeah. Same guy. Name is Kent somebody."

*The guy with the girl at the rally . . . the girl I'd been praying for all summer . . . the "female member of the hate group" who'd probably turned him in.* I wondered what had happened to her. Newspaper still hadn't released the informant's name. Did the police have her in protective custody? What happened to members of White Pride who ratted on the group?

"Hey. Enough doom and gloom. What happened tonight? Is Chanda the proud owner of a time-share in Hawaii? Did she get her free Hawaiian vacation?"

"Oh, yeah. She got it all right. Paid twenty-two thousand five hundred for it."

Denny nearly fell off the swing. "Whoa! For a three-day *vacation*?"

"No. For the one-week time-share she bought on Maui. But I got the feeling that the perks of the 'free' vacation depended on whether she bought a 'bargain' time-share, or whether she opted for one with real class." I shuddered. "They know how to lay on a real guilt trip. Made *me* feel like I ought to whip out our credit card and—"

"Jodi!" Even in the dim light, Denny looked stricken. "You didn't take the credit card with you!"

I popped off the swing. "Don't know how to break it to you easy, Denny, but—"

He grabbed at me. I danced out of the way. "—once you get there and see how beautiful it is, you'll hardly notice how much—"

"Jodi!" There was a hint of alarm in his voice. "If you . . . I'm gonna . . ." He launched himself off the swing and grabbed for me again. I squealed, pulling open the screen door as Denny's hand closed around my arm. I jerked away and made it inside the screen door, laughing, fumbling with the hook to latch it.

"Mom! Dad!" Josh's voice behind me in the dark kitchen made me screech. "What are you guys *doing*?"

I leaned against the doorjamb, still laughing. The look on Denny's face! I caught my breath and pinched Josh's cheek. He hated that. "Just playing, sweetie." I sashayed through the kitchen, calling back over my shoulder, "Just playin' with you, Denny dear. Had you going, though." The tiredness I'd felt ten minutes ago had totally disappeared.

Josh's voice floated after me. "You guys are really *weird*, you know that?"

IT OCCURRED TO ME on a trip to the bathroom in the middle of the night that maybe there was another reason Denny had been sitting on the back porch in the dark. That phone call from the high school. Was he worried? I should have asked him.

But the next morning I hesitated. Why make a mountain out of a molehill? He'd call, they'd tell him they couldn't find the equipment inventory he turned in a month ago, and he'd have to go in and do it again. Something annoying but minor. I'd just wait and see. Besides, I hadn't told him what Avis said about budget cuts for the elementary school district. No point in getting him all worked up on two fronts.

Or me, for that matter.

*"Don't be anxious about anything. But make your requests known to God, with thanksgiving."* Oh, yeah. The "with thanksgiving" part . . .

"So did you call the school?" I asked when Denny and Josh came through the door that evening. So much for wait and see.

"Uh-huh." Denny pulled open the refrigerator door, grabbed the orange juice, and chugged it straight from the carton.

Josh headed for the shower. I could hear him pounding on the door. "Hey, squirt. How long you gonna be in there? I gotta leave in thirty minutes!"

I looked at Denny. "Where's Josh going?"

Denny wiped his mouth. "Said something about Edesa's birthday."

My eyes widened. "Josh is taking Edesa *out* for her *birthday?*" Edesa was three years older than Josh! Starting her junior year in college. Not to mention she was *my* Yada Yada sister. I thought Josh had gotten the message when he'd invited her to his senior prom and she'd said no. Smart girl.

"They're just friends, Jodi." Denny headed for the front room and the newspaper.

*Yeah, right.* I trailed behind him. "So what did the school want?"

He settled into the recliner in front of the fan and tilted it back with a *whump.* "Wanted to make an appointment for me to come in 'at my earliest convenience.'" He shrugged. "I'm going in at four o'clock tomorrow afternoon."

"Did they say what . . .?"

Irritation flickered at the edges of his voice. "They want to discuss some staff changes. That's all they said."

Alarm bells started ringing in my head. "Staff changes! Oh, Denny, you don't think—"

"No, I'm not thinking. No point in going there, Jodi." He closed his eyes. Denny's code for *Leave it alone, will ya?* I headed for the kitchen.

Amanda stood barefoot in the hall, wrapped in a towel, arguing loudly through the closed bathroom door. "You're going to celebrate Edesa's birthday without *me*?! She's my friend, too, Joshua Baxter! In fact, she was my friend *first*! She was *my* Spanish tutor, remember? She came to *my* birthday last year, not yours. That is so unfair, stealing *my*—"

"So come with us," said the muffled voice on the other side of the door.

Even I stopped short in the archway between hall and dining room. Did I hear right? Amanda gaped at the closed door. "Really?"

The door opened a crack. "Really. But only if you can be ready in ten minutes, squirt." The door slammed.

Amanda didn't move. "I—I can't. I've got to babysit tonight."

The shower turned on behind the closed door. "Oh. Too bad," Josh yelled. "Another time."

He sauntered through the kitchen ten minutes later in cargo

shorts, a sleeveless tank showing off that "sanctified" tattoo, his short sandy hair toweled dry—but not combed—and jingling his car keys. "Bye, Mom." He planted a kiss on my cheek.

I looked at him sideways. "Joshua James Baxter." I kept my voice low. "Did you know your sister had to babysit tonight?"

He just grinned at me and whistled his way out to the garage.

DENNY SPENT THE EVENING in front of the TV. But he was in one of his *leave-me-alone-I-just-wanna-veg* moods, so I holed up in the kitchen to make dinner for Nony's family—my turn to take something tomorrow. Didn't really want to turn on the oven. Too hot. What could I make that didn't actually need to cook?

A quick inventory of the fridge and cupboards turned up some decent romaine lettuce, three frozen boneless chicken breasts, a can of mandarin orange segments, a few forgotten slivered almonds, and a large can of crunchy Chow Mein noodles. *Voila!* The makings of a chilled oriental salad. Maybe even enough for two salads. Could even pick up some crusty bread at the Dominick's bakery on my way to Nony's house tomorrow.

As I sliced up the chicken for a quick stir-fry, I suddenly stopped, knife in midair. *Edesa's birthday.* I'd told Delores we would celebrate at the next Yada Yada meeting. Better send out an e-mail and give the sisters a heads-up before I forgot.

With the chicken sizzling in the frying pan turned low, I booted up the computer in the dining room and opened our e-mail. *Sheesh.* How come we were still getting all these ads for Viagra!? I deleted as much junk mail as I could, moved e-mails for Amanda and Josh into their own folders, and scanned the rest. Denny's parents, emailing their latest travelogue from Europe . . . a reminder from Uptown Community Church about the monthly men's breakfast this coming Saturday . . .

A sputtering sound arrested my attention. *Ack! The chicken!* I ran into the kitchen and pulled the pan off the stove. OK, so the chicken would be a little crispy. I went back to the computer, temporarily deleted Edesa's name from my Yada Yada group list, called up a new message, and began to type.

To: Yada Yada
From: BaxterBears@wahoo.com
Re: Edesa's birthday

We're all getting older and wiser, ha ha, even the younguns among us. Our dear Edesa has a birthday this week—can we celebrate at the next Yada Yada? Avis, you're next on the list to host. This is the first time since you and Peter got married—let us know if you want to take a pass. You can always send him over to keep Denny company.

As an afterthought, I added prayer requests from our last meeting: Florida's family, still looking for a larger apartment, preferably in Rogers Park . . . Chanda, who was moving in less than two weeks . . . a job for Becky Wallace . . . Mark Smith's full recovery . . . safety for Ruth and her unborn baby . . .

I stared at the last thing I'd written. *Safety for Ruth and her unborn baby.* What, exactly, did that mean? Ben was in a dither about the risks—or so he said. Ruth had already had a couple of miscarriages, but she was into her fourth month now. What *were* the risks, actually, for a woman Ruth's age? I didn't have a clue.

The TV was still blabbing away in the living room. I sent my e-mail, then called up Google and typed "older women," "pregnancy," and "risk" into my search field. Hundreds of hits. I pulled up Web site after Web site, my insides sinking as I read.

*Oh God . . . I had no idea . . .*

Fifty percent of pregnancies after age forty ended in miscarriage. *Fifty percent!* Risks to the mother included high blood pressure, onset of diabetes, preeclampsia (or toxemia as it used to be known), even the risk of death from hemorrhage or hypertensive disorders. Risks to the baby—low birth weight, premature birth, birth defects, a 1-in-30 chance of a Down syndrome baby . . .

*Oh God, please God, don't let that happen to Ruth and Ben!*

My heart felt stuck in my throat. I couldn't read any more. I was just about to shut down the Internet when the words "Jewish women" on the list of sites caught my eye. What about Jewish women? I opened the Web site. It was titled, "Tay-Sachs Disease." What in the world was Tay-Sachs disease?

I read the article. I wished I hadn't.

# 9

The stuff I'd read on the Internet bothered me all the next day. Was Ruth really in danger? And Tay-Sachs disease sounded like a parent's worst nightmare. But what was I supposed to do with it? Ben was already in a dither; no point raising the ante. Talk to Ruth? Was she in total denial?

That, and knowing that Denny had a meeting to discuss "staff changes" that afternoon, made me totally oblivious to the fact that I had no car to deliver my oriental salad to Nony's household. *Duh.* How was I going to get this stuff to north Evanston?

When five o'clock rolled around and still no Denny, I decided to ask Stu if I could borrow her Celica, but a quick check of the garage told me she wasn't home yet either. *Rats.* What was I going to do now?

I dialed Nony's number. "Nony! I'm so sorry. I have your supper ready, but Denny's not home yet with the car. He's usually home by five in the summer—day camps, you know—but he had a meeting at four, and I don't—"

"Jodi, calm down. It is all right." In spite of Nony's soothing words, she sounded distracted. "We can manage. We still have left-overs from Adele's fried chicken."

"Um, it's a main dish salad, already made it. Just wanted you to know I might be a little—" In the background, I heard Mark calling her name.

"Jodi, I have to go. Don't worry. It's all right." The phone went dead just as I heard our garage door go up.

Nick of time. Denny was home.

I grabbed the covered plastic bowl holding Nony's salad and the bottle of celery-seed dressing and hustled out to the garage. He was locking the car. "Denny, wait. I have to take this food up to the Sisulu-Smiths. I'll be back as soon as I can."

No response. He jerked his duffle bag out of the backseat.

"Oh. The meeting. I'm sorry, Denny. What happened?"

"That's what I wanted to talk to you about. But if you've gotta go . . ."

*Argh!* I did have to go. But I wanted to stay and hear what happened. Unless—"Denny, come with me. We can talk in the car. I promise we won't stay long at the Smiths, but it'd be a chance to see Mark for a few minutes too. I know he'd rather see you than just me."

Denny was silent a long moment. I knew he didn't want to get back in the car after a long day. *Plus* a meeting with the principal. Maybe I should forget the salad, phone Nony, and tell her to go with the leftovers.

"OK." Denny walked around to the other side of the car. "But you drive."

I hopped in the driver's seat before he could change his mind. Decided to skip the bread. No way was I going to ask Denny to wait ten minutes in the car while I stood in line at Dominick's. "So.

Tell me about your meeting." I glanced sideways at him as we waited at a red light. "Bad news?" I steeled myself.

"No."

"No? Then what—?" A car horn blared behind me. The light had turned green. "Don't be so impatient, buddy," I muttered. We crossed Howard Street and headed north into Evanston. Within a few blocks, we were passing a rash of new condos going up.

"Good news, actually . . . I think."

"Denny Baxter!" I felt like slugging him. "For somebody with good news, you're acting like your dog just got run over! *What* good news?"

"Turns out the AD quit. Resigned. He's already gone. Kinda funny. They didn't say why." He frowned, as if rolling the information over in his mind.

*Huh?* I opened my mouth to say, *"That's it?"* But Denny started up again. "The district offered me the position of athletic director for West Rogers High. They'd like me to start ASAP."

My mind did a spin. "Denny! *Athletic director?* That's wonderful!"

"Yeah, guess so. I hardly know what to think."

"You *guess* so! It's awesome! They knew your talents were being wasted as an assistant coach. Wow. A big pay increase, right?"

He snorted. "Don't know about *big*. This is still public high school. But, yeah, definitely an increase. To tell you the truth, Jodi, I don't know how I feel about it. The job I'd really love is head coach. But . . . AD? That's mainly administrative. I wouldn't be out there coaching. I'd be hiring and firing, wrestling with schedules, dealing with conflicts. What I like is working with the kids. Coaching."

"Oh, Denny." I hardly knew what to say. We drove in silence as

Chicago Avenue merged into Sheridan Road along Northwestern University. I finally put on my left-turn blinker at Lincoln and pulled up in front of the Sisulu-Smith's ivy-encrusted home in the middle of the block. I shut off the engine. My insides danced with excitement, but I tried to sound sympathetic. "Look. We can talk about it some more after we drop off this food. But I just want you to know—I'm really proud of you, Denny."

I didn't dare say more. But what I was *thinking* was, maybe this was God's 'ram in the bush' if my job got sacrificed on the altar of budget cuts.

NONY TOOK THE SALAD with a warm hug. "Thank you, Jodi. The meals help a lot." I followed her into the kitchen while Denny dropped into the front room where Mark was parked in a recliner.

"Hey, man," I heard Denny say. "What's with the double eye patches? You're taking this pirate thing too far."

*Bad joke, Denny.* But I grabbed Nony's arm. "What's happening, Nony? Why does Mark have both eyes patched? I thought . . ."

She sighed. "I'm sorry, Jodi. I should have called somebody, let Yada Yada know. Asked you to pray. But it's just so . . . crazy sometimes."

"But what happened?"

She set the plastic bowl in the center of the square wooden table in the kitchen and got out five stoneware plates. Her usually sculpted hair was hidden beneath a black silk head wrap, matching a pair of wide-legged, silky black pants. "Mark's doctor referred him to an eye specialist at the University of Illinois. I took him today; we were down there almost four hours." Her lip trembled. "They did a dozen different tests, but . . . the ophthalmologist doubts that they can save his left eye. He has major retinal detachment and . . . lots of hemorrhage from the beating. They did some laser staples today—oh, Jodi. It was so painful. I could hardly bear to watch."

I took the flatware from her hand and set the table. "But why are both eyes bandaged? I thought the right one—"

"It's all right. But the doctor bandaged both eyes to keep the left one totally still. He's supposed to stay immobile for the next five days, which on top of everything else . . ." Her voice broke.

"Oh, Nony." I wrapped her in a hug and let her cry for a few minutes.

She sniffed, grabbed a tissue, and wiped her face. "We'll be all right. It's hardest on Mark, because he's more aware now. But he can't see, and he's not supposed to move."

"Hard on you too." I got glasses from the cupboard and filled them with ice and water from the dispenser in the door of the top-of-the-line refrigerator. "You end up having to be his eyes, his hands and feet, his link to the world. Right?"

She looked at me gratefully. "Exactly." The front door opened, and I heard Marcus and Michael tromp noisily into the house. "Oh, there's Hoshi and the boys. She took them to the park."

"That's OK. We've really got to go. I've got hungry kids at home too. Oh." I grimaced sheepishly. "I meant to bring some crusty bread to go with that salad, but . . . it's a long story. Sorry."

She took the cover off the bowl and smiled. "Looks fabulous. We'll be fine."

I stopped into the living room. Denny was leaning forward, elbows on his knees in a straight-back chair, talking to Mark. I gave Mark a hug. "Sorry to take Denny away, Mark. Did he tell you his good news?"

"What good news?" Mark's speech was still slow, a little slurred.

Denny cut his eyes at me, then turned back to Mark. "Well, don't know yet if it's good news. Got offered the AD job at West Rogers High. Total surprise."

Mark seemed to digest this. Then a grin slowly lit up his battered face. "Athletic director?" He held out his hand, searching for Denny's. The two men's hands met in a street grip. "Awesome, man. Congrats."

"JODI, PLEASE," Denny said when we got back in the car. "Don't tell a lot of people about this job offer yet, OK? I'm not sure what I'm going to do. I need to think about it. *We* need to pray about it."

"I'm sorry." Was I? I wanted to get on the phone and tell Yada Yada the good news. Tell my folks, tell Denny's folks—yeah, the Senior Baxters would be happy. *"About time,"* his father would say. But I needed to respect Denny's process. "Just . . . talk to me, Denny. Let me in on what you're thinking, OK?"

"I will."

But he didn't. Not much, anyway, for the next few days. "Wish I could talk to Mark," he said. "I mean, *really* talk to him about it. I need a brother who can give me some advice. But I don't know if he's up for that kind of thing yet."

That hurt. What was I? Chopped liver?

*Wait a minute, Jodi. You've got a whole circle of sisters you talk to, talk with, pray with. Don't deny that kind of input and support for Denny.* OK. I decided not to be offended. "What about Peter Douglass? Or Pastor Clark? You'll see both of them at the men's breakfast on Saturday."

He nodded thoughtfully. "Yeah. Maybe so."

The weekend rolled around. Third Saturday in July. Josh took off early, catching the el to Jesus People. JPUSA was refurbishing the emergency shelter the group managed for homeless women with children and needed all the volunteer help they could get. I dropped off Denny at Uptown so I could have the car, then called Ruth. In one way, it felt like a reckless thing to do. What if all that stuff I'd found on the Internet came popping out of my mouth? On the other hand, I really wanted to stay close to Ruth during this pregnancy. She was going to need all the support she could get.

"Ruth! It's Jodi. What are you doing this morning? Can I take you out for coffee or something?"

She groaned right in my ear. "Coffee, schmoffee. The smell still makes me want to puke. But you can take me shopping. Will Ben take me? No. He says to buy baby furniture is foolishness right now. So what, I said. Then he says—"

I laughed. "Shopping would be great, Ruth. I'll pick you up at ten."

SHOPPING FOR BABY FURNITURE with Ruth was dizzying. And exhausting. We started out at Lazar's Juvenile Furniture on Lincoln Avenue, with a swing through Target's collection, then ended up at Golf Mill Shopping Center, gawking at cribs, bassinettes, and car seats at J. C. Penney. At her command, a harried sales clerk took apart an amazing contraption that was a stroller, infant carrier, and car seat all in one and put it together again to show her how it worked; then rolled her eyes when Ruth didn't buy. "*Nudnik,*" Ruth huffed as she propelled me to the next store. "We have to compare quality and prices at other stores, don't we?"

"Only the best for the new grandchild, right?" gloated a greedy male clerk as we hunted for price tags on matching oak furniture.

Ruth nailed him with a look. "We want your opinion, we'll ask." Chastened, he backed up and tried to fade into the next display, the same furniture in cherry. "So. How much for just the crib?" Ruth hollered after him.

I pulled Ruth toward the infant clothes. Onesies and booties would be safe.

"Do you know the sex of the baby?" a young female clerk tried pleasantly as Ruth held up a blue outfit, then a pink outfit.

"What is this, an I.Q. test?" Ruth shot back. "I'll take one of each."

This was getting ridiculous. "No, she won't. Here." I handed the clerk the same outfit in mint green. "Pay up, Ruth, then let's find a place to sit down before your feet fall off." Or mine.

We found the food court in the mall and gave in to the temptation of a magnificently huge, gooey cinnamon bun, which Ruth sawed in half with a plastic knife. Coffee for me, milk for Ruth. She blathered on about baby this and baby that, due near Christmas, wouldn't that be fun—then suddenly she stopped in midchew.

"I have to find the restroom. Right now."

She headed toward the sign for Women so fast I lost sight of her by the time I grabbed her bulgy purse and her purchases. "Ruth?" I called to the row of stalls. "Are you OK?"

No answer. Then a stall door swung open and Ruth came out, her eyes terrified, her face pale beneath the frowsy dark hair.

"Jodi. Drive me to the hospital. I'm . . . spotting."

# 10

*S*hould have called an ambulance. I didn't have a clue where the closest hospital was! But Ruth said "Golf Road and Gross Pointe" through gritted teeth, so I headed that way and ended up at Rush North Shore Medical Center. Pulled right up to the emergency room entrance, ran in, and gasped, "Pregnant . . . bleeding . . . " Two orderlies immediately ran out with a wheelchair. They seemed momentarily confused when they saw Ruth, but they gently lifted her out of the car, into the chair, and whisked her away.

I parked and called Ben. Then I called home and left a message on the answering machine, all the while praying, *Oh God, Oh God, don't let anything happen to Ruth or her baby.* Ben showed up in twenty minutes, groused, "I'm the husband," and they let him into the inner sanctum. I saw the intake nurse and the receptionist lift their eyebrows at each other, then follow him with their eyes as his white wavy hair and slight stoop disappeared beyond the double doors.

Yeah, well, guess it wasn't every day a pregnant woman came in whose husband looked like he qualified for Social Security.

Ben came out half an hour later. "They're going to keep her overnight for observation. She told me to tell you to go home."

"But what about the baby? Did she . . . miscarry?"

Ben shook his head, his face a big frown. As he turned away, I heard him mumble, "Better if she had. Better to lose the baby this way . . ."

I WAS STILL STEAMING WHEN I GOT HOME.

"Ben Garfield makes me *so mad*, Denny. I mean, he practically said he wished Ruth would have a miscarriage! That is so . . . so . . ." I couldn't think of a word terrible enough. Not one I dared say aloud, anyway. "That man is so selfish. Just doesn't want to be bothered with a baby."

Denny looked at me sideways. We were sitting on the back porch swing munching tuna sandwiches and washing them down with iced tea, while I tried to catch him up on what had happened that morning. "Take it easy on Ben, Jodi. Seems to me like you freaked a couple of weeks ago when I mentioned us having another kid."

"That's not fair." I stuck out my lip. "We were talking hypothetical. Ben and Ruth have an actual muffin in the oven."

Denny dropped it. We finished our sandwiches, idly pushing the swing back and forth. After a while, he said, "Wonder what Ben meant by 'better to lose the baby *this* way'?"

I didn't have a clue. Come to think of it, it was a strange thing to say. I decided to change the subject. "You guys have a good time at the men's breakfast?"

"Yeah. Nobody showed up from New Morning, though. I was kind of disappointed, but as it turned out, it was for the best."

"What do you mean?"

Denny drained the last of his iced tea. "Well, Pastor Clark brought up the fact that we've maxed out our space at Uptown. Sometimes we even run out of chairs, and people have to stand."

I snickered. "They're the lucky ones. I really hope we don't buy any more of those terrible folding chairs."

"That option *did* come up." Denny grinned. "But Pastor Clark said the real issue is whether it's time to sell the building and buy a bigger space."

"Whoa. Isn't that something *all* the members should talk about?"

"Don't get bent out of shape, Jodi. The pastor just brought it up as something we should be praying about. Except . . ." His words retreated, as if having a private conversation in his head.

"Except what?" I prompted.

"Oh. Except Peter Douglass was there, and he said there was another option, one that God had already been speaking to him about the past couple of months."

I held my breath. Peter Douglass's "suggestions" usually had the effect on you of being dangled over a roaring river from a high cliff. Either sink or fly.

"The option being to sell the current building and invest the money in New Morning—to finish off the remodeling of their new space, buy chairs and equipment, so that it can be used sooner."

I blinked. "You mean . . .?"

"Yeah. Merge the two churches. That's what he meant."

HAD TO ADMIT I WAS STUNNED. True, Peter Douglass had brought up the idea of a merger before, when Mark Smith had been attacked after that White Pride rally. He said the incident could drive us apart, or we could thwart the devil and let it bring us together. But sell our building and put all the money into New Morning? I couldn't imagine the folks at Uptown agreeing to something that radical! I mean, that committed us big-time. With no escape hatch if things went south.

The idea stirred up both excitement and fear in my spirit. But I couldn't think about it now; had to send an e-mail to Yada Yada about Ruth ending up at the hospital. But the moment I hit Send, I realized some sisters might not look at their e-mail before Ruth got sent home. Had to make phone calls. We needed to be praying.

Mostly I got answering machines. Not too surprising on a Saturday afternoon. But as I dialed Avis's number, the excitement and fear in my bones took on a new face: excitement about Denny's job promotion, fear about losing mine. OK, so why didn't I just *ask* Avis? Be done with the guesswork. Might help Denny make his decision if he knew we were on the cusp of becoming a one-paycheck family.

*"Hello, you've reached the Douglass household,"* said a masculine voice. Recorded. *"Please leave a—"* I hung up. No way was I going to ask about my job via voice mail. Then I realized I hadn't left the message about Ruth either, so I had to call back.

Becky Wallace was one of the few Yada Yadas who actually answered the phone. "So Ruth's goin' to be OK, right?" she asked. "She must want that baby real bad. Don' know what I'd do if I was in her shoes. But I'll tell Stu when she comes in. Say, Jodi. You or Denny heard of any jobs yet? My PO says I gotta have a job interview or appointment to go to; I can't just go wanderin' around lookin'."

I stifled a groan. Only jobs I knew about were with the public school system. No way Chicago schools would hire someone with a violent felony on her record. Stu's contacts at DCFS wouldn't be much better. "I'm sorry, Becky. I really don't." Silence on the other end. "Becky?"

"Yeah. OK. It's just—*damn* it, Jodi. I wanna get a place of my own so I can get Little Andy back. I gotta get a job first, save some money. But I can't get no job with this"—she blistered my ear with a string of profanity—"around my blasted ankle. Might as well be hog-tied and dumped in the Chicago River."

I felt really bad for Becky, but helpless too. She was caught in a web that *seemed* like freedom at first hoot—getting out of prison on early parole—but at this point felt like checkmate. Can't move this way; can't move that. Was tempted for a flash second to remind her that Stu's apartment was a presidential suite compared to a cell at Lincoln Correctional, but then I remembered how I felt when Denny and I "lost" Little Andy at the Taste of Chicago, how one minute without that little boy had felt like a hundred hours. Must be even worse for his mother.

DREAMED ALL NIGHT ABOUT SPIDER WEBS—mesmerized by their intricate patterns, delicate and iridescent in the morning dew. But in the dreams when I tried to move, I felt as if I was swimming through a gossamer maze. Deadly beauty . . .

Couldn't shake the dreams even as I woke to a beautiful Sunday morning—cloudless, low humidity, pearly pink sky, a sweet warm breeze off the lake rustling the leaves along Lunt Avenue. Not bad for late July. But the dreams—what was *that* all about? The feeling of wading through the webs persisted even as I let the dog out, filled the bird feeder, and started the coffee. Made me want to get into the shower and wash off all the sticky, clinging mess . . .

As I stood under the tepid water, letting it pour over my head, flattening and parting my dark brown hair into shoulder-length rivulets, I realized Becky wasn't the only one caught in a web that wasn't as shimmering as it first appeared. Look at Chanda. Bright-eyed and bushy-tailed about her lottery winnings, but when we'd finally staggered out of that time-share "sales reception," seemed to *me* she'd gotten herself into a silver-lined trap. But what could I say? She seemed happy, so maybe that's what counted. Maybe I shouldn't worry . . .

Then there was Denny's job. I mean, seemed like we ought to be shouting and praising God for such a wonderful promotion. But we were still tiptoeing around the subject, like a relative who'd come to visit we were slightly ashamed of. *"Not sure if it's good news."* Denny's words. Even though the budget-cutting axe was hanging over my job. Of course, I hadn't told him yet. Probably should. We needed to get this thing in perspective.

And Ruth. So ecstatic that she was finally pregnant. Should be a happy time for her. Baby showers. Pregnant woman jokes. Starting a college fund. Except, it was beginning to feel like a ticking time bomb instead of a baby that she was carrying around. How many more times would she end up in the hospital before—

I shut off the water. Ruth was laying up there in the hospital all by herself! Or maybe Ben was there, which could be worse, the old grouch. Either way, she had to be worried. Maybe frightened. While the rest of us just went off to church to sing praises.

*Uh-uh. No way.*

Wrapping a towel around my wet body, I scurried down the hall to our bedroom. Denny was sitting up on the side of the bed, only half awake. "Denny, can I drop you and the kids off at church? I want to go see Ruth in the hospital."

"Oh. S'pose so," he mumbled. "Can't you go this afternoon?"

"Nope." I didn't say she'd probably get discharged by noon. For some reason it seemed important to go see her in the hospital this morning. For Ruth's sake? Or mine?

"HEY, YOU. Are you awake?"

Ruth's eyes were closed when I peeked into her room at Rush North Shore Medical Center. But they immediately popped open, adding spitfire to the pale face and dark hair propped up on two starchy-white hospital pillows.

"How you doing?" I asked.

Ruth beamed. "Never better. Especially since I put Ben on my 'visitors not wanted' list. Blood pressure went right down."

I giggled, setting the pink azalea I'd picked up at the grocery store on the windowsill. "Wow. A private room. How do you rate?"

"Ben insisted. Me, I'm grateful. Fewer *nudniks*. Every nurse who comes through that door thinks she's the first one to notice I'm not twenty-five."

I dragged a chair over to the bed and took her hand. On the way to the hospital, I'd decided not to beat around the bush. "Ruth. I want the real deal. How are you? How is the baby? And 'fine' is not an acceptable answer."

She looked annoyed. "What, you want bad news? We *are* fine."

87

"No, no, I don't want bad news! I just don't want a one-word answer. What does the doctor say? Why were you spotting? Is the baby growing all right? How's your blood pressure? Any—"

"All right, all right. I get it." She rolled her eyes at me. "As far as I know, everything is fine. So my blood pressure is elevated. What's to worry? I can't feel it. But salt I have to give up. What's food without salt? Like sex without love. But . . ." She fluttered her other hand. "For the baby, I give it up." She winked. "Salt *and* sex."

"So the baby is . . . ?"

She kissed the tips of her fingers. "Good, good. They hear the heartbeat. I told my doctor I didn't want any of those tests, but here, they insist. The heartbeat they must hear. Everybody wants to listen—the nurse, the doctor, another nurse, another doctor—"

A knock on the door was followed by Stu's face and red beret. "Aha. I guessed right. Come on in, Flo."

I looked at my watch. Ten fifty. Church wasn't over yet. "What are you guys doing here?"

"Same as you." Florida bounced into the room, pecked Ruth on the cheek, and swiveled her head, taking in the cheerful hospital room done in pastel colors. "Mm-mm. Nice crib. How long you get to stay up in here, Ruth?"

"We saw Denny and the kids come in without you," Stu said to me. "Figured you must be here. Florida and I decided to skip church too. Hang out with you two. Cheer up Ruth in case she needed cheering up."

*Nice timing*, I thought. Ruth was just beginning to open up. But by the rosy blush on Ruth's cheeks, I could tell the visitors were good medicine.

We had *schmoozed*—as Ruth called it—about ten minutes when

two white coats with stethoscopes came in. There the similarity ended. The female doctor looked to be late thirties, pallid skin with no makeup, no-nonsense hair tucked behind both ears. The male doctor was dark in comparison: jet black hair combed straight back, black eyes, smooth coffee-no-cream skin, maybe Indian or Pakistani. The woman held out her hand to Ruth. "Mrs. Garfield. I'm Dr. Kloski. This is Dr. Anand." She looked at the three of us. "Do you ladies mind?"

"I mind." Ruth's tone was mild, with a dash of horseradish. "Unless it's a matter of national security."

Dr. Kloski shrugged. "All right. It's just a bit crowded. We'd like to check the baby's heartbeat with the fetal Doppler." She took a small instrument from her pocket. Stu, Flo, and I crunched ourselves into the corner by the window.

I caught a flicker of anxiety in Ruth's eyes. My own heart caught in midflop. "Again?" Ruth said. "Half the hospital listened to it last night."

Dr. Anand spoke for the first time. A gentle voice. "Don't worry, Mrs. Garfield. The reports say there's a good heartbeat. But your case is a bit, ah, unusual. We would like to check it again."

Ruth looked resigned. "Be my guest." She pulled up her polka-dotted hospital gown. "Belly up." Florida poked me in the side with her elbow; I didn't dare look at her or Stu, or one of us might start giggling.

Without benefit of bedsheet or clothes, Ruth was definitely starting to look pregnant. Dr. Anand squirted some clear gel on Ruth's rounded tummy, then holding the monitor in one hand, he moved the Doppler wand here and there, concentrating on Ruth's left side. We all held our breath, trying not to make a sound.

Then he nodded to his colleague. "Got it," he said. "Now over there."

What was going on?

Now both doctors were using the small monitors, one on each side of Ruth's belly. Dr. Kloski nodded and finally straightened. "Definitely. Two heartbeats."

"*Two?!*" Ruth actually choked on the word.

Dr. Anand nodded, a slight smile on his lips. "That's right, Mrs. Garfield. Twins."

# 11

For a nanosecond, the doctor's pronouncement sucked all the air out of our systems. Then Florida screeched, "*Twins?* Two babies in the cooker? Oh, Jesus. Glory hal-le*lu*jah! Ain't God somethin'. Your cup just runnin' over, Ruth. My, my."

I found my voice. "Ohmigosh. Ruth! That's amazing!"—or something like that. All I heard was babble.

Dr. Kloski glared at us. "Ladies, *please*." She turned back to Ruth, whose mouth hung open in a state of shock. "Mrs. Garfield, I'd like to say congratulations. But, medically, this actually presents us with a challenging situation, which I'd like to discuss with you privately."

Little red flags sprouted in my brain. But Ruth fluttered her hand at us. "All right. But don't go far away," she croaked. "And don't call Ben. Yet."

"*Huh*," Flo snorted as the door closed behind us. "What they gonna talk at her about? She needs some armor bearers in there—

Jesus! Put a hedge of protection 'round that sister right now. Don't let her get bowled over by all that doctor-speak. An' we wanna pray for those two little babies in there. Oh my Lord. Put a hedge of protection 'round them too."

Florida had her eyes fixed on Ruth's door, so it took me a second or two to realize she was praying. "Amen to that," I murmured.

Stu seemed unusually quiet. "Stu? You OK?"

She shrugged. "Yeah. Just thinking about . . . David. My baby."

Florida and I exchanged quick glances. Stu rarely mentioned her baby, the baby she'd aborted almost four years ago, not since that weekend last spring when she'd almost taken her own life, crushed by the burden of trying to pretend she had everything under control. She'd never told her family; had just disappeared out of their life. Most of the Yada Yada sisters didn't know about it, either, but Florida and I had been there last spring, stayed with her night and day to make sure she didn't do anything drastic. Encouraging her to talk about it. Cry. Grieve. We'd even named the baby together: David. *Beloved.*

That's why Stu going to a family reunion had seemed so significant. "Stu? What happened at the reunion? Did you see your parents? Talk to them about . . . you know."

She shrugged again. "They didn't come. I was relieved, I guess. I could just relax; enjoy my cousins and their kids. But disappointed too. It took a lot of courage for me to go to a family get-together. Thought it might be easier to relate to my parents in a crowd. Wouldn't get too personal. Now . . . I'm not sure what—"

The door opened; the two doctors came out. Dr. Kloski swept by without a glance, but Dr. Anand tipped his head pleasantly at us. "Ladies."

"Later, OK?" I whispered to Stu as we piled back into Ruth's room.

"Girl, what them two doctors have to say, anyway?" Florida scolded.

"Sit me up," Ruth mumbled. Stu pressed the buttons that raised the bed and found another pillow to stick behind Ruth's head. Ruth's frowsy hair clung damply to her pasty forehead. She still seemed in shock.

"Ruth," Stu urged. "What'd they say?"

The patient fluttered her hand in the air. "The usual. Pictures they want to take. Test this, test that—"

"Sounds like a good idea," Stu cut in. "They've got great technology now to monitor the babies' progress. Ultrasound pictures, stuff like that." She grinned. "Bet they could even tell you the sex of your babies."

"I said no." Ruth pressed her lips into a determined line.

*"No?"* we chorused.

"No. No pictures. No sonogram. No amnio . . . whatever." Ruth threw out her hands and leaned forward. "What for do they need pictures? I eat right, I don't smoke, I don't drink, I sleep too much, I take my prenatal vitamin with folic acid, I give up salt. I even walk around the block like a dog on a leash. I do everything they say except fetch." Her voice hiked up a pitch or two. "'Oh, but Mrs. Garfield, there might be problems. We need to take tests.' What am I, a dimwit? I know about Down syndrome, birth defects, blah blah blah. So? If I miscarry, God's will be done. If I *don't* miscarry, what does it matter if the babies aren't perfect? Perfect is overrated. I'll take my babies however they come—even if they look like Ben." She smirked. "Big hair, big nose, big mouth . . ."

We couldn't help snickering. Poor Ben.

Ruth's eyes suddenly widened, and she pawed the air for Stu's hand. "*Oy vey*. Did they really say . . . *twins*?" She smacked her forehead and fell back against the pillows. "*Ay-ay-ay*. A heart attack Ben will have."

STU FUSSED ALL THE WAY TO THE PARKING GARAGE. "I've met stubborn fools before, but Ruth Garfield takes the blue ribbon. Why *not* get a sonogram? It's just a picture! It doesn't *do* anything. It's just a way to monitor the babies, tell if anything is going wrong."

"What they gonna do if something's wrong!" Florida laid it out like a statement, not a question.

Stu opened her mouth, then closed it. We all knew the answer. Continue the pregnancy—or end it. Which Ruth obviously had no intention of doing, no matter what.

"Look," I said. "Didn't we just pray with Ruth for protection for her and her babies? So do we believe God can do it or not?" *Ha! I sounded like Avis*. Well, Avis wasn't here. Somebody had to do it.

We parted at the elevator. "You guys going back to the church? I've got to pick up Denny and the kids."

"And Carla and Cedric," Florida added.

"What?"

Florida beamed. "Stu gonna run me by a house she saw for rent. Realtor meetin' us there at one o'clock. Your Amanda said she'd watch the kids for me till we done."

I didn't ask the whereabouts of the Hickman daddy and big brother. Back home in bed, probably.

"Hey!" Florida called after me as the down elevator arrived and I stepped in. They were waiting to go up. "Think those twins really might look like Ben?" Our laughter stretched between us like shared taffy even as the door closed and the car sank down the elevator shaft.

CARLA SEEMED GENUINELY EXCITED to be going home from church with Amanda; Cedric less so. "I wanna play with my friends," he whined. "Why Mama hafta go look at a stupid ol' house, anyway?"

Josh had gone off "somewhere," but we took Becky Wallace and Little Andy back to the house, too, so she could get there by her check-in time. We all ended up in the backyard grilling hot dogs and bratwurst, which I found miraculously still in the freezer. Amanda got out an old soccer ball from the garage and played keep-away with the three kids, who ranged in age from three (Andy) to twelve (Cedric). Willie Wonka got excited and tried to play, which mostly meant getting in the way and tripping everybody up, easy to do in our shoebox of a backyard. Even Becky joined in. Falling down amid squeals of laughter seemed to be the highlight of the game.

I did a quick inventory of the serving tray. *Hot dog buns, mustard, melon slices, potato chips, lemonade—that oughta do it.* I put the tray down on the small rickety table on the back porch and sat down on the porch steps. "It's twins," I said as Denny nursed the hot dogs and brats on the grill.

"The Reilly twins?" Uptown's youth leader and his wife had ten-year-old twins. "What about them?"

95

I shook my head. "Ruth's twins."

Denny dropped the barbecue tongs he was using to turn the food. He grabbed for them before they hit the ground, but they bounced off his hand and went sailing into the flower garden. Muttering, he fished them out of the bushy marigolds and wiped them off on his shorts. I was enjoying this. Finally, he stood in front of me, pointing the tongs at my face, like a prosecutor cross-examining a witness. "You're kidding, right?"

I grinned big. "Nope. *Our* Ruth. Twins."

"Twins." Denny sank down on the steps beside me. "How's Ben taking it?"

"Don't know. She hadn't called him yet when we left the hospital."

"Oh, Lord, help us," he groaned. But the smell of charred meat soon launched him off the steps. "Uh-oh!"

We'd pretty much finished eating the charred hot dogs and brats when Stu and Florida arrived to pick up Carla and Cedric. "Might as well take Andy back home now too," Stu offered as Florida gathered up her kids.

"That house ain't his *home*," Becky huffed before disappearing up the stairs to get Andy's things. Stu and I exchanged glances. Andy's paternal grandmother was likely to give Becky a fight when she tried to get custody back.

We'd agreed not to say anything about "twins" in front of our kids until we got an OK from Ruth, but Florida had plenty to say about the house they'd looked at. "Not only does it got *three* bedrooms," she gushed, "but the back of the second floor got a nice little apartment—a studio kind of thang. We could rent it out, help with our own rent. Not that far from here either—half a mile, wouldn't you say, Stu? Close to Adele's Hair and Nails. Gotta get Carl up here, see if he like it."

"Hope he's handy." Stu pulled off her red beret and twisted her straight hair into a single braid to get it off her neck. "Needs a lot of repairs and a lot of paint. But the price is right—say, you got any of those burned hot dogs left? I'm starving." She took a shriveled, blackened hot dog, dipped it into the mustard jar, and munched on it without benefit of a bun. "What happened at church, Denny?"

"Why should I tell you backsliders?" he smirked. "Oh, but one thing you need to know. Pastor Clark announced that Uptown and New Morning are going to have another joint worship service next week. He's suggesting we do it the last Sunday of each month as long as New Morning is using our building."

"Well, thank ya, Jesus. That'll get Carl up here on a Sunday morning." Florida raised her voice. "Carla! Cedric! Leave that dog alone! We gotta go!"


I'D BEEN PATIENT ENOUGH. Denny had been offered the job of athletic director four whole days ago. Didn't he need to give them an answer?

After running Amanda over to the Reilly home for youth group, I marched into the living room where Denny was cooling off in front of the fan and a Cubs game on TV. "Denny? Can we talk about this job offer? Don't you need to give the school an answer?" I knew I was breaking one of the Baxter Ten Commandments: Don't start deep discussions in the middle of a baseball game. Or any other sport, for that matter.

Denny reluctantly hit the Mute button on the remote. "I've got two more weeks of sports camp to finish out. Couldn't start till the beginning of August anyway. They can wait a few more days."

I sat down on the ottoman. "But . . . what are you thinking? It seems like a wonderful promotion. You could develop a really fine athletic program at West Rogers. All your good ideas the other AD kept scrubbing. And we could certainly use the money." I almost added, *"After all, Josh will be going to college soon"*—except he wasn't. Not yet, anyway. That was another discussion for another day. Or another year.

Denny sighed. "I know. It's just . . . I need to find some peace about taking this job, Jodi. Or get a vision for it. Feel like I'm being skipped over two grades instead of one. Not sure I'm ready to be AD. Like I said before, I'd love the job of head coach. Don't know if I want to end up behind a desk."

Frustration niggled at my gut. "But you're not being offered the job of head coach, Denny! If you don't take the AD job, you'll still be an assistant coach. Is that what you want?"

Denny scratched the back of his head. "No. Not really. But if I don't take it, maybe they'll offer it to Kramer, then the head coach position would be open . . ." I gave my husband a look, and his voice trailed off. "Yeah, yeah, I know. Wishful thinking."

"Right. If they wanted Coach Kramer for AD, they would've asked him."

Denny snorted. "He's not going to like getting passed over either. Could get touchy—oh, hey! Homer! Homer!" Denny hit the sound and the roar of Cubs fans at Wrigley Field filled the living room as Sammy Sosa rounded the bases with clenched fist in the air. "Can we talk later, Jodi? I'd like to, you know . . ." His eyes glued once again to the TV.

"Sure. Later." But I felt unsettled as I headed toward the kitchen to find something to eat that might qualify as supper. Why didn't I just tell Denny that I was worried about my job? *Well, for one thing, Jodi Baxter, you don't know anything for sure.* I pulled open the refrigerator and stared into it blankly. Still hadn't asked Avis outright. But I should. I had a right to know, didn't I, if my job was going to get cut?

I shut the refrigerator door and picked up the phone.

# 12

*I* hung up the phone ten minutes later. *Well, that was fruit-less.* I came right out and asked Avis if I was going to lose my job. I knew she felt put on the spot. I mean, Avis and I had a rather complicated relationship. She was my boss at school—all business, authoritative but fair. But on weekends she was my Yada Yada sister and fellow church member—my spiritual mentor, if I was honest about it. And here I was calling her on a Sunday night with school business. Which hat was she supposed to wear?

"Jodi," she'd said, "I simply don't know how the school board is going to handle the proposed budget cuts. Yes, we might have to reduce staff. But that's not a foregone conclusion. There's also talk of closing a couple of schools."

*"No!"* Might as well have stuck my finger in an electric socket. "Oh, Avis. They wouldn't close Bethune Elementary, would they?!"

Avis sighed, like air squeezed out by a heavy weight. "I don't think so, Jodi, but as I said, I don't know. I think we both need to trust the Lord here. I know it's hard, but this is the time we need to claim God's promises."

"Like what?" I hated the challenge in my voice, but right then what I wanted was answers, not promises.

"Like Psalm 138, the last verse. 'The Lord will perfect that which concerns me.' Also Proverbs 3:5. 'Trust in the Lord with all your heart . . .' Both of those scriptures have been a resting place for me the past couple of weeks—not just with the budget uncertainties, but the stuff going on with my daughter too. Look them up."

"OK. Sure." *Jodi, you jerk. You've only been thinking about yourself. Avis has her own worries.* "How is Rochelle? And little Conrad? They still at your house?"

There'd been a brief hesitation. "No. No, she went home. Peter had a talk with her and Dexter. Told them to get counseling. They promised they would. So maybe Rochelle leaving him for a few days was the wake-up call Dexter needed to realize they should get help. But please keep them in your prayers."

Well, at least that was good news. I hoped. But after I hung up the phone, I just stood in the doorway between the kitchen and dining room. *Argh!* Still no answers. And Denny was in the living room glued to the TV, avoiding a decision that would impact our family big-time. My gut still wanted to march in there and scream, *"Look, Denny Baxter. I'm next in line at Bethune Elementary to get axed by budget cuts. We're one hiccup away from being a one-income family. Take the darn promotion!"*

I pressed my fingertips to my temple. Supper. I'd come in here to make some supper. I gave up on creativity and pulled out a frozen pizza, struggling to come up with a New Jodi response, not give in to Old Jodi fear and frustration. Decided the first step was to look up the scriptures Avis had suggested. While the oven was heating up for the pizza, I took my Bible out to the swing on the back porch and turned to Psalm 138.

My translation was a little different from Avis's, but the last verse read, "The Lord will fulfill His purpose for me . . ." Wow. God's purpose. For me.

I could feel my knotted-up spirit easing. I flipped pages to the book of Proverbs. This one was more familiar. "Trust in the Lord with all your heart; do not depend on your own understanding. Seek His will in all you do, and He will direct your paths."

I shut the Bible. A flock of sparrows and house wrens hopped around on the ground under the birdfeeder out by the garage, snatching up spilled birdseed. The feeder must be empty—

*Trust Me, Jodi.* The Voice deep in my spirit was so strong, I stopped pushing the swing with my foot to listen. *Trust Me. Seek My will . . . and I will direct your paths. I have a purpose for you—for Denny too. And I will fulfill My purpose. Can you trust Me?*

My eyes suddenly got wet. I'd been focusing on the problems, when I needed to be focusing on the promises. In fact, I'd been jumping ahead, assuming problems even before they happened. *Trust Me,* God said. Could I do that?

The back screen door banged. "Is that frozen pizza for dinner? Want me to stick it in the oven?" Denny lowered himself to the swing beside me. "Game's over. Did you, uh, want to talk some more about the job offer?"

Had to give him brownie points for willingness.

*Trust Me . . .*

"Nope." I smiled ruefully. "But that frozen pizza is about as appetizing as painted cardboard. Let's . . ." I felt reckless. If I was going to trust God with our jobs and our money, maybe God could spring for a pizza. "Let's walk over to Giordano's and get the real thing. Before the kids show up."

AT LEAST DENNY CALLED THE HIGH SCHOOl the next day, told them he was giving the job offer serious consideration and would give them a definite answer in one week. Could they wait that long? According to Denny, sure, they were happy to wait—if he said yes. But they let him know if he dragged his feet and then turned it down, it'd be difficult to find another applicant in time to get the athletic program up and running before school started. *"We want you, Baxter,"* the principal had growled. *"Step it up."*

I called Ruth at least twice that week to find out Ben's reaction to the news that Ruth was carrying a double blessing and to ask when we could leak the news. The first time, Ben answered the phone. He said nothing about twins, just growled that Ruth was on bed rest for a week ". . . where I can keep an eye on her." The second time Ruth said, "No, no, don't tell Yada Yada. I—I haven't told Ben yet."

"You haven't told Ben?" I screeched into the phone.

"I will! I will! Timing is everything."

News that big wasn't going to stay a secret for long. Especially when a bunch of Yada Yadas got together at Chanda's apartment a couple of evenings that week to help her finish packing. But Florida and I were models of restraint and didn't say anything. Had to admit Chanda's apartment was twice as clean as my own house. Guess she hadn't cleaned North Shore homes for years for nothing. Most of her furniture, however, was destined for the Salvation

Army or the dumpster. Chanda had already ordered all new furniture for the new house. *Must be nice . . .*

Nope, nope. Wasn't going to go there. I wouldn't trade Denny and my own family for all of Chanda's "lottery winnin's," even if the most you could say about my decorating style was Early Attic.

Florida took Chanda's three kids home with her Friday night for a sleepover, to get them out of the way when the movers came on Saturday—though where they were going to sleep was a mystery to me. Florida didn't even have enough room in the Hickman apartment for her own kids. "Jodi," Florida said when I dropped them off. "Think your Amanda be willin' to help me ride herd on these rugrats tomorrow? Maybe we can go to the zoo. Run off all that energy."

"Just call her," I said sweetly. I hoped Amanda would say yes. That would be my contribution to the zoo trip.

When I walked in the back door twenty minutes later, Amanda was on the kitchen phone with Florida. "Sure," she was saying. "José is coming over to hang out with me tomorrow. Can he come too?" I rolled my eyes. For two fifteen-year-olds who, according to Baxter rules, were still too young to date, Amanda and José managed to spend a lot of time together.

With Amanda off to the zoo the next day, Josh still in the bed after coming in who-knows-when, and Denny meeting at the church with volunteers involved in Uptown's homeless outreach, Willie Wonka and I had Saturday pretty much to ourselves—something I needed after chasing Ruth around the mall last weekend and ending up at the hospital. I could've cleaned out closets, hauled junk out of the basement, or tackled the mending basket piling up in our small bedroom. But the thermometer on the back porch crept steadily toward ninety degrees. Wonka had the right idea—he found a shady corner of the yard and zoned out.

I finally settled for making a humongous pasta salad that would feed my own family plus enough to take to the Sisulu-Smiths *and* drop off at Chanda's new house. My mother would be proud of me. Taking covered dishes when people were sick or moved or had babies was the backbone of the church I'd grown up in. Had to do *something* to show for my day's work.

I was adding chopped red and yellow peppers to the three large bowls of rigatoni pasta I had lined up on the counter when Josh came wandering through the kitchen still with that bed-head look, tank top hanging out over his wrinkled cargo shorts, looking for something to eat. "Don't wait supper on me, Mom," he mumbled from inside the refrigerator, his tattooed arm holding the door open. He backed out with the orange juice. "Don't know when I'll be back. Edesa's meeting me at Jesus People; she wants to see the shelters they run for homeless women and children."

He faded out the back door, disappearing for the rest of the day. Had we spoken more than thirty words to each other *per day* for the last three weeks? Seemed like I hardly ever saw my son anymore, and he was still living under our roof. Like Denny, he had one more week working with the city summer camps. Then what?

"He should be getting ready to go to college, that's what," I muttered, chopping up all the ham and turkey lunchmeat I could find. But that was a moot point, since he hadn't followed up on U of I's acceptance. He kept talking about "volunteering at Jesus People" for a year, but what did that mean exactly? And then there was Edesa. Where did she fit into his plans?

I stopped in midchop. Edesa! I'd told Yada Yada we were going to celebrate Edesa's birthday at the next meeting, which was tomorrow! But what? We were meeting at Avis's house, but I couldn't ask her to come up with a cake at the last minute. Yo-Yo could bring one from the Bagel Bakery, but they weren't cheap. I leaned my forehead against the nearest cupboard. No, no, no, I really didn't want to make a cake—

"You OK, Jodi?"

Becky's voice at the back door startled me. I hadn't heard her coming down the back stairs. "Um, sure. What's up?"

"Just wanted to know if the washing machine is free." She held up a bundle of laundry in her arms. "I know it's not my regular time slot, but . . ."

"Sure. No problem. Neither of my kids are here to do their laundry. Guess they'll be wearing week-old clothes for a while." Come to think of it, when *was* the last time Josh had done his laundry?

I suddenly had a brilliant idea. "Becky, would you like to make a cake for Edesa's birthday? We're celebrating at Yada Yada tomorrow night."

Becky just stared through the screen door. "Me? Bake a cake?" Her face slowly widened into a grin. "Really?"

*Bless her.* Becky making the cake would give me time to hunt for the meaning of Edesa's name on the Internet. Had the dickens of a time finding it, though. Not on any of the traditional baby name Web sites; couldn't find "Edesa" under Spanish names either. And, OK, by the time Becky got done borrowing ingredients and asking questions about oven temperatures and pans and recipes, I could've made that stupid cake myself.

But I'd started the "meaning of the name" tradition at Yada Yada birthdays; I didn't want to drop the ball with Edesa. I'd missed her birthday altogether last year when I was still laid up after the accident.

I finally Googled her name—and smiled just as Becky hollered from the back porch, "Hey, Jodi. Wanna see my cake?" The top layer of the chocolate cake looked like it might slide right off to make two zeroes, but, hey. It was her first-ever cake. And I'd finally found a meaning for *Edesa*. Becky and I slapped each other's hands in a high five.

Mutual success.

THE LAST SUNDAY IN JULY promised to be another scorcher. New Morning Christian Church provided the setting for our joint worship service—the spacious "store" they'd leased—but Uptown Community provided the time: nine thirty, the time we normally met on Sunday mornings. Josh left early to help with moving and setting up Uptown's sound system. Had to bite my tongue when he headed out the door "ready for church," still wearing those jeans that looked like they'd been through a paper shredder. What *was* it with Josh?! First a shaved head, then a tattoo, now he looked like he'd just crawled across America.

Teenagers.

But it sure felt good to breeze into a parking space in the shopping center lot instead of driving around and around the narrow streets off Morse Avenue, trying to find enough space to shoehorn our minivan. The butcher-paper sign on the new store still boasted FUTURE HOME OF NEW MORNING CHRISTIAN CHURCH—ALL ARE WELCOME! Denny and I made our way through the double-glass doors, propped open in lieu of central air-conditioning, which hadn't been installed yet. A crew of volunteers from both Uptown and New Morning were still setting up chairs. Uptown's sound-board rested on two sawhorses, wires running every which way like a spilled bowl of spaghetti; Josh was busy testing microphones and wire connections.

"Brother Denny! Sister Jodi," called a voice that seemed vaguely familiar. Swiveling my head, I saw the New Morning couple who sat with us at the Second Sunday Potluck two weeks ago coming toward us.

"Debra?" I ventured. "And Sherman . . . Meeks, right?" Sherman beamed. The men shook hands. Debra gave me a hug. *Oh dear. I'd practically promised to come to a New Morning service some Sunday afternoon.*

Debra must have read my mind. "We didn't make it to your service either. Maybe this"—her hand swept around the room—"is even better."

Wheezing, Sherman sucked on his inhaler. "I'm going to sit down. Let the young ones do the muscle ministry. Care to join me, Brother Denny?"

"Uh, was just going to help out a while. Save me a seat." Denny, suddenly animated, grabbed a couple of chairs off the dolly and whipped them into an unfinished row.

Debra and I cut our eyes at each other and grinned. "Guess your Denny isn't ready to be classified with the geezers who sit and watch," she chuckled. We chatted a few more minutes, then hustled to our seats as the combined praise teams from both Uptown and New Morning struck up the first song. Instead of a lively gospel song as I expected, the first song started out slow and simple . . .

*I love to worship You,*
*I love to worship You . . .*

A lot of Uptown people seemed to be missing. Were they on vacation? Forget we were having a joint service? Florida and Carl came in a few minutes late with kids in tow—no Chris, though. As Florida had predicted, Carl was more likely to show up at our joint service. Across the room, Avis lifted her hands in praise, eyes closed, singing the words from deep inside. Peter Douglass, her more reserved husband, nodded in time to the repeated words. I felt that familiar tug in my gut, realizing that Peter Douglass and Carl Hickman would naturally be more at home in a church where they weren't the "token black men"; at the same time, I was afraid Uptown would lose their wives—my Yada Yada sisters, my friends—who'd been brave enough to grace our little church with their presence, nudging us toward becoming a "house of prayer for all nations," even if we weren't there yet.

*I love to worship You,*
*I love to worship You . . .*

Somehow I missed seeing Nony come in with her two boys. But a flash of a royal blue head wrap caught my eye and there they were, sitting near the front. She, too, seemed to be embracing the words of the song with her whole self, oblivious to those around her. I didn't see Mark or Hoshi. The Japanese student must have stayed behind so Nony could make it to church. *Bless her, Jesus.* She had such a servant heart.

*I love to worship You,*
*I love to worship You . . .*

I squeezed my eyes shut. *Stop it, Jodi Baxter. Think about the words. Are you here to count noses or worship?* I kept my eyes shut and just soaked up the voices all around me, singing from their hearts. "I love to worship You . . ."

*Yes, yes. I do love to worship You, Jesus.* I lifted my own arms, and found myself reaching up, up. *Yes, yes, I love to worship You . . .*

But when the joint service was over a couple of hours later, I realized the missing Uptown people never did show up.

# 13

The missing Uptown people bothered me all afternoon. It was just a "brotherly" worship service with the church that was using our building, for Pete's sake! And yet, maybe the idea of a "church merger," though only mentioned at the men's breakfast, had gotten around. Denny told me not to make too much of the absentees—after all, it was midsummer. Sunday attendance was often down this time of year.

They'd missed some great worship, though. The joint service lasted a good two and a half hours, but that still got us out around noon. Theoretically, anyway. "Hug somebody! Hug somebody!" Pastor Cobbs encouraged after the last prayer. He and Pastor Clark had shared the service, focusing on how worship itself can bring people together across our differences, because the attention is on God, not on ourselves. A good message for two churches sharing the same space, even temporarily. Most people seemed eager to stand around and talk afterward. Some kind soul from New Morning had plugged in a huge coffeepot, and I think we drained the tank, in spite of the muggy heat.

When Denny realized Yada Yada was meeting at the Douglass's apartment that evening, he called Peter and offered to liberate him, go to the Heartland Café for iced coffee or something. "I've got something I'd like to talk to you about, anyway," I heard him say into the phone.

Denny dropped me off, along with Becky and the lopsided cake, and told us to send Peter down. Stu was driving Little Andy home after his Sunday visit, said she'd meet us there. We had to walk up to the third floor, but at least Avis and Peter's apartment was air-conditioned. "Thank ya, Jesus!" Florida said when she arrived, plopping into one of Avis's beige-and-black armchairs. "Hot day like this is a good reminder I don't wanna go to hell. Mm-mm. Avis, can I sleep on yo' couch tonight? This cool air sure does feel good."

Frankly, I was kinda surprised Avis and Peter had decided to stay in her apartment after they got married—the same apartment where Avis and her first husband, Conrad Johnson II, had lived happily with an "empty nest." But it was a lovely apartment, nestled among the tops of the elms lining the narrow street, with polished wood floors, bookshelves covering whole walls, pictures of her grandkids, and framed artwork. Just being there made me feel so . . . peaceful, even when it filled up with our motley crew of Yada Yada sisters.

And fill it up we did! Even Nony and Hoshi. A couple from New Morning Church had offered to visit Mark that evening, Nony explained. "Mark would be livid if he suspected he was being babysat," she added sheepishly. "I convinced him Sister Debra and Brother Sherman had come to play with the boys."

*Debra and Sherman Meeks. Of course.* The sweet older couple from New Morning just went up another two notches in my estimation.

A conversation in rapid Spanish floated up the stairwell, then

Delores and Edesa burst into the apartment. Edesa immediately kicked off her sandals and padded across Avis's wood floor in her bare feet. *"Edesa's birthday?"* Delores Enriques mouthed at me, her back to the younger woman.

*"Sí,"* I whispered, using up half of my Spanish vocabulary.

The black Honduran college student spun around on her bare feet, arms wide as she gazed admiringly at the spacious front room. "Ah. Someday I will have an apartment like this, so *mi familia* can come to visit. My apartment is—how do you say? *Pequeño,* like a dollhouse."

"You are so tiny, *mi hermana,* a dollhouse is all you need." Delores gave me a wink. One birthday celebration, coming up.

I was surprised to see Ruth, though. Wasn't she supposed to be on bed rest? She arrived muttering and out of breath. "Would an elevator be asking too much?" She collapsed into another over-stuffed armchair. "Next time, Yada Yada better be ground level, or Ruth and her cargo stay home."

Yo-Yo, bringing up the rear, hooted. "Yo, Ruth. Cussing out each stair in Yiddish didn't help any."

Ruth sniffed. "I wasn't cussing."

"Ha. I know cussing when I hear it. No matter what language." Yo-Yo plopped on the floor beside Ruth.

I tried not to laugh. *Ruth's "cargo."* She better tell the big news to the rest of Yada Yada tonight. I, for one, couldn't keep my mouth shut much longer. And I knew Florida was itching to spill the beans.

Chanda was the last to arrive. "Dat taxi could be taking me to de moon an' back, as much he charged," she complained. "Don' know no babysitter in me new place, had to drop off Thomas and de girls at me sister's place." But her face brightened. "Soon as mi get settled, Yada Yada can meet at *mi* 'ouse, what you tink?"

"We'd love to meet in your new home, Chanda." Avis took a seat in an elegant rocker that breathed *antique*, while the rest of us found places to sit or perch on her modern beige-and-black furniture. "We have a little celebration tonight, but I thought I would read a scripture to encourage all of us." Avis reached for her modern-language Bible. The rustling around the room hushed.

"From Isaiah 44 . . . 'Listen to me, Jacob my servant, Israel my chosen one. The Lord who made you and helps you says: O Jacob, my servant, do not be afraid. O Israel, my chosen one, do not fear. For I will give you abundant water to quench your thirst and to moisten your parched fields. And I will pour out my Spirit and my blessings on your children. They will thrive like watered grass, like willows on a riverbank. Some will proudly claim, "I belong to the Lord." Others will say, "I am a descendant of Jacob." Some will write the Lord's name on their hands and will take the honored name of Israel as their own.'"

I grinned. I had told Avis what I'd found out about Edesa's name, and she'd found the perfect scripture. I glanced toward the door into Avis's dining room where Becky was waiting to bring in the cake—but sudden sobbing from Ruth's armchair caught me off guard. Becky peeked into the room, looking confused.

We all gaped at Ruth. "Ruth?" Avis said gently. "Are you all right?"

Ruth nodded, rummaging in her roomy bag for a wad of tissues. She cried and blew her nose and cried some more. Sitting on the floor by her feet, Yo-Yo looked worried. Delores, sitting next to her, put an arm around Ruth's shoulder and prayed quietly to herself, her lips moving.

Ruth blew her nose again and dabbed at her blotchy face. "Don't mind me. I'm not dying. It's just that scripture . . . where is that, Avis?"

"Chapter 44 of Isaiah."

"Read that part again about 'blessings on the children.'"

Avis nodded. "Let's see . . . verses three and four. 'I will pour out my Spirit and my blessings on your children. They will thrive like watered grass, like willows on a riverbank.'"

"And the next part," Ruth insisted.

"All right. 'Some will proudly claim, 'I belong to the Lord.' Others will say, 'I am a descendant of Jacob.' Some will write the Lord's name on their hands and will take the honored name of Israel as their own.'"

Ruth beamed through her tears. "That's my promise! My children will thrive like watered grass, like willows by a riverbank. And they'll treasure their Jewish heritage too. And write Yahweh's name on their hearts."

"Your *children*?" Yo-Yo grinned up at Ruth. "You an' Ben plannin' to pop more kids in the cooker?"

I winced. Yo-Yo's teasing of Ruth needed to stop. I opened my mouth to say something, but Ruth patted her tummy under the dark, shapeless dress she was wearing. "Already did. Doc says it's twins."

She said it so matter-of-factly, nobody reacted for a full two seconds. Then—Chanda screeched. "Say again, Sista Ruth? You got an A an' B selection in dere?"

115

That cracked everyone up, and suddenly we were all talking at once. After several minutes of laughing, hugging, and shaking heads, Adele took charge of the conversation. "How's Ben taking it, Ruth? Seems like this good news could be a major challenge for you two. I oughta know. Taking care of MaDear is like having a toddler around the house, and it ain't no picnic at *my* age." *And I'm younger than you are* hung unspoken in the air.

The room fell silent. Ruth studied the ceiling and tapped her foot. "Oh. Uh . . ." She cleared her throat. "Ben doesn't know yet."

I couldn't believe it! Apparently, neither could the rest of the Yada Yadas, who opened their collective mouths and gasped, "He doesn't know?!" But Avis rescued Ruth from a corporate scolding and moved us directly to prayer, thanking God for the new life He had created, praying protection for Ruth's health, asking God's grace to cover the challenging situation facing Ben and Ruth. Since we were already in prayer mode, Avis suggested we delay our celebration a few minutes and add other prayer requests.

"Well, I got one," Becky said, still leaning in the doorway between front room and dining room. "Can anybody get me a job? Parole officer says I can work, but somebody gotta set up an appointment for me first; can't just go out lookin'."

Yo-Yo snorted. "Yeah. Never woulda got my job at the Bagel Bakery if Ruth hadn't—hey!" Yo-Yo jumped to her feet. "The Bagel Bakery needs a counter girl! Why didn't I . . ." She whirled on Ruth. "Ruth! Ya think ya could, ya know, put in a good word for Becky?"

Ruth shrugged, seemingly relieved that her pregnancy was out of the spotlight. "Sure, sure. Why not? I'm already dangling on the edge of a limb. Might as well saw it off—ack!" Ruth struggled under Becky's embrace, as our newest ex-con threw her arms around Ruth's neck from behind the couch.

So we prayed for a job for Becky and threw in Florida's plea that the Hickmans would get approved by Section Eight for the house rental they'd found over near Clark Street. "Just a couple of blocks from Adele's Hair and Nails. Won't have any excuse lookin' like somethin' the cat drug in," she snickered. "An' if we get approved, we movin' in two weeks. Gotta get the kids registered in they new schools 'fore school starts."

New schools? Well, of course. Chris was in high school, Cedric in middle school, Carla in—

*Whoa!* Would that put Carla Hickman in the Bethune Elementary school district? She'd be going into fourth grade, not third, but still, that'd be great if Florida could have one of her kids in Avis's school.

If the school board didn't axe the school first. Or my job.

After prayers, Becky finally brought out her cake, complete with flaming candles, and we sang "Happy Birthday" to Edesa. She seemed genuinely surprised. Well, OK, her birthday had been a week and a half ago. She probably thought we'd forgotten. "Sorry we're late," I said, giving her a hug.

"Oh, no, it's wonderful." Edesa's dark eyes misted even as her smile widened. "Birthdays in my village in Honduras are not so important. In my family, I have two brothers and three sisters younger than myself. I am the oldest. No money for parties or gifts. Everything goes to send us to school."

"Blow, Edesa!" Becky butted in. "Candles almost drowning in the frosting!"

She blew, we laughed, Becky cut the cake—which tasted like

chocolate-coated sugar—and I brought out the card we'd all been signing surreptitiously under Edesa's nose. I'd found a picture of Niagara Falls on the Internet and printed it out on heavy paper. "Edesa, if you know a different meaning of your name, you better tell me now! Because the closest I could find was . . . Avis, could you read that verse from Isaiah again? Listen for the clue."

Avis found the verse again. "For I will give you abundant water to quench your thirst and to moisten your parched fields. And I will pour out my Spirit and my blessings on your children. They will thrive like watered grass, like willows on a riverbank."

Edesa looked at the picture of Niagara Falls that had our signatures scrawled all over it, little hearts, words of love. "Abundant water? That is my name?"

"Well, the only Edesa I could find was spelled E-D-E-S-S-A, and is the name of an ancient city in Macedonia, which is now Greece. And the name means 'abundance of water,' or 'life' because of how water nourishes life."

"Oh," breathed Delores. "That is perfect. Edesa has brought so much life to our family, so much happiness to *mis niños*."

"To all of us, I'd say." Adele's voice was surprisingly husky. "If I had a daughter, I'd want her to be like you, Edesa."

To my surprise, a tear dribbled toward Edesa's chin. Her mouth quivered. "I . . . wish it were true. *Mi familia*, they sacrificed so much to send me here to school. I have so little to send them. I don't know. Maybe I should be a business major or computer programmer—something to make money instead of public health."

A chorus of protest bounced around the circle. "You listen to me, sister girl," Adele commanded, unlocking her arms, which had been resting across her ample bosom. "You made a good decision to switch to public health. Women and children need you—whether here or back home in Honduras. Their health is more important than money."

"That's right, that's right!" Florida clapped and we all joined in until it sounded like welcome rain.

Edesa hugged the photo card to her chest. "Thank you so much, *mis hermanas*. Yada Yada is my second family here in America. After the Enriques *familia*, that is." She dimpled at Delores.

"So." Becky cleared her throat. "What y'all think of the cake? Made it myself."

A loud buzzer in Avis's foyer saved us from having to do more than make a few murmurs of appreciation. Avis frowned. She walked over to the intercom next to the front door and pushed a button. "Yes? Who is it?"

From where I was sitting, all I could hear was static. Or was it—crying?

"You all go on. I'll be back in a minute." Avis disappeared out her front door; we heard her feet scurrying down the three flights of stairs. We all just looked at each other, then busied ourselves with Becky's cake.

A couple of minutes later, a babble of voices floated up the stair-well—Avis's low voice trying to soothe . . . the high-pitched questions of a child . . . and the gulping sobs of a young woman. "He hit me, mama. He *hit* me! I . . . I . . ."

"Oh, baby. Oh, baby. Shh, shh. Here, give me Conny . . ."

The trio wedged through the door. Avis held her grandson, a strapping toddler almost too big to carry. Behind her, her daughter Rochelle stopped, startled, when she saw us, her eyes big, her face a bloated mess. "Oh. I-I'm sorry. I . . . I didn't know." She tried to take the child from Avis's arms. Her chest shuddered with incomplete sobs. "I'll leave. You're busy, mama."

"Girl, you'll do no such thing!" Adele stood up. "We were just leaving, weren't we, sisters? We'll be out of here 'fore that baby can count to three."

Little Conrad giggled. "One!" he shouted. "Two! Free!"

# 14

We hustled down the stairs as quietly as a dozen women could manage, with Yo-Yo propping up Ruth and saying, "Take it easy, take it easy." Nony said she would take Ruth and Yo-Yo home so they wouldn't have to wait outside for Ben to come. Becky and I caught a ride home with Stu.

Stu was furious. "Rochelle shouldn't have gone back to that jerk the first time! I could've told her that."

"They were going to get counseling," I pointed out.

Stu slammed her fist on the steering wheel. "Oh. So we wait until hubby beats her up before we tell her to leave him."

"I just meant—"

"Jodi, shut up. You're married to Denny the teddy bear, for heaven's sake. What do you know?"

I pressed my lips together and looked out the window. Car windows were up, air-conditioning on. I longed to roll the window down and let the wind blow over my face. I felt like crying. *Why?* Because Stu jumped on me? No. I knew she was upset. I wanted to cry for Rochelle. For Avis. For little Conrad. For Conrad senior and the grandson he'd never know and wasn't there to protect. For Peter Douglass, who was going to arrive home and find his step-daughter and stepgrandson in his home again. This time bruised and desperate.

*Oh God, why does this happen even in the best families? Why does Satan keep messing with people I love?* Avis was probably the woman I admired most in the whole world. I wanted to be like her. Seemed like she'd done everything right. But I knew her mother heart was breaking for her daughter. How would *I* feel if Amanda got slapped around by—

I felt like throwing up. *Oh God, please don't let anyone abuse my daughter! Protect her, Lord! Protect all our daughters! Emerald Enriques and her little sisters . . . Chanda's Cheree and Dia . . . Carla Hickman, who's already had her life turned upside down twice in her nine short years . . .*

And Ruth. Did she have baby girls in her womb? Ruth would be seventy and Ben eighty years old by the time those babies had their twentieth birthday. I'd been thinking, *If they're born safely, all will be well.* Would it? What would life hand them by the time they were fifteen? twenty? thirty? Was that what Ben was afraid of?

Fear twisted my gut. Fear for all our children. For Chris Hickman, maybe out on the street tonight, "just hangin'," getting himself into who-knows-what trouble and worrying Florida to death . . . for Yo-Yo's half brothers, growing up without parents except a big sister who cared . . . for my Josh, basically a good kid, who was morphing into a stranger, hot-wired to "make a differ-ence" but with no real direction, floundering . . .

The garage door went up. Stu drove the Celica inside. Our

Dodge Caravan wasn't back yet. The three of us got out and walked silently up the walk to the back porch of our shared two-flat, lost in our own thoughts. Lights were on inside the first floor. My kids must be home from youth group.

At the steps I stopped. A breeze off Lake Michigan a half mile away shifted the sultry air. I turned to my housemates. "I . . . can't go in yet. I feel so torn up. Do you think . . . could we pray?"

DENNY GOT HOME while Stu, Becky, and I were still on the back steps, holding hands, praying. Not exactly powerhouse prayers like Avis and Florida and Nony might pour out. Or Adele. Just three white chicks, our ages spanning two decades—married, single, single mom . . . me raised in the church, Stu with her master's degree, Becky just out of prison. But I felt strength as we gripped each other's hands and just talked to God about our fears, our anger, our helplessness for Avis and her daughter, whose similar feelings must be magnified ten times over.

After the last "amen," Stu and Becky said goodnight and climbed the back stairs to their apartment. Denny, who'd been leaning against the handrail the last two minutes, sat down beside me in the dark. "What in the world happened over there tonight?"

I could see his features outlined by the streetlight in the alley. Frowning. Confused. "Didn't Peter tell you?"

Denny shook his head. "I brought him home; he said he'd send you down. But he came back out two minutes later and said all the Yada Yadas had gone already. And that he had a 'situation' upstairs."

I sighed and told him about Rochelle arriving in hysterics, her face swollen. Saying Dexter had hit her. Denny put his head in his hands. "Oh my God." It was a groan. A prayer. He sat that way for a long time. I sat beside him, not saying anything. What was there to say?

After a while, Denny went inside. I heard him rummaging in a cupboard, then water running in the sink. I thought he was headed for the living room, to numb the pain with the TV, but he came back out with a glass of water and sat down beside me on the steps. He took my hand. "Jodi. I think I should take the AD job. What do you think?"

"You do? I mean, I think it's great! But what changed your mind?"

"Peter Douglass. Well, no. God did. But Peter was a good sounding board. As businesslike as he seems most of the time, he really has a heart for kids. I saw that at our Guys' Day Out last spring. Mostly he just listened, but he also asked good questions. What would I really like to see happen with the sports program at West Rogers High? Where would I have the most influence? Stuff like that. Kinda surprised me that he didn't even mention the raise in pay or what would look good on my résumé. He focused on the opportunity to bridge the gap between academics and the sports program, develop good communication between staff—stuff like that."

I squeezed his hand. "All the 'stuff' that's been sending you up the wall the last two years, especially because you've always felt helpless to do anything about it." My voice caught a little. *Oh God, I've been so self-centered about this whole job thing. Wanting Denny to take the job to give us some financial security, a cushion in case my own job went south.* I studied my husband's face in the shadows. "You're good at that kind of thing, you know."

"What kind of thing?"

"Being a bridge."

Denny didn't answer immediately. Then he cleared his throat, as if embarrassed. "That's what Peter said."

Suddenly I knew that the AD job was God's gift, not just to us but to West Rogers High School. In fact, I felt like laughing. They had no idea they'd just unleashed God's man on their public school!

"Hel-loo? Parents?" Amanda's sing-song voice cut into the darkness from inside the back screen door, tinged with exasperation. "'Say, kids, do you know where your parents are?' No, we don't, because they forgot to tell us when they got home. So here we sit, Wonka and me, imagining all sorts of gruesome headlines in tomorrow's paper—"

"Oh, quit." Denny's laugh cut off her dirge. "You didn't come into the kitchen to look for us. I bet you were gonna sneak the last of the mint-chocolate-chip ice cream. Right? Right? But I'm gonna get it first!"

Amanda screeched as her dad launched himself toward the screen door, both of them yelling, "*My* ice cream! Mine! Mine!"

DENNY CALLED THE HIGH SCHOOL Monday morning, accepted the job, and said he'd be in the office first thing the following Monday. When he hung up, he looked at me apologetically. "Just realized we usually have a couple of weeks in August before preseason practice starts. But with this new job . . . it doesn't look like the Baxters are going to get any vacation this summer."

That thought had occurred to me too. Not that we'd actually bought tickets to Alaska or Paris or anything—*yeah, right*—but we had talked about going camping at Starved Rock or maybe Kickapoo

State Park. But I shrugged. "Well, my accident put the *kibosh* on our vacation plans last summer. So now we're even, buddy." I kissed the dimple in his cheek. I was so grateful for Denny's new job, no way was I going to complain about not camping in the middle of bee season.

Denny and Josh had just left for their last week of coaching summer camp when the phone rang. "Jodi." It was Avis. Calm, cool, and collected. No hint of the melodrama going on at her house. "Can you come by the school office today? The local school council met last Friday and I have some answers to your questions. Of course, nothing's official until—"

"Avis! Just tell me! Do I have a job or not?"

"Eleven. How about eleven? All right? See you then." *Click.*

*Good grief.* I changed out of my shorts and pulled on a denim skirt. No way was I going to dress up for a meeting with Avis in the middle of summer, even if we were meeting at the school office. I even allowed myself a half hour and took Willie Wonka with me for his morning walk. But as we made our way toward Bethune Elementary in typical Wonka fashion—*walk, stop, sniff, pee*—I realized something extraordinary.

I didn't feel anxious. In fact, that old spiritual I'd come to love stepped once more in slow rhythm through my spirit . . .

*We've come this far by faith*
*Leaning on the Lord*
*Trusting in His holy Word*
*He's never failed me yet . . .*

Only three cars sat in the parking lot, one of them Avis's black

Camry. Wonka and I stepped into the cool hallway of the school, its polished floors wearing silence like an ill-fitting shroud. School hallways weren't supposed to be quiet. They were supposed to be full of running feet, childish voices, stern commands to "Slow down and walk!"

No one was in the outer office, but Avis's door was open. I half-expected to see her in one of her typical school-day outfits, usually slacks with a soft blouse and a jacket, that somehow managed to seem professional and feminine at the same time. But she was actually wearing a lightweight running suit, pale blue with white stripes down the leg, a tank top, and lightweight jacket. "Hey," I said.

She looked up. "Hey yourself." She peered over her reading glasses. "I see you brought along some company."

I sank into the armchair on the business side of her desk. "Yeah, thought I might need the moral support." Wonka, totally fatigued from his half-hour walk, sank to the floor with a grateful wheeze.

Avis set aside the papers she'd been working on and folded her hands. "Well, first the good news. They are *not* going to close Bethune Elementary."

I sat up. "Avis! That's great! That's wonderful! Praise God! Oh! That is really good news." It was. I smiled big at Avis. She had poured so much of herself into making this "a school that worked." But we all knew nothing was guaranteed. Political pressure and back scratching made their way into school-board politics as well.

Then my smile faded. "Oh. You said, 'first' the good news. Now comes the bad news, right? It's my job, isn't it. They're cutting my job."

"No." She smiled. "More good news. We're keeping all our teachers."

127

This was too much. I jumped out of my chair. "Halle*lu*jah! Oh, Avis, you just made my day!" I laughed. I did a little jig right there in Avis's office. I wished all the Yada Yada sisters would burst through the door right that moment and bring some music so we could "get down" and do some *real* praising.

"Jodi." Avis interrupted my little jig, her voice sober.

*Uh-oh.* I sat down. "What?"

"There is bad news. They—"

"Oh, Avis. Is it Rochelle?"

She looked momentarily confused. "No, no. I mean, yes, that too. We can talk about that later. But I'm talking about what the school board has decided to do. They *are* closing three schools— one north, one south, one west."

"But you said *not* Bethune Elementary," I prompted. I wanted to keep a tight grasp on the good news.

"That's right. But *all* the remaining schools, including Bethune, will need to take in the displaced students. Most of them are under-achieving, needing lots of help to pull them up to grade level." Avis drew in a big breath. "What this means for you, Jodi, is an influx of students into your classroom—temporarily anyway, until we add another class."

I just stared at her. Add *more* students to my classroom? No! That was crazy! I already had twenty-five, give or take. I didn't know where we'd put more desks, much less teach more students who sounded like they'd need a lot of extra attention.

*He's never failed me yet . . .*

"OK, LORD," I muttered fifteen minutes later as Willie Wonka and I did the *walk, stop, sniff, pee* routine on the way home. "I wanna be happy about still having my job. But it *really* feels overwhelming to add more students. I don't want to just *have* a job. I want to do it well." But that song just wouldn't leave me alone.

*Oh! O-o-o-oh! O-o-o-oh! Can't turn around*
*We've come this far by faith!*

# 15

The house was empty when I got home; Amanda had a daytime babysitting gig all that week and wouldn't be back until six. The light was blinking on the answering machine though. *Uhh.* Didn't want to be bothered by the phone. Too much had happened in the last twenty-four hours. Rochelle showing up at Avis's house last night in a state . . . Denny accepting the new position at West Rogers High . . . Me still having a job, but with too many students . . .

I needed time to calm down. And pray.

But the blinking light nagged me. I hit the Play button, telling myself I didn't have to call the person back. But at least I'd know who called, could call later—

"Jodi? Ben Garfield here. Thought you Yada Yadas ought to know I had to take Ruth back to the hospital last night. I *told* her not to go to the Douglass's. Climb three flights up? *Oy*, she just spent a week on bed rest. But does she listen to me? Such a *shmegege!* Maybe she'll listen to you. Just wish somebody would pound some sense into her head before this pregnancy kills her. OK, that's it." The machine clicked off.

I sank into a chair at the dining room table, head in my hands. *Oh God.* Guilt nibbled at my concern. We should've realized stairs would be a problem. *Good grief.* Why didn't we just meet somewhere else last night?

I sighed. On the other hand, it was a good thing Avis was home and not somewhere else when Rochelle and the baby showed up last night, wasn't it? *Argh.* Why did everything feel like a catch-22?

*So who's in control here, Jodi Baxter?* The Voice in my spirit stifled my whimpering. *Stop beating yourself up. You know what to do. Get your focus back. Pray for Ruth. Pray for Rochelle. Pray for the kids coming into your classroom this fall. Pray God's promises over these situations. Then call Ben.*

Right. I took a deep breath. At least my "stewing" time was getting shorter.

Half an hour later, fortified by a gospel CD belting out "I Go to the Rock," a reading of Psalm 103, ten minutes of out-loud prayers, and a fresh cup of coffee, I dialed the Garfields' number. *Maybe he's at the hospital with Ruth,* I thought hopefully.

"Yeah? Ben here."

"Oh. Hi, Ben. It's Jodi. Got your message." Silence. "Is Ruth OK? What's happening?"

"She's all right, I guess. She got dizzy last night, blood pressure way up, heart beating funny. Scared the heck out of me. But they got her stabilized, just keeping her for observation overnight."

"Oh, Ben. I'm sorry. We were thoughtless, meeting at Avis's house last night. Not used to thinking of Ruth being pregnant, I guess."

He snorted. "Yeah, well, you and me both. Still rocks my boat. Look here, Jodi. Might as well say what's on my mind. I like you ladies. Yada Yada's been good for Ruth. She needs female company. Gives her somebody else to talk to. *Huh*. Used to think my ears were going to fall off. But—"

I braced myself with another gulp of coffee.

"—you're not helping us here. She's too old to be pregnant. *I'm* too old. I was hoping to talk her into early retirement so we could enjoy a few years together. Now this. *Mishegoss*. That's what it is."

My heart melted. "I know. Must be tough thinking about parenthood at your age."

"Parenthood!" The word came out strangled. "We'll take up *that* one if she makes it that far. Don't you Yadas get it? This is a risky pregnancy! She should have ended it when she had the chance. I know, I know, all you good Christians have a heart attack if anyone brings up abortion. Look, I'm a Jew. I don't like it either. But when it comes down to life and death—*my* wife—sometimes you gotta do what you gotta do. And I'd like a little moral support from our so-called friends." Ben stopped, breathing hard.

A lump tightened my throat. "Oh, Ben." I didn't know what to say.

Ben Garfield heaved a sigh into my ear. "Yeah, well, sorry for dumping on you, Jodi. Just . . . feel like I'm going crazy sometimes."

Without knowing where they came from, words tumbled out. "Ben, I worry about Ruth too. I pray for her constantly. But you know as well as anyone how much she's longed for a child—for years! Now, it's like a miracle. A dream come true for Ruth."

"More like a nightmare," he mumbled. "I'm husband number three, remember? Wasn't supposed to happen on my watch."

"Ben." He hadn't hung up on me yet. Might as well blunder onward. "I know there are some risks. But she's getting good medical care. She'll probably be fine! And when those babies are born, you'll forget all the worry and—"

"*Babies!* Whaddya mean, babies?"

A horrible realization hit me right between the eyes. Ruth hadn't told Ben yet. But it was too late. "Uh, you know, babies." I pushed the word out. "Twins."

"*Twins!*" What followed was a string of Yiddish no doubt meant to blister my ear. Then—the phone went dead.

"Oh God," I groaned, clicking the Off button and slumping against the kitchen door jamb. "What have I done? What do I do now?"

Willie Wonka, somehow sensing all was not right, roused himself from the floor and pushed his nose into my dangling hand. I pushed him away, alternately feeling mad at myself, then furious at Ruth for not telling Ben like she should have when she found out. Irritated, I yanked open the dishwasher door and started putting away yesterday's dishes, though they seemed in danger of not making it unscathed into the cupboards.

Half an hour later the phone rang. The caller ID said Garfield. "Hello?"

"So when was Ruth going to tell me, huh?" Ben's voice snapped over the wires with no introduction. "Do all you Yadas know? Whaddya think this is, some kind of joke? That was cruel. Not what I expected from you, Jodi Baxter."

Tears sprang to my eyes. Why was he blaming *me?* "Ben, she only told the prayer group last night." *Well, mostly true, though Stu, Florida, and I were at the hospital when the docs told Ruth.* "We thought she'd told you too." *Well, sorta true. Ruth told us last night she hadn't told him yet, but I, for one, assumed she'd have to tell Ben once she'd spilled the beans to the whole group. Didn't I?*

"Well, she didn't. Makes me feel about as significant as roadkill. But I got one thing to say to you. You think I'm just being selfish. A grouchy old man. You think I don't know how you Yadas talk?" I winced as he plunged on. "But give me some credit. Bottom line, I don't want Ruth to end up with a broken heart."

"Oh, Ben. Ruth knows the risks. She does! But she's choosing to leave it with God, to walk with this miracle as long as she can."

"No she doesn't." He said it under his breath.

"Doesn't what?"

"Doesn't know the half of it—look, Jodi. I gotta go." The phone went dead.

I stared at the phone in my hand a long time. *Doesn't know the half of—what?*

I TRIED TO PUT BEN'S PHONE CALL BEHIND ME and think about supper instead. I'd blundered, but it wasn't really about Ben and me. He and Ruth would have to deal with her zipped lip. Besides, we had our own family issues. Josh, for instance. Here it was almost August already, and he was still like a fish flopping around on the beach.

Denny jumped in the shower when he and Josh got home that evening, but Josh appeared in the kitchen with his old skateboard under his arm. "Uh, mind if I eat supper later? Thought I'd go to the lake, do a little skateboarding. Gotta catch the daylight, ya know." He snitched a handful of grapes from the fruit bowl and headed out the door. A moment later, I heard the skateboard rattling down our bumpy alley.

I shook my head, plopping spoonfuls of shredded potatoes-eggs-flour mixture on a hot griddle for potato latkes and giving the sliced, smoked kielbasa sausage a stir in the frying pan. Skateboarding? Hadn't seen that old thing since Josh was a freshman. What was up with that?

Amanda called to say she wouldn't be home until ten; the parents had just called and asked if she could feed the kids and put them to bed too. "Sheesh, Mom. What could I say? I'm here already. Just wished they'd asked me earlier. Hope this doesn't happen every night. I've got a life, too, ya know."

Yeah, teenagers with "a life" were what turned their parents' hair gray. At least I knew she was safe and bored for the next four hours. I had way too much potato batter for just Denny and me, but it'd turn brown if I didn't cook it up. Josh would just have to figure out how to heat them up later.

"Hey, this is nice." Denny came in, eyeing the two plates on the table. "No kids? Hm." He kissed me on the back of my neck as I loaded latkes on a plate, then nibbled my ear. He smelled delicious after his shower. "Can this supper wait?" he murmured. "We could . . ."

I giggled in spite of myself. "Look, Romeo. I'm a much better lover when my stomach's not growling. And these are hot. Do you take rain checks?"

He threw up his hands in mock resignation, fished a bottle of Merlot from the cupboard, and got out a corkscrew. "Thought we were saving that for a special occasion," I said. "Our anniversary's coming up."

"What's more special than having my girl all to myself? A few potatoes, a bottle of wine, and thou"—he waggled his eyebrows—"after supper."

*Huh.* Just about the time Josh would walk in. I looked at the potato latkes. I looked at my freshly scrubbed husband, smelling of alluring aftershave. "On second thought . . ." I grinned, pulled out a sheet of aluminum foil, and covered the plate of hot latkes. "These can wait."

JOSH CAME IN AROUND EIGHT THIRTY, just as daylight was fading. Denny and I were clothed once more and still at the table, plates pushed back, sipping that no-reason-at-all glass of wine, just talking. I was glad I'd had a chance to tell Denny about my meeting with Avis this morning and the phone call with Ben before Josh got home. Now, sweaty and rumpled, Josh filled the dining room doorway. "Told you guys not to wait for me." He rubbed one hand over his sandy hair, which had grown out about one shaggy inch.

"We definitely did not wait for you," Denny deadpanned, twitching one corner of his mouth at me. "Just having a late dinner. Come on. Sit."

Josh filled a plate with leftover latkes and sausage from the warming oven, slathered them with applesauce and sour cream, and sat down. He looked at us suspiciously. "Whassup?"

Denny shrugged. "Mom and I were just saying it'd be good to talk about your plans for the rest of the summer since this is the last week of sports camps. Your plans for the rest of the year, actually. Not going to college this fall is one thing. But . . ."

"Yeah, yeah, I know." Josh stuffed a forkful of latkes into his mouth and chewed thoughtfully. "Actually, that's why I took the skateboard—to get out by the lake and think. I kinda want to spend a year at Jesus People, but . . . I dunno. It's pretty intense. Most of them live right there in an old SRO hotel, pretty much like dormitory living. Not just singles; families too. Nobody has jobs—I mean job-jobs out in the city, like regular people. They support themselves with their own roofing business. But I like the kinds of ministry they do—housing for the elderly, an after-school program, weekly meal for the homeless, stuff like that. Plus they staff at least three shelters—some for women and children, some homeless, some abused, even a couple of floors for families, trying to keep them together. That really got Edesa excited. She's been visiting some other women's shelters in the city, too, realizing how few of those women have any kind of health care. Or even basic knowledge about self-care. But . . ."

Josh stopped long enough to tackle the rest of his supper. Edesa? Interesting how Josh just slipped her name in there hand in glove. All sorts of questions popped into my head. But the Voice in my spirit overrode my mouth. *Just listen, Jodi.*

Josh finally pushed his plate away and gulped the last of his milk. "OK. I know this sounds stupid, but I'm kinda waiting for God to tell me, 'This is it. This is what I want you to do.' And . . ." He shrugged. "I don't feel sure. I don't know what I'm supposed to do. Maybe I should just get a job. I'm trying to pray about it."

I looked at Denny. Couldn't read his face. A job. Glad *that* got mentioned. Couldn't see Josh hanging around the house for a year, sleeping in, coming in at two in the morning, wasting his time. Uh-uh. No way.

Denny scratched the back of his head. "I've never been to Jesus

People here in the city. Just Cornerstone a couple of times." He grinned at me. "Back when we still had eardrums. But it'd be easier to talk about this if we had a little firsthand experience ourselves. Maybe go with you a time or two."

To my surprise, Josh brightened. "Good idea. How about this Saturday? Edesa and I volunteered to help with their Saturday meal for dinner guests."

"Dinner guests?" I was confused. "I thought they did a weekly meal for the homeless."

Josh grinned. "That's it. Dinner guests."

I FINALLY WORKED UP COURAGE to call Ruth that week and apologize for spilling the beans about the twins to Ben. Silence thickened on the other end of the phone. "Ruth?" I'd told myself not to wallow in guilt, that the real problem was Ruth not telling her own husband when she found out. But her silence killed me. "I'm really sorry. It just slipped out."

She sighed. "Tell me something I don't know. When he starts speaking to me again, I'll let you know if I forgive you. So—what's this I hear about the Baxters moving to Jesus People? A little off the deep end for you, Jodi, no?"

OK. If Ruth was still speaking to *me*, I'd take that as forgiveness. Just had to set her straight about Jesus People. "Not *moving*, Ruth. Just volunteering this Saturday."

When Amanda heard what we were going to do that weekend, she wanted to come too. *And* José. Josh called to make sure it was all right and was told some youth group from Indiana had to cancel, so "come on down."

We arranged to meet Edesa and José at the Wilson el stop—they had to come from Little Village on the West Side—and walk over to the JPUSA shelter. We still had a transit card from the last time we'd ridden the el—on July Fourth weekend, with Little Andy. Not many suit-and-tie commuters on Saturday, but the trains were still half full—Latino grandmothers with giggling grandchildren; teenagers of all shades plugged into their music; young women in short tops and hip-hugging shorts or jeans, their tummies bared to the world; middle-aged shoppers heading downtown. The doors slid open at Bryn Mawr, loaded and unloaded, then slid closed again. Florida's stop. *Wonder how the packing's going...*

I tugged on Denny's T-shirt. "Um, forgot to tell you. The Hickmans are moving next Saturday. They found a house to rent near Adele's shop. Can you help?"

Denny gave me that Look. The one that said, *I used to lead a quiet life until you Yada Yadas filled up my schedule.* He sighed. "Yeah, guess so. Far as I know."

Four more stops. "Wilson," crackled the speaker. "Wilson and Broadway."

We piled out and waited until the train pulled away. Edesa and José weren't on the opposite platform. "Let's go down to street level," Josh urged. "They'll find us there."

Correction. We found *them* on street level. They'd already arrived and were standing in front of a long concrete wall beneath the el station, gazing at a mural of sorts. Edesa, dressed in a breezy summer shift of yellow and orange, colors that brought out gold tints beneath her mahogany skin, waved us over. "*Hola!* Not your usual gang graffiti, eh?" she said, waving a hand at the wall. "Some of these taggers are pretty good."

José was gazing intently at a figure spray-painted on the wall, surrounded by some kind of gang signs. He traced something with his finger. "Josh! *Venido!*"

Amanda, not to be left out, hustled over with her brother. The trio studied something on the wall, talking in low tones.

"What?" I said when they rejoined us.

"Uh, can't really be sure," Josh said.

José stuck out his lip. "I'm sure."

"What?" Denny, Edesa, and I sounded like a Greek chorus.

José pointed at the life-size drawing of a brown youth on the wall, muscled arms, arms folded, legs apart. "I thought I recognized that drawing—well, the style anyway—but I wasn't sure. Then I saw the signature." He pointed. Our gaze followed. It wasn't a name. Just a *C* with a slash through it. "I saw it at Cornerstone. That's his signature."

We looked at each other. "Who?"

José hesitated as several people walked by. Then he lowered his voice. "Chris," he said. "Chris Hickman."

# 16

Serving JPUSA's "dinner guests" for the next several hours in their community center chased my emotions around like a cross-country race. At first I felt awkward, feeling rich and privileged and conspicuous even in my jeans and T-shirt beneath the clear plastic apron we each put on. A woman in a security vest greeted people at the door and waved them toward the long tables where we served from big aluminum pans of rice, chicken-something in a sauce, iceberg lettuce salad with a smattering of grated carrots and tomatoes for color, and a yellow sheet cake with chocolate frosting. I thought the greeter was one of the Jesus People, but it became apparent that she herself was a "dinner guest" who had found a way to give back by helping out. The same was true of several men—a hard life on the street outlined in their faces and scruffy clothes—who wiped tables, folded them up, and swept the floor afterward.

My heart ached for some of the younger adults who came through the line. Too young to be living on the street; too old too soon. Some dinner guests ate alone; others chatted with each other, like old friends meeting at the local coffee shop. As far as I could tell, anyone could come to dinner—those living in the shelters or those who just needed a meal. No one was turned away.

The volunteer coordinator—a woman who said she'd been at Jesus People at least twenty years—offered to show us around. The community center had an after-school program and a childcare center for children of shelter residents, so moms (and sometimes dads) could look for work or sell the *Streetwise* newspaper or apply for welfare benefits. I was delighted to see the bright colors of the toys and equipment and the artwork by the children. But my heart sank to my knees again when the coordinator showed us the large residential room for women with children—a sea of bunk beds, the only privacy provided by a sheet or blanket pinned to the top mattress marking off two bunks as "family space." We were told some of the women were simply homeless, a litany of hard-luck stories or chronic drug abuse. Others had been abused by husbands or boyfriends. *Like Rochelle*, I thought. I couldn't imagine Avis's beautiful daughter here, even though the room was surprisingly tidy.

At midafternoon, the room was mostly empty, except for two little boys playing with action figures on one of the bunks. I stopped to talk. Dwayne and Tremaine, they said. Brothers. First and second grade. I wanted to sit down and read them a story—but we moved on. Just visitors passing through. It made me feel like a window shopper of human misery.

The "family floor" had individual rooms and parents of both sexes. A mannerly black man, maybe thirty, greeted us politely in musical French. Staff? No, said the coordinator. He and his wife and child were shelter residents, immigrants from French-speaking

Senegal with no place to go. The floor for single women (no children) occupied two conjoined rooms—one with rows of single bunks, like an army barrack; the other a day room, brightened with colorful walls, comfy couches, a TV, a small kitchen in one corner. At night, the coordinator said, the day room floor was covered with mattresses for overflow who came in from the street "just for the night."

Later we sat and talked with the volunteer coordinator in her little office. I felt overwhelmed. How did Jesus People deal with this level of stress, day after day after day? Even more, how did homeless women—especially the women with children—survive in a shelter for two, three, even six months?

No wonder Avis didn't want to see Rochelle end up in a shelter. But the tension on her face when we'd talked in the school office several days ago punctuated her words: *"I have to admit, Jodi, I feel caught between my daughter and my husband. I don't know how to do what's best for both of them. A few weeks is one thing. But long term?"*

I reined in my thoughts and tried to concentrate on Edesa's questions about the health needs of the shelter residents. "I am still a student, third year, and have just changed my major to public health. Is there some way I can help?"

"To tell you the truth," said the coordinator, "we've got a fair number of resources lined up for our residents, and a lot of available staff. Oh, I don't mean we can't use volunteers—there's always *something* to do and toilets to clean!" She laughed. "But there are other shelters that are woefully understaffed. A new one, Manna House, here on the North Side, is desperate for volunteers . . ." Edesa and Josh leaned forward, listening intently. Amanda and José too. Denny and I looked at each other.

Only on the way home, as we passed that brooding figure spray-painted on the long wall of the Wilson el station surrounded by gang symbols, did I think about Chris Hickman again. The wall bumped my emotions over one last set of muddled hurdles: the art-work on that figure was *good.* The kid ought to have art lessons! But was Chris part of the gang that had taken over this wall? *Oh God, please no.* Should I tell Florida? Wouldn't she want to know? But what if José was wrong?

I leaned against the cool window of the elevated train as it squealed out of the station heading north. The Hickmans were moving in two weeks. Maybe the move was the answer. Give Chris a fresh start . . .

TEMPERATURES HAD COOLED OVER THE WEEKEND to the midseventies by the time we climbed the stairs to the second floor at Uptown Community Church the next morning. Good thing, because by the time kids, teenagers, and visitors crowded into the rows of chairs along with the usual adults, we barely had elbow room. Add muggy hot and we'd probably get mutiny. A couple Uptown women were setting up the Communion table at the front of the room with its special embroidered cloth depicting children around the world. First Sunday of August. Communion Sunday.

Avis, Bible in hand, was talking to Rick Reilly, who played lead guitar in our praise band; she must be the worship leader this morning. Didn't see Peter Douglass—or Rochelle and Conrad the Third for that matter. I swallowed a big sigh. *Here we go again, back to our separate churches, same space, different times . . .*

Stu came in with Becky and Little Andy. The toddler with the chocolate-and-whipped-cream complexion waved at me and my heart squeezed. We Baxters had offered to help pick him up each Sunday from his paternal grandmother, who had temporary custody, but Stu had never asked for our help. Just as well. From what I'd heard, his grandmother was rather recalcitrant about getting Andy ready for his weekly visit with Becky. Stu probably put on her *I'm-DCFS-and-he-better-be-ready* persona to get results. Never mind that she wasn't Andy's caseworker anymore.

Avis Johnson-Douglass, dressed in a black sheath with a black-and-white scarf at the neck, set her Bible on the simple wooden stand that served as a pulpit and called out, "Good morning, church!"

Andy Wallace yelled back, "Good morning!" then collapsed in giggles on his mother's shoulder. People laughed. Becky's face turned beet red.

Avis smiled. "Andy's got the right idea. Talk to me! Makes me feel at home. I came up in the black church, you know, where talking back to the preacher was part of the worship flow."

"Got that right!" called out Florida. "An' if you didn't talk back, you were asleep." More laughter. I caught her eye and gave her a thumbs-up. Could count on Florida to talk back to the preacher, worship leader, or whoever was up front. That was one of the gifts Florida and Avis brought to Uptown, nudging us away from being an audience to being participants in all parts of the worship.

"So let's encourage one another this morning," Avis continued, "to bring our cares and burdens from the week and leave them at the altar, so that we can freely worship our Lord and Savior, Jesus Christ. Listen to the words of the apostle Paul . . ."

I marveled at Avis. Joy seemed to leak from her pores as she read from Galatians 5, verse 1: "It is for freedom that Christ has set us free. Stand firm, then, and do not let yourselves be burdened again by a yoke of slavery." *Huh.* If my married daughter showed up at my house nursing a black eye and a cut lip, I don't think I could dredge up joy. Or could I? What did that verse mean anyway—the one that said, "The joy of the Lord is my strength"?

"—old devil likes to bind us up any way he can," Avis continued. "Sometimes it's religious 'rules' that get in the way of a relationship with Jesus. Or money—having too much or too little. Or maybe it's that son or daughter who keeps you awake nights. Satan wants us to *worry* instead of *worship.* But let's tell Satan this morning that he's a liar. It is for *freedom* that Christ has set us free! Come on, church, let's sing praises to the God of our salvation!"

The worship band—keyboard, guitars, drums—did their best at launching into the Richard Smallwood song, "I Will Sing Praises." *New Morning's saxophone would be nice,* I thought. But as we sang, several phrases stood out: "Lord, You are my joy . . . whom shall I fear? I don't have to worry, I won't be afraid. For in the time of trouble You shall hide me . . ."

That was Avis's secret. *Oh God, I want to have that kind of joy. The kind that doesn't depend on my circumstances. The kind that encourages others who are struggling.* I opened my mouth and poured my voice into the song: "I will sing praises! Praises unto You! . . ."

After an extended time of worship, the children and teens were dismissed to their Sunday school classes. But instead of preaching a sermon or serving Communion, Pastor Clark surprised us by announcing an ad hoc congregational meeting. "We have several pressing matters that need our immediate attention. We won't be voting on anything; that can come later at a regular business meeting. Rather than call you back for an extra meeting, it seemed a good thing to weave these matters right into our worship—for that is the issue at hand."

I looked sideways at Denny; he met my gaze. Both of us had an idea what "the issue at hand" might be. I noticed Josh was still at the soundboard; he hadn't left with the teens. Well, he'd graduated. Time for him to transition to adult responsibilities.

Pastor Clark, in shirtsleeves and tie, squeezed his eyes shut. "Lord, we invite You to be part of the business at hand. Our only desire is to love You, serve You, and bring glory and honor to Your name. Show us Your purpose for our presence as a church in this neighborhood. Amen."

People shifted uneasily in their seats; murmurs rustled across the room and then settled down as Pastor Clark waited for quiet. "Most of you know we're outgrowing our space here on Morse Avenue. This building has served us well for almost twenty years. But give us a few more months and even a shoehorn won't help."

"That's what I been sayin'!" Florida snorted. "An' these chairs don't help neither."

Nervous laughter, more rustling.

"We have several options to consider. We can stay where we are—but like a too-tight shoe, that will stunt our growth. We can sell our building and hunt for a new one. That seems like the most obvious solution. Or—there is another possible option." Pastor Clark paused. All the rustling ceased. "In other words, rather than treat our shrinking space as just a financial issue, as just a building size issue, I'm suggesting we use this opportunity to ask, what is God doing among us right now? What does it mean for us? Is God wanting to do something new?"

"I don't get it. What are you talking about, Pastor?" A voice spoke from the back of the room.

Pastor Clark smiled. "Bear with me a moment. This summer God brought a new relationship into our lives as a church—a relationship with New Morning Christian Church, which has been sharing our building as they looked for new space. Two churches, one building."

"That's right, Pastor!" I said. Stu gave me a smirk. I ignored her. Avis told us to talk back to the preacher, didn't she?

"Then, as we all know, tragedy struck. One of their members— Dr. Mark Smith, who also happens to be a close friend of several in our congregation—was brutally attacked by members of a hate group, trying to sow seeds of hatred, distrust, and fear among the races and ethnic groups in our city."

"Jesus! Help us!" Florida cried.

Pastor Clark didn't miss a beat. "Throughout this summer, both churches have made a conscious effort *not* to succumb to the enemy's schemes. We have invited their members to our men's breakfast and our Second Sunday Potluck; a few of us have visited each other's worship services. When they found a new space for their services, they invited our whole congregation to join them in thanksgiving and worship—something we decided to continue once a month as long as we are sharing this building."

I saw several heads nodding.

"Soon, we could just go our separate ways. But God has been stretching us, teaching us what it means to be *His* church, not just *our* church. As your pastor, I think it's worth asking, what has God been doing among us? What does God want to do now? How does our need to move on from this building figure into *that*?"

No one spoke for several moments. Then a familiar voice piped up from the soundboard. Josh. "We could sell our building and invest the money to renovate New Morning Christian's new space—"

"What?" a woman behind me gasped. "Just throw away our church assets?"

"Somebody said the same thing at our last men's breakfast," a man snorted. "But it's crazy. You can't be serious."

"—and merge the two congregations. Just be one church," Josh finished.

A babble of surprise and dismay followed, though some people actually clapped. I gripped Denny's hand. Peter Douglass should be here. Wasn't this his idea? But he wasn't a member of Uptown, even though Avis was. And Josh was still a teenager. The idea would *never* fly unless the leaders of the church supported it 100 percent.

To my surprise, Pastor Clark laughed. "You stole my punch line, young man." People laughed. For some reason, this broke the tension that had us all by the collar. But a lot of hands shot up, too, with a lot of questions and comments.

"What does New Morning think about this idea? They might be a little surprised if we all showed up—for good."

"Yeah. Maybe they don't want us!"

"Who would be the pastor? Can't see Cobbs stepping down."

"Visiting their services is one thing—but every Sunday? Not really my style."

To my surprise, Denny stood up. "Pastor? May I say something?" At Pastor Clark's nod, he made his way to the front of the room.

I tilted my chin up. *You go, Denny.*

But for a moment, Denny just stood staring at the Communion table, not saying anything. Then he picked up the cloth covering the elements, the cloth with embroidered children from around the world all along the edge—*"red, brown, yellow, black, and white"* as the children's chorus went.

"Pastor . . . brothers and sisters . . . The events of this summer opened my eyes in a new way to those verses in First Corinthians that talk about the church being the body of Christ. Especially the part that says we can't say to different parts of the body, 'I don't need you.' No, Paul said, the different parts of God's body *need* each other. But do we? Do we *need* New Morning Christian Church? Do they need us? We don't act like we do. We're so used to staying in our own little church corner, doing things our way, that I, for one, have no idea what it would be like to actually function as a whole body. But . . ." My husband tore off a piece of bread from the loaf on the table and then picked up the cup of wine. "Seems like I remember that just before Jesus died, right after He shared broken bread and wine with His disciples, He prayed that all His followers would be *one*, just as He and His Father in heaven are One."

Denny looked up, holding the piece of bread and the cup. "Don't we have a chance here to take one giant step in that direction—to be *one* with another part of Christ's church?"

# 17

They should've included the teens in that meeting."
Amanda pulled a pout on the way home from church.
"We have opinions, too, you know."

I could practically hear my father: *Some things are for adults to decide.* But Amanda had a point. Whatever we decided would impact everyone at Uptown Community, big-time. Even the kids. Maybe especially the kids. *Huh.* Hadn't thought about it that way before. But the decisions we adults made said a lot about what our priorities were—spiritual and otherwise. Our kids were watching.

"Nothing was decided," Denny said, "except everyone agreed we need to sell our building. Pastor Clark asked all of us to take one month to pray, and we'll make a decision next Communion Sunday." He cocked an eyebrow in Amanda's direction. "You can do that, too, you know, kiddo. Pray about it."

Josh was quiet on the trip home. I wondered what he was thinking. In fact, we hadn't really talked since our visit to Jesus People yesterday—and tomorrow was the first day of his jobless-schoolless life. As soon as we pulled into the garage, Amanda ran into the house—to call José and tell him Uptown was falling apart, no doubt—but I grabbed the little stepladder and a scooper of birdseed to fill my neglected bird feeder. Josh steadied the ladder for me. "Can I talk to you and Dad a few minutes?"

"Uh, sure. Give me a minute." Was I ready for this? I poured the birdseed slowly into the feeder. By the time I stowed the ladder and scooper, Josh and Denny were already ensconced on the back porch swing with glasses of iced tea. My glass sat on the porch railing. I unfolded a lawn chair by the railing and sat, studying my two men. Denny, casual in his khaki slacks and pale green short-sleeved dress shirt, a new job title tucked in his pocket, had reined in all the practical questions about a merger with New Morning and taken us to the core issue: did we really *need* the other parts of the body of Christ? Josh, still wearing those pathetic shredded jeans and a wrinkled T-shirt—OK, at least it was clean—had taken Pastor Clark's buildup and reduced it to the bare bones of what our gentle pastor was trying to say: sell the building, give the money to New Morning for renovation, and merge the two churches.

Now this six-foot fruit of my womb wanted to talk. I had no idea what to expect.

"OK." Josh blew out a breath. "I'm not sure how all this fits together, but I know you guys don't want me just hanging around."

*Good. We had one thing straight.*

"I'm really interested where this idea of merging with New Morning Church is going to go. Far as I'm concerned, we could have made the decision today. But . . ." He shrugged. "Guess people gotta think about it."

"And pray," I said. "We sometimes forget to ask what God wants us to do. At least," I admitted, "I know I do."

He nodded. "Well, yeah, that too. Still, if we *do* go that direction, I'm real interested in Pastor Cobbs's vision for reaching out to the kids in the Howard Street area—gang kids too. Not just church kids, like Uptown. I'd like to get involved. Don't know how. But that means waiting till Uptown makes a decision, unless . . ." He frowned. "Guess I could just change churches."

Denny and I looked at each other. Josh was lost in thought for half a minute. Then he said, "But I'd like to wait till the next meeting, anyway, see what happens. As for Jesus People, I had a long talk with Edesa on the phone last night. She's really interested in that Manna House. It's not like Jesus People—the staff isn't residential. So if we volunteered at that shelter, I'd still have to live at home— if that's OK with you guys."

*Long talk with Edesa . . . if "we" volunteered . . . Um, God? You've got this under control, right?*

Josh put up his hands. "OK, I know what you guys are thinking: all that's fine and good—"

*Were we?*

"—but what about a job? Well, I've been thinking about that too. Remember when Peter Douglass asked what I was planning to do after I graduated? Said he might have a job for me if I was willing to go full time. So"—he blew out another breath, like the last five minutes had taken more energy than he had stored up— "thought I'd go see him tomorrow at his company, see what he's got. Work the volunteer stuff around the job. I could maybe pay you guys rent or something."

Josh collapsed against the back of the swing and drained his glass of iced tea as if saying, *Done.*

Denny and I were both silent for a few moments. Kinda iffy on all counts. But Denny caught my eye and raised an eyebrow. I gave a short nod.

"All right. Guess that's OK for starters. We'll talk again if you get the job." And that was that. My two men got up and wandered back into the house.

But I sat on the porch a few minutes longer. *Pray first, Jodi, not later.* "OK, God," I murmured, "You've heard it all. I don't understand what's going on with Edesa and Josh. She's at least three years older than he is, sailing through college, but it almost sounds like they're making decisions together. At least about this Manna House thing. A job with Peter Douglass, well, that would be great. But he made that offer to Josh months ago. So, God . . ." I searched my heart. What did I want for my son? Or was that the right question?

Suddenly I remembered what Nony had said about Josh several weeks ago as we all kept vigil for Mark in the ICU. *"God has plans for that young man. Not your plans. Don't stand in his way. I believe God will use your Joshua like the Joshua of old, to fight a battle that the older generation did not fight."*

This time I was the one who blew out a breath. Give up my own expectations for Josh? My ideas of what was best for my kids? Hard to do. But I tried again. "So, God, please, work out *Your* purpose for Josh—and don't let him get caught or led astray or . . . or hurt along the way."

DENNY GOT UP, PUT ON A TIE, and went to work at West Rogers High School as the new athletic director the next morning.

Josh left the house and came back a few hours later—*ta da!*—employed. Working in the shipping department at the Chicago branch of Software Symphony, Inc., as assistant to Carl Hickman, starting tomorrow. Amanda got a call from one of her babysitting parents wanting to know if she'd be a daytime nanny for their three kids for the month of August. When she hesitated, they upped her hourly rate. I saw her eyes go big.

To celebrate the new jobs, I made one of our favorite summer salads—bow-tie pasta with grilled chicken, lemon, nuts, and grapes—served with sliced melon and grilled bread, and invited Stu and Becky downstairs to join us for supper. "Yeah, well, hope you can be celebrating for me soon," Becky said. "Yo-Yo and Ruth got an interview for me at the Bagel Bakery next Monday. Don't know much about baking stuff, though. Might have to start by sweeping floors or something."

We clapped and cheered as if she already had the job. *Oh God, thank You. You are so good . . .*

Stu was serving up banana splits with three kinds of ice cream, hot fudge, fresh strawberries, and whipped cream—her contribution to the celebration—when the phone rang. Amanda, always the first one to jump at the phone, said, "Oh. Hi, Mrs. Hickman," and handed it to me.

"Jodi! What's all that laughing? You guys havin' a party without me?"

I giggled. "Hi, Florida. Come on over! We're just celebrating the new jobs. Did Carl tell you Josh is going to be working for him?"

"Yeah, he tol' me and he's real glad too. Some nights he been so overworked, he don't get home till eight or nine. And you know we movin' this Saturday. I need that man around here bad. Anyway, that's why I'm callin'. You guys comin' to help out?"

I covered the mouthpiece. "Hickman move. Saturday. Everybody on? . . . Yeah, you can count on four Baxters and Stu. Becky says, sorry, she's grounded by the State."

"All right. Say, Jodi, can you do your e-mail thang and ask the rest of the Yada Yadas? We need all the help we can get."

WE FOUR BAXTERS AND STU showed up at the Hickmans' third-floor apartment at eight o'clock on Saturday, along with Peter Douglass and a couple of guys from Software Symphony, Edesa Reyes, and José Enriques. (José brought regrets from his mom—Delores had to work pediatrics at the county hospital that weekend.) Even Ben Garfield showed up in his big Buick with Yo-Yo and her kid brothers, grumbling about the narrow streets and nonexistent parking.

Not Avis. She begged off, saying she had to take care of grandson Conny. Didn't say where Rochelle was.

Not Ruth—for obvious reasons. *"But ask Ben, Jodi,"* she'd said in response to my e-mail. *"Do him good to get out of the house. OK, OK, I'm lying. Do ME good to get him out of the house."*

Not Nony and Hoshi. In fact, I didn't even ask. They already had their hands full at the Sisulu-Smith house.

Not Chanda, who knows why. She still didn't have e-mail and didn't return my call. Maybe the kids picked up the message and didn't give it to her.

Not Adele. Saturdays were her busiest days at Adele's Hair and Nails.

We still had a good crew. The men and teen guys lugged furniture down the outside stairs of the apartment building to the rented moving van in the alley, wrestling couches and mattresses around sharp landings, while Amanda and Edesa helped pack the kids' bedroom (still looking as if a cyclone hit it). Stu and Yo-Yo volunteered to clean the stove and refrigerator, leaving Florida and me to tackle the bathroom.

Every now and then, we heard shouts from the furniture crew: "Watch it! Watch it!" "Chris! Grab that corner!" "*¡Espere un minuto!*" . . . and stupid jokes: "Hey, Hickman! Why don't we just toss those mattresses over the side and drop everything else on top?"

Taking a break from the strong ammonia fumes in the bathroom, I gulped fresh air at the back door of the apartment before tackling the medicine cabinet. "Chris seems to be working well with the guys out there," I said to Florida, who was scrubbing the life out of the tub. "He doing OK?" I still felt a little guilty that I hadn't said anything to her about the spray-painted wall at the Wilson el station with Chris's "signature." But I didn't *know* it was Chris, did I? Only had José's word, and he could be wrong.

"Yeah. Guess so. He's pretty mad we're movin'. Doesn't want to go to a new school. But guess he resigned himself. He's still only fourteen. Not like he's grown."

The bathroom squeaky clean, Florida disappeared for half an hour and returned with doughnuts and store-bought lemonade. "Break!" she yelled out the door to the men. "Oh, mercy. It's starting to rain."

Indeed. Gray clouds and a light drizzle had settled in over the city. We all crowded together on the third-floor back porch, downing doughnuts and gulping lemonade, talking and laughing. Chris, José, Yo-Yo's brothers, and Josh and Amanda huddled in one corner and I heard "Cornerstone" at one point. That was the last time they'd all been together; probably comparing notes on the bands they liked or hated. I smiled. Good that they had that experience in common.

The wind picked up, warm and wet. "Mr. Hickman!" José called out. "The rain's blowing into the van! I'll close it." The boy ran down the stairs and out into the alley, passing a couple of black teenagers on the way. *"Hola."* His easy greeting floated back up to the movers on the porch.

I watched curiously, licking the last crumbs of the blueberry doughnut off my fingers. The boys glared at José, as if he'd insulted them. But they turned back, shielded their eyes against the drizzle, and hollered up. "Hey, Hickman!"

Carl Hickman leaned over the railing. "What you boys want?"

The boys smirked. "Uh, hi, Mr. Hickman. We came to see Chris. He here?"

Beside me, Edesa's body tensed. *"¡José! Venido aquí. Ahora!"*

Chris swore under his breath and started down the stairs. "Chris!" Florida hollered after him. "Don't you go runnin' off now!"

The roll-up door of the rental moving van slammed shut, and José headed back toward the building, running through the rain. We saw him lift his hand as if greeting Chris in passing—and the next second stumbled off the narrow sidewalk as Chris, hands in his pockets, shouldered past him—almost as if he'd given José a shove with his body.

"Chris!" his fathered hollered. "You get back up here!"

But the fourteen-year-old put his head together with the other two—and disappeared down the alley.

# 18

osé made no comment when he got back to the third floor, but I noticed he seemed withdrawn the rest of the move. He even avoided Amanda, which put a kink in her ponytail. I didn't think Florida had seen the body language that went on between José and Chris; she was just fussing that he disappeared. "That boy done cut out for the last time! He gone be lucky if I let him back in the house."

"But Mama!" Carla's face puckered. "What if he don't come back 'fore we move? Does he know where our new house is?"

Florida was unmoved. "*Humph.* That his problem, now, ain't it?—Carl! You ready for boxes now?"

Edesa tried to say something to José, but he just shrugged her off and started lugging boxes down the stairs. "What went on out there?" I murmured to her a few minutes later as we tackled the boxes stacked in the hallway, when I was sure Florida or Carl wouldn't overhear. "Chris acted like he didn't even know José—no, worse than that. As if he didn't exist."

She hesitated. "I'm not sure. But the way those boys looked at José, I was frightened. That's why I called him to come back. Black and Latino gangs are at each other's throats on the West Side. Maybe here too."

"But José isn't in a gang! Remember, he stood up to some gang-bangers, maybe it was even Latin Kings, when they were selling drugs in the park where his kid brother and sisters played! Then that rival gang showed up . . ." I swallowed. *That was the phone call that glued us together as a prayer group at the women's conference where we first met—Delores's son in the hospital! Caught in gang crossfire, try-ing to get his siblings out of harm's way.* "And he and Chris were both laughing and talking not thirty minutes ago."

"*Sí.* But Chris's friends don't know that. I suspect Chris acted that way to save face."

Now *I* was mad at Chris. "What kind of friend is that? Couldn't he have just said, 'Hey guys, this is my friend, José, he's helping us move'—or something?"

Ben Garfield's voice sailed down the hall. "Jodi Baxter! You and Edesa gonna jabber all day? We need some more boxes!"

Edesa grabbed a box labeled Carla's Stuff. "All I know is, the Enriques family is like *mi familia.*" Her eyes teared up. "I don't want José to get hurt again."

THE TRUCK GOT LOADED BY NOON, and Carl asked Denny to drive the rental truck to the Hickmans' new address on North Ashland in Rogers Park. That was the first time I realized that Carl Hickman didn't have a driver's license. *Duh, of course. No car, no dri-ver's license.* Peter Douglass, who somehow ended up with a carload of teenagers, showed up at the new house with a couple of buckets of Buffalo Joe's hot wings and five liters of soda. José seemed to have snapped out of his funk. He and Amanda were sitting together on the front steps, sucking the life out of those hot wings.

The frame house was old, badly in need of paint, and looked tiny squeezed between three-story apartment buildings. But it had two small bedrooms downstairs and two upstairs, plus a separate second-floor "apartment" in the back. "An' a front porch!" Florida crowed. "I'm gonna get me a wicker rocking chair, jus' like my grandmama used to have back in Memphis. Mm-hm." Her eyes got dreamy, her upset at Chris momentarily forgotten.

Fed and sassy, the teenagers came up with a brilliant idea, lining everybody up from the truck to the front door, passing boxes hand to hand. "*Huh*," Yo-Yo snorted. "Takes me longer than that to get Pete outta bed in the mornin'." Even unloading the furniture seemed to go faster on this end of the move.

"Yada Yada still meetin' at my crib tomorrow?" Yo-Yo asked hopefully as we finally dragged our weary bodies to our cars.

"What about Ruth?" I asked. "You know, stairs." Yo-Yo's motel-like apartment building had one flight of outside stairs to the balcony walkway in front of the second-level apartment doors.

Ben, waiting on Yo-Yo to get in the monster Buick, snapped, "Ruth's not coming. Even if you lived in a basement. Doctor's got her back on bed rest."

Yo-Yo, Edesa, Florida, and I looked at each other. How did we miss this new development?

BUT BEN WAS RIGHT. I called Ruth the next day when we got home from Second Sunday Potluck, and she said, yes, she'd been ordered back on bed rest at her last prenatal appointment if she didn't want to miscarry. "A few sick days I've still got. So I call the office; my boss has a snit. Can the man find anything when I'm not there? Make his own phone calls? *Oy.* Helpless as a *goyim* in a Yiddish restaurant." She sighed. "I was hoping to use all my sick days when the baby—uh, babies arrived. But I don't know, Jodi. My job might be kaput when all this is over. One more thing to upset Ben."

For the first time since she'd announced she was pregnant, Ruth sounded discouraged. And frankly, I didn't know how to encourage her without stomping all over Ben's concerns. The tension between Ruth and Ben made my head ache.

*What are friends supposed to do in a situation like this, anyway?* I thought, riding with Stu and Becky toward Yo-Yo's apartment a couple of hours later, half-listening to their chatter in the front seats.

"Kinda cool to see more people from New Morning at the potluck," Becky said. "What? Roll up the window? But it's hot!— Oh." She fiddled with the power window as Stu turned the AC on full blast. "Preacher Cobbs's wife even asked me my name, called me 'Sister Becky,' like I was a regular saint. What's that people call her? First Rose somethin'?"

"First Lady Rose." Stu pulled her Celica into the parking lot of Yo-Yo's apartment building. "I think it's a black church thing. Sign of respect for the pastor and his wife, I guess. Would take getting used to, though." Stu came from the school of first-name egalitarianism. No titles.

"Huh." Becky chewed on that a while. "Guess it's good Pastor Clark ain't married if Uptown and New Morning do that joining thing. Can't see *two* 'first ladies' in the White House, the doghouse, or any house."

We were still laughing about that as we punched Yo-Yo's doorbell, then trooped into her barely furnished apartment. "Hey, Becky." Yo-Yo gave Becky a high five. "Glad your PO gave you the OK to pray with Yada Yada. Guess the penal system finally figgerin' out that religion helps."

As I hugged Chanda, Delores, Edesa, and Nony, who had already arrived, my mind strayed to Yo-Yo's comment. Funny. Didn't think of my faith as "religion." Other people had religions: Muslims, Buddhists, Hare Krishnas. Christians and Jews were supposed to have a *relationship* with God. Big difference in my mind. But Yo-Yo had a point. Ex-cons who went to prayer meetings—Yada Yada or otherwise—probably lowered the recidivism rate.

Yo-Yo's furniture consisted of one ancient couch and several mismatched dining room chairs, which meant more of us had to join Yo-Yo on old bed pillows on the floor. Besides Ruth, several others were missing. Florida, who never skipped, was too overwhelmed with unpacking. ("Mi still not unpacked," Chanda sniffed. "What de big deal?") Florida hadn't been to church either. *"We still callin' Chris's friends, tryin' to find him,"* she'd told me on the phone, her tone rippling between worry and fury. *"That boy! Lord, give me patience!"*

Adele wasn't coming; she'd had an upset with MaDear.

"And Hoshi stayed home with Mark and the boys so I could come," Nony said. "I wish . . ." But she didn't finish. Just picked at her nail polish.

Avis arrived last—with her daughter Rochelle. "I'm sorry I didn't call ahead. Rochelle is staying with us for a few weeks. I told her she'd be more than welcome." A smile tickled Avis's face. "Peter's babysitting Conny. It'll be good for him."

Rochelle cast her eyes down as if embarrassed. Didn't blame her.

After all, her abrupt arrival two weeks ago had disrupted our *last* Yada Yada meeting. To our credit, though, everyone said "sure" and kept the greetings low-key, not making Rochelle's presence a big deal. She settled on a floor pillow near her mother, a vision even in slim faded jeans, sleeveless top, and toe sandals. Her hair was a long, thick fall of kinky curls with rusty highlights. Her nutmeg skin showed little sign of the bruises she'd had two weeks ago. But her sad eyes were a window into the bruises in her heart.

Delores, who'd come straight from work at the county hospital, leaned over, gave Rochelle a hug, and whispered, *"Dios le bendiga.* God bless you, my daughter."

Avis cut through the usual chatter. "Sisters, let's spend a few minutes in worship before we share requests. Try to lay aside all the pulls and tugs for our attention, and consider who it is who hears our prayers. *Immanuel,* God with us. *Jehovah-Jireh,* our provider. *Jehovah-Rapha,* our healer. *Jehovah-Shalom,* our peace. We have so much to be thankful for, in spite of the concerns we have." She began to pray aloud, just worshiping; others joined in. But without Florida and Adele, and with a subdued Nony, our worship seemed more restrained than usual. Or maybe it was just me. Funny how I let how others worshiped influence my own expression to God.

Well, I wasn't going to let it. I grabbed my Bible and opened it to Psalm 139, paraphrasing as I read along, adding my voice to the other prayers. "Lord, You know all about me. You know when I'm resting and when I'm working. You even know what I'm thinking—"

"Ouch," Yo-Yo muttered. Chanda giggled. The other prayers dropped to a murmur. I seemed to have the floor.

"Everything I do is familiar to You. You know what I'm going to say even before I say it, and You protect me from every side. How can I even begin to understand how wonderful You are?—"

To my surprise, another voice cut in. Nony, her Bible closed, took up the familiar psalm straight from her heart. "Where can I go from Your Spirit, O Lord? Where can I flee from Your presence? If I go up to the heavens, You are there; if I make my bed in the depths, You are there too."

For some reason, Psalm 139 broke open our worship. We sang "thank You" hymns and songs, read Scripture, added prayers . . . until Avis herself brought worship to an end. "Nony? How can we pray for you?" she asked gently.

Nony's face was wet. "Oh, sisters. I am tired of bringing my sorrows to you. I feel so selfish. Mark is improving little by little—for that, I do thank God. But it will be a long time before our family is back to normal, before we can think of other things. And . . . I feel so useless. Like God has put me on a shelf. I wanted to help my suffering people in South Africa, and now I'm just . . . a nursemaid." She smiled ruefully. "See? I told you my thoughts are selfish. Pray for me, my sisters, that I would grow in patience. That I would learn to wait on God."

I reached out and held Nony's hand. *Good grief, Lord, I'm the one who's selfish. How easy I get caught up keeping my own household running and forget to call Nony and Hoshi.* I still had a couple of weeks before school started. Maybe there was something else I could do.

"Yeah, you can pray that waitin' thing for me too," Becky chimed in. "Y'all know I been goin' nuts just hangin' around Stu's house. Drivin' Stu nuts too—"

"Amen to *that*." But Stu's smile took away any sting.

"—but the good news is, Yo-Yo and Ruth put in a good word for me at the Bagel Bakery, an' I got an interview tomorrow. Y'all can pray about that. Kinda nervous." Becky seemed embarrassed at the "Yea, Becky!" and "You go, girl!" comebacks.

"Uh, speaking of Ruth . . ." Yo-Yo stuffed her hands into the bib of her overall shorts. "Tell ya the truth, I don't know how to pray 'bout her. Sometimes . . . I dunno. Almost agree with Ben. Not sure she should push this pregnancy. Heck, the lady's almost fifty!" She made a face. "Sorry. Tryin' to clean up my language . . . but she's already been in the hospital twice. I think Ben's scared. Grouchy ol' goat is still the closest thing to a father I ever had. He's been real good to me an' the boys. He's got his reasons for thinkin' like he does."

I tensed. Yo-Yo was practically saying Ruth should end the pregnancy! I expected a flurry of protests, with Bible verses flying through the air. But there was only silence. I was shocked. Was everyone in Yada Yada thinking the same thing?

# 19

Stu cleared her throat, breaking the silence. "Uh, I know Ruth's being real stubborn, maybe even stupid about not getting any of the tests they want to do because of her high-risk pregnancy. But I just want to say that I, um, I . . ." She cleared her throat again, struggling to find words.

My skin prickled. Leslie Stuart *never* had trouble saying exactly what she thought. But last spring Stu told me she'd share her story with the rest of Yada Yada "when the time was right." Only Florida and I had been with Stu the weekend we discovered the secret she had carried for so long. Was she going to—?

"—I mean, we all know Ruth has always wanted a family but had all those miscarriages, and the foster girl she wanted to adopt was returned to the parents. But I mean, at a deeper level *I understand*. You see . . ." Stu took a deep breath. "I once *chose* to end a pregnancy. I had an abortion, and it is a decision I have regretted every day of my life since. I . . . thought I knew what was best for me at the time, but . . . *nothing* hurts like knowing you threw away the life of your own child." Tears slid down Stu's face and dripped off her chin.

"Oh, *mi amiga*. God knows," breathed Delores, handing her a tissue. Becky's eyes were wide with shock.

Stu mopped at her face but didn't stop. Her tone became fierce. "Ruth has lost several children—*not* by her own choice. You think she's going to choose to end *this* pregnancy, risky though it is? I, for one, understand why she's willing to take those risks. *All* the risks. I would give anything, *anything*, even risk my life, if I ... if I ..." She mopped the flood of tears again. "... if I could hold my baby David in my arms for even one hour." Stu buried her face in her arms, her shoulders shaking. Delores wrapped her arms around her.

My own face was wet with tears. *David.* *"Beloved."* The name I'd suggested for her aborted child, a name she'd embraced like salve to a wound.

The room was quiet, except for a few sniffles ... and then Avis began to hum. The tune seemed familiar, but for a moment, I couldn't place it. And then Nony began to sing the words quietly. "A saint is just a sinner who fell down ... and got up."

There. Stu's secret was out. I was glad. The look on Stu's face as we joined in the song reminded me of a parched field after a good rain.

We spent a lot of time praying for Stu and Ruth and Becky and Nony, throwing in other concerns and thanksgivings on top of them. Delores said José had applied to Lane Tech College Prep High School. "Pray he will be accepted." *Huh. Wonder whose idea that was.* But Ricardo's threat to take José out of school had galvanized Delores to do just the opposite: send her firstborn to college.

Chanda said she was heading for Hawaii the following week. "T'ree days and t'ree nights, all *free!*" she giggled. "I'm taking de boy, but you can pray about me girls. Me sister gone back 'ome to Jamaica, so mi needing somebody take care o' dem." She looked directly at me, and I had a feeling . . .

Sure enough. Chanda grabbed me as Yada Yada broke up and began to disperse. "Sista Jodee! What about your Amanda? I pay her good to come take care of my girls. Mi hear she de best babysitter in Chicago." Chanda laughed appreciatively.

*Aha. She wanted Amanda!* But my relief drained out the sieve of reality. "Ah, I'm sorry, Chanda. Amanda has a nanny job the whole month of August. Otherwise, I'm sure she'd be glad to . . . What?"

A gleam still shone in Chanda's eye. "Den, what about she mama? Such a short time; only t'ree days—"

"Five, Chanda. It takes a day to get there and a day to get back from Hawaii."

"Oh." She shrugged. Then she smiled slyly. "Well now, mi knows you don' want to leave dat Denny mon to sit at mi 'ouse. So mi girls, dey could come to your house, eh? Mi pay you too!"

"Ah, uh, I . . ." My mind scrambled. Surely I had something to do next week. Our anniversary! No, that was this week. Amanda's birthday, that was it! But we had said just cake and ice cream this birthday, even if it was her "sweet sixteen," since she'd had a huge Mexican *quinceañera* at fifteen-and-a-half. "I need to check my calendar, Chanda." And buy some time.

"No problem! Mi call you tomorrow. De girls, dey be *so* happy to stay wit you!" And Chanda bubbled out the door to a waiting taxi.

DENNY WAS ON THE PHONE when I got home. Sounded like the August men's breakfast was turning into a workday at New Morning's facility. I studied the kitchen calendar. Five days taking care of Chanda's girls would pretty much kill my last full week at home before the required professional development days just before Labor Day.

I poured myself a glass of iced tea and went out to the swing on the darkened back porch to think. Everybody else in Yada Yada was either working or had *really good reasons* not to nanny-sit two extra kids. What was my excuse? I was off for the summer. Was I just being selfish wanting to salvage my last few days of summer break? Once school started, I'd have a classroom full of eight-year-olds— *more* than full, if Avis's predictions were accurate—five days a week for the next nine months!

But if I didn't take the girls, where would that leave Chanda?

The cicadas, invisible in the darkness, struck up a rousing chorus. Denny came out onto the back porch, iced tea in one hand, a candle jar in the other. He set the flickering candle on the porch railing and sank into the swing beside me.

"Hey," he said, reaching out a hand and twirling my limp brown locks around his index finger. "Why don't you make an appointment at Adele's shop, have her do that twisty thing with your hair again for our anniversary?" A slow grin spread across his face in the candlelight. "You looked pretty hot, gotta say that. And wear that slinky black dress I got you. We'll do dinner and a show on Thursday, OK?"

OK, OK. Had to figure out Chanda first. "Um, Denny? Chanda asked me if I'd be willing to take care of Dia and Cheree when she goes to Hawaii next week."

Denny snorted. His touch in my hair disappeared. "Hawaii! How many days are you talking about? You didn't say yes, did you?"

I was startled by his reaction. "Well, no. But I don't really have a good reason not to. School hasn't started yet, and—"

"Well, I can give you some good reasons. One, I've just started a new job. It's stressful. I don't want a houseful of little kids underfoot for a whole week."

"You! You'll be at work all day. I'd be the one taking care of them. Why is this about you?" I could feel my back stiffening.

"OK. Reason number two. School starts in a couple of weeks. Don't you have lesson plans to do? If you end up babysitting for a week, I know you; you'll be up half the night after everyone's gone to bed in order to be ready. Then you'll be tired, cranky, burn the coffee—"

"Oh, *stop*. See, it is about you. You just don't want a cranky wife." I meant to say it jokingly, but it came out nasty.

He flinched. "Of course it's about me—and you, and Amanda, and Josh. When are you going to realize that your Yada Yada friends sometimes have to take a backseat to your family? You don't have to say yes to everything."

I felt my defenses rising. "Of course our family comes first! But just how terrible would it be to spread some of our blessings around a little bit? We've been married twenty years—"

"Twenty-one next Thursday."

"*OK.* Twenty-one! My point exactly. A grace Chanda has not enjoyed for even a day. She's got three children by three different daddies, not one of whom offered to marry her. She likes our family. I'm sure she thinks the girls would be safe here. Not only that, Denny Baxter. Before Chanda won the lottery, before she had scads of money at her disposal, while she was still cleaning houses on the North Shore, struggling to make ends meet—it was Chanda who showed up at our house after my car accident and cleaned it from top to bottom, *no charge*. Wouldn't this be a way to thank her?"

Denny zipped his lip and looked away. The cicadas were deafening. Then he got up, sending the swing wobbling. "Fine. Do what you want to do." The screen door banged behind him.

We slept that night two feet apart, backs to each other.

AMBIVALENCE BOUNCED ALL OVER MY THOUGHTS the next morning: Mad at Denny for turning a simple request into major marriage muck. Mad at Chanda for giggling her way to Hawaii, oblivious to everything but her own greedy pleasure. Mad at myself for not knowing what I should do. I felt caught between Chanda and Denny and my own mixed-up motives.

"OK, Lord," I muttered, taking my Bible and a mug of coffee out to the back porch swing after the three worker bees had scuttled out the door. "How did this get to be such a big deal?" I sat quietly, my Bible closed, watching the sparrows fight over the dwindling birdseed in the birdfeeder. *Argh*. Hated to admit it, but Denny was right. I was feeling like I "ought" to do it. But was "ought to" such a bad thing? If we only did what we wanted to do, it'd be a pretty selfish world.

On the other hand, maybe I "ought to" consider my husband more. If he said it'd be stressful having two little girls underfoot all next week so soon after starting a new job, why didn't that weigh more with me than doing Chanda a big favor? And he was right.

That would be my last chance to get my lesson plans in order, do all my preparation for school, set up my classroom . . .

But how could I say no to Chanda? If I didn't take the girls, who would?

Then I started to laugh. Here I was, wrestling with my "problem" in good Old Jodi style. Didn't Scripture say we could ask for wisdom? I flipped open my Bible to the book of James. There it was in the first chapter: "If any of you lacks wisdom, he should ask God, who gives generously to all without finding fault, and it will be given to him."

I took a deep breath and blew it out. "OK, God, I need some wisdom. I don't know what to do. I don't really want to take care of Dia and Cheree for five whole days, but kinda feel I ought to. But what's right for my family? What's right for Chanda? Will You show me?"

No big answer thundered from the clear blue sky. Even the Voice in my spirit was quiet. But I suddenly felt untangled. OK, the problem was in God's lap. I didn't have to solve it right this minute. I felt . . . free.

I popped out of the swing, startling Willie Wonka who was already deep into his first nap of the day at my feet. I called Adele's Hair and Nails to make an appointment for Thursday morning to get my hair done. Maybe I'd go early and take MaDear for a walk in her wheelchair. Only ran into one hitch. Adele's assistant was sick, and she had to reschedule all this week's appointments. Didn't have anything free until Saturday morning, and that was because she just got a cancellation. *Saturday!* Oh well. Denny would have to take his bride "as is" this time—or go out on Saturday evening instead.

*Hm. Not a bad idea, actually.*

173

I DIDN'T REMEMBER when Becky said her interview was, but I happened to glance out the kitchen window in midafternoon and saw her on her knees, pulling weeds out of the flower garden as if they were one of the ten plagues of Egypt.

"Hey, Becky!" I yelled from the back door. "How'd it go?"

No answer. Just a *so-so* waggle of her hand before jerking out another weed.

So-so? I poured two glasses of "swee'tea" over ice and headed down the steps and across our undersized backyard. "Here." I handed her the tea. She rocked back on her heels and took the glass, mumbling, "Thanks." The baggy T-shirt she was wearing over a pair of sweat shorts stuck damply to her skinny body, the electronic monitor she always had to wear strapped to one ankle of her bare leg. Not exactly "dressed for success." I suddenly had an awful thought. Had *any* of us thought to ask Becky if she had anything to *wear* to this interview?

"Um, so did you go to the interview? Taking the bus go OK?"

A nod. Another weed went sailing.

I lowered myself to the patchy grass, amazingly green for August. Had to be Becky's doing. I knew neither Stu nor we Baxters were good at remembering to water it. "So how'd it go? Did you get the job?"

"If I want it." She jerked another weed.

It wasn't the answer I was expecting, not the way she was acting. "Becky! That's great! Is there a problem? When do they want you to start? Don't they pay enough?"

Becky gave up on the weeds and wiped the back of her hand across her forehead. "Right after Labor Day. And pay's OK, I guess. Can't expect more doin' what I'd be doin'—wiping tables, washing

174

dishes, takin' out trash, stuff like that. But the man said if I stuck it out for six weeks, he'd train me on the cash register, do counter stuff. I'm OK with that. I know I gotta prove myself, work my way up. But . . ." She flicked a ladybug off her arm, sent it flying. Took several long swallows from her glass of iced tea.

"Becky." I laid a hand on her arm. "Tell me what happened. You don't seem too happy. But I know how much you wanted a job. This seems like an answer to our prayers. *Your* prayer."

The long sweep of her Adele haircut fell over one side of her face. "Yeah." She pushed back her hair and turned angry eyes at me. "So tell me, Jodi. How come God answers prayers but He don't go the whole way? Huh? Can you tell me that? I get out of prison early. God gets three cheers. But I end up on house arrest, can't go nowhere. Then Stu offers me a place to live. Sweet. But she gets a burr up her butt 'cause I'm not Martha Stewart. Finally, parole officer says I can get a job. I get an interview. Hooray, God. Then the Jewish guy tells me they ain't open on Saturday, I gotta work Sunday." She spit out gutter words that would've earned a *bleep* even on today's TV.

My mind was spinning. *Sunday?* Becky had a problem with working on Sunday? Avis maybe, or Nony. I was brought up that way too. But I hardly thought it'd be a problem for Becky. Yo-Yo worked Sundays. We all thought it'd be good when she got a different job, could go to church on Sunday. But one thing at a time.

And then it hit me. "You mean . . . Little Andy?"

She nodded. "I ain't gonna give up my boy's visits." Becky's eyes narrowed, her voice fierce. "Not for one minute. Had to fight too hard to get what I got already."

"Oh, Becky. Maybe DCFS would change the day to Saturday. You never know."

She snorted. "Maybe. But Big Andy's mama gonna put up a hissy fit, make it as hard as she can. She don't want Andy to visit me—period. She wants to take Little Andy away from me if she can."

Becky's shoulders sagged. "An' that's not the only thing. I like takin' Little Andy to church. Makes me feel like we're a . . . a family. He gets to see everybody, play with other kids, learn about Jesus in Sunday school." Her eyes filled with tears. "That's what I want, Jodi. To be a family. And for Andy to be part of God's family too."

# 20

*I* felt badly for Becky. What a choice! An actual job offer—nothing to sneeze at when you're an ex-felon—versus her hard-won Sunday visits with her son. But sounded like Becky had already made her choice. Little Andy came first.

*Too bad she wasn't clear on that before she messed up her head on heroin.*

Not knowing what else to say, I took her hand, grubby from tackling weeds barehanded, and we prayed. In the middle of praying that "God would make a way out of no way," I stopped.

Becky opened her eyes and looked at me. "What?"

"I'm sorry. I just . . ." I felt like laughing. Was this wisdom? God's loving answer? "I just had an idea. Even if you took the job at the Bagel Bakery, it wouldn't start for a few weeks, right? How would you like a job for five days *next week* you could do right here at home? For pay?"

BECKY JUMPED AT THE IDEA. Denny acted like I'd just come up with a peace plan for the Middle East. Even Stu the Magnanimous said sure, why not, sounded like fun, though she pulled me aside and asked if we'd keep an eye on things when she was at work.

When Chanda called that evening, I told her I had lesson plans and school prep and couldn't take the girls—but I knew someone who'd like the job. She sounded put out at first but perked up when she realized that we'd just be downstairs. "Dat's good, dat's good," Chanda said. "And Becky needs de money. Tell her I pay her good."

"You tell her! It's between you and Becky now." I simpered at Denny, who could hear my side of the conversation. He gave me a thumbs-up.

But my qualification for the Nobel Peace Prize was short-lived—about as long as it took me to wonder why I hadn't heard from Florida by Tuesday morning. It'd been three days since the move. Had Chris come home? Maybe their phone wasn't hooked up yet. Did the Hickmans even have the same number? I dialed the old one just in case.

Florida answered. "Hey, Jodi. Glad you called. What's the number of Bethune Elementary? I gotta get Carla registered."

"Uh, sure, Florida. But what about Chris? Is he home yet?" I couldn't imagine my fourteen-year-old being gone for three days without reducing me to gibberish.

"No, he ain't, and he ain't comin' home till he gets a thing or two straight in his head. Carl found him coolin' his heels at some kid's crib, felt like smackin' him good. But ya can't do that nowadays, ya know. Anyway, Chris said he knew we'd be mad, him runnin' off like that during the move, that's why he didn't come home. Carl said, yeah, we mad as hot pepper sauce, but if he wanted to come home, he'd just have to face it like a man. That, or he could just live at the homeless shelter."

"Uh, Florida? I don't think they take minors at shelters. And you can't just leave your kid out on the street. What if he gets in trouble? You know, stealing to get food or something. They've got all those laws now making parents responsible for what their minor children do."

Florida snorted. "Yeah, we know that. Chris just don't know it. We countin' on him to show up today or tomorrow. The mama where he at said he could stay one more day *max*. Then she was kickin' him out."

I blew out a long breath. Would I have the guts to exercise that kind of tough love? "Still feels kind of risky, Flo. He could just go from friend to friend, a night here, two nights there, for a long time." *Or get caught up by some pimp.* I shivered.

"Jodi, you with me on this thang or not? I don't need no friend tellin' me I gotta let my kid run all over me. Got better things to do, like get Carla and Cedric registered for school. You gonna get me that number or not?"

I mumbled my apologies and got her the number.

I HAD A HARD TIME not getting tangled up in my feelings the rest of the week. Why did friendships have to get so complicated? And Becky's question about half-answered prayers had been bothering me too. Wouldn't mind a few answers myself. Like why Nony's husband woke up from that coma in answer to our fervent prayers, but he still struggled to tie his shoelaces. And take Florida and Carl, who'd come so far getting their family back together, which was nothing short of miracle upon miracle, but now their teenager was spinning out on the street. And why my job got a reprieve from the budget ax—*thank You, Jesus!*—but Bethune Elementary was getting a dump of underachieving kids from other schools that would stress my classroom to the max.

*Yeah, what about those half-answered prayers, God?*

Decided to hold off on calling Florida for a few days. She could call *me* if she wanted to fuss about Chris. I tried to pray for Florida's family, though; tried to pray for Becky and Little Andy, tried to pray for Ruth and Ben—even remembered to pray for "that girl" in the White Pride group, the one who probably fingered Mark's assailants and was in protective custody. But sometimes it felt like I was just praying in circles. How did I know what was best?

*Huh.* Sometimes felt like I hadn't learned anything about prayer in the last year and a half. But I did know one thing: God was God all by Himself. His ways were not our ways; His thoughts not our thoughts—all that stuff. Somewhere along the line, I had to trust that God was going to "work all things together for good."

*Hm.* Just to be sure, I looked up that well-worn verse in my modern-language Bible. Romans 8:28—"We know that God causes everything to work together for the good of those who love God and are called according to His purpose for them." Hm. *His* purpose.

*OK, God. I need to trust You for my friends, as well as for myself. For their children too. I know stewing and worrying doesn't help. Work out Your purpose in each of their lives. Just . . . give them wisdom, Lord. And me too.*

"Mom?" Amanda interrupted my thought-prayers Wednesday evening as I tossed some chilled pasta with olive oil, sun-dried tomatoes, yellow peppers, and still-crunchy broccoli for supper.

"Has Dad asked Mr. Enriques to the men's breakfast yet? He's still riding José really hard. *Somebody's* got to talk to him."

"That's putting a lot on your dad, isn't it?" Olives. And feta cheese. That's what this pasta salad needed.

"But he's a *man*! He's not going to listen to *me*."

I kept a straight face. I could well imagine the disaster if Amanda, hands on hips, gave Mr. Enriques a piece of her mind about his "unreasonable" demands on José. "Smart thinking," I allowed. "But I don't think your dad wants to invite Ricardo to the men's breakfast *just* to confront him about José. It takes time to build a friendship."

"Yeah, well, he could *start*."

If only teenagers ran the world . . . "Oh, just remembered. Don't think there's going to be a men's breakfast this Saturday. Heard your dad talking to Pastor Clark about the Uptown guys showing up at a workday at New Morning instead."

"So? Dad could ask Mr. Enriques to that!"

Amanda flounced out of the kitchen. I hollered after her, "Well, don't talk to me about it. Ask your dad!"


AS IT TURNED OUT, Denny almost seemed relieved to switch our anniversary night out to Saturday instead of Thursday. Still new to his job as athletic director at West Rogers High, he sometimes didn't get home until six thirty or seven. And Amanda must have used her daddy's-girl charm on him, because he did call Ricardo Enriques and invite him to the doughnuts-coffee-and-hammer work fest with the Uptown and New Morning guys. "I tried, kiddo," he told Amanda. "But he said he can't make it."

The workday at New Morning was a nice gesture—no, more than a gesture; maybe essential for two congregations considering a merger—but I felt sorry for Denny and Josh heading out the door Saturday morning in scruffy sweat shorts and old T-shirts. The weatherman promised temperatures in the nineties, and as far as I knew, New Morning didn't have central air in their new building yet.

At least Adele's Hair and Nails had AC, lucky me. The bell tinkled over the door of her shop as I pulled it open; a blast of arctic air nearly knocked me back outside. *Sheesh!* I should have brought a sweater! Three women in the waiting area flipped through Oprah's magazine and *Essence* as they chatted, their skin coloring ranging from honey to ebony. The chatter momentarily died when I came in, and I felt my cheeks grow hot at the once-over I knew I was getting. *"Who's that white chick coming in here?" "I don't know, girl, but that hair needs help bad!" "Hair? I thought it was a Halloween wig."* . . . Well, maybe they weren't.

Adele, who'd gone "natural" with her short 'fro, looked up from the weave she was doing in the first chair. "Jodi Baxter." Adele had a way of saying my name that made me feel like a schoolchild caught ditching. "Didn't I tell you eleven o'clock? I got three people ahead of you and only one of me."

"I know." My voice squeaked. "Your shop is air-conditioned, and my house isn't." Nobody laughed at my little joke. "Just kidding. I came early to play with MaDear. Is she here?"

Adele pursed her lips. "Yes, she's here. Not sure she'll want to go out in the heat, though. What's that thermometer say?"

I peered outside the front window. "Uh, eighty-four."

"*Humph.* Not too bad yet. It'll be good for her to get out." A

# 21

*B*ecky Wallace was blowing smoke rings on the back stairs leading up to Stu's apartment when I got home from the beauty shop. "Oh. Hi, Becky." I jiggled my keys, eager to get inside before my "party" hairdo frizzed up. "Sure is muggy. Say, any news from DCFS about Andy's visiting day?"

Becky shrugged. "My case worker's workin' on it, I guess. Stu said she'd put in a good word for me too." She blew another smoke ring. "Got mixed feelin's 'bout it, though. Hate to give up Sundays."

"Could you talk to the guy at the Bagel Bakery? Or did you already?"

Becky frowned. "I'm not so good at stickin' up for myself—not as good as I was stickin' up you guys." The second those words spouted out of her mouth, Becky looked at me, horrified. But when I snickered, we both started laughing. Howling, actually. Becky Wallace had just made a *joke* in the middle of her pain.

My phone was ringing. "Gotta go," I gasped, and gave her a quick hug. "It's going to work out, Becky, I know it will. Somehow."

I got the kitchen phone just as the answering machine kicked in. "Hi! I'm here!"

"*Hola,* Jodi. I am so glad you are home."

My heart warmed to hear Delores's voice. Delores Enriques and I were probably around the same age, but she had a mothering heart that made me feel safe. Loved. "Me too! We haven't talked in a while."

"I'm sorry. I'm working extra hours to help with—well, you know. But I just called to say *gracias* to Denny for asking Ricardo to the workday at New Morning."

"I'll tell him, Delores. But Ricardo said he was busy."

Her sigh was deep. "*Lo sé.* But, still, I think it meant something to be asked, though he wouldn't admit it. I'm not sure what he's 'busy' with this morning, but his band is playing at La Fiesta tonight. Maybe they're practicing."

We were both silent. *Should I ask?* Curiosity overcame me. "What about, you know, the dog? Does he still have it?" What I really meant was, *Is Ricardo still fighting that scary pit bull in those illegal dogfights?* That was what had started the whole mess about Ricardo saying they had to get more money *somewhere*—if not betting on the dogfights, then José had to drop out of school and get a job.

"Just pray for us, *mi amiga.* The good news is, José was accepted at Lane Tech. A long commute from Little Village, but that boy wants to go to college. And he will."

"OK. I'll pray now." It was becoming more natural for me to "pray on the spot." And we did, right there on the phone. Delores prayed too. That woman. She had so much faith in the middle of circumstances that would knock me over.

When we hung up, I looked at the clock. One o'clock. Denny

and Josh would be home at three, they said. I had two hours to myself, time to put on my makeup and paint my nails. Denny hadn't said where we were going for dinner. Maybe he hadn't decided.

And then a wonderful thought danced into my brain. *La Fiesta.* The largest Mexican-American restaurant in Chicago, famous for its authentic cuisine and colorful atmosphere. And Ricardo's band was playing tonight . . .

"WOW." Denny looked me up and down, then turned me around. "Nice. Very very nice—for forty-four."

"Forty-*three.* My birthday's not for another month." But my cheeks flushed at the light in his eyes. I did look nice. The mirror said so. Not exactly my everyday bangs and ordinary brown hair brushing my shoulders. Little twists, anchored by a row of glitter pins, pulled my hair back from my face, releasing the bouncy fall of waves behind my ears. The hairstyle my Yada Yada sisters had picked for me last year at my first makeover at Adele's Hair and Nails made my brown eyes stand out, especially with some liner and mascara. And the slinky black dress Denny got for my last birthday slimmed down the few pounds I'd put on the last couple of years.

But Denny's eyebrow went up when I suggested we go to La Fiesta Mexican Restaurant for dinner. "Hm. Isn't that where Ricardo Enriques's mariachi band has a regular gig?" I'm sure I looked guilty. "Jodi Marie Baxter. I smell a Yada Yada scheme. Can't we do something just *us* on our anniversary without involving the trials and tribulations of your Yada Yada sisters and their families?"

I protested. It wasn't a scheme. Honest. But didn't he remember the wonderful music Ricardo and his band played at Amanda's *quinceañera?* And Avis's wedding? So romantic. Why *not* go to La Fiesta and hear him play? Ricardo probably wouldn't even know we were there.

But a few hours later, when we asked for a table for two, the hostess led us to a table not ten feet from the band. "Oh, well," I whispered to Denny as he pulled out my chair. "So much for anonymity." To my surprise, Mr. Bump-on-a-Log Enriques, dressed like the rest of the mariachi band in a short black and silver jacket, white shirt, and black pants, actually smiled when he saw us sit down. Then he once again bent over the large *guittarón* he hugged like a lover to his chest, coaxing the lilting music from its heart.

We were halfway through our *combinación* plates when the band took a break. Ricardo stopped by our table and shook hands. "So glad to see the Baxters at La Fiesta." His smile was genuine. He tipped his head at me. "The lady is beautiful tonight. What is the special occasion?"

Denny grinned and laid an arm across the back of my chair. "Our anniversary. Twenty-one years."

Ricardo's smile broadened. "Congratulations. Enjoy."

We did. The restaurant walls beamed with brilliant shades of orange and yellow. Sombreros, piñatas, and other Mexican trappings decorated the walls and ceilings. We lingered over *café de olla*—a pot of coffee with chocolate and cinnamon—so we could hear the band play again. I was glad Denny seemed to be enjoying himself.

I was just about to whisper, "Shall we go?" when Ricardo Enriques took the microphone. "We have *un ocasión especial* tonight." His eyes twinkled, and he swept a hand in our direction.

"Mr. and Mrs. Baxter are celebrating their twenty-first anniversary at La Fiesta—"

People started clapping. The tips of Denny's ears turned red.

"—and we are going to play a special song in their honor—a song for lovers." His smile got bigger and he motioned to us. "Come, come, Jodi and Denny. For you, we are going to play while you do the *jarabe*, the dance for lovers—otherwise known as the Mexican Hat Dance."

I could tell Denny was starting to panic. Denny would *never* voluntarily dance in public. But Ricardo was insistent. "Come, come, I will show you." He tossed a sombrero on the floor and snapped his fingers to set time for the band. "*One*, two, three, *one*, two three . . ." And then Delores's husband took my hand and led me in a startling dance around the hat on the floor. The other dinner guests clapped and yelled encouragement. I was laughing so hard, I had no idea what I was doing, but it was *fun*.

After a few minutes, Ricardo bowed to me and handed me off to Denny. "Now you, *mi amigo*."

I was sure Denny would say no, afraid of making a fool of himself, but to my surprise he shrugged and flashed his two big dimples. "Can't dance, but I can't let *mi amigo* have the only dance with *mi amor*." He took my hand, the band swept back into the dance music, and the two of us, laughing, stumbled and fumbled around that big hat to cheers and clapping all around us.

Inspired, other patrons got up and danced as Ricardo and his band introduced other dance music: *la raspa*, a sort of square dance with a little hopping step all its own . . . *jarana*, a complicated fast dance that put *us* out of commission . . . and everyone's favorite, *la bamba*. It didn't seem to matter whether anyone could dance or not.

For the next hour, all the strangers who'd come to La Fiesta that night were knit together in the joy of a culture and a people whose history was so entwined with our own.

Denny and I finally pooped out. We giggled at ourselves all the way home. I couldn't remember having so much fun since . . . maybe never.

Only one thing bothered me. I was having a hard time matching up *this* Ricardo—Ricardo the talented mariachi musician, brightening the lives of La Fiesta dinner guests each weekend with his flamboyant guitar—with the Ricardo Enriques who kept a pit bull in his garage for illegal dogfighting. It didn't make sense.

THE EXHILARATION of our anniversary night out stayed with me right through church at Uptown the next day. *Why don't we dance more in church,* I wondered, *responding with our bodies to the joy of the Lord?* Then I realized that's what Avis and Florida did in their own way, whether anyone else did or not.

I was still smiling inside on Monday, in spite of spending all day sorting out old lesson plans and doing back-to-school shopping with Amanda that evening, gasping at the price of brand-name jeans. Even had a big grin on my face Tuesday when I heard Stu and Becky's doorbell. I peeked out my front door. A taxi was double-parked in front of the house, its hazards flashing, while Chanda fussed over Dia and Cheree on the porch.

"Oh, Becky. Mi hope dey got all dey need for five days wit'out dey mama." She ticked things off on her fingers. "Jammies. Toot'brushes. Swimsuits. Sandals. Shorts and T-shirts—"

"They gonna be fine, Chanda! Just go. Go!" Becky squatted

down, making eye contact with the two girls. She tweaked the nose of Dia's stuffed dog. "Who's this? Does he bite?" Dia giggled. Twelve-year-old Thomas smirked at the girls behind his cool sunglasses, obviously thrilled not to have his little sisters tagging along to Hawaii.

I poked my head out the door. "Chanda! You and Tom have a wonderful time." Everyone waved. "Bye! Bye!" And the taxi was gone.

Becky worked hard at entertaining the girls the next few days— if the board games, kid videos, markers, and scratch paper she kept borrowing were any indication. I could hear them out in the backyard squealing as they ran through the sprinkler, and at least once a day, the girls knocked at our back door and asked if Willie Wonka could come out to play—which good ol' Wonka was happy to do, providing it didn't require doing more than panting in the sun.

By Thursday, Becky looked a little ragged. I'd already planned a trek up to Evanston to give Nony a break. Why not take Cheree and Dia along? They could play with Nony's boys while I visited with Mark and folded some laundry. Nony and Hoshi took the opportunity to go out for lunch and do some shopping. Both were laughing when they came back. But I struggled with sadness when I left. Mark's left eye was patched again—another surgery to clean out the hemorrhage—and he seemed to tire quickly. I didn't ask but I wondered . . . would he ever see with that eye again? Would his body and spirit ever really recover from the beating?

Since we were out, the girls helped me shop for Amanda's birthday, then we dropped by the Hickmans' house to deliver a hanging plant for Florida's front porch. Carla immediately took the girls to her new bedroom on the first floor, a NO BOYS ALLOWED sign on the door. Florida made a big fuss over the plant, as if it hadn't been almost a week since she'd yelled at me on the phone. She tipped her head toward Carla's bedroom. "That girl in heaven havin' her own room. The boys too."

Boys—as in plural? Florida grinned. "Yeah, that's what got Chris back home. We told him he had his own room now—the boys' rooms are upstairs. He behavin' himself so far, even got him registered over at Sullivan High School. Right now he's cleaning out the garage as punishment for runnin' off." She winked. "Never can tell when the Hickmans gonna get us a car, the way God is blessin' us. Oh, thank ya, Jesus!"

Becky was zonked on the couch when I brought the girls back home, using Stu's extra key to let ourselves in. Dia and Cheree clamored to watch TV, so Becky popped in one of our ancient kid videos and followed me to the back door. "Man, Jodi. I didn't know keepin' up with two little girls was gonna be so hard! They good, but—man! They always wantin' me to *do* somethin' with 'em."

I grinned. "Welcome to parenthood. Maybe that's why they come out as babies instead of kids. Gives us parents time to fall in love before we have second thoughts."

She glared at me. "Second thoughts? You mean about Andy? Never."

I had a last-minute inspiration. "Do you and the girls and Stu want to come to Amanda's birthday supper tomorrow? Maybe the girls could help decorate." I knew Amanda wouldn't mind. It'd feel more like a party than the "no-frills birthday" we'd promised, even if the guests were only six and eight.

As it turned out, given construction paper and rolls of crepe paper, the decorating kept Becky and the girls busy for hours. They made cards and plastered signs and streamers everywhere I'd let them stick tape. And just as we were lighting the sixteen birthday candles on the fudge chocolate layer cake, José "just happened" to come by with a present for Amanda—a big white teddy bear with Sweet Sixteen embroidered on its heart—so it turned out to be quite a party after all.

Lots of chatter and laughter. Family. Friends. Simple gifts. *Thank You, Jesus.*

Josh offered to take Amanda and José to a movie after supper as his birthday gift, and Becky tried to drag Dia and Cheree upstairs to get ready for bed, but the girls begged for a story first. "Mr. Denny! Mr. Denny! You read us a story!"

For two seconds Denny looked like a deer caught in the headlights, but then he grinned. "Sure. That means I don't have to do dishes, right?" I chased all three of them out of the kitchen with a snapping dishtowel.

Stu and Becky helped me clean up the kitchen, then I peeked into the living room, where Denny was reading *The Wind in the Willows* with Cheree and Dia cuddled up on either side of him. I turned to leave silently when I heard Dia interrupt the story. "Mr. Denny? I wish you could be our daddy."

*Oh Jesus.* My heart squeezed. *Out of the mouths of babes.* I wondered what Denny would say. Tell them he was married to *me*, not their mama, so he couldn't be their daddy. Then I heard him say, "Tell you what, snicklefritz. I could be your uncle, how about that? Uncle Denny. How does that sound?"

The giggles coming from the living room told me it sounded just fine.

SINCE BECKY COULDN'T LEAVE THE HOUSE, I took the girls to the airport to meet their mama and brother on Saturday, even though we had to meet at United's baggage claim. Thomas showed up in a colorful Hawaiian shirt, new shorts, and the ever-present sunglasses. Chanda wore a teal Hawaiian sarong with a creamy orchid print and flip-flops. The girls squealed as Chanda lifted fresh-flower leis from her neck to theirs.

"Ooo, Sista Jodee, so glad you come to get us," she said as we waited for the luggage carousel. "Mi got more suitcases comin' dan goin', and dem taxi mons all want a big tip. So how de girls behave for Becky?"

"They were great, Chanda. I think she enjoyed them very much. But I'm eager to hear about your trip. Was it everything you hoped for?"

Chanda rolled her eyes. "Oh, girl, don't get mi started! What dey offer for 'free' more like a budget motel wit' a dinky pool six blocks from de beach! No chocolate on de pillow; no complimentary breakfast buffet. When mi complained, dey say, 'Oh, you can upgrade! Only pay a little more!' Better hotel, better food, better view—till mi spending four, five hundred dollars on me 'free' vacation. Dem big mout's at Glass Slipper Vacations ina big badda touble wit' Chanda George!"

"Oh, Chanda. I'm so sorry. I was hoping you would have a really good time."

The baggage carousel hiccupped noisily to life and started spitting out all sizes of bags and suitcases. Chanda heaved a large sigh, then leaned toward me in a low voice. "*Huh.* A cut-rate vacation to Hawaii wit'out no mon. No chocolate, no sex—what kind of vacation is dat?"

# 22

The phone started ringing Sunday morning while I was in the bathroom trying to salvage what was left of my week-old "party 'do." Denny pounded on the door. "Jodi! It's for you. I've gotta shave anyway." He handed me the phone as I came out.

"Jodi, how ya doin'?" Florida was altogether too lively for this early in the morning. "Yada Yada comin' to my house this evening for a house blessing, right?"

I racked my brain. Had we talked about this? "Uh, fine with me, Flo." It would be the first time we met at Florida's home. Did that mean we had to call everybody?

"Well, help me remember to tell Stu and Avis at church today—Oh. Is Uptown meetin' with New Morning at the shopping center today? It's the fourth Sunday."

I squinted at the kitchen calendar, suddenly annoyed. Why was I information central for Yada Yada, anyway? Today was the fourth Sunday all right, but August had five Sundays. I'd written on the fourth Sunday, "Meet w/ New Morn." And on the fifth Sunday: "Uptown Bus Mtg."

*Yikes. The church business meeting was only a week away.* The decision about selling our building and merging with New Morning. Had I been praying about it? Seeking God, as Pastor Clark had urged? I blew out a breath. "Yeah, you're right, Florida. Thanks for the reminder."

"Good. That means Nony and Hoshi will be there too—that's half the Yada Yadas right there! Hey, gotta go. See you in an hour or so."

Well, at least I hadn't offered to make all the calls, and Florida hadn't asked me to. But I'd no sooner hung up than the phone rang again. Nony this time. My heart gave a lurch. "Nony? Is everything all right?"

"Oh, yes, Jodi. God is good. Mark even wants to come to worship this morning—we are meeting at the new building, yes? He can't do the stairs at Uptown when New Morning meets there."

Nony had said Mark hadn't been going to church, but I hadn't realized Uptown's stairs were such a barrier. *Duh. Of course.* Another reason for New Morning to get into their own building quickly. Maybe a good reason for Uptown to merge with New Morning, for that matter. How many other folks with disabilities were kept away from our worship services by those steep stairs?

"I'm calling because—just a moment, Jodi." I heard a door close. Nony came back on the line, her voice lowered. "Can you still hear me? Hoshi is in the next room. It's her birthday next week. Remember? That's why her parents came to see her last year about this time. Can we do something for her at Yada Yada tonight? I will be glad to purchase a cake—"

"Fine with me." I was starting to feel like a parrot, repeating myself.

"—but I was wondering, Jodi. Could you look up the meaning of her name? It might not be easy, since it's Japanese, but—"

"Sure." Doing a meaning-of-the-name card would be fun, especially since nobody was asking me to bake a cake. "I'll see what I can do."

IT WAS GREAT TO SEE MARK SMITH at worship that morning. Nony drove their minivan and unloaded Hoshi and her family at the door of New Morning's shopping-center church. Marcus and Michael ran ahead to open the double-glass doors, but Mark walked into the large sanctuary-in-progress on his own steam. A black patch over his left eye made him look a bit suave and mysterious, but I noticed that he found a chair quickly and stayed anchored during the entire two-hour service. He'd always looked slender and fit; now he just looked thin and fragile. But he was there. Smiling.

I apologized to the Lord for my snippy attitude that morning, but I still couldn't shake the feeling that something felt "off" during the whole service. I shut my eyes, trying to close out my normal distractions, enjoying the combined praise team—especially that lovely wailing saxophone—as our two congregations filled the house with "We bring a sacrifice of praise!" and "What a mighty God we serve!" followed by a few quieter worship songs: "I love to worship You," and a new one to me, "This is the air I breathe . . . Your holy presence living in me."

*That's what I want, Lord,* I thought, breathing my own prayer. *Your holy presence living in me.*

So why did I feel so edgy today? Couldn't put my finger on it until Debra Meeks, my new friend from New Morning, came up to me after the service and gave me a hug. "It's a strange time, isn't it?" the older woman commented. "Both of our congregations trying to decide whether we want to merge." She gave a little snort. "What if you say yes and we say no?"

I was startled by her matter-of-fact honesty. But I sensed nothing tense between us in her use of "you" and "we." She was sharing with me. Pulling me into her circle. I raised an eyebrow. "Or vice versa."

She laughed. "Guess it's a good thing we've got the Holy Spirit. God may need to be the tiebreaker." With another hug, she was gone.

But Debra's comment brought my feelings into focus as I climbed into the Baxter minivan for the twelve short blocks home to Lunt Avenue. As much as I'd enjoyed the monthly services with New Morning this summer, even shared the excitement of possibly merging our two churches, I'd really wanted to be "just us" that morning, to soak up another Uptown worship service as I'd grown to know and love it in the past two years before we bid it good-bye. If I was honest with myself, my feelings were a tangled mess: anticipation mixed with loss, blessings mixed with uncomfortable change, trust in God's direction mingled with fear of the unknown.

I took Willie Wonka for a walk along the lake that afternoon, praying aloud, confessing all my mixed feelings to God, and trying to ignore the weird glances I got from the walkers and bikers and baby-stroller pushers who passed us. "Yeah, Wonka. Notice that they *all* pass us."

But by the time I pried myself out of Stu's car in front of

Florida's house that evening, I felt better for having confessed it all to God and actually *praying* about the upcoming business meeting rather than stewing about the decision we had to make.

Florida must have gotten the word around, because we had a good turnout that night at Yada Yada. Ruth huffed into the house, proudly wearing a bubblegum pink maternity smock that looked straight out of the eighties—probably left over from one of her early pregnancies and kept hopefully in the back of her closet the past twenty years. I almost commented on it, but Delores took one look at her and started scolding. "Ruth, *mi amiga,* you are too thin. What are you eating?"

"Thin, schmin!" Ruth patted her tummy under the pink bubblegum. "What do you think this is, my bed pillow?"

"That's *not* what I mean. Your face, your arms . . . how many pounds have you gained?"

Ruth rolled her eyes. "How many *ounces* do you think these babies weigh at twenty weeks? Not even one pound. I'm fine. Not to worry. Ben worries enough for both of us."

How Nony smuggled a cake into Florida's kitchen when she also brought Hoshi was beyond me. But Nony lifted an eyebrow at me as if to say, *Did you find her name?* I grinned and patted the tote bag holding my Bible and water bottle. Did I ever.

Avis arrived alone. "Rochelle didn't come this time?" I asked.

Avis shook her head. "Dexter agreed to move out and get counseling. Rochelle seemed relieved to be able to go back home. She and Conny have to get back to something resembling a normal life, even with the marriage in trouble. Have to admit, so do we." She allowed a wry smile. "It was getting a bit tense at home."

I hadn't realized Stu had overheard, but she cut in. "Did she change the locks? No? Avis, I'm telling you. Tell Peter to change those locks."

By the time Chanda blew in, everyone else had arrived. "'Scuse my fancy coffee table," Florida smirked, setting chips and salsa on an overturned packing box. "We gettin' there; just ain't there yet."

Chanda loaded a paper plate with potato chips, complaining that she'd been in her new house longer than Flo and we hadn't had a house blessing for *her*. "Well, just invite us, girl!" Florida said. "You can't wait around for ever'body to be thinkin' about you all the time. If you want somethin' to happen, speak up! We'll be there."

My hand paused with a potato chip halfway to my mouth. *Sheesh*. Why couldn't I "speak the obvious truth" as Florida had just done without a tinge of irritation or self-righteousness? She made it look so easy. *Huh*. Maybe that's what the apostle Paul meant about "speaking the truth in love." Not such a big deal, really.

Avis flopped open her big Bible. "Don't sit down, sisters. In a minute, we're going to bless this house from basement to attic. But if you've got your Bibles, turn to Psalm 127." I dug my Bible out of my tote as she began to read: "'Unless the Lord builds the house, its builders labor in vain. Unless the Lord watches over the city, the watchmen stand guard in vain.'"

"Jesus! Help us!" Florida said, shaking her head.

Ruth begged off from the blessing tour, saying she'd pray blessings right where she sat. Avis got out her little bottle of anointing oil, and we started first in the living room, asking God to "build this house" and watch over the family within its walls. Avis anointed the doorways as we went from room to room—the kitchen, the dining room, the dark and damp basement where empty spaces sat next to the laundry tubs. Carla, playing with a doll in her first-floor bedroom, watched wide-eyed as Avis anointed her bed, her toy shelf, her CD player, and her desk as Delores poured out her heart for God's blessings in Spanish. The only words I recognized were "*muchacha preciosa*"—precious girl.

"Are the boys here?" I whispered to Florida as she led the way upstairs.

She shook her head. "Carl took them to the park to play ball, to get them out of the way." But her eyes twinkled. "Now *that* ain't happened since I can't remember when."

We prayed a long time in the boys' bedrooms—each room hardly bigger than Chanda's new walk-in closet—then Florida unlocked a door and we crowded into the tiny "apartment" that made up the back half of the second floor: closet-sized kitchen, one room for living room and eating in, a small bedroom, and a tiny bath. Adele prayed that God would send "the right someone" to rent the apartment, and that it would be a blessing to whoever lived there.

As we all shuffled out, I noticed that Becky lingered, just standing there as if memorizing the four walls.

I hadn't noticed when Nony slipped downstairs, but when we wiggled ourselves in a long line down the narrow staircase to the first floor, Nony and Ruth were already lighting candles on a gorgeous bakery cake sitting precariously on the upturned packing box. Adele launched the group into "Happy birthday to youuuu . . ." as fingers gleefully pointed to Hoshi, who was blushing beneath her fall of shiny black hair.

"Hey, look at that." Yo-Yo pointed to the cake. "Is that your name in Japanese or somethin', Hoshi?" I did a double take. Sure enough, a Japanese character in mint green frosting graced the top of the cake—the same character I'd worked so hard to copy onto a card when I'd finally discovered the meaning of Hoshi's name. *Huh.* So much for my surprise.

"Look, nothin'," growled Adele. "Make a wish an' blow 'em out, Hoshi, or we're all gonna be eating wax with our frosting."

Hoshi blew, Ruth cut, and Nony passed out mint green paper plates of raspberry-filled chocolate cake. I took out the card I'd made and showed off the front with its Japanese character, which looked somewhat like a leaping stick figure with a pigtail. "I thought I was so smart discovering how to write Hoshi's name in *kanji* script, but it looks like Nonyameko beat me to it. How'd you find it, Nony?"

She laughed. "Hoshi's been teaching the boys bits of Japanese. I found a scrap of paper with 'Hoshi' written on it and that drawing. Decided to take a chance."

Ruth rolled her eyes. "That could mean 'quit bugging me, you little *nudnik*,' for all you know."

Hoshi burst out laughing, spraying cake crumbs everywhere. "No, no . . ."

I grinned. "Well, I'm sure Hoshi already knows the meaning of her name, which means 'star' in *kanji* script. In fact, her name *is* Star in Japanese, right, Hoshi?"

"Star? Oh, so beautiful." Edesa, her own dark eyes alight, gave Hoshi a hug. Hoshi, blushing big time, nodded.

I opened the card, showing the words to a scripture verse on the inside. "I found a verse in First Corinthians that I thought fit Hoshi very well. 'The sun has one kind of splendor, the moon another and the stars another; and star differs from star in splendor.' So, sisters, I'm going to pass this around, and I want all of you to write a note of appreciation for how Hoshi's splendor shines in our lives."

I'd just started to pass the card around when a loud commotion at the back door caught our attention. Male voices, sharp and angry. "But I din't *do* it, Dad! Why would I do that to our own house?"

"Then who did? Why our garage? You better tell me, boy!"

"I don't know!"

"Like hell you don't!"

Florida's face got dark. She started to get up, but Carl burst into the room, one hand gripped tightly around Chris's upper arm. A frightened Cedric, clutching a basketball, slipped quickly up the stairs.

"Carl! Whatever it is—"

Carl looked ready to explode. "If you don't wanna hear it, Flo, you better go see for yourself." He disappeared up the stairs pushing Chris ahead of him.

To my surprise, Florida just stood in the middle of the bare floor, as if rooted to the spot, afraid to move. "Come on, girl." Adele lifted her big frame off the straight chair she'd been sitting on. "I'll go with you."

"Me too," I blurted. Meekly, Florida let herself be herded through the kitchen, out the back door, and down the rickety back steps. It was still light outside, only six o'clock, the pavement and alley still holding the heat from the day. The three of us rounded the corner of the one-car garage, badly in need of some paint, and stared at the garage door.

The letters *BD* had been splashed across the garage door in fresh, black spray paint, sitting above a scrawled six-pointed star and crossed pitchforks.

# 23

A low moan rose to Florida's lips from deep in her belly. "They found us, found my baby. Oh Jesus, noooo . . ."

"Flo!" I grabbed her and held on, afraid she was going to fall to the ground.

"Lowlife gangbangers," muttered Adele. "Cockroaches have more decency. Come on, Flo. Come on, baby, it's all right. We'll get that mess off your garage." She circled Florida's waist with her arm, and the two of us slowly walked her back to the house.

At the back door, Florida halted. "Maybe—maybe they not markin' our house on purpose. Maybe some taggers jus' picked our garage, randomlike. 'Cause I *told* Chris not to give our address to any of those gangbangers in our old neighborhood. Want him to get a fresh start, leave all those friends behind."

Adele snorted. "Girl, you only moved a couple of miles. You would've had to move all the way to Lake Forest or maybe Canada to shake the dust of that neighborhood off your feet! These gang-bangers, they're everywhere. But come on; it's not the end of the world. I've had my shop defaced at least three times since I opened up. It happens. You deal with it. You go on."

Florida frowned in the glow of the dim yellow bulb above the back door. "I know. But, what if those BDs *are* leavin' a message, like, 'We know who lives here'?"

That's what I wanted to know. Was it just vandalism—or a threat?

Adele pulled open the screen door. "Maybe, maybe not. Chris said he didn't do it; that's one good thing. I believe him too. But doesn't surprise *me* if his old friends know where he lives. Still don't mean this won't be a good change for y'all." She waggled a finger in Flo's face. "What you *do* know, Florida Hickman, is our God is bigger than all those gangbangers put together. Your family is under the blood of Jesus—an' we just anointed all the doorposts in this house under God's protection. Now you claim that, girl. You think the devil ain't gonna fight back? He might try, but he's *not* gonna get that child. Now, c'mon. These skeeters are eatin' me up somethin' fierce!"

Well, that was the second time in a month a family crisis erupted in the middle of our meeting. The others had pretty much guessed what the trouble was. But when we got back to the front room, Adele took over. "Don't anybody leave, now, 'cause there ain't anything we can do about that graffiti tonight—and we don't want that ol' devil to score any more points than he already got."

Yo-Yo wagged her head. "I dunno. If this keeps up, I'm gonna think twice 'bout havin' Yada Yada at *my* place. I'm too young to have a heart attack." I don't think she meant to be funny, but the tension broke and we all had a good laugh.

Then we prayed. Adele led us into a passionate prayer, putting

Chris Hickman and all our children under the blood of Jesus. "No more!" she cried. "We gonna take back what that ol' devil tryin' to steal from us!"

After a while, we added prayers about Chanda's mammogram and Becky's job search. When Ruth heard us mention the schedule problem at the Bagel Bakery, she muttered, "Not to worry, young lady. You leave Mr. Hurwitz to me."

As we finally left the Hickmans' house, which had been blessed and battered in the same evening, Stu said, "If you need any help painting over those gang symbols, Flo, just let us know."

Florida snorted. "'Preciate it. But I think Chris gonna be slinging a paintbrush tomorrow. Maybe paint the whole garage! Needed it, anyway—Jodi, wait!" She grabbed me. "Speakin' of tomorrow, any way you could pick up Carla an' take her to Bethune Elementary? Avis wants to do some testing since she comin' into a new school, make sure she put in the right class. Test at ten, but I don't get off work till three."

I shrugged. "Sure. Was going to start working on my classroom this week anyway. What time should I pick her up?"

I TOOK DENNY TO WORK the next morning so I could keep the car, which had definite advantages. Besides picking up Carla, I could load all my school supplies and take them to school in one trip. And later I could shop for Amanda's school supplies—*Oh Lord, is she really starting her junior year?*—though I didn't dare get any school clothes without her along. *That* much I knew.

I was tempted to drive through the alley behind Florida's house to see if those menacing gang symbols had been painted over yet, but I stuck to business and picked up Carla, who was wearing new jeans and a pink "Girl Power" T-shirt, and drove straight to Bethune Elementary. I glanced over my shoulder into the second seat of the Caravan. "Do you know why our school is called Mary McLeod Bethune Elementary School?" No answer. But I chatted away, telling the story about the teacher who ran a school for little girls from the railroad camps in Florida, about her motto over the doorway that said ENTER TO LEARN on the outside and DEPART TO SERVE on the inside, and the college that eventually grew out of that little school.

Carla said nothing until I pulled into the parking lot. Then, "*My school was a lot bigger than this dinky school.*" I did my best not to roll my eyes and simply herded her into the office and turned her over to Ms. Ivy, the secretary.

As I unlocked the door to my classroom, I was startled to see that my storage cabinet had been removed and replaced with another row of desks. I groaned. "Oh Lord, I forgot about all the additional students. What am I going to do?" Had to admit my immediate concern was where I was going to store all my supplies, not how I was going to teach a classroom of thirty-one kids.

*Place these children in My care, Jodi.* The Voice in my Spirit didn't seem as concerned about where I put my store of construction paper, pencils, and scissors.

I grinned inwardly, my frustration knocked down a few notches. "OK, Lord, here we go." I didn't have my class list yet, but I walked up and down the rows of empty desks, touching each one, praying for the girl or boy who would sit there in one short week. As I touched the desk where Hakim Porter used to sit, I paused. Something was different—what? And then I knew.

The jagged scar he'd scratched into the desktop last year had been sanded off.

Unbidden, my eyes felt wet. Hakim was truly gone from my life.

TO MY SURPRISE, the week sped by quickly, in spite of two professional development days sponsored by the school district and a teachers' institute for Bethune Elementary. Avis—whom I had to start calling "Mrs. Douglass" again—handed out our class lists at the end of the institute day on Friday, and I ran my finger down the long list of names. Did I have time to look up all their name meanings and do a Welcome Bulletin Board for this new crop of students, as I'd done last year?

*Abrianna Jones . . . Adam Smith . . . Bowie Garcia . . . Carla Hickman . . .*

I blinked. *Wait a minute. Carla's supposed to be in fourth grade.* I sidled up to the group of teachers crowding around Avis, who was trying to field half a dozen earth-shaking questions. "What happened to the copy machine in the teachers' lounge? We can't *all* use the one in the office." "Why do teachers have to supervise the lunchroom? I thought we were going to get parent volunteers this year!" "I was supposed to get new marker boards, but the old ones are still in my room! They're impossible!"

The crowd thinned. Avis finally turned to me. "Jodi, you have a question?"

"Um, just a misprint, I think. Carla Hickman. She's on my class list, but she's supposed to be in fourth grade."

Avis massaged her temples. "I'm sorry, Jodi. I should have called you. Carla's test results were too low for fourth grade. I recommended she repeat third grade, especially since she's starting a new school. None of the other children will know she's repeating. It's an ideal situation to help her catch up."

"But—"

"And when I had a conference with the Hickmans, Florida requested that Carla be put in your class. At least she'll know her teacher as she starts a new school."

"Oh." *Huh.* Wasn't sure how I felt about that. Carla could be a little snit! That's the last thing I needed—a troublemaker in class whose mother was one of my best friends. *Sheesh!* What if I had to discipline her or send home a note from school?

On the other hand, I was touched that Florida asked for me to be Carla's teacher. That said a lot about our friendship. Maybe it would work out . . .

I picked up the mail when I got home, rifling through the stack as I let Willie Wonka out into the backyard. Not sure why I bothered. Since the advent of e-mail, nobody wrote letters any more. Like today: Dominick's ad, water bill, L. L. Bean catalog, Mr. Coupon, a reminder from Uptown about the business meeting this Sunday, a letter for Josh—

*Whoa.* A letter for Josh. OK, so I was wrong. I squinted at the return address: Mr. and Mrs. Harley Baxter. Why were Denny's parents writing Josh? They were pick-up-the-phone people—when they bothered to call. Probably a belated graduation card. They'd been on a cruise last June and couldn't make Josh's graduation. But why a business envelope?

I shrugged, put the letter on the dining room table, and stuck some chicken in the microwave to thaw. By the time my motley crew straggled in, I had lemon-and-thyme chicken breasts on the grill, a fruit salad with kiwi garnish, and fresh corn on the cob I'd picked up at the Rogers Park Fruit Market. My personal kickoff to Labor Day weekend! The end of summer! The beginning of the school year!

Amanda kicked off her sandals, threw her backpack into a corner, and squatted down to hug the dog. "My nanny days are over, Wonka! I'm a free woman!" she crowed, nuzzling his face and getting a face licking in return.

"Free until Tuesday anyway," I said mildly, handing her a tray with paper plates, paper cups, and napkins. Maybe the bees would leave us alone long enough to eat on the back porch.

She took the tray, rolling her eyes. "Mo-ther! School is *nothing* compared to the torture of babysitting three aliens disguised as children for a whole month!"

"Yeah, but you're rich now, pipsqueak, so quit complaining." Josh snitched a kiwi slice from the fruit salad on his way through the kitchen. "Can we eat now, Mom?"

"Sure, as soon as your dad changes his clothes. And Josh— there's a letter for you on the dining room table. From your grandparents." I herded Amanda out to the back porch, following her with the food, proud of myself for not hanging over Josh's shoulder.

Silence in the other room. Then Josh banged the screen door and flopped down on the porch swing, his face a big scowl. "What?" I asked.

He jerked a thumb inside. "Dad's got the letter. Talk about pressure."

Well, if Denny could read it . . . I hustled inside. Denny, stripped down to running shorts and a T-shirt, stood in the dining room, holding Josh's letter, his face gathered in a huge frown. *"What?"* I said again. Denny handed me the typed letter—and a check.

"Dear Josh," I read aloud. "Don't be foolish, son. Get a good education, *then* do your Good Samaritan thing, travel, live in a kibbutz, whatever. Don't waste that brilliant mind of yours. If money's the problem, let's just say we're investing in your future. This check should cover your first year at the University of Illinois. Love . . ." The letter was signed, "Harley and Kay."

I looked at the check. Made out to Joshua James Baxter for twenty thousand dollars.

# 24

*wenty thou—!"* Denny put his fingers to my mouth and shook his head.

"Not now. Let's eat. We can discuss it later." Right. Let's eat chicken with our fingers while twenty thousand dollars lay on the dining room table. Josh didn't say much during supper, just hunched over his corn on the cob, ignoring the bee that was investigating the short, sandy hair he was letting grow out. *A bit shaggy, but at least it's hair,* I thought, swatting at the bee with a napkin.

Amanda filled up the silence with a running monologue about her monthlong babysitting marathon. "Did you know that Donald *insisted* on wearing his shirts *and* shorts inside out? He thought the seams sticking out looked cool. *Huh.* What does he know. He's only eight." She waved her half-eaten cob of corn in the air. "And Deanna. She would *not* eat anything touching anything else. She took apart her PB and J, licked off the peanut butter, licked off the jelly, *then* ate the bread." She rolled her eyes. "Oh, puh-leease . . . Dad, can I have that piece of chicken? Thanks. Davy was cute, though."

We let Amanda celebrate her new freedom by cleaning up the kitchen. "Oh, right. *She* gets to clean up when we use paper plates," Josh grumbled. But Denny herded him into the living room with me right on their heels. Wonka, torn between the kitchen and the living room, opted to keep Amanda company in case any leftovers fell to the floor.

Josh parked his gangly frame in a corner of the couch. I sat on the other end, my thoughts tumbling over each other. Would this change Josh's mind about going to school this year? I'd be glad about that, except—*dang it!* What right did Denny's folks have going around us, not even discussing it, dumping that much money in Josh's lap?

Denny pulled the recliner closer but sat on the edge, leaning forward. He handed the letter to Josh. "Just want you to know, your mother and I didn't have anything to do with this. A surprise to us too."

Josh heaved a big sigh. "Yeah, well . . . I guess I'm supposed to be grateful, but honestly, it makes me mad! I don't *want* to go to U of I this year. So what am I supposed to do now? Throw it back in their face?"

So much for changing his mind. "Maybe they'd let you put it in the bank, save it till next year." I knew it sounded lame, but twenty thousand dollars was nothing to sneeze at.

"Mom." Josh looked at me with exaggerated patience. "If *I'd* made the decision to go to school—this year, next year, whatever—and *then* they offered to help out financially, that'd be one thing. But I don't like being pushed into doing something, just because they're offering to pay for it. Feels like emotional blackmail: 'Do what we want or look really ungrateful.'"

I glanced at Denny. Time for Dad to say something. After all, Harley and Kay were his parents. But Denny just frowned, as if sorting out his thoughts.

"Look." Josh eyed us both. "Why can't everybody respect what I want to do this year? I've got a good job at Software Symphony, starting to save some money. I'd like to be around for this merger with New Morning if it happens. And I'd like to volunteer at Manna House—you know, that new shelter they told us about at Jesus People. Edesa's going there on Labor Day to do some kind of health assessment of the women and kids, find out what the needs are. I told her I'd help—entertain the kids or whatever while she talks to the moms."

I looked at my son. His skin was the color of warm sandstone from working in the parks most of the summer. Still all elbows and knees, he hadn't filled out yet—but he seemed confident. Bold. A man.

Denny took a deep breath and then blew it out. "You're right. It's a lot of money to turn down"—I knew he was thinking of having to come up with that much on our own if Josh did end up at U of I—"but we do need to respect your decision. Would still like you to consider college. Skipping that step could narrow your options down the road."

Josh threw out his hands. "Fine! I am still considering it. I'd just like some real-life experience first. I don't even know what I want to study yet."

"So . . ." Denny made a face. "What do we do about this money?"

I lifted my chin. "We send it back. *We*"—I pointed to Denny and myself—"send it back. We tell your folks we appreciate the gesture, but we stick up for Josh, tell them he's not going to school this year; he's got other plans, so he can't keep the money." Tears lurked behind my eyes in spite of myself.

Josh looked at me, mouth agape. "Thanks. That means a lot, Mom." I realized this was the first time I'd truly stood on his side about not going to school this year. Then he grimaced. "But maybe I should do it. They sent it to me. Don't want them to think I'm hiding behind you guys."

"You're not! The point is, your grandparents need to know that *we* support your decision not to go to school this year." I couldn't believe what was coming out of my mouth. "The only way to do that is tell them ourselves."

Denny allowed a half grin. "OK, OK. Compromise. Josh should write his own letter saying thanks but no thanks, and we should include a letter saying we support his decision." He clapped his hands. Meeting over. But once Josh was out of the room, Denny eyed me sheepishly. "Uh, Jodi, would you write our letter? I'm so angry with them right now, I'd be tempted to tell them where they can jump off on their next cruise."


DENNY AND SOME OF THE OTHER UPTOWN MEN spent most of Saturday helping New Morning guys plaster drywall and add more electrical outlets at the new space. The day was blessedly cool for end of August, only midseventies. Cool enough to turn on the oven. I made cinnamon rolls to take to the work crew for a snack, and while the dough was rising, I went online and started my search for the meaning of names from my class list. I worked my way through Abrianna, Adam, Bowie, Caleb, then Carla . . .

*Carla—"one who is strong." Also Old German, meaning "free woman."*

Ha! That was Carla, all right. Just wasn't sure how free I wanted that little woman to feel. Might make her think she didn't have to obey the rules.

By Sunday I'd found the meaning of most of the names on my class list. Hadn't figured out how to make a bulletin board, but at least I still had Labor Day to work on it. As we Baxters climbed the stairs to the second floor of Uptown Community Church, the thought haunted me that we'd probably be selling the building, regardless of what we decided about merging with New Morning. Every worn stair and creaking floorboard suddenly took on a nostalgic veneer.

No nostalgia for the dreadful folding chairs, though. I hoped we'd vote them out of existence.

Florida leaned over my shoulder from the row behind us. "Lot of Uptown folks decided to stay in town, I see, spite of it bein' a holiday weekend. Even Carl got himself here. Now is that a good sign or a bad sign 'bout this vote we takin' today?"

"Good sign, I hope," I whispered back, waving at Little Andy, who was riding on his mother's hip, flapping his hand and grinning at everybody as Becky and Stu found three seats together.

Peter Douglass sat on the far side of the room, no doubt feeling responsible for bringing up the idea of a merger in the first place. Avis led worship that morning, taking her call to worship from Psalm 139—the same psalm I'd prayed at Yada Yada a few weeks ago. "Read along with me, church! 'Where can I go from your Spirit? Where can I flee from your presence? If I go up to the heavens, you are there; if I make my bed in the depths, you are there.'"

Avis's voice rode on the words. "'If I rise on the wings of the dawn, if I settle on the far side of the sea, even there your hand will guide me, your right hand will hold me fast. . .'"

The words soaked deep. Was Avis thinking about the merger with New Morning when she chose that scripture? But the words were comforting. No matter what happened, no matter how the decision went, God would be there.

The praise team launched into "Shout to the Lord"—though I had to admit, they sounded a little thin after the combined praise team last week. A while later, the younger children filed out to their Sunday school groups, but Pastor Clark kept his sermon short, almost as an introduction to the business at hand. He read the prayer of Jesus for His disciples from John 17: "I pray also for those who will believe in me through their message, that all of them may be one, Father, just as You are in me, and I am in You."

Pastor Clark cleared his throat, making his Adam's apple bob up and down. "I think it's important to keep Jesus' prayer for unity and oneness in mind as we approach the decision on the table today. The Christian church today is so divided—by race, by culture, by denomination, by leadership struggles. Let's have a minute of silent prayer, each of us asking the Holy Spirit to speak to us as a church today."

The room quieted. Thunder rolled over the city somewhere, not real close, and rain started to patter against the windows. Well, at least nobody would be antsy, wishing they were out at the lakefront barbecuing on this last weekend of summer. I squeezed my eyes closed, trying to shut out my stray thoughts. *Jesus, we need You now. Merging feels downright scary. But not merging doesn't feel right either. So what am I afraid of? What do You want us to do?*

A sudden loud clap of thunder made us all jump, laughing self-consciously as Pastor Clark drawled, "Guess that's a good amen. Why don't we open the floor for discussion?"

Rick Reilly got to his feet. "Uh, point of order, Pastor. Just who is making this decision today? We've got members and nonmembers here, no disrespect intended. But we ought to be clear."

"Good point. We want to hear thoughts from everyone, even our teenagers, but the decision will be made by the voting members of this church."

There was a long silence. Finally Bob Whittaker stood up. "Pastor, I know you mean well, but equating this decision with that scripture about all of us being 'one' in the body of Christ—well, that feels like a lot of pressure to go one way."

Pastor Clark cleared his throat. But Denny spoke up first. "I don't think Pastor Clark meant to put pressure on anybody. He was just pointing out that a merger with a church different from our own would bring some reality to that scripture—at least, that's how it spoke to me."

Brenda Gage waved her hand, her baby asleep over her shoulder. "I agree with you, Bob. After all, churches *are* different from each other. What's wrong with that? Why do we have to get so radical about this?"

Nods and murmurs rippled across the room. Comments flew, even as the rain outside drummed harder on the windows. "Why don't we just keep things simple? Sell our building, buy something larger." . . . "Merging two churches isn't the only way to be in unity" . . . "Yeah. We could do things with New Morning from time to time but still be two different churches." . . . "Wouldn't it be irresponsible to just hand over the money from the sale of our building to another congregation? After all, most of us have invested years of our tithes in this place." . . . "If we merged congregations, would we merge leadership too? Or would New Morning just take over?"

Carl Hickman winced at that one. I couldn't read Peter Douglass. His chin rested on his clasped hands, elbows on his knees. Avis sat beside him, her eyes closed, her lips moving, as if covering the room in prayer.

Josh spoke up from the soundboard. "Uh, just want to say, I'm excited about this. For one thing, there are a lot of kids just hanging out there on the street who need the church. We might do a better job reaching them if we were more diverse."

Some of the teenagers and adults clapped. Denny squeezed my hand.

"Uh, my name is Leslie Stuart." I twisted my head. Stu was standing, long blonde hair tucked behind one ear, the one with the row of tiny pierced earrings. "Most of you know me as Stu. I've been a member of Uptown a little over a year. And I've had more change in my life this past year than I know what to do with!" Becky, beside her, rolled her eyes and snorted. Several people chuckled. "But I have to admit, change can be good. How long has Uptown Community been here on Morse Avenue? Twenty years? I think Pastor Clark is saying that Uptown is ready for some change. Would stir us up. Maybe new ideas and new ministries would come out of it."

Florida popped up. "That's right, that's right. An' let's not forget why we're talkin' about this! We didn't just open the phone book and point a finger. God's been doin' something with New Morning and Uptown this summer—somethin' nobody planned. Seems like the Holy Spirit to me."

I heard several hearty amens. Now the discussion bounced back

and forth, pros and cons, questions about petty details, doubts . . .
but for some reason I was acutely aware of Avis and Peter on the
other side of the room, and Carl and Florida behind me. Those two
couples had more on the line than anyone else in the room. But
they'd never say so. It would seem too whiny. But if we decided to
"just be Uptown," would Peter end up at New Morning? Would
Avis be forced to choose? Same with Carl and Florida.

*So speak up on their behalf, Jodi.*

I wanted to stop my ears. I argued with the Voice nudging my
spirit. *I wouldn't know what to say! What if I embarrass them? People
would probably dismiss what I said, anyway, because both couples are
friends of mine . . .*

The Voice in my spirit interrupted my thoughts. *Speak up, Jodi.
Say what you think . . . what you know in your heart.*

I stood up, my knees wobbly. Someone else was speaking, but I
knew if I didn't stand now I'd probably chicken out. After the other
speaker sat down, Pastor Clark said, "Jodi?"

I kept my eyes on Pastor Clark. "Um, I'm not quite sure how to
say this. But I don't think most of us know what it feels like to
always be a minority. Those of us who are white are used to being
the majority. But, praise God, sisters like Avis Johnson-Douglass
and Florida Hickman put themselves here at Uptown—I'm not
sure why. Maybe out of obedience to God. And Uptown has gladly
received them. But I think"—I swallowed—"maybe we're kind of
proud of ourselves because we've got a couple of black folks. Maybe
that's enough for us. Sure, folks are welcome—as long as we don't
have to *really* change, as long as we're still the majority."

My voice started to waver. Denny's hand found mine and
squeezed. I took a deep breath. "Uh, I may be going way out on a

limb here, but I think it's especially hard for our African-American brothers to be 'the only one,' or even two. But we *need* these men—brothers like Peter Douglass and Carl Hickman. And these families need to worship together. I think . . . it would strengthen these men and strengthen families like the Douglasses and the Hickmans to merge our church with New Morning, so we could truly be equal partners in the kingdom of God."

I sat down and closed my eyes. There was no clapping. Only silence. My insides felt like slush. *Why did I do that? Oh God, did I hear You wrong?*

And then I heard a strange sound. Like a . . . groan, or stifled cry. My eyes flew open. Peter Douglass was bent forward, head in his hands, his shoulders shaking.

# 25

"Labor Day . . . no kidding," I muttered to Willie Wonka, who had graciously accompanied me to Bethune Elementary the next day, while Denny, Josh, and Amanda accepted an invitation from one of Denny's coworkers to go sailing on Lake Michigan. After yesterday's storm, the day was sunny and breezy—*"Perfect for a great sail!"* Denny had gloated. I noted that word, *breezy*, and was just as glad to have an excuse not to go. "Heeling up" on a sailboat always scared the bejeebers out of me.

Now the dog snored under my school desk while I arranged my new "supply cabinet"—six plastic, stackable dairy crates, which sell like hotcakes to college students and teachers who have their supply cabinets hijacked. I spent a lot of time decorating my Welcome Bulletin Board, wisely forgoing cutout bubble letters this year in favor of printing my students' names and their meanings with colored markers, which sped up the process. But I caught myself several times just staring out the window of my classroom, not even seeing the playground equipment, thinking about what had happened at church yesterday . . .

Actually, we'd taken two votes. Whether Uptown Community Church should merge with New Morning Christian Church, and whether we should donate money from the sale of our building (after paying off the mortgage) to New Morning's building fund.

It still felt unreal. *What happened?* Listening to the overall tenor of the discussion, I didn't think the merger would happen, no way, no how. But at the very end, Rick Reilly had said, "I see two ways to approach this vote. We can add up all the pros and cons and vote whichever list is longer. Or we can vote what God is speaking to our hearts and trust Him to work out the details."

Both votes passed with the two-thirds majority required for major decisions.

Only after the final tally did Pastor Clark tell us that New Morning members had met the night before to vote on the same issue of merging. *Their* meeting had lasted till midnight! I heard Florida snicker behind me. But Pastor Cobbs had called our pastor early that morning to extend an official invitation to copastor Uptown–New Morning and bring our members with him. Nothing had ever been said about money.

That was when our so-called business meeting had erupted into clapping and tears and shouts of "glory."

Denny thought what I'd said had helped people look at it a new way. I don't know; nobody said anything to me. Just Peter Douglass, and all he did was give me a big, wordless hug.

I shook my head and turned away from the window. Well, like Rick Reilly said, we'd have to work out the details later. And right now, I had a more immediate merger on my plate: thirty-one third graders piling into my classroom tomorrow.

THE NEXT MORNING I flew out the front door with my bulging school tote bags for the first day of school—and nearly collided with Becky Wallace, who was stooped over on the front porch tying the shoelace of her orange athletic shoes. She stood up. She was wearing hip-hugger slacks and a simple V-neck knit top. Cranberry and pink.

"Where are you going?" I gasped. "You look fabulous! Except"—I giggled—"for the shoes."

She blushed, adding color to her normally pale face. "Goin' to work! At the Bagel Bakery. Meant to tell you yesterday, but all you Baxters was gone all day. Guess Ruth roughed up Mr. Hurwitz. Anyway, he called Sunday, said he'd offer me a part-time job—twenty-five hours or somethin' like that. Can't give me benefits, but"—she grinned—"I got Sundays off."

I hugged her. "That's great! I want to hear all about it, but I gotta run. First day of school, you know."

"Hey, Jodi," she yelled after me. "You look great too. Except for the shoes!" And she laughed.

*Huh.* Well, I had to walk to school. I'd change to my clogs when I got there.

I got to school half an hour before the first bell rang. *Yea, good start.* I poked my head into the school office, where Avis, smartly dressed in a navy pantsuit with a red-and-white silk blouse, was talking to two of the secretaries about schedules. "Happy first day of school, Mrs. Douglass," I said. "Here we go!"

She looked up. "Oh. Jo—Mrs. Baxter, wait." She excused herself and walked me out to the hall. "Jodi, I'm sorry about your storage cabinet. The janitor just moved it out when I asked him to move the desks in. But I want you to know that as soon as we can hire another teacher, we'll take some of your students and put together a third- and fourth-grade class. Might have to meet on the stage in the auditorium . . ." She frowned, as if sorting thoughts in her mind. "Anyway. Thanks for hanging in there."

I opened my mouth, but she was already gone. Oh, well. I'd dearly love to know what she and Peter thought about the humungous decision to merge with New Morning, but this obviously wasn't the time. I unlocked my classroom, set out my lesson plans for the first day, and then tried to quiet the butterflies in my stomach.

*Pray for your students, Jodi. By name. Cover your classroom in prayer.*

Right. Today especially. I walked slowly up and down the rows of desks, each of which had a colorful nametag taped on it. "Lord Jesus, I don't know some of these children yet, except Carla Hickman. But You do. So I ask for Your blessing on Abrianna . . . for Caleb . . . for Orlando . . ." I touched each chair. When I got to Carla's desk, I stopped. "I pray a special blessing on Carla, Lord. She's starting a new school. She has to repeat. She's still adjusting to being back home with her family after foster care. Have to admit, Lord, I feel kind of anxious about Carla. Help us both, Lord, to get a good start."


NOT SURE WHAT HAPPENED TO MY PRAYER, but when I brought my new class of third-graders in from the playground, Carla balked at the classroom door. Literally folded her arms across her pink knit top, stuck out her lip, and wouldn't come in.

Sorely wishing I had a teacher's aid this year, I asked the rest of the children to find the desk with their name on it and to sit quietly—*yeah, right*—keeping one foot in the door while I coaxed Carla. "Hey, sweetie. I'm really looking forward to having you in my class this year. We're going to have a good time." Who was I trying to convince? Her or me?

The lip stuck out further. "This is a baby class. I'm s'posed to be in fourth grade. Everybody's gonna laugh at me."

*Help, Lord!* "Oh, sweetie. Nobody's going to laugh. Because nobody else knows—just you and me and Mrs. Douglass. It'll be our secret, OK?" I knelt down, letting the door close with a *click*. "And I want to tell you something. People learn at different speeds, did you know that? Even adults! It doesn't really matter if you learn fast or learn slow. Everybody should learn at the level that's right for them. Why, even in this class, some kids are probably already reading at fourth-grade level, others might be still at second-grade level."

"So why do *they* get to be in third grade? Why don't *they* have to repeat?"

*Well, that backfired.* The noise level inside the classroom was rising. "You know what? I don't know. All I know is that I think it's special that you're in my class. I think you'll make some good friends *and* we're going to have a good time." *And you better get in here before I have to drag you in!*

Carla just looked at me. "Maybe."

"Maybe" was good enough for me. I opened the door and we walked in together, interrupting a sword fight with two rulers in progress between Demetrius and Lamar.

IT TOOK A GOOD WEEK for the Baxter household to adjust from the more relaxed summer schedule into our school year routine, which started with the daily challenge of one bathroom to accomodate four showers. Amanda started snatching breakfast on the fly in her hurry to catch the early bus to Lane Tech. (Denny snorted. "Wouldn't have anything to do with José Enriques attending this year, would it?") Denny usually dropped Josh off at Software Symphony before heading for West Rogers High with the car, leaving me to walk the half mile to Bethune Elementary—which I didn't mind until the weather turned nasty.

Willie Wonka, poor baby, was lucky if we remembered to leave his food and water crocks full, and he probably spent the next eight hours heaving doggy sighs and feeling abandoned—all of which was forgotten, of course, when the first person got home. Usually me. Nothing like the joy of being smothered with doggy kisses and tail wagging in return for some rump scratching—and a quick exit into the backyard to take care of doggy business.

"What's going to happen when Wonka gets too old to hold his bladder all day?" I murmured to Denny on Friday evening as we did supper dishes, being careful not to let Amanda hear me.

Denny cocked an eyebrow at me. "Keep him in the yard when the weather's nice. Cut a doggy door. I don't know. We'll deal with it when the time comes."

I stroked Wonka's silky, floppy ears that had betrayed him, leaving him almost deaf. Wonka had been part of our family for the last sixteen years. I could hardly imagine the Baxter family without him.

The phone rang once, cut off short as it was picked up, then a yell tinged with disappointment. "Mo-om. It's for *you*."

Chanda was on the line. "Sista Jodee! Mi got a computer now. Top of the line, high-speed Internet, all dat. Got e-mail too! Set up de account today." She laughed. "Everybody will know it's Chanda when dey see mi address. Are you ready, Jodee?"

"Sure . . . wait." I scrambled to find a piece of scratch paper. "Um, why don't you just send it to me by e-mail. That's the best way."

"Jodee, Jodee. Dat's why mi calling! Mi don't have *your* e-mail address—nobody's for true. Can you send dem to me?"

I stifled my irritation. It was probably my own fault I ended up being the Yada Yada secretary. Maybe I should take it as a compliment, though sometimes it felt as if some of my sisters thought I just sat around waiting to take calls and send e-mails and keep the group up to date.

"OK, I'm ready . . . what? You're kidding!" I burst out laughing as I scribbled "Million$Mama@online.net" on the scrap of paper. "OK, got it. I'll send you everybody else's. Welcome to cyberspace—oh, wait! Chanda? Chanda?"

But she was gone. *Rats.* I wanted to ask about her mammogram. Last I'd heard she had an appointment for this week.

# 26

It was Saturday before I got online to add Chanda's e-mail to my e-address book. Our inbox was stuffed; hadn't checked e-mail since school started. *Grr.* Most of it was junk. Didn't want to deal with it now. So I called up a new message and began to type:

To: Yada Yada
From: <u>BaxterBears@wahoo.com</u>
Subject: Chanda's got e-mail!

Hi sisters! Everybody survive the first week of school? The Baxter Barn is still standing, in spite of barnyard squabbles over our solitary bathroom. (I'm thinking of running for president of the U.S. on a platform of "a chicken in every pot and TWO bathrooms in every house." Probably won't get the vegetarian vote, but it'll be a landslide with parents of teenagers.)

Wish we were meeting this weekend to pray over all our

school kids—that fifth Sunday in August throws us off, making it THREE weeks between YY meetings. But guess we should stick to the schedule. Second Sunday at Adele's, right?

Speaking of that fifth Sunday last week, Uptown Community had a business meeting accompanied by dramatic drum rolls (well, thunder). But we made an awesome decision: to merge Uptown Community with New Morning Christian (Nony and Mark's church), which has been using Uptown's space for worship Sunday afternoons all summer. It seems God has been putting our two churches together for a reason. Have to admit, I'm still astonished at this turn of events, have no idea what it will actually mean, but I think it's a big HALLELUJAH!

Oh, don't want to forget: Chanda's finally got e-mail! Here's her addy: <u>Million$Mama@online.net</u>. When you get this, please send her a howdy and *your* e-mail address, OK? I think that makes us 100% online now! Yea!

Hugs! Jodi

I hit Send, feeling smug that I'd thought of a way for Chanda to get everybody's address without me having to go to all that work copying them into an e-mail for her. Then I reread all that "barnyard" and "howdy" stuff and groaned. The hick-chick from Iowa in me was leaking out.

Denny had to be at school all day Saturday—still working out kinks in the high school schedule between academic classes and sports—which meant he couldn't make it to the workday at the new building. We'd gotten a letter that week from Pastor Clark and Pastor Cobbs inviting everyone handy with a hammer or a paintbrush to join the Saturday work crew the month of September, hoping to have the building habitable by the first Sunday of October for our first worship service as a combined congregation.

Rick Reilly rounded up the Uptown teens, however, and they put in three hours sanding drywall in exchange for several buckets of hot wings and a case of soda. I figured Josh and Amanda counted for the Baxter contribution today; I'd go next week when they were ready to paint.

My e-mail about the church merger sparked a flurry of Yada Yada messages. Nony said she hadn't gotten to church at all last weekend and only just now heard the news. "Mark had to have a laser treatment on his 'good' eye; the doctor discovered some tiny retinal tears," she wrote. "Losing the sight in his left eye is frightening enough. Please pray, sisters, for protection of his other eye! But I am so glad to hear about 'two' becoming 'one.' Praise Jesus! He is true to His Word that every valley shall be exalted, and every mountain and hill brought low! Let us pray that the crooked places ahead for this church merger will be made straight and the rough places smooth."

Hadn't thought about Isaiah 40 in this context, but it sure fit. *How does Nony pull out just the right scripture?* I wondered, clicking on Avis's message, which was short and to the point: "Please keep Rochelle, Dexter, and Conny in your prayers too."

Over the weekend there were also e-mail messages from Florida ("Carl still pinching himself, can't believe Uptown voted themselves out of a church"), Becky and Yo-Yo, basically saying "Welcome, Chanda" and giving up their own e-addresses, and Delores asking,

"Anyone know how Ruth is doing? I tried to call but only got the answering machine."

Ruth. *That's* what I wanted to do after church: go see Ruth! She hadn't called or anything the last two weeks. That wasn't like her. Ben either. He and Denny and some of the other guys—Peter Douglass, Carl Hickman—had become pretty close this past summer after the attack on Mark Smith. I knew Denny was all geared up to watch a football game on TV that afternoon, but I asked him anyway if he'd go with me to visit Garfields. "I think Ben needs our support during this pregnancy as much as Ruth, but if I go alone he'll just leave us girls to ourselves. Hey, maybe we could meet them at the Bagel Bakery or something, like we did that first time when we met Ben."

Denny had that sour look on his face, that feeling-put-upon-by-good-deeds-when-his-heart-wasn't-in-it look. "*Man*, Jodi. Not fair to spring that on me at the last minute. You knew I wanted to see the Bears play the Forty-Niners."

"Fine. I'll go by myself." I started off to look for my purse.

"Oh, great. You make me feel like a jerk if I don't go."

"I did not. I just asked. You can say no." Well, I had laid it on pretty thick. "Isn't the game usually over by three? We could go after that."

Denny rubbed the back of his head. "Problem *is*, they're playing in San Francisco, which means the game won't start till around three . . . OK. Look. I'd like to see Ben. If he's planning to watch the game, we can go over there. We'll watch the game while you and Ruth visit. Deal?"

Which is how we ended up in the Garfields' compact brick bungalow in Lincolnwood that Sunday afternoon, Ben and Denny totally absorbed in armchair quarterbacking, snarfing up bowls of chips and salsa, not to mention a couple of cold beers. Ruth made tea for us, and we sat in the dining room making small talk. I didn't like what I saw. Her face and hands were puffy, and at the same time her skin looked sallow, hanging loosely on her arms. She was into her sixth month, but it was hard to believe she was carrying twins. She wasn't that big.

"—have to visit this product of a mixed marriage," Ruth was saying, referring to the church merger I'd just told her about. "Will you hyphenate your name, like they do nowadays? Uptown Community–New Morning Christian Church . . . or maybe New Morning Christian–Uptown Community Church." She poured herself another cup of peppermint tea. "Always wondered about those hyphenated names. If Jimmy Smith-Jones marries Susie Brown-Miller, will their kids go to school with names like Oscar Smith-Jones-Brown-Miller? Now *there's* a teacher's nightmare, Jodi Baxter." She snorted, blowing tea out of the cup and having to wipe it up with her napkin.

"Don't you usually put honey in your tea?" I asked her, noticing its absence.

She fluttered her hand. "Too many calories. Had to give it up."

"Ruth!" Ben's voice yelled over the sports announcers in the living room. "We got any more chips? Baxter here cleaned me out."

Ruth started to push herself up. "Let me get them, Ruth," I said. "Where are they?" But she shook her head, disappeared into the kitchen, then walked through with a bag of chips in her hand. A moment later, I heard Ben say, "Put that back, Ruth! No salt, remember? Baxter! How'd your wife keep her girlish figure after two kids? Maybe the trick is to have them one at a time!" I heard Ben guffawing at his little joke.

*Of all the rotten . . .* For one nanosecond I hoped Denny would knock his teeth in. *Just kidding, Lord,* I hastily amended. "Ruth," I hissed, when she lowered herself back into the dining room chair, "what are you eating? *Less* salt, not *no* salt. You don't look so good. And is Ben always like this? That was mean."

Ruth fluttered her hand dismissively again, but the spitfire wasn't there. "Don't mind Ben; he means well. Watching I don't eat too much, just because I'm carrying twins. And this . . ." She patted her puffy cheeks. "Like a goldfish bowl I look. But Jodi. Did you ever try to eat food without salt?" She crossed her eyes, made a gagging noise, and I burst out laughing.

But when we left a couple of hours later, my insides were frowning. Something wasn't right.


THE SECOND WEEK OF SCHOOL included an anniversary I dreaded: 9-11. If I closed my eyes and ran backward with my thoughts, I could still see the horrific images of passenger planes crashing into the Twin Towers in New York, the mighty buildings crumbling into mere particles of dust, carrying thousands of lives with them.

It wasn't a day I wanted to remember. But how could I avoid the issue when replays of crashing planes and terrorist mugshots flooded the TV with 9-11 images? My problem, I told Avis in her office, was that my third-graders were only *six years old* when 9-11 happened and probably had no memory of those events. Why pour fear and horror into their souls? Not to mention that several kids in my class were Middle Eastern. Kids could be cruel.

"It could be a teachable moment, Jodi," Avis said. "A chance to say that here in the United States, here in our school, we *can* live together with respect, no matter what we look like or where we're from."

I rolled my eyes.

"Well then," she said, "just observe the minute of silence and say we are honoring the people who died when the Twin Towers collapsed. Maybe they won't ask questions. Sometimes we tell kids more than they want to know."

I did as our venerable principal suggested, but I should have seen it coming. An eight-year-old is curious by definition, especially about the adult world. The questions flew thick and fast after the moment of silence. *Why did the buildings fall down? Who was in the planes? Did any kids die? Was it an accident? Why would somebody do that?*

"Because they hate us, that's why," Carla said, nose in the air.

"Yeah. They hate Israel too. I heard on TV that somebody blew himself up at a bus stop in Jerusalem and killed lots of people." Caleb Levy's voice squeaked.

*That* nearly scrambled the rest of the day. *Oh God! I wish I could use a scripture like 'God so loved the world' or 'love your enemies.' Or just gather all these kids into a big circle and hold hands and pray for all the people who are hurting.* But this was public school, so I did my best to make it a teachable moment, telling them that it was important to respect differences, that violence was never the way to solve problems, that "tolerance" didn't mean everybody had to agree about everything, that in fact "tolerance" was most important when you *disagreed* with someone.

By the time I got home from school, my emotions were frayed. If I ever thought teaching third grade was a walkover, I revised my thinking: I'd just been walked over.

235

Which is why I probably shouldn't have punched the blinking New Message button on the answering machine.

"Jodi?" Adele's contralto voice was tight and off-tune. "You got a car? Somebody might want to get over to Florida's place. There was, uh, some trouble on Clark Street in front of my shop not fifteen minutes ago when Sullivan High School let out. I called the cops, wanted to nip it in the bud before somebody got hurt. But"— I heard Adele suck in a breath—"I think I saw Chris Hickman get tossed in the backseat of a squad car."

# 27

*M*y insides twisted. *Oh no, oh no, oh no.* But I guess adrenaline kicked in. I called Adele at the shop to get more details.

*What happened?* . . . She wasn't sure, big melee mostly between black kids and Latino kids, probably gang wanna-bes trying to be tough . . . *Does Florida know?* . . . Yes, she'd called Florida, who needed to get to the police station . . . *Can't help, the car's not home.* But I did call Denny at his office (of course he wasn't there; it was four o'clock, so he was probably out on the athletic field somewhere) and left a message to come straight to Florida's house. Then I half-ran, half-walked the ten blocks to the Hickmans' new home, sending warning messages up my thigh from the rod screwed into my left leg.

Only when I rang the doorbell and no one answered did I think to fuss, *Wait a minute. Why me? What did Adele think I was supposed to do about it? She was the one who called the cops. I don't even understand what it's all about.*

I sank down onto the front steps. Why hadn't I called Florida first? *Now* what? But no way was I going to walk all the way back home. Besides, I'd told Denny to come here. I'd just wait on the porch until Florida or Carl got home or Denny arrived—whoever showed up first.

I leaned against the slightly wobbly handrails. Florida's fantasy of white wicker porch furniture would be nice about now.

*Pray, Jodi,* prodded the still, small Voice in my spirit. *You don't have to know what it's all about to know that Chris and his parents—and maybe a lot of other kids and families too—need a lot of prayer right now.*

So I prayed, glad that God was *El Shaddai*, all-powerful, all-sufficient, able to handle problems too big for me—which certainly described the problem of the moment.

Denny got there first. Giving him the sketchy information I had, we decided to go down to the Clark Street police station, just a mile or two from Adele's shop. If the boys who'd been arrested weren't there, we'd probably have to drive all the way to "Twenty-Sixth and California"—everybody's shorthand for the main Criminal Courts Building and Cook County Jail on Chicago's South Side.

I got a queasy feeling as we pulled into the parking lot behind the neighborhood police station, even though the compact building was modern and attractive with fancy bricks spelling out POLICE in an arch over the large half-moon window facing Clark Street. The last time I'd been here, almost a year ago, I'd come to reclaim my wedding ring that "Bandana Woman" had stolen at knifepoint. *Oh God, You've worked some mighty miracles since then,* I breathed. *We may need a few more.*

Florida Hickman, hair tucked under a worn knotted scarf, was pacing in the lobby near the L-shaped front desk, sucking on a cigarette. No chairs. Guess they didn't want people to think of it as a waiting room. "Was hoping you'd be Carl," she started in, without even a hello. "Told him to get himself here. When that boy comes out that door, I want his daddy to be the first person he sees."

"When he comes out?" That sounded hopeful. "Does that mean they're not charging Chris with anything?"

Her brows furrowed. "Oh, that boy's in trouble, all right. But . . . could be worse. It's a first offense, so they're releasing him to us, but he has to pay for removal."

"Uh, Florida?" Denny loosened his tie. "Remove what? We really don't know what happened. Just came to see if you needed some support, a ride, whatever."

"Tagging, that's what!" she muttered. "Don't got the whole story. But what they sayin' is that *somebody* tagged an alley near Adele's shop with Black Disciple gang symbols, some other stuff. Latino kids saw it on the way home from school, said it was disrespecting Latin King territory, started yellin' an' pushin' the black kids around. Cops came, busted the crowd an' some of the younger black kids got scared, said it was Chris did it—oh. That's gonna be Carl."

I caught a glimpse of Peter Douglass's black Lexus turn into the parking lot, three men inside. The third person turned out to be Josh.


"LOOKS LIKE CHRIS'S WORK ALL RIGHT." Josh stood in the alley in the fading light. "Gotta admit, Mrs. Hickman. He's good."

Peter Douglass had offered to stay with Carl to wait for Chris, bring them home. Josh wanted to stay, too, but Denny said too many people might be humiliating. Florida had elected to leave with us, leave Chris to his daddy and Big Bad Peter, but she wanted to see the start of all this trouble.

"Whatchu mean, looks like Chris's work?" Florida glared at the brick wall, covered in spray paint, depicting a powerful black man, muscles bulging, dripping attitude, like a superhero in shades and gold jewelry. The now-familiar six-pointed star, crossed pitchforks, and a bold, black *BD* decorated the man's shirt. The letter *C* with a slash through it had been slyly worked into the man's pant leg.

I shot a grim glance at Josh. *Thanks, buddy.* We'd never told Florida about that mural we saw at the el station or what José had said about Chris's "signature." But we did now, apologizing for not saying anything earlier—though we had no proof at the time that it was Chris and didn't want to be passing rumor.

"But the style is the same, Flo." Denny's voice carried a note of admiration. "Like Josh said, he's good."

"Don't 'good' me, Denny Baxter. We don't need this kind of trouble. Where we gonna get the money to pay the city to remove this, tell me that?" She angrily brushed away tears that threatened to spill over.

I put my arm around Florida as we walked back to the car. "I don't know, Flo. But we're not going to leave you caught up in this alone." Though I felt some of her panic. What would it be? Five hundred bucks? A thousand?

ACCORDING TO ADELE, the mural was defaced during the night with the Latin Kings' five-pointed gold crown and *LK* in fancy script letters. Another melee erupted on the street after school; one boy was badly kicked and beaten—Latino? Black? No one seemed to know for sure. The cops came; a few more kids got hauled away for disorderly conduct. Fortunately, Chris was nowhere near Clark Street since Florida had showed up at Sullivan High School after work, went straight to his last class, and hauled him out before the last bell. Ha! I could imagine Chris slouching behind bushes all the way home.

Fortunately, that was Friday. No more school for two days. But I shouldn't have been surprised that everybody was talking about it at the workday on Saturday. After polishing off a blueberry dough-nut and a cup of Dunkin' Donuts coffee, I had been handed a bucket of ivory paint and assigned the woodwork around the doors of offices and classrooms. Well, *doors* plural might be stretching it. I'd forgotten how careful one had to be painting trim when the walls were a contrasting color. Slow about summed it up.

But in the large room where a bright coral was going up on one wall, contrasting with a light salmon on another, I heard snatches of conversation between some of the men and teens. "We ought to have a neighborhood presence on Clark Street after school, diffuse some of this violence." . . . "But that's three o'clock, man! We're all still at work!" . . . "Yeah, but some of the little kids are gonna get caught up in this mess." I recognized Josh's voice. "They go to Clark Street after school to get snacks." . . . "Yeah, all the vendors are still out. Maybe we oughta man one of those carts ourselves!" That last was met with general chuckles. "Don't let Pastor Cobbs take a turn. He's got a weakness for those little doughnut balls—what do you call them? *Bunuelos*, I think."

I thought about what the guys were saying while I finished the trim on another door. Thought about it again the next day during worship, when Pastor Clark preached on "Living with Divine Interruptions," using the ministry of Jesus as an example of the Holy Spirit interrupting our schedules with opportunities to pour out God's love on hurting people. *Huh.* Street violence was an interruption all right—to the Hickmans, whose son ended up at the police station . . . to Adele's Hair and Nails . . . to the kids walking home from school, who clumped naturally in groups but could easily get caught up in the anger and violence of a few . . .

"*What* are you thinking about, girl?" Florida said at the potluck after worship, it being the second Sunday of September. "Bunch of New Morning folks are here, but you sittin' there like a bump on a log, not talkin' to nobody. An' you ain't even tried my greens yet."

I squinted my eyes at her. "Lemonade."

"*Lemonade*? Just go get yourself some! In that pitcher over there—whup, sorry. Too late. It's empty. You a sad case, girl." Florida moved off. "See you at Adele's tonight. We got some serious prayin' to do."

"LEMONADE."

My Yada Yada sisters looked at me as if my lightbulb was dimming. We hadn't even started our meeting yet, but already Chanda and others wanted all the details of what had happened near Adele's shop a few days ago. Adele, bless her, left out Chris Hickman's role when talking about the gang signs—a mural, really—decorating the alley nearby. It was irrelevant, in a way. Rival gangs and the flotsam of young lives floating around their edges didn't need much provocation to get in each other's faces. If it wasn't tagging on rival gang territory, it was somebody's sister dating a rival.

"We gotta do somethin'!" Florida fumed. "Too many kids gettin' caught up in this gang mess. Chris too! That boy's grounded again, but you all know that's about as effective as expectin' yo' man to remember your birthday."

That got several hoots. I was momentarily distracted by Delores, who had steered Ruth into the hallway and seemed to be giving her an animated lecture. Ruth looked confused, but she was listening. I tried to refocus on the discussion at my own elbow.

"Lemonade," I said again. "Lots of kids walk along Clark Street on the way home from school because they can buy snacks. All the street vendors are still out, selling flavored ices, sweet corn, burritos—stuff like that. What if . . ." I tried to hold on to my idea in spite of cynical looks all around me. "What if we set up a lemonade stand near Adele's shop, where the trouble started, and give out *free* lemonade to kids on the way home from school? We might get to know some of the kids that way, while adding an adult presence on the street."

"Whoa, sister. I don't want no lemonade stand in front of *my* shop." Adele stood in the center of the room, hands on her hips. "Just what I need, forty kids clogging the sidewalk. Scare my customers away for *sure*."

My heart sank. I'd actually been hoping we *could* put the stand in front of Adele's shop, use her water, even say she'd given us permission to be in front of her store if anyone asked. So much for—

Edesa spoke up. "Maybe not so, Adele. If I saw a lemonade stand outside a beauty shop, I would think what a great person, she must have a heart for kids, maybe I will go there!"

"For true." Chanda flashed her own spiffy nails. "All de young girls get dey nails done now. Dey tell dey mamas 'bout your shop, you get *double* de business."

Adele snorted.

Florida shook her head. "Jodi, that's gotta be one crazy idea. *Lemonade?* We're talking gang fights, girl!"

"I dunno. Makes sense to me." Yo-Yo eyed Adele from beneath her spiky hair. "Didn't you say your shop's been tagged a couple of times already? My guess is, if we give out free lemonade in front of your shop, it's never gonna happen again. Word gets around."

Avis looked dubious. "Sounds like a lot of work to me. *I* can't help, I know that. And . . . I'm not sure it's safe. Not with the recent tensions."

We argued about the idea for the next ten minutes. Skepticism gradually backed down in favor of responding to the after-school violence with something positive. Even something ordinary and kid-friendly, like a lemonade stand. "Not just leaving it to the cops," as Stu put it.

Yo-Yo waved her hand in the air. "How many days ya wanna do this, Jodi? I gotta work tomorrow. But I'm off Tuesday."

"*Sí.* My classes are in the morning. I can help," Edesa offered.

Chanda stuck out her chin. "Mi toss in some monies for de lemonade. Dat be me contribution."

"It would take a lot of coordination, Jodi," Avis warned. "Are you up to that?"

I gulped. "Well, let's just do it a couple of days. Monday and Tuesday. See what happens. But we could use some guys too. Any ideas?" *Humph. Count Denny out. He'd balk at the whole idea.*

Ruth, released from Delores's clutches in the hallway, poked her nose into the conversation. "Take the grouch. Anything to get him out of the house and off my back. Just don't let him drink all the lemonade. His prostate's not too good."

"I'll help you, Jodi," Stu said. "We can do it." And for the first time since Leslie Stuart had flipped her superior attitude into my face, there wasn't a trace of one-upmanship in her offer or in the gratitude I felt.

"All right." Avis opened her Bible. "We can talk about this some more after prayer. But right now let's give God some praise that *He* can take five small loaves of bread and two fish and bless a multitude." She slipped a grin. "In your case, Jodi, maybe five lemons and two cups of sugar."

Everyone laughed.

Becky Wallace just wagged her head. "You guys are a trip, you know that?"

# 28

Our meeting lasted late that night. Nony and Hoshi were both absent, but no one had gotten a call; so we prayed the protection of the blood of Jesus over the Sisulu-Smith household. Edesa shared about her visit to Manna House, the women's shelter on the North Side. "So many health needs," she said, shaking her head. "So many poor life decisions, too, not realizing how soul and spirit affect the body. The Bible even talks about that." The young Honduran woman paged through her Bible. "The book of Proverbs, chapter three. 'Do not be wise in your own eyes; fear the Lord and turn away from evil. This will bring health to your body and strength to your bones.'"

"That's in the Bible? Show me." Becky leaned close and squinted at Edesa's Spanish Bible. "Wait a minute. Didn't you just read it in English? How'd you do that?"

Yo-Yo snickered. Leaning forward, Avis asked several pointed questions about the shelter. Did women with children stay there? How much privacy did they have? How long could they stay?

Adele finally had to "ahem" and suggested we hear from others. "Like you, Chanda. You get the results of your mammogram yet?"

Chanda casually picked at a fingernail. "Nah. Mi taking driving lessons now; had to cancel." Her cinnamon face slowly beamed, like a dimmer switch turned up full. "*Den* you see what mi gonna park in me driveway! It's on order!"

No one smiled. Her grin faded and she picked studiously at that nail. Adele spoke gently—well, gently for Adele. "Chanda George. I don't give a rat's tail for what kind of car you park in your driveway. But I do care about you. And you need to get that lump checked out. Tomorrow!"

To my surprise, a tear rolled down Chanda's cheek. "But mi so scared."

"*Chanda!*" Several voices chorused at once.

"But Chanda!" I protested. "We offered to go with you, and you pooh-poohed us, said it was no problem!"

Chanda's lip trembled. "It's not de mammo puts fear in me heart. De lump—it's bigger."

"Oh, Chanda," Stu moaned. Adele rolled her eyes. But it was one of those moments when everyone instinctively gathered around our sister, laid our hands on her head, her shoulders, her arms, her back, and began to pray. Avis got out her bottle of anointing oil and touched the oil on Chanda's triple-D chest, generously exposed by the low-cut spandex top she wore.

"Jesus!" Avis appealed to heaven, both in word and posture. "Your Word says that by Your stripes we are healed! We praise You that You forgive all our sins, You heal all our diseases, and You redeem our lives from the pit . . ."

I wasn't sure where Avis was going with this, but Chanda

247

seemed comforted. We ended the meeting with a lusty rendition of "The steadfast love of the Lord never ceases, His mercies never come to an end . . ." It was obviously a new song to both Yo-Yo and Becky, but they seemed to be drinking it in as much as Chanda. ". . . They are new every morning! New every morning! Great is Thy faithfulness, Oh Lord . . ."

After our worship and prayer time, those who could stayed to talk a bit more about the lemonade stand idea. (Could we really pull this off *tomorrow*?) A horn blared outside. *Honnnk. Honnnk. Honnnk.* Ruth pushed herself off her chair and stomped to Adele's open front window. "I'm coming already!" she yelled. She turned back, muttering, "Such a *nudnik.*"

But she beckoned to Yo-Yo and they headed for the door. "By the way, you won't see me at Yada Yada next time," Ruth tossed over her shoulder. "Rosh Hashana it is."

"Happy new year!" a few of us tossed back.

"Wait, *mi amiga.* I'm coming with you." Delores quickly gathered up her stuff, then eyed me. "Jodi. You come too. I need moral support."

I opened my mouth to protest since I was the one organizing the lemonade stand, then realized that Delores, she of great wisdom, would never ask me frivolously. I followed the trio down the short flight of stairs and out the front door where Ben Garfield's big Buick was double-parked in front of Adele's apartment building. Delores marched up to the driver's side window and made circles with her finger to roll it down.

"Shalom, Mrs. Enriques. You look ravishing today." Ben could pour on the charm when he wanted to.

But Delores was in no mood. "Well, your wife doesn't look rav-

248

ishing, Ben Garfield. She's too thin for six months pregnant. The babies are too small for six months. She needs to eat! Eat!"

Ben's charm immediately turned sour. "She eats, she eats."

"He says I'm too fat," Ruth chimed in.

"Ha! You're the one who gorges on—"

"*Silencio!*" Delores shook a finger in Ben's face. "I don't care who says what. She's not getting enough nutrition. Look at her face! No color. Look at her skin! Sagging. She's already a good candidate for preeclampsia. If she gets toxemic, they'll take those babies early. Is that what you want? Two babies weighing just a pound or two, fighting for life?"

Ben's expression darkened under the tongue-lashing. Yo-Yo had backed up a few steps and was standing on the curb, jaw dropped. But Delores's demeanor softened. "Ben, I'm not picking on just you. I said all this to Ruth a couple of hours ago. But both of you"—she hooked a finger at Ruth—"listen to me. Before I took a job as a hospital nurse, I was a midwife. Sometimes the medical approach overlooks the benefits of the natural approach. Don't overdo the bed rest—she needs exercise to get that appetite back. And don't limit her diet for fear of weight gain! Those babies *need* the nutrition, and Ruth does too. She *can* carry those babies to term, good size babies too. But the two of you need to work together. Promise me?" She tempered her words with laughter. "See? I've got witnesses."

Ben grunted. Who knew what he meant. Ruth heaved a sigh, walked around the car, and got into the front seat. Yo-Yo ducked into the back of the Buick like Peter Rabbit hiding in Mr. MacGregor's watering can. Delores and I watched until the big car turned a corner and was gone.

I cleared my throat. "Well, um, that was interesting. Think you dented their stubborn skulls?"

Delores's round face broke into its own sunshine. "*Quien sabe?* Who knows? But they haven't heard the last from me yet!" She took my arm as we walked back into Adele's building together. "But, Jodi, we must pray. The time is critical. It is not too late to turn things around, but if they don't . . ."


I'M STILL NOT SURE WHY ADELE RELENTED and let us set up the lemonade stand in front of Adele's Hair and Nails. But it never would have worked without her shop as an anchor. For one thing, she already had a card table on site that she kept in the back room. Not to mention a couple of folding chairs and a bathroom for emergencies.

Wouldn't have worked without Stu either. Somehow, between DCFS clients on Monday, our very own miracle worker managed to pick up plastic cups, a ten-pound bag of ice, and eight half-gallon cartons of off-brand lemonade—Chanda had given her two twenties—and get them over to Adele's Hair and Nails. There they were, packed like sardines in Adele's small, back-room refrigerator when I showed up after school, sweating in the mid-September sunshine and clutching the used-on-one-side, neon-green poster board I'd liberated from the teachers' workroom. I'd also snatched a ride from one of my fellow teachers, an early escapee after the two thirty dismissal bell.

Edesa Reyes, bless her, showed up not two minutes later, and together we set up the table, the cups, the ice, the lemonade, and the loud sign: FREE LEMONADE TO STUDENTS (ADULTS $1). I was counting on the staggered release times between the K–8 schools and the high school to give us time to set up.

Edesa pointed at the "$1" amount and lifted a quizzical eyebrow.

I shrugged. "Never can tell. Might start a fund to clean off that alley wall."

Edesa looked at me sideways from beneath the corkscrew curls popping out of her wide turquoise headband. "It was Chris Hickman, wasn't it?"

I didn't confirm or deny.

She smiled, a bit sadly. "Stopped to take a look in the alley on my way here. Saw Chris's 'signature' even though most of it had been spray-painted over with Latin King signs."

I'd forgotten Edesa had been with us when we saw Chris's "artwork" at the el station near Jesus People several weeks ago. That was when she and Josh first got interested in Manna House. *Edesa and Josh* . . . Should I ask her about their friendship? I mean, was it more—

But I was distracted by a trio of African-American boys—*really big* boys—slouching toward us in oversize T-shirts, low-slung jeans, and backward caps, lugging battered book bags. They kept looking over their shoulders and muttering to one another. I suddenly decided this had to be the dumbest idea in the world. *What was I thinking?!* One flip of a hand could send our lemonade table flying if these boys had a mind for mischief. But the boys barely gave us a glance as they passed, clearly not interested in lemonade, free or otherwise.

"We need to offer it," Edesa murmured, nodding toward the next group of teenagers, a cluster of girls not in a hurry to go anywhere, cracking gum, sluffing on shoes with the backs mashed under their heels, two on cell phones. "*Hola!*" Edesa's warm mahogany face broke into sunshine as the girls came closer. "Would you like some lemonade?"

A few of the girls stopped, reading the sign suspiciously. "Free?" said one. "Whazza catch?"

"No catch." I made my voice as light as possible. "Help yourself."

"OK." Three of the girls shrugged, took the lemonade. One even asked for a refill. Nobody said thanks.

Down the street, we saw a large group of Latino boys clustering at the alley that had been double-tagged with gang signs. They milled about, waiting for—what?

"That's where we need to be," Edesa said. The next thing I knew she had grabbed two cups of lemonade in one hand and one in the other, and was scurrying down the sidewalk. Torn between leaving the table unmanned and sticking with Edesa, I grabbed three more cups of lemonade and hustled after her.

She was laughing and speaking Spanish to the boys, who looked at one another, smirking like, *Who is this nut?* But several took the proffered drink. Encouraged, I held out my cups, which were lifted from my hands, poured down laughing throats until empty, then tossed on the ground.

I flinched. *Uh oh. We're going to get it for littering.*

"*Venido!*" Edesa beckoned with her hand to the other boys, grumbling because they didn't get any. They trailed behind us to the table, and basically drank us out of four half-gallons of lemonade.

We were folding up the card table when Ben Garfield's big Buick slid alongside the curb, the window down. "The fun's over?

Ruth told me I should come check on you." He looked relieved that nothing more was expected of him.

*Sweet.* I gave him my biggest smile, momentarily forgetting I was permanently annoyed at him. "Hi, Ben! Yeah, we're done. Thanks for checking up on us, though."

Ruth's silver-haired husband craned his neck, casing the street up one way, then down. The largest mass of after-school teenagers had drifted away, and Clark Street had resumed its everyday cacophony of impatient car horns, vendors with their carts on the corners, and a colorful mash of sidewalkers lugging plastic sacks of groceries or pushing strollers and speaking everything but English. He frowned at me. "So Denny let you two ladies do this all by your-selves?"

My annoyance popped back up like a jack-in-the-box. *LET me?* I wanted to scoff. *This isn't Saudi Arabia, buddy.* But I stopped short of mouthing off, suddenly squirming.

That was the thing of it. I hadn't told Denny. Not a word.

# 29

We stored the card table and extra plastic cups in the back room of Adele's Hair and Nails; kissed MaDear, who was parked in her wheelchair near the front of the shop dozing in the sunshine; and waved our thanks at Adele, who was rolling a pink plastic curler into the hair in the chair. Adele, pins sticking out of her mouth, just rolled her eyes at us as the bell tinkled over the closing door.

"Want to come by the house?" I asked Edesa. "Stay for supper if you'd like. I know Amanda would love to see you." The moment the words were out of my mouth, I wanted them back. *Why didn't I say "Amanda and Josh"? Now if I add, "Josh would too," it makes too much of him—or them.*

"*Gracias*, Jodi. But I need to study. I've already got research papers! But I'll try to come again tomorrow. Three o'clock?" Edesa hugged me and was gone, heading for the Loyola el station about eight blocks away.

Actually, I felt relieved. If she came home with me, we'd definitely end up talking at the supper table about what we'd been doing
that afternoon. As it was, I'd probably still get home before anybody
else, cook dinner, nothing needed to be said. After all, it wasn't a big
deal, even if it came up later. *"Oh, yes, we had a lemonade stand for
after-school students in front of Adele's shop. Didn't I tell you?"*

But as I headed north on Clark Street and turned right on Lunt
Avenue, my insides squirmed again. Why was I reluctant to say
anything to Denny? *Huh.* Because I knew what he'd say, that's why.
*"Jodi! That's crazy. Who knows what kind of confrontation might hap-
pen next between those wanna-be gangbangers? I don't want you anywhere near that area till things settle down. Don't you remember what
happened with that crowd at Northwestern?"*

Actually, I had forgotten about *that* melee when I came up with
the lemonade stand idea. I just wanted to do something positive,
reach out to those kids. Weren't we all proud of Josh's speech at
graduation when our son said, "We *can* make a difference. It has to
start with me." What was wrong with that?

*You didn't tell your husband. That's what's wrong with it.*

Stubbornness thickened like pulled taffy in my gut. So? Nothing
bad happened. Maybe we even made a difference. Didn't those kids
milling around the alley leave it and drink up half the lemonade?
But if I'd told Denny ahead of time, too bad. We wouldn't even have
had a chance to find out.

*Besides,* I told myself as I hefted my school tote bag to the other
shoulder, turned off Clark, and hiked down Lunt Avenue. *I really
didn't have time to tell Denny. We didn't decide to do the lemonade stand
until last night, then Yada Yada ran late, and this morning was the usual
hurry-scurry out of the house.*

I squashed the uneasy feeling that if things *had* gotten out of hand again between the Latino and black kids, Edesa and I would have been sitting ducks. I'd hoped for at least five or six of us Yada Yadas "being a presence." Still . . . nothing happened. Maybe more of us would show up tomorrow. It was going to be just fine.

ON TUESDAY, Carla Hickman decided her name ("one who is strong") gave her permission to punch Miguel ("who is like God") in the nose during morning recess when he grabbed the rope during a game of double Dutch and tripped her down on the playground pavement. "Teach him not to mess with *me*," she muttered as I marched both of them to the principal's office, where we also kept the first-aid kit. "'Sides. Ain't *nobody* like God. That's a dumb name, anyhow."

*Hmph.* Maybe it was time to take down my Welcome Bulletin Board, which proclaimed all the names of my students and their meanings.

I had to make calls to both parents after school to explain Carla's skinned elbow and Miguel's bloody nose. Florida sounded breathless on the phone. "What? Carla fightin'? Look, Jodi, I just got home from work, now I gotta get over to the high school to pick up Chris. Call me tonight; we can talk about it." Then, like an afterthought, "She punched him a good one, huh?"

Was that a chuckle I heard as she hung up?

So I was late getting over to Adele's Hair and Nails. Kids of all ages were already cruising the sidewalks, supposedly on their way home. But the card table was set up, Yo-Yo and Ben Garfield were pouring plastic cups of lemonade, and Edesa, bless her, was taping up the garish green sign. The day, which had started out at a comfortable sixty-five degrees, had inched up to a muggy eighty—typical for mid-September. Perfect for lemonade.

The after-school crowd seemed surprised to see us back. More girls stopped by. Less suspicious. I realized Yo-Yo and Edesa talked easily to the teenagers. Why not? Yo-Yo looked like a teenager herself in her signature overalls and tinted, spiky hair. Edesa bubbled easily to the Latino kids. "*Hola! . . . Un poco de limonada?. . .* How was school today? *El agujerear?*" She laughed and poked Yo-Yo. "*Sí,* school is sometimes boring."

Ben and I faded into the background while the two younger women chatted up the girls (and a few boys) who accepted cups of lemonade. "Hey, thanks for bringing Yo-Yo today," I told Ben. Why was it I could be so mad at the old goat one day and want to hug him the next? "And thanks for hanging with us. Really helps."

"Nah. You gals got it covered. Good excuse to get out of the house, though."

Better tiptoe there. "Um, how is Ruth doing? She OK?"

He shrugged, his features sagging. "I don't know. I guess. The pregnancy is hard on her. Should've never happened . . ." He faded into his own thoughts, and I decided to leave it alone.

We handed out the remaining four half gallons of lemonade easy—and we hadn't even seen the large group of Latino guys who'd drunk our stash yesterday. "Uh-oh," I said, shaking the last carton. "Ben, do you think you could drive up to Howard Street and get us some more?"

Ben had no sooner left than a familiar trio appeared—from nowhere it seemed. The three oversize boys in baggy pants who had swaggered past yesterday with barely a glance. One of them picked up the last empty carton. "Whassup wid dis? You ain't got no more lemonade?"

I bit my tongue. What grade was he in—junior? senior? Didn't the school have some minimum standards for speaking English?

Edesa just kept smiling. "*No problemo.* More is coming."

A hand shot out and gripped her upper arm. My alarm bells didn't even have time to go off. "Why a sweet-lookin' Afro chick like you speakin' Spanish? Huh? Tell me dat, woman!"

The other two boys chimed in. "Yeah. You wit de Kings?" "You dissin' us?"

Yo-Yo's eyes had gone wide. She seemed frozen in time. Me, too, for that matter. All we had to do was tell them she's from Honduras, right? Everybody—blacks, brown, white—speaks Spanish there. I opened my mouth but couldn't breathe. *Oh God! Help us!*

A bell tinkled. The door to Adele's Hair and Nails whooshed opened and Adele marched out, a curling iron in her hand trailing its cord. "You boys get outta here—*now!* Before I hit you upside your heads. And this baby's still *hot!*" She thrust the curling iron six inches from the bully's face.

The boy flinched; his eyes narrowed. His buddies shouldered in. But just then three of Adele's customers spilled out into the street, hair in curlers, one wrapped in foil, the third with half her hair sticking straight up in sections, held by white goo. The yelling and arm waving probably lasted for only thirty seconds, but the boy let go of Edesa's arm and the three slouched off, muttering.

Adele stood in the middle of the sidewalk, fists on her wide hips, still gripping the curling iron. Her eyes glared at their backs from beneath her short, silver-black Afro. The customers disappeared back inside, muttering. Adele slowly turned to us. To me, actually.

"Pack it up, Jodi. This business is over." And she stalked back inside.

HURRICANE ISABEL hit the East Coast that week, but we had our own category five at the Baxter house. I was trying to figure out a way to tell Denny what happened when Josh got off the phone Tuesday night and poked his head into the kitchen, where Denny and Amanda were doing dishes and I was putting leftovers away. "Yo, Mom. Edesa just told me about the lemonade stand you Yadas had on Clark Street today. Did I miss something? Got a bit tense, she said."

A silence dropped into the kitchen, like the warning calm just before a tsunami. All movement stopped. All eyes turned on me.

"Um, not really. Just a last-minute thing." I nervously spooned leftover tossed salad into a plastic container and snapped the lid. "We came up with the idea Sunday night, and . . . it was, uh, such a rush to put together, I guess I forgot to let you guys know."

Denny's eyebrows lowered until they practically met in the middle.

"Lemonade stand, Mom?" Amanda snickered. "How dorky is *that*. I mean, sure, did that when I was *five*. But a bunch of old ladies?"

"Shut up, squirt." Josh came to my defense. "Edesa said you guys were trying to diffuse the after-school tension along Clark Street, where that alley got tagged last week. Personally, I think it's a cool idea, except . . ." His face clouded. I noticed a golden shadow along his jawline. Facial hair. Was Josh shaving? Or not shaving, more like it. When did that happen? "I dunno," he went on. "Don't take this the wrong way, Mom, but seems kinda risky to do something like that, just a bunch of women."

"Why? It was just a lemonade stand, for heaven's sake! Besides, Ben Garfield was there." Well sort of there. Today. I kept my eyes on Josh, ignoring Denny.

"Oh right. A sixty-year-old white guy with an attitude. Sorry, Mom, don't mean to put you down. But it could've gotten nasty. Edesa said a black kid—big dude—got on her case because she's black and speaks Spanish. I mean, that's what the clash was about last week, right? Rivalry between blacks and Latinos?"

*Got on her case?* Edesa must have left out the part about his grabbing her arm.

Denny slowly turned his back and resumed loading the dishwasher. He still hadn't said a word. Josh snitched the last cookie before the platter disappeared into the dishwasher. "Anyway, mind if I steal your idea? Rick Riley and Pastor Cobbs are trying to think of ways to meet kids along the Howard Street strip. If we had something like a free lemonade stand, then we could invite them to teen activities at New Morning Church, right there in the shopping center, or heavy metal concert, stuff like that . . ." Josh was still rattling off ideas as he headed back toward his bedroom and his earphones.

Amanda snatched the phone. "Dad, can you finish up? I gotta make a quick phone call."

"Homework first!" I yelled after her.

The kids disappeared. Silence settled over the kitchen again like putrid air. Denny poured powdered dishwasher soap into the little cups in the door, banged the door shut, and turned the knob. The old dishwasher chugged away. Then he turned and leaned back against the counter, arms folded. I stood in the middle of our small kitchen, still holding the plastic container with leftover salad, like a caught rabbit.

"I want to know just one thing, Jodi. Why didn't you tell me what you were up to the past couple of days?"

I avoided his eyes. How did this get to be such a big deal? What could I say to lighten this up? It just happened. My intentions were good. Nothing bad happened. End of story.

I must have taken too long to reply. Denny pushed himself off from the counter and stalked out of the kitchen, his body language dripping aggravation. I stood staring at the leftover salad I still held in my hand. With sudden fury I hurled it into the trash basket, container and all.

# 30

*I told* Denny I was sorry I didn't tell him about the lemonade stand. He said, "OK." But the rest of the week felt as if we were acting in silent movies on two different screens. A peck on the cheek as he went out the door in the morning. "Pass the salt, please." . . . "Any clean laundry?" . . . "Staff meeting tonight." . . . A lot of TV.

*Sheesh,* I muttered to myself as I walked to school Friday morning. *It's my birthday today, for heaven's sake, and Denny's treating me like . . . like I maxed out our credit cards or posed in* Penthouse *magazine or something. Good grief.*

In fact, it was easy to work up a good mad about the whole business. For one thing, Edesa and Yo-Yo were the only Yada Yadas who actually showed up to support the enterprise. Well, OK, Stu did the shopping with Chanda's contribution. But what happened to Florida? And Avis? They both lived nearby. Actually, I never expected Avis to show up—but Florida? *Her* son was the one caught up in the middle of the mess. *She* was the one who kept saying, *"We gotta do somethin'."* And Adele—even though she grudgingly let us set up outside her shop, I never felt like she was behind it 100 percent. Not even 50.

So much for unity.

And yeah, yeah, I should've told Denny. But I said I was sorry, didn't I?

A gift bag was sitting on my desk when I got to school that morning. Cheerful orange and yellow tissue paper hid a birthday card and some yummy melon lotion from Avis. I screwed off the cap and squirted the silky cream into my hand, smoothing it over my skin. It had been a long time since I'd taken care of my hands. Rough skin. A broken nail. A tear dribbled down my cheek and dripped off my chin.

Some birthday. A present from Avis. That might be it.


BUT I WAS WRONG. Amanda chased me out of the kitchen when she got home from school and actually made my lemon-and-thyme chicken recipe—one of my favorites. It easily passed the Baxter five-star test: super easy, super yummy. Stu and Becky came downstairs for dinner, bearing Becky's second-ever birthday cake. Didn't matter that it came from a box. It was chocolate.

I took a swipe of the frosting with my finger and gave her a big hug.

Stu and Becky actually helped thaw the deep freeze, and we all laughed and joked at the dinner table—me the butt of most jokes, of course. I didn't care. It felt good to laugh. While Becky cut cake and Stu dipped up vanilla ice cream, I opened presents. A crocheted winter scarf from my mom. (I already had three.) A CD from my dad: *Best-Loved Hymns by Top Country-Western Artists.* ("Yep. That's Grandpa," Josh snickered.) A pair of silver dangle earrings from Amanda and Josh. One from each, wrapped separately, the nuts. A fat candle with fall leaves embedded in the wax from Stu and Becky.

And a silky burgundy scarf from Denny in a Ten Thousand Villages gift bag.

I held the filmy scarf against my cheek and looked up at my husband, sitting at the other end of the table. Our eyes locked for a second—the first time in days. "Thanks, honey," I whispered.

He smiled. "Happy birthday, babe." But his smile seemed . . . sad.

Once again we slept that night with our backs to each other.

"DID YOU CALL HIM, DAD? What did he say?"

When I came into the kitchen the next morning, Amanda was grilling her father, who was getting ready to jog over to the men's breakfast at Uptown Community before heading over to the Howard Street shopping center to put in another Saturday workday laying floor tile in our new sanctuary.

*Our* and *sanctuary* still felt a bit of a stretch.

"Yes, pumpkin, I tried to call Mr. Enriques—twice last night." Denny poured himself a second slug of fresh coffee. "Left one message on voice mail, one with some little sweetheart—Emerald, I think. But he hasn't called back." He touched a finger to her nose. "I don't think he wants to come, Mandy. I don't want to bug him."

"But Da-ad! You said he was real nice to you and Mom when you went to that Mexican restaurant on your annivers—oh, rats."

The front doorbell sounded unnaturally loud at eight o'clock on a Saturday morning. "That's my ride. Gotta babysit all day for the Three Terrors." She pulled a long face. "They better pay me *good*."

I was grateful when the house emptied, except for Josh, who had come in after one o'clock and would probably sleep until eleven. I knew something was desperately wrong, and I needed to figure out what it was. For one thing, I hadn't even touched my Bible that whole week. My prayers had been one-liners. "Quiet time" was a joke. A hole seemed to be growing inside me—empty, yawning, slowly sucking my soul into a bottomless pit.

Willie Wonka followed me outside while I filled the birdfeeder. *How long had it been since I'd filled the birdfeeder? Had the birds given up? Would they come back?* I settled on the porch swing with my Bible and a large mug of coffee, Wonka sprawled at my feet. Tears blurred my eyes. I didn't even know how to start.

"Can I back up, Lord?" I whispered. "Where did I get off?"

*You've been rushing, Jodi.* The Voice in my spirit whispered back. *Not taking time to listen.*

I sighed. *But it's hard during the school week. Every day is so hectic.*

*No, even before that. Last weekend. You were so busy with your thoughts, your ideas, your plans, you didn't stop to ask for My wisdom.*

I thought about that. The lemonade stand. Hadn't God given me that idea? *It seemed so . . . brilliant. Corny, yes. But simple, a way for us ordinary women to make a connection with kids in the neighborhood. What was wrong with that?*

The Voice continued. *Stop it, Jodi. The idea's not the problem! But you ran with it in your own strength. Admit it. You pushed that one through Yada Yada in spite of some serious doubts from others.*

*Well, yeah . . . but—*

*And you didn't trust your husband. That should have been a clue.*

*Trust? What does trust have to do with it? I just knew he'd get all worried and think of all the things that could go wrong. Don't know what he's so mad about. Nothing happened! We managed just fine.*

*Did you? Weren't you grousing five minutes ago because not enough Yada Yadas showed up? Did you really have enough people "to be a presence on the street" if any violence had gone down?*

I kicked the swing into motion, uncomfortable with how this inner chat was going. *But it was a good idea,* I thought stubbornly. *And I think we made a difference.*

*Maybe. But you got all caught up in your good works, Jodi.*

Good works? The words jogged my memory bank. "Not by works of righteousness that we have done but according to His mercy He saved us." Must be one of those Sunday school verses I'd memorized back in sixth grade to get my Bible Warrior pin. Was that how it went? Maybe I could find it . . . Titus something.

I paged through the Bible on my lap and there it was: Titus 3:5. My modern language translation said, "He saved us, not because of the good things we did, but because of His mercy."

My Old Jodi response tried to dismiss it. *Nah, doesn't apply. Paul was talking to Titus about our salvation.* But I pondered. If good works couldn't "save" us, maybe the same principle did apply to other things. Like the lemonade stand. My good idea. Maybe . . . maybe the only reason "nothing happened" was because of God's mercy.

I dug deeper for a little honesty. To be truthful, Yo-Yo, Edesa, and I would've been no match for those bullies if they'd gotten rough. If Adele and the Curler Brigade hadn't marched out there . . .

*God's mercy.*

It suddenly hit me, like a Saturday morning cartoon when a

piano falls out of nowhere on a passerby below. Got my attention. *If* they'd gotten rough? They *had* gotten rough. That big kid grabbed Edesa's arm. Had practically accused her of being a race traitor, on the wrong side. That in itself had been frightening. And I'd been so busy justifying to myself and my family that everything went fine, what was the big deal—did I even call her later to see how she was doing? She must have been terrified!

Pianos must have kept falling on my head, knocking sense into me, because I suddenly knew why Denny was so upset. I'd shut him out. Yes, I knew he'd be concerned, wouldn't think it was such a hot idea, and I'd basically said I didn't care. Didn't even give him a chance. I wanted to do it my way. I'd pronounced it "good" and nobody—not Denny, not Yada Yada, not even God—was going to change my mind.

My head sank into my hands. "Oh God," I groaned. "I'm so stupid, stupid." Denny wasn't mad. *He was hurt.* How would *I* feel if *he'd* done something behind my back? Without wanting my input? If he'd shut me out?

"Uh, Mom? You OK? Didn't you hear the phone ring?"

I raised my head. Josh was standing behind the screen door in his sweat shorts, bare chested, tattoo bulging on his bicep, with a serious case of bed head. I shook my head. *No, I didn't hear it ring.* Then nodded. *Yeah, I'm OK.*

He opened the screen door and handed out the phone. "Anyway. For you."

I grimaced, covering the mouthpiece. "Sorry if it woke you up." He just waved me off and disappeared back inside.

I took a deep breath to rein in my bucking thoughts, then ventured, "Hello?"

"Sista Jodee?" The voice was high, almost hysterical.

"Chanda? Chanda! What's wrong?"

I waited several moments while Chanda broke into muffled sobs. Then she blew her nose. "Dey just got mi test results back, Jodee. Mi doctor is very concern. He tinks dat lump . . . it might . . . it might be . . ." The sobbing started again.

But I knew what was coming before she managed the word.

". . . c-cancer."

# 31

*C*ancer?! Wait, wait—she'd said, *"might be."* I shored up my own ragged emotions, which had already been close to tears even before the phone rang. "Chanda, now wait. Don't run ahead of the facts. Sounds like they don't know anything for sure yet. What do they want to do?"

Between sobs and nose blowing, Chanda managed to tell me her doctor had ordered both a mammogram *and* an ultrasound earlier that week. It was *not* a cyst. She had to go back the next day for a "core needle biopsy," taking some cells from the lump . . . just got a call from her doctor . . . cells were abnormal, but inconclusive . . . but her doctor and the radiologist agreed: the lump should come out.

"Dey want me to talk to a surgeon next week. Surgeon, Sista Jodee! Dat mean dey going to cut it out! Oh, Jesus, Jesus, help mi, Jesus!"

I didn't know what else to do, but I offered to pray with Chanda on the phone. Felt like a hypocrite, when my own prayer life had been suffering big-time lately. *Oh God, forgive me,* I prayed, a silent rider hanging on to my out-loud prayer.

"Tanks, Jodee," Chanda sniffled. "Uh, one more ting. Mi really don't want to go alone talkin' to dis new doctor. Could you . . . do you tink—?"

"I teach every day, Chanda. It'd have to be a four o'clock or something. Don't know if they make appointments that late."

"Mi try dat. Let you know. Tanks." And the phone went dead.

I sat a long time on the swing, feeling like my emotions had just been run through a spin cycle. I tried to unscramble my brain and refocus on what God had been saying to me just before Chanda called. I'd taken my "good idea" and run with it. I'd shut Denny out. And maybe my idea wasn't that good after all. Good intent, maybe. But poor implementation. Maybe even poor context. So we gave the kids lemonade. What kind of follow-up was possible?

Zero. Nada. None.

Willie Wonka lumbered up with difficulty and stuck his wet nose into my lap. "Whaddya think, Wonka," I murmured, stroking the white hairs sprouting around his mouth and eyes. "Am I ever going to quit tripping over my own goody-two-shoes?"

The dog just licked my hand. Good ol' dog. Always there. Like God's forgiveness. *Just for me, just for me, Jesus came and did it just for me . . .* "The words of a Donnie McClurkin song caressed the soreness in my spirit. I soaked in it for a while, letting the tears run free. *Thank You, Jesus. Thank You.*

But I also had some apologies to make—starting with Denny.


THE FOURTH WEEK OF SEPTEMBER bumped along over the usual rocky road of worldwide and hometown turmoil. The U.N. arms-inspection team reported no WMDs had been found in Iraq

. . . Earthquakes devastated Hokkaido, Japan . . . Uptown Community was down to the last two Sundays before our official merger with New Morning . . . Carla got in another fight at school, this time with Mercedes LaLuz for "stealing" her mechanical pencil . . . and Chanda made an appointment with the cancer surgeon for four o'clock Friday—on Josh's birthday.

But my wheels had been greased by my talk with the Lord Saturday morning and my talk with Denny Saturday afternoon, and to me the difference between last week and this one was like January and June.

Denny had dragged in about four o'clock that Saturday, covered with plaster dust, obviously weary. I considered a big hug and kiss then discarded the idea. He wasn't exactly huggable in that state; even more to the point, we needed to clear out the garbage between us first.

"I'd . . . like to talk," I'd said, handing him a glass of ice water. "Maybe after you get cleaned up?"

He took the water and hesitated. Then tipped the glass and drank. Stalling. I knew I was asking a lot. He was beat, and a "talk" probably seemed as appealing as scooping up after Willie Wonka. A nap in front of the TV would be more like it.

But he came out of the shower looking less like a survivor from a chalk factory explosion and more like my husband. Shaved. Clean. Good smelling. Downright yum—

Nope. Couldn't go there. Yet.

Actually, our talk didn't take long. We sat on the swing on the back porch, more ice water on hand, and I told him I was wrong. I'd suspected he wouldn't like the lemonade-stand idea, so I deliberately didn't tell him until afterward to prove him wrong. But God had showed me my motives were full of pride. Worse, I'd shut him out. Had practically shouted that what he thought wasn't important. A violation against our marriage really. And I was sorry, so sorry for hurting him like that.

I blew out a breath when I was done, and we sat silently in the swing, letting it drift in a small breeze coming in off Lake Michigan. A few birds fluttered to the birdfeeder hanging from the corner of the garage, then flew off. Probably empty again. Then Denny put down his glass of ice water, drew me into his arms, and just held me tight, not saying anything for a long time. But his embrace spoke volumes.

"Thank you, babe," he finally whispered into my hair. "Funny thing is, I couldn't even pinpoint why I felt so bad. Kept asking myself, what *was* the big deal, anyway? But when you said, 'I shut you out'—it was like you touched the sore spot on my heart. That's what I was feeling and hadn't even known how to put it into words."

We sat on the swing like that for a long time. Then Denny murmured, "Kids gone?"

"Yup."

I felt him grin.

JOSH'S BIRTHDAY ALWAYS SNUCK UP ON ME, only a week after mine. Nineteen! But I tried to get things ready the night before for a birthday supper, and Denny said he'd pick up our gift for Josh— several music CDs and a CD case with a shoulder strap. Good thing he was taking care of that, because Chanda had left a message on our voice mail, saying she'd pick me up at Bethune Elementary on Friday afternoon at three thirty.

*Pick me up? That must mean . . .*

Sure enough. There she sat in the school parking lot behind the wheel of a sleek, brand-new, slate gray Lexus. "Wow!" I said, sliding into the front seat. That new car smell—part leather, part ocean breeze, part excitement—kissed the interior. "You did it! You got your license, you got your car . . . Congratulations, girl!" I leaned over and gave Chanda a hug, then double-checked my seat belt, wondering if I was a guinea pig for Chanda's maiden voyage as a driver.

*"Surprise!"* I jumped—well, jerked is more like it, given how tight I'd pulled the seat belt—as Thomas, Cheree, and Dia all screeched from the backseat, where they must have scrunched down, hiding from their prey. "Do you like it?" "Isn't it fancy?" "We got the bestest car on our whole block!"

I needn't have worried about Chanda's driving. She crept along at twenty-five miles an hour, the kids chattering the whole way, until she reached Evanston Hospital and pulled into the small parking lot next to the Kellogg Center. The cancer unit. She didn't say much to me, but while we sat in the waiting room, she pulled out snacks, activity books with mazes and puzzles, even Dia's favorite stuffed animal, a snuggly black and white dog. "To-mas!" she ordered when a nurse called her name. "You kids be quiet here, now. Mama in no mood to give you t'ree a whippin', but mi will, from bigg'un to little'un if you don' behave. Sista Jodee going wit mi." All three kids meekly nodded.

In the consultation room, the nurse gave Chanda one of those ugly hospital gowns—the kind that make you feel sick just putting it on—and she hugged it around herself as she sat shivering on the paper-covered examining table. I took her hand, trying to reassure her. It was icy cold. When the doctor came in, I faded into a corner with a pen and notebook. As scared as Chanda was, I was pretty sure she wouldn't remember a thing the doctor said afterward. He seemed like a kind man, even gentle as he examined Chanda's breast. Her eyes were squeezed shut. "I'd like to do another needle biopsy," he said. "This lump is very suspicious, and I don't want to take any chances." He smiled warmly at Chanda. "And neither do you, Ms. George."

While the doctor did the biopsy, I took the elevator to check on Chanda's kids. I peeked into the waiting room. All three were immersed in the books their mother had brought. I left without disturbing them, anxious to get back to Chanda. "Like they say," I murmured, punching the elevator button, "if it ain't broke, don't fix it."

We waited a long time for the doctor to come back after the biopsy. We even started singing, "Hold to His hand, God's unchanging hand!" to pass the time, giggling as we tried to sing a belt-it-out gospel song in quiet hospital tones. At which point the doctor came back in, catching us in the middle of "If by earthly friends forsaken—"

The doctor said the biopsy was still inconclusive but troubling. "The best thing to do is schedule a lumpectomy and send it to the lab on the spot. If it's not cancer, we're done! Sew you up, you can go home the same day." He allowed a brief smile. "But if there are cancer cells, we will need to remove the sentinel, or gateway, lymph nodes, and get those analyzed. If the cancer has not spread, again, we're done." He cleared his throat, not exactly looking at Chanda. "But if the cancer has spread to the sentinel nodes, we will need to assume the cancer has spread to other lymph nodes, remove them, and, ah, if necessary do a mastectomy. It all depends what we find when we go in there."

Chanda just stared above the doctor's head. She seemed to be in shock.

I spoke up. "Do you mean that Chanda won't *know* when you put her under whether or not she'll have a breast when she wakes up?"

The doctor looked truly regretful. "Well, we could just do the lumpectomy and then do a second surgery if we need to do a mastectomy. But surgery is surgery, Mrs. Baxter. There's always a risk. You don't want to do two if you can do it all in one."

He scheduled surgery for the following week.

Chanda was so shook after we left the Kellogg Center, she handed me the keys to the new Lexus. "You drive, Sista Jodee." And she climbed into the front passenger seat. The three kids, sensing all was not well, climbed wordlessly into the backseat and put on their seat belts without being reminded. I realized arguing was useless. But now *I* was the one driving twenty-five miles an hour back to Rogers Park. No way was I going to be the first one to put a scratch on Chanda's dream car.

But when I pulled up in front of our stone two-flat, I took one look at Chanda and realized there was no way in good conscience I could let her just drive back home. "Chanda?" I laid a hand on her arm. "You and the kids want to stay for supper?" I knew I was crawling out on a limb—waaay out—inviting the George family to Josh's birthday supper unannounced. But I felt the Holy Spirit prodding me, and I figured, *Hey! If God's kicking my rear, He'll make it all right with Josh too.*

But just in case God was busy taking care of Chanda and Josh and didn't have time for the new Lexus, I parked it in our space in the garage and double-checked the garage doors to make sure they were locked.

# 32

Ha. Should've known God's plans were bigger than my plans. Cheree and Dia were beside themselves with glee that they were "eating over," and clamored immediately to run up the back stairs to see Becky the Babysitter. When Chanda and I got in the house, Amanda poked her head into the kitchen. "Mom! You better listen to—oh, hi, Mrs. George. Anyway, there's a phone message from Josh. Birthday's off."

Birthday's *off?* What in the world? I punched the blinking button on the answering machine. *"Mom? Dad? Anybody? This is Josh. I'm just leaving work—Mr. Douglass let me leave early. Got a call from Manna House. They had a break-in last night; a lot of the women and kids are scared. They're asking two or three of the male volunteers to sleep over tonight till they get security tightened up. Sorry about your birthday plans. Can I take a rain check tomorrow? If you need to reach me, here's the number down there . . ."*

Chanda's face puckered into a disapproving frown. "Nah, nah, Sista Jodee. You didna tell mi it was de boy's birt'day! What business you got inviting we to stay for dinner, an' he not know?"

I shrugged, pasting on a nonchalant smile. "Well, see? It all works out. He won't even be here tonight." Though I intended to call my son tonight *and* tomorrow morning to be sure *he* was safe. Break-in? What kind of break-in?!

WE THREE BAXTERS and Chanda's crew did a complete number on the szechuan noodle salad I'd made ahead of time—a new recipe I'd wanted to try out on Josh, who loved pasta anything—which was supposed to be our "farewell to summer" birthday feast. Didn't matter that there were no leftovers. Joshua elected to stay through the weekend at Manna House " . . . just as a precaution. Edesa says to tell you she'll try to make Yada Yada Sunday night, though."

Should've guessed that Edesa would be there too.

All of which meant that Josh missed the last Sunday worship service at Uptown Community. It would be New Morning's last Sunday using Uptown's space as well. The following Sunday, the first Sunday in October, we would meet together as one church for the first time.

*Whew. Was this really happening?* I plunked into a chair in the third row beside Denny, almost feeling nostalgic about the torture chairs. Had to keep telling myself we'd outgrown the building and would be selling it anyway, even if we weren't merging with New Morning's congregation.

We'd been at Uptown Community Church as a family for over two years. Felt like two lifetimes. To the casual observer, the Baxter family probably looked pretty much the same as we did in Downers Grove, with the exception of a few more gray hairs and one garish tattoo. But to me, our whole lives had been turned upside down—or maybe rightside up—in those two years. And it was about ready to go into another dizzy—

"Jodi!" Florida whispered over my shoulder. "What'd the doc say about Chanda's lump? Didn't you go with her?"

"Yeah. She'll probably tell everybody at Yada Yada tonight," I whispered back.

"Tell me now!"

But just then Avis's voice rang out from the front. "Good morning, church!"

Little Andy Wallace yelled, "Good morning, Miss Avis!" from somewhere behind me, outdoing all the other "Good mornings" put together and winning chuckles.

"No wonder Jesus said, 'Become like little children,'" Avis teased. "For our call to worship this morning, I'm taking a few liberties with Psalm 118, adapting the psalmist's praise to this time and this place and this people—and, church, I want you to imitate Little Andy's gusto with your part of the litany." She smiled and began: "Oh, give thanks to the LORD, for He is good!"

"For His mercy endures forever!" we all responded.

"Let Uptown Community Church now say . . ."

"His mercy endures forever!"

"Let Pastor Clark now say . . ."

Pastor Clark's large Adam's apple bobbed as he called out: "His mercy endures forever!"

"Let the Uptown teens now say . . ."

The teens yelled: "His mercy endures forever!"

"Let the Hickman household now say . . ."

"His mercy endures forever!" Florida shouted. Carl and Cedric ducked as if embarrassed.

Avis continued naming different families and singles for whom "His mercy endures forever," and a wonderful thing happened: The rest of us grew quiet and only family or solitary voices responded: "His mercy endures forever!"

"Let the Baxter family now say . . ."

Denny squeezed my hand, and we spoke together: "His mercy endures forever!" Yes, it was true. So true.

Finally Avis said: "Let *all* those who fear the Lord now say . . ."

"His mercy endures forever!"

"Oh give thanks, Uptown Community Church, for He is good . . ."

And we all joined in: "His mercy endures forever."

It was inevitable that we would sing, "The steadfast love of the Lord never ceases, His mercies never come to an end . . ." I turned slightly and tried to make eye contact with my Yada Yada sisters—Avis, Stu, Becky, Flo—scattered among the congregation. We'd sung that song at our last prayer meeting. And it hit me: out of thirteen Yada Yadas, there were already five of us at Uptown. When we merged with New Morning next Sunday, there'd be two more, Nonyameko and Hoshi—*seven* of us, all in the same church! What was God doing?

Pastor Clark preached on the third chapter of Philippians, where the apostle Paul said, "I am still not all I should be, but I am focusing all my energies on this one thing: Forgetting the past and looking forward to what lies ahead, I strain to reach the end of the race and receive the prize for which God, through Christ Jesus, is calling us up to heaven." In a gentle voice, he recalled many of the good things God had done at Uptown since the beginning twenty years ago. "But if we only look back, and not forward, the row we're plowing will get crooked and off track." His craggy Ichabod Crane face smiled. "Forgive the farming metaphor, but I grew up on a farm, unlike most of you . . ."

Our pastor didn't speak long. Instead, he said he wanted to allow time for others to share their thoughts at this important juncture in the life of our church, one that had few precedents in our modern time. "That's all right, Pastor." Florida waved her hand in the air. "Jus' means we gotta trust God all the more."

The room stilled, with only the creaking of plastic-and-metal chairs as people tried to relieve their backs. Then Bob Whittaker stood up. "Well, might as well get this over with. Me and Ann"— he indicated his wife—"we've been talking and praying, and want you all to know this is our last Sunday with you all." Dismay murmured across the room. "This church votes by majority, and the majority decided to merge with New Morning. We don't feel bitter about that; it was a fair vote. But we voted no with the minority, and we still do not feel called to make this move. We're disappointed, because we've been here at Uptown for almost ten years. I just ask one thing: don't judge us; don't make us wrong because we're going a different way. We bless you; we wish you all the best. We ask the same from you."

Before Pastor Clark could respond, Brenda Gage stood up, jiggling her baby, who was drooling all over her arm. "Uh, that goes for the Gages too. This is our last Sunday. We stayed out the month, but we won't be going with you all to New Morning. It's . . ." She searched for words. "Well, just not the right fit for us. But we want you to know we love you all." She sat down and burst into tears.

To my shock, two other families and three singles got up and announced they were leaving as well. This was good-bye.

I was floored. Eleven people, *good-bye*, just like that? I felt upset, but wasn't sure at whom. How could I have been so oblivious? I knew it was a stretch for some folks—for all of us in one way or another—but I'd presumed folks who intended to leave would have drifted away before now. My upset was a little mad too. How many got the courage to bail out just now when they realized a few other folks weren't going along?

Pastor Clark beckoned to Avis, as worship leader, to join him, then called those who had just spoken to join them at the front. "You have each been an important part of our body here at Uptown Community, and we thank God for you. But we release you with our blessing. Come on, church. Let's gather around our brothers and sisters and thank God for their faithful service here, and send them out with our blessing."

*OK, I needed that.* My mad melted, and I joined the circle at the front as hands were laid on bent heads and shoulders. I heard tears along with the prayers. For some reason, I thought of the tears the prostitute cried over Jesus' feet: No words were adequate really, just washing away the dust of our road together, aware of our own fallenness. At the same time, tears of gratitude—gratitude for all God had done already and was going to do.

I WAS STILL TRYING TO SORT OUT MY MIXED FEELINGS about the members who'd parted ways with Uptown as I headed up to Stu's apartment later that day for Yada Yada—and ran into Josh and Edesa dragging up the front steps from their long weekend at

Manna House. Josh looked like he'd hardly slept the last two nights. "Hi, Mom," he mumbled. He gave Edesa a tired hug. "Bye, Desa." And he disappeared into the house.

Great timing. He'd be zonked by the time I got home from Yada Yada, and we still hadn't celebrated his birthday yet. I peered at Edesa closely. "Josh looks like he just crawled off the Sahara. What about you? Should you even be here tonight?"

She smiled briefly, but the usual sparkle was missing. "*Sí.* I'm all right. I got more sleep than Josh did. But . . ." Edesa shrugged, slim hands thrust into the pockets of her jeans, overnight backpack slung over one shoulder of her jean jacket. "Two nights at the shelter was difficult, with the *niños* crying at night. But I have an apartment waiting for me. I used to think it was small, but I won't complain again. I heard many sad stories. Some of those women . . ." She bit her lip. "They have no *casa*, no place to go."

I gave her a hug and opened Stu's screen door to get us inside. The temperature, which had only hit fifty that day, was starting to fall and I didn't have a jacket on; I thought I was just going to bop out my front door and up to Stu's apartment. But just then a North Surburban Yellow Taxi pulled up and Chanda climbed out. "You go on," I said to Edesa and waited for Chanda.

"Where's the Lexus?" I teased as I followed her up the stairs. Chanda didn't answer. "Chanda? You OK?"

She threw me an irritated glance over her shoulder. "Why should mi be OK, Sista Jodee? Dey going to carve mi up like de pumpkin heads at Halloween, dat's all!" And she stalked into Stu's living room, plopping herself down on Stu's futon couch.

I followed. "Chanda," I whispered. "You need prayer, and that's why we're here—to pray." She nodded, puddles in her eyes, and helped herself to some apple slices and caramel dip on the coffee table.

By the time we'd cleaned off Stu's plate of apple slices and caramel dip, almost everyone had arrived—even Nonyameko and Hoshi this time. Good. I wanted to ask Nony about the mood at New Morning. Were people there leaving too?

Yo-Yo was the last to arrive. "Ruth says Happy New Year to y'all," she said, flopping on a floor cushion. "Beth Yehudah is celebrating Rosh Hashanah, ya know."

Becky snorted. "Never heard of Rosh Hashanah till I started workin' at the Bagel Bakery. Still don't get why Jews got their own new year."

Yo-Yo made a face. "Ask Ruth next time. She'll talk your ear off."

Everybody was there who was going to be there, but Avis made no move to start us off. In fact, she seemed off in the ozone somewhere. Finally Delores said, "Avis, if it is all right with you, I will begin with prayer, *sí?*"

And she did. I loved to hear Delores pray, peppered with Spanish words and phrases, as if she was most comfortable praying in her primary language. ". . . and we invite Your presence tonight, *Espirito Santo.* Lace our hearts together and make us one people. *Gracias, Jesús.* Amen."

That *prayer was right on the money,* I thought.

Somebody started "Blessed be the name of the Lord!" which we sang with gusto: "The name of the Lord is . . . a strong tower!" Afterward Nony opened her Bible and read the verse in Proverbs 18 it was based on: "The name of the Lord is a strong tower; the righteous run to it and are safe." So we sang it again: "The righteous run into it . . . and they are saved!" Even Chanda.

The song died away. We all looked at Avis. Finally Adele *har-rumphed.* "Sister Avis. You got something we need to pray about?"

Avis looked so surprised it was almost comical. "I'm sorry. I . . ." She shook her head, then allowed a big sigh. "I'm sorry. I just—"

"Girl! Quit apologizin'!" Florida cut her off. "You see anybody in this room ain't got problems? Just spit it out. We're listenin'."

Another sigh. "It's Rochelle again. She showed up an hour ago with Conny, just as I was leaving to come here. Dexter came back; another big mess, I guess. I probably should have stayed home to find out what's going on, but Peter insisted I keep going and he'd take care of it." She grimaced. "I'm just a little worried what 'take care of it' means."

# 33

e will pray right now. *Venido!* Come!" Delores waved us out of our seats to gather around Avis. "Nonyameko. Pray protection for Avis's daughter and the baby."

Nony led out with pieces of Psalm 91: "O Lord, we say on behalf of Rochelle and little Conny, that *You* are their refuge and fortress, their God in whom they trust! Cover them with Your feathers; under Your wings they will find refuge. *Your* faithfulness will be their shield and rampart—"

Yo-Yo poked my leg. "What's a *rampart?*" she whispered.

"It's, uh, some kind of wall, I think," I whispered back. "I'll look it up."

As we found our seats after our prayers, Delores pointed to the door. "Avis, go home. That's where your heart is right now. It's all right."

We all murmured assent. Avis hesitated about two seconds, gathered her stuff, and slipped down Stu's front stairs.

Delores spread her hands. "So, now, who else needs prayer?" She smiled. "We are 'warmed up,' as you say here in the States."

"Mi be needing de prayer big-time!" Chanda blurted. The puddles lurking in her eyes spilled over as she recounted the visit to the cancer doc and the upcoming surgery later that week. "He—he tink it might be de cancer," she hiccuped. "Won' know till he get in dere—mi might wake up wit'out me breast!" She really blubbered then as several other Yadas passed her tissues. "Why God be letting dis 'appen to mi?" she wailed. "Everting goin so good for we now! Dis not s'posed to be! Oh pray, sistas! De devil be attacking me body—an' what mon want a 'oman wit only one breast? Ohhhhhhh . . ." And fresh tears flowed.

Hoshi and Stu, sitting on either side of Chanda on the futon, murmured words of comfort and held her hands as she cried. But no one prayed. What was going on? I was hoping someone else would pray, because I wasn't sure how—or for what. For healing? Well, sure. That it was a misdiagnosis and not cancer? Still a possibility. But I wasn't sure about what Chanda said. Was God "letting" this happen? If so, for what reason? Was it an attack from the devil? Or just "bad things happen to good people too"?

The Voice in my spirit seemed to whisper in my ear. *God doesn't waste anything. He uses everything to accomplish His purpose. So pray.*

OK. That's right. It was our job to pray and God's job to answer in His own way. So I prayed aloud for Chanda, asked God for healing, asked for a good report of no cancer. But I also prayed that God would work His purpose out in Chanda's life. "Bring her closer to You in this time, Lord," I prayed. "Closer, closer, closer . . ."

I was surprised at the hearty amens from others as I closed my prayer.

Our prayers continued—for Ruth and her unborn babies, we praised God for Becky's new job, prayed for the merger of Uptown and New Morning churches, for continued healing of Nony's husband from his severe head injury, patience for Adele as MaDear slipped further into senility, for the high school students who had stopped by the lemonade stand . . .

That last prayer from Edesa jiggled my private stash of good intentions. I had told God I needed to apologize to Yada Yada for pushing the lemonade stand idea so hard without adequate confirmation and preparation. As the prayers tapered off, I told myself I should really do that tonight—though Avis wasn't here now, and she'd had the most reservations.

But Hoshi's soft, cultured voice broke into the momentary silence. "Lord Jesus, I want to pray for the girl named Sara in my honors history class. She sits by herself, doesn't talk to anyone, yet she is obviously very bright. She seems so alone. Give me an opportunity to show her Your love—as Nonyameko and Dr. Smith did for me."

As we ended our prayers, I leaned toward Hoshi to ask, "Tell us more about Sara," but never got a chance, because just then Stu and Becky came waltzing into the room carrying a frosted cake with candles blazing. "Happy birthday to youuuuu . . ." they sang. Others joined in as Becky thrust the cake in my face. "Happy birthday, dear Jodeeeeeeeeeeeee . . ."

I was dumbfounded. My birthday seemed like weeks, maybe months ago, overshadowed by Josh's *un*-birthday.

"Blow!" Becky hissed. "Them candles ain't gonna last all night."

Did I have a wish? Couldn't think of anything on the spot, so I just blew. Out they went. "That's not forty-four candles," I joked.

"Yes it is," Becky insisted. "See? Those make a 4 and the rest make another 4."

287

Stu handed me a computer-made card with a flourish. "To our very own naming expert." She grinned. "Your name."

The card said *Jodi Marie* in a beautiful flourish on the outside, and the words *Grace* and *Rebellion* on the inside. The second word startled me so much I didn't even see the little love notes and signatures of my Yada Yada sisters all around the inside of the card. Was that the meaning of Marie? Why had I never looked *that* up?

I offered a wry grin. "Guess we oughta be careful what we name our kids, huh?"

"I *told* Stu not to include your middle name." Becky glared at her housemate.

"Hang on to your booties," Stu said. "I thought Jodi would get it—see? Without 'grace' you're just 'rebellious'—"

Florida snickered. "Now you're sayin' it."

"—but the meaning of *Jodi*—'grace'—changes everything!"

Yo-Yo nodded. "Hey, that's kinda cool."

I managed a smile, still a bit taken aback. "Uh-huh. Guess you're right, that's who I am without God and who I am *with* God." I looked at the card again. "Aw, these notes are sweet."

After Becky cut the cake and passed it around—her *third* chocolate cake creation—people started drifting home. But before Nonyameko and Hoshi left, I pulled Nony aside. "Nony, how do people at New Morning feel about the merger next week? Several people are leaving Uptown because of it." I knew my anxiety was leaking, but I was starting to wonder: *Are we doing the right thing?*

Nony, slipping into a simple black jacket with gold buttons, made a face. "I have to confess, Jodi. We have not been going to worship at New Morning."

She must have seen the alarm in my eyes, because she chuckled.

"Only because Mark has not been able to manage the steep stairs at Uptown. Once New Morning begins to meet regularly in their new space, we will come." Her eyes twinkled. "Next week, right? Mark is very excited about our two churches becoming one."

I nodded. At least *somebody* was excited. I gave her a hug, catching a whiff of an alluring perfume. Sandalwood or something. "Thanks, Nony. See you Sunday then."

Stu made me take the rest of the cake downstairs to Denny and the kids. I set it on our dining room table and stared once more at the inside of the handmade card. What was my mother *thinking* when she gave me "rebellious" for a middle name?!

WE FINALLY KINDA SORTA HAD A BIRTHDAY DINNER for Josh on Monday night. I baked a chicken with an apricot jam-mustard glaze and made mashed potatoes, and Denny picked up a French silk chocolate pie at Baker's Square on the way home. Josh said, "Sweet!" when he opened the CD case from us and made a huge fuss when Amanda gave him three *autographed* CDs from bands they'd heard at Cornerstone. "You got these autographed? Wow, Amanda." Then he clutched his chest. "You mean you've had these stashed away since last July? When I could've been listening to them for three whole months? Oh, you're cruel! Cruel!"

Amanda rolled her eyes. "Mom, he's adopted, right?"

I handed him a package from my parents and a card from Denny's. "Aha," Josh said, pulling out a long, knitted winter scarf which looked alarmingly identical to the one my mother had made for me, except longer—much longer. He wrapped it around his head like an untidy turban and opened the next gift, a book about "how to keep your faith in college" and signed, "Love, Grandpa."

Amanda patted him on the shoulder. "They mean well, bubby." Which cracked all of us up—until Josh opened the card from his other grandparents. A card simply signed "Harley and Kay" and a check for twenty-five dollars. I saw Denny's lips tighten. Guess "Harley and Kay" were still annoyed about the college tuition check we'd sent back.

But Josh just grinned and waved the birthday check in the air. "Now *this* one I'm gonna keep." He pushed himself away from the table. "Well, thanks, people. Can I use the car tonight? A buddy at work invited me to see a movie. Not a prob, is it?"

Well, so much for lingering at the table. But I smiled. "Sure, go, go. You need some fun after your stressful weekend. Who's your buddy?"

"She works in accounting. Her name's Sue."

YOU COULD'VE KNOCKED ME OVER with a limp noodle. A *buddy* named *Sue*? "Well, could be a good thing," I told Denny as we cleaned up the kitchen. "I mean, for him to go out with other girls, not be so fixated on Edesa."

Denny was tackling the encrusted roasting pan with a bedraggled wire soap pad. "I think," he grunted, scraping away, "Josh and Edesa are just good friends. Hasn't she made it pretty clear?" He scowled at the pan and left it to soak.

I snorted. "What do I know? They're awfully chummy. But this Sue would have to be a quality person if Peter Douglass hired her, right?"

"Yeah. Maybe. I'd say Josh has a good eye for quality himself."

Denny snickered and snapped me on the rear with his dishtowel. "But I sure never called you my 'buddy' when *we* were going out. Nope. Nope."

CHANDA'S SURGERY WAS SCHEDULED for Friday to give her time to do all the pre-op stuff—a complete physical, chest X ray, EKG, blood work. "What dey need all dat stuff for, Sista Jodee?" she complained when I called her midweek. "Seem like de only ting mi do all week is go to de doctor!"

We scrambled to cover things for Chanda—a bit tough, since most of us worked or went to school. "Doesn't Chanda have any family here in Chicago?" I complained to Avis in her office that week. "She used to leave the kids with a sister, I thought. But where is she now, when Chanda really needs her?"

Avis shrugged. "Chanda said her sister went back to Jamaica. But whether that was just for a visit or for good, I don't know. We'll just have to cover somehow."

To my surprise, Nony offered to take Chanda to the hospital on Friday and stay until she was out of surgery. *Mark must be doing better for her to leave him all day,* I thought—though I found out later that Hoshi only had one class on Friday, leaving "Dr. Smith" alone only a couple of hours. Still, the fact that Nony felt she could be away all day was good, I hoped—for both Nony and Mark.

Florida offered to keep Chanda's kids over the weekend but didn't know how to get them after school in north Evanston down to Rogers Park. I wasn't any help; Denny usually didn't get home with the car till six or six thirty, earliest. They could stay in afterschool care, but . . .

My brain ached as I headed for school Friday morning. I felt badly that Chanda's kids had to stay in after-school care so late. Best-case scenario, Chanda might be able to go home that night, the lumpectomy done as an outpatient.

Or not.

It all depended on what the doctors found when they went in.

# 34

Avis appeared at my classroom door twenty minutes after the dismissal bell as I was cleaning off the marker-boards. Still had to straighten desks and toss left-behind lunchboxes, sweaters, and jump ropes into the Darn Lucky Box before I could leave for the weekend. The principal of Bethune Elementary leaned against my desk, arms folded across her soft, rust-colored sweater-tunic. "Nony called," she said. "The lump was malignant."

I stared at my boss, openmouthed.

"That's the bad news. The good news is that the lymph nodes were clean. It hadn't spread. So all they did was take out the lump and sentinel nodes. But they're still going to keep her overnight for observation. She was pretty sick when she came out of the anesthesia."

My insides sank. "Poor Chanda." *OK, God, what happened to the "no cancer" report we prayed for?* Still, there was some good news. She'd been so afraid of waking up with only one breast. And they'd found it before it spread. Then I had a memory jolt. "Wait a sec.

That's exactly what you went through, wasn't it, Avis? A lump that was malignant but hadn't spread? I mean, you didn't have a mastectomy, and you're fine now."

"That's right." Her businesslike manner softened. "I'd like to run up to the hospital to see her, give her some encouragement. Want to ride along?"

Ten minutes later, I met Avis in the parking lot and we headed north toward Evanston Hospital in her black Toyota Camry. Wasn't often I had Avis to myself for five minutes, much less fifteen. Might as well stick my foot in it. "Um, how's Rochelle, Avis? You and Peter doing OK?"

Avis was a long time answering. *Uh-oh,* I thought. "Sorry. You don't have to—"

"No, no, it's all right, Jodi. I'm just not sure how to answer." She concentrated on spiraling the Camry up the ramps of Evanston Hospital's huge parking garage. We finally found a space on the roof.

Avis turned off the ignition and sighed. "Let's just say Peter and I don't see eye to eye on how we should respond to Rochelle 'when she comes crying to us about Dexter,' as he says. He gave her an ultimatum last weekend—told her we're not a halfway house; she needs to get an order of protection, and if Dexter violates it, she needs to call the police or go to a shelter."

"So what happened?" I gasped.

Avis shook her head. "Rochelle was so mad, she just left, was gone before I got home from Yada Yada. Went to stay with a friend, I guess. Called me to say Peter wasn't her dad, and he had no right to boss her or tell her she couldn't come home to Mama. Hung up on me when I didn't immediately take her side. At least I have her cell number, but . . ." The pain in Avis's eyes was almost more than I could bear. "What do you think, Jodi? Feels like I'm having to choose between my husband and my daughter."

I had no idea what to think! "Oh, Avis," I moaned, and gave her a hug. A few moments later, she picked up her Bible and purse, got out of the car, and marched into the hospital. All-business Avis again.

We got lost coming into the hospital from the top floor but finally found Chanda in the right wing. Ruth Garfield sat in the corner of the private room, a garish orange maternity top announcing her expanding tummy, knitting away on what vaguely looked like baby booties. Chanda snored gently against a pile of pillows, clear liquid from plastic bags dripping into her arms, bandages peeking out of the top of her hospital gown.

"Hey," I said to Ruth, leaning over to give her an awkward hug. "How are you?"

"How should I be?" she grunted. "Not yet seven months and already seven tons. That Delores, she better be Solomon."

"The eating must be working. You look better," I teased. All I got was a *humph*.

On the other side of the bed, Avis was anointing the sleeping Chanda from a little bottle of oil she always carried with her and starting to pray. "Where's Nony?" I murmured to Ruth. "Is Ben here?"

"Left when we arrived, Nony did. To pick up Chanda's children and bring them here to see the mother." The knitting needles never paused. "Ben, he's noshing on bagels and coffee in the cafeteria. He doesn't do hospital rooms too good."

ONLY ON THE WAY HOME with Chanda's kids belted in the backseat, headed for the Hickmans, did I realize how beautifully God had smoothed out all the complicated juggling for Chanda's children. Ruth "just happened" to arrive in perfect time to sit with Chanda so Nonyameko could pick up Chanda's kids from after-school care and bring them back to the hospital to see their mother. Chanda managed to wake up long enough "to kiss me t'ree babies," after which Avis and I offered to transport them to the Hickmans, who were waiting for the kids with open arms and home-fried chicken, no doubt. I started to hum a little thanksgiving to God.

"Sing it," Dia demanded from the backseat. "I know that song from Sunday school."

I grinned. "God is so good . . ." I started. Dia joined in, practically yelling in my ear. "God is so good! God is so good! He's so good to us!" I couldn't remember the verses, so we made some up. "He loves my mommy" . . . "He gives us friends" . . . We added "our family," "new cars" ("Mommy's Lexus!" the kids shouted), "lunch-boxes" ("Lunch *money*," Thomas corrected). From there it got a little silly—pizza, birthday parties, toilet paper (giggles from the backseat). At the end of each "verse," even Avis couldn't resist smiling as the kids shouted the rousing last line: *"He's so good to us!"*

When we'd delivered our lively cargo to the Hickman abode, Avis and I rode home in silence, grateful for the golden hush. I wondered what she was thinking. About Rochelle, no doubt. About her new marriage and the stresses bombarding it so soon. But an echo still seemed to fill the car: *God is so good . . . He's so good to us.*

CHANDA HAD SOME "MINOR COMPLICATIONS" that she declined to describe, and the surgeon kept her in the hospital until Sunday. Yeah, I knew about those "minor complications." Probably just trying to "go" again to the nurses' satisfaction, who said inane things like, "Did we have a BM yet, sweetie?" *("We"?)* But just as well. I'd offered to bring a lasagna for Chanda's first night home, but Nony called on Saturday. She said Pastor Cobb and Pastor Clark wanted to have a special "fellowship hour" after the worship service tomorrow with coffee, tea, and munchies, and could I make something? I decided on chocolate-chip cookies—who didn't like chocolate-chip cookies?—so ended up Saturday afternoon mass producing two lasagnas, two foil-wrapped bullets of garlic French bread, and a double-recipe of my mom's best-ever chocolate-chip cookies.

She'd be proud.

We arrived at the Howard Street shopping center at nine forty-five Sunday morning—fifteen minutes before the new starting time of ten o'clock. OK. So we were on New Morning time. Couldn't help wondering just how many things would happen New Morning's way just because *we* were joining them in *their* building.

"Does New Morning know we're going to donate the proceeds from the sale of our building to help buy this building or help pay for the renovation?" I murmured to Denny out of earshot of the kids.

Denny shrugged. "Probably. We voted on it. I'm sure Pastor Clark has told Pastor Cobb by now."

*Yeah,* I thought. *But do the folks in the pews—er, chairs—know?*

Josh had already disappeared inside the large storefront, but Amanda hung back and walked with us. "You OK, sweetie?" Denny asked, putting an arm around her.

"Guess." She leaned into him, her loose butterscotch hair catching highlights from the bright October sun. It was one of *those* days. Bright blue sky. A nip in the air. But enough sunshine to beckon one outside with promises of a lingering Indian summer. "Just feel kinda funny, not ever going back to Uptown Community anymore."

"I know, honey," I heard Denny say. "Guess we have to keep reminding ourselves that the 'real' Uptown—the people—came along with us. We just left behind the building."

*Most of them,* I thought, trailing behind my husband and daughter, my hands full with the two plastic cookie containers. *But not all.* My heart squeezed. *Oh Lord, why does this merger feel good and sad at the same time?*

But the moment I walked into the large storefront sanctuary, sadness evaporated. Someone had made a large banner in various shades of blues and sea green, which hung at the front of the worship space facing a long sidewall. Inside a large circle on the banner, hands in all shades of brown, tan, beige, and peach clasped wrists in the middle. Felt words arching at the top said, PRAISE GOD FOR HIS BODY, and a similar semicircle at the bottom said, UPTOWN & NEW MORNING.

My eyes got wet. I felt . . . welcome.

The Sisulu-Smiths were already there, dad and sons wearing their South African dashikis and Nony wearing my favorite blue-and-gold caftan. Denny immediately attached himself to Mark, who was sitting at the end of a row. Denny chatted, one hand resting on Mark's shoulder; Mark nodded, a half smile on his face. Mark looked . . . good. Basically. He was still wearing a patch over his left eye. But he didn't seem like the same Mark who had stood up in the middle of the plaza at Northwestern University and dissected the bogus invective of the White Pride group. Coming out of the coma had been a miracle! But maybe he'd never be the same after that vicious—

*Wait a minute.* The Voice in my spirit stopped me in my mental tracks. *Are you still praying for Mark's healing? Praying like you did when he was in the coma? Didn't I answer your prayers? Where are those prayers now? Have you given up?*

I was so stunned that I had to sit down. Didn't even notice it was one of Uptown's torture chairs. *Oh God, forgive me for my faithlessness. Yes, yes, I want to still pray—*

Small, cool hands covered my eyes at that moment. "Boo!" I turned to see Carla, Dia, and Cheree giggling like carbonated bubbles, while Chanda's Thomas and Florida's Cedric made a beeline for Marcus and Michael Smith. I waved at Florida and Carl, who were talking with some of the New Morning folks. Even Chris Hickman was hanging out on the edges of a clump of teenagers.

And there was Becky with Little Andy strangling her neck . . . Avis and Peter acting as greeters . . . Stu talking to Hoshi. This was amazing! Half my Yada Yada sisters and their families were ending up in the same melded church. Nothing we had planned. Nothing we'd even *imagined* when we met at that women's conference the first time.

New Morning's pastor, Joseph Cobbs, and Uptown's Pastor Clark walked to the front of the restive congregation—a study in contrasts, if ever there was one. Short and tall. Brown and white. Married and widowed. Snappy dresser and cardigan sweater. Vigorous and sedate. Mutt and Jeff.

"This is the day that the Lord has made!" Pastor Cobbs boomed.

"Let us rejoice and be glad in it!" Pastor Clark croaked in response.

Immediately the praise band launched into an ear-splitting rendition of "These Are the Days of Elijah." The saxophonist seemed to make the words leap right off the coral-colored wall where the overhead displayed them, as New Morning and Uptown voices melded in our first song of praise as "one body."

> *... though these are days of great trial,*
> *Of famine and darkness and sword ...*

"Help us, Jesus!" shouted a familiar voice. Florida.

> *Still, we are the voice in the desert crying,*
> *"Prepare ye the way of the Lord!"*

Next to Florida, I saw Carla Hickman and Dia George giggling and pointing toward the broad expanse of windows running alongside the double-glass doors. Sunday morning shoppers heading for Dominick's super-size grocery store and kids hanging out at the mall were stopping along the sidewalk and peering in the windows. I grinned. *"Prepare ye the way of the Lord" indeed!*

And then the band and praise team, a delightful mix of Uptown and New Morning faces, served up the chorus:

> *... Lift your voice! It's the year of jubilee!*
> *And out of Zion's hill salvation comes.*

All over the room, voices shouted "Hallelujah!" and hands lifted into the air—brown and white in all shades, sending praise to God. Even Denny had one arm lifted! I raised my own hands upward. It was as if I couldn't help it! All things seemed to fade away as the electric basses thrummed, taking our praise upward . . .

*There's no God like Jehovah.*
*There's no God like Jehovah! . . .*

Again and again, like ancient drummers sending messages from hilltop to hilltop: *"There's no God like Jehovah . . ."*

I FELT WEAK-KNEED AFTER THE SERVICE. How many prayers, how many tears, how many sacrifices had been offered to see this day come about? Mark Smith, for one. The vicious beating he'd barely survived had been the catalyst that had made both congregations ask, *Will prejudice and hatred drive us apart into our own safe little worlds? Or bring us together?*

I looked around for Nony, remembering what she'd said when Mark first came to worship after that scary coma: *"Take that, devil!"* But I didn't see her; the Sisulu-Smiths must have slipped out and gone home. Maybe Mark had tired out.

Most folks headed for the long table loaded down with everything from chocolate-chip cookies to sweet potato pie. Maybe it was easier to meet and greet with coffee in one hand and pie in the other. Like weather and baseball, you could always talk about the food. "Isn't this good?" "Oh, child! My grandmother used to—" But the long service was too much for my bladder, and I made a beeline for the women's restroom.

Three stalls! That was luxury. I stepped into the handicapped one—always larger—dumped my Sunday tote bag, and started to pull out a paper seat cover. Just then, the door opened and two voices using stage whispers filled up the room.

"—that awful sweater. What's with *that*? Doesn't the man have a suit?"

I froze. Did they know someone was in here?

"Girl, I know what you mean. Didn't seem respectful, know what I'm sayin'? And that tall kid with the short, shaggy hair—did you see his raggy jeans? Now I *know* his parents can afford better'n *that*."

What? Tall kid, shaggy hair . . . were they talking about *Josh*?

I was sorely tempted to come out of the stall, pin their loose lips to the wall with a stony glare, and tell these backbiters where to stuff it. Or wait until they were gone, tuck my tail between my legs, and slink out of there, never to return.

Old Jodi responses.

But I knew better now. Knew Satan would like nothing better than to derail God's people getting together, using careless talk to hurt our feelings and trip us up before we'd even left the starting line.

And if I was *honest* . . . I'd thought the very same thing about Pastor Clark wearing that awful sweater—on this Sunday, of all Sundays! And I'd had to stitch my own lips shut that very morning when Josh showed up at the breakfast table in those raggy jeans. Had reminded myself to be glad he was going to church.

I decided to do what I came in here to do. Didn't *normally* make that much noise pulling out the paper seat cover and arranging it artfully on the toilet seat, hanging on lest the automatic flush pulled it into the abyss before I had a chance to sit down. But a moment later the bathroom door closed with a whisper, and I was once more alone.

And then the tears crowded to the surface.

*Oh God! This merger is going to be harder than I thought!*

# 35

lorida hijacked Josh-of-the-raggy-jeans to take Chanda's kids home after the service, but I made a separate trip later that afternoon with my pan of lasagna, foil-wrapped garlic bread, a salad—did Chanda eat salad?—and a few chocolate-chip cookies I'd left at home on purpose. When I arrived at the Georges' new home in the quiet neighborhood straddling the Skokie-Evanston border, the steel gray Lexus was parked out front, a parking ticket decorating the windshield.

A short woman with straight black hair pulled back from a pale, round face opened the door after I pushed the doorbell. "Uh—" I glanced at the house number. This *was* the house Chanda had moved into, wasn't it? But just then Cheree poked her braided head around the strange woman and yelled, "Mama! It's Ms. Baxter!"

The woman smiled, took the food from me, and disappeared.

Chanda was propped up like a queen in the living room, surrounded by pillows, a puffy comforter, and empty glasses with straws, watching TV sitcom reruns. She turned the volume down with the remote and fanned herself with the TV guide. "Oh, t'ank you, Sista Jodee. Hope all dat cheese don't give mi gas. What's dat?" She pointed at the parking ticket I'd brought in. "Oh! Dat make mi so mad! Dis neighborhood don' want dem 'outsiders' parking here, so all up and down dis street, all de cars need a special resident permit. But does dis lady look like she can run down to city hall an' get dat permit? *Humph*!" Chanda fanned faster.

I pulled up an ottoman, trying to ignore the annoying drone of the TV. "Why don't you just put the car in the garage, Chanda?"

"Oh, dat. Dat be full of boxes still."

The woman at the door turned out to be a nanny-housekeeper Chanda had hired for a week—a sweet Romanian woman named Yohanna who barely spoke English, which I thought was hilarious, since it was sometimes hard to understand Chanda's mix of Jamaican patois and black English. I could just imagine them trying to communicate by pointing, nodding, and inflection. But when I used the half bath off the kitchen fifteen minutes later, Yohanna had the girls setting the table and Thomas was doing his homework at the bar counter.

Talk about serendipity. Chanda the housecleaner now had her own household help! I had an idea Yohanna wouldn't be going anywhere at the end of the week.

Chanda was perfectly willing to give me a blow-by-blow complaint about her hospital stay—soggy food, bossy nurses, medication at midnight—but seemed to be avoiding the obvious. "Chanda," I finally interrupted. "What is the doctor saying about the cancer?"

Her face fell, like a glob of silly putty that suddenly lost its shape. Her eyes puddled, and I handed her a couple tissues. "Oh, Sista Jodee. Why God be mad at me? Dey saying mi got to have dat

305

radiation. Is all mi hair going to fall out? Mi tought all dat lottery money make ever'ting work out good for we." She wagged her head, trying to stifle the wail I could see building up. "What mi do wrong, Jodee? Eh? Eh?"

Wrong? I had my own opinion about the statewide lottery, preying mostly on the people who could least afford to sink hundreds of dollars into those weekly get-rich-quick tickets. Except that, whoopsy-daisy, Chanda actually won. What was *that* all about, God? But who could argue with Chanda being able to take her kids to Disney World or buying her own home for the first time in her life? Things other people, lots of white people, did all the time without batting an eye.

I licked my lips and chose my words carefully. "I don't know if you did anything wrong, Chanda. That's not for me to say, anyway." *OK, OK, so I was thinking it. New Jodi responses took time.* "But if you think this cancer is about God punishing you for something— nope. Don't believe it." I reached out and took her plump, manicured hand. "God never wants somebody to have cancer. He's not like that. Ever. But God will use things like this. To get our attention, maybe. To teach us something. To cut through our headlong dash through life. Maybe give us a course correction." Definitely how God had used that car accident on me. "Want me to pray? Let's pray that you'll hear God's still, small voice speaking to you during this time."

"Yes, yes," she sniffled. "Dat be a good prayer. You pray, Sista Jodee."

"Sure. Wait a sec." I grabbed the remote and turned off the TV. How could anyone hear God's still, small voice with all that racket on?

# The y a d a y a d a Prayer Group Gets Caught

MONDAY I HAD A NOTE in my office mailbox that two of my students—Jessica Cohen and Caleb Levy—would be absent that day for "religious reasons." I checked the school calendar. October 6. Yom Kippur.

*Huh.* Last year Ruth had invited Yada Yada to attend one of the Jewish high holy days that Beth Yehudah—the Messianic congregation she attended—celebrated in the fall. I had dragged Denny to a Rosh Hashanah service last year, choosing the festive Jewish New Year over Yom Kippur, the more somber Day of Atonement.

But Ruth hadn't said anything about inviting us this time. Didn't I tell her last year that *this* year I would attend Yom Kippur with her, find out what it was all about?

Guess she had other things on her mind.

So did I, frankly. The conversation I'd overheard in the bathroom Sunday morning niggled at me. The nerve! Talking like that in the bathroom like a couple of teenagers, when anyone could have overheard them.

*Oh,* I realized, as I went out on the playground and brought my third-grade class inside at the morning bell. *Maybe they were just a couple of teenagers.*

*Grace, Jodi. Grace,* whispered the Voice in my spirit. *Love covers a multitude of sins.*

Well, yeah. And to tell the truth, maybe I needed to talk to Josh about those raggy jeans on Sunday morning. If New Morning thought dressing up a bit more on Sunday morning was a sign of respect, weren't we supposed to be culturally sensi—

"Ow! Ow! My eye!" The screech of pain was so high-pitched I was startled to see Bowie Garcia, a toughie if there ever was one, holding his eye and hopping up and down by his desk. Standing two feet away, a braided and beaded Carla Hickman clutched a pencil in her fist, glaring at the boy jerking like a puppet in front of her.

"She stabbed me! Ow! Ow!" Bowie howled.

"It's *my* pencil, an' he tried to grab it from me."

*Oh Lord. Help me here!* I told Carla to *sit and don't move*, while I tried to assess the damage. "Bowie! Stand still. Let me see your eye." I peered closely. A small graphite dot, like a stray black freckle, decorated Bowie's eyebone below his eyebrow, just millimeters from his eyeball. I blew out a sigh of relief. No real harm done.

But it might have been.

I told my class to sit at their desks and be quiet or there would be two extra math pages for *everyone* if I heard even a squeak. Alerting the teacher next door that I had to leave my classroom, I marched Carla to the office. "He started it," she pouted, pulling back on my hand until I was practically dragging her. "Why only *me* in trouble?"

"I will deal with Bowie later," I said, sitting her down in the time-out chair in the school office. "Grabbing is one thing. But poking someone's eye with *anything* is very, very dangerous."

Carla folded her arms across her tiny chest and stuck out her bottom lip. No penitence there. I wanted to shake the stubborn snippet. But I simply left the office, then leaned against the wall in the hallway. To tell the truth, I could use a time-out myself, give myself time to think. *Lord, how do I handle this?* Teachers were supposed to report to parents any hitting or violent behavior and ask for a parent-teacher meeting.

Not exactly a call I wanted to make to Florida. Last time she practically laughed when I told her Carla had given that kid a bloody nose.

But I tried to call her from the office before I left school for the day; only got Cedric. "Nah, Miz Baxter, Mama's not home. She workin' double shift now."

"Oh." Double shifts? What was *that* about? "Who's taking care of Carla?"

"Me an' Chris—till Daddy gets home anyway."

I called the Hickmans later that evening, got Carl this time, who said Florida wouldn't get off until eleven."You say the boy's OK? He sounds like a bully to me, but . . . Can't you just handle it, Jodi? Do what you need to do . . . I know Flo don't got time for a parent-teacher meeting, not till we get this bill from the city paid off."

If I'd been talking to Florida, I would've asked, *"What bill from the city?"* But I just said, "Sure. I'll handle it, Carl. Don't worry about it," and hung up. Only later that evening, while waiting at the back door for Willie Wonka to finish his final "business" of the day, did it hit me.

Bill from the city. *Of course.* For the cost of cleaning off that alley wall Chris had tagged.


I DIDN'T WANT TO ASK FLO how much the city was charging them for the alley cleanup, but it worried me all week. Hundreds? Thousands? How did the city expect a kid like Chris to pay that off? It got dumped in the parents' lap, that's what, which made sense theoretically—but it killed me to think of Florida working from 7 a.m. to 11 p.m. five or six days a week. Might kill *her* was more like it.

Seemed like the rest of us should help somehow. I wasn't sure where an extra hundred bucks would come from, but Denny *did* get a raise with the AD position this fall. Would a hundred dollars even make a dent? We'd need to multiply that somehow, but I wasn't sure Florida would want me calling around, drumming up money. The Hickmans had their pride. Especially Carl.

I was so caught up with the Carla problem and mulling over our church merger that the call from Ruth on Thursday surprised me. "So are the Baxters coming Saturday or not?"

"Coming where? What are you talking about, Ruth?"

"To our Sukkoth celebration. Ben was supposed to call you."

"Um, not to my knowledge. Maybe he talked to Denny. You know how guys are about messages. Sukkot is . . .?"

"Sukkot, Jodi! The Feast of Booths. What, you don't know your Old Testament? First Yom Kippur, the Day of Atonement for our sins. Now we are rejoicing that God has been with us while wandering in the wilderness, living in tents. Seven guests we must have—Abraham, Isaac, Jacob, Joseph, Moses, Aaron, and David. You Baxters make four, and Yo-Yo and the two rascals make seven."

I wasn't sure I was following all this, but I finally figured out she was inviting us over Saturday evening, the first day of the Feast of Booths—"To party!" I heard Ben yell in the background.

It didn't take much to convince Denny to give up a Saturday evening "to party" with Ben Garfield. The kids were another story.

"Mo-om!" Amanda wailed. "I love Mr. and Mrs. Garfield, don't get me wrong. But hanging around with *your* friends on a Saturday night—sheesh, Mom!"

I cocked an eyebrow. "Do you have other plans?"

"Well, no, but . . ."

Josh, however, *did* have other plans. "Sorry, Mom. Can't do it."

310

"Why? Another overnight at Manna House?" *Ouch.* I immediately regretted the two imps of sarcasm that snuck into my tone.

Josh hesitated, trying to read me. "No. But I already told Sue—"

*Sue again.* "Oh. Well, just thought it could be fun. Pete and Jerry are coming." Unless Yo-Yo was having this exact same conversation with her two half brothers.

"Oh." Josh made a face. "Well, sorry about that. But . . ." He shrugged.

But Amanda's ears picked up. "Pete and Jerry? Hey, Mom, if Josh isn't coming, can I invite José?"

SO THERE WE WERE, seven honored *goyim* sitting on the deck behind the Garfields' modest brick bungalow, eating chicken schnitzel and potato knishes, talking and laughing under a plastic tarp that had been strung up over the deck to represent the temporary "booths" or "tents" of the wilderness. Strings of tiny white lights were wrapped around the deck railings and strung overhead under the tarp, making this "festival of booths" festive indeed. The October weekend weather cooperated beautifully, hitting a high of seventy-eight degrees that afternoon, and cooling off to the midfifties as the sun went down. The four teenagers—Pete and Jerry Spencer, seventeen and thirteen respectively, and Amanda and José, both sixteen—lolled about in the tiny backyard, holding their plates of seconds and thirds in one hand and kicking around a basketball, brought by Pete in the unrequited hope that there would be a hoop in the alley.

"You guys sleepin' out here on the deck tonight?" Yo-Yo looked at Ben. "Mr. Hurwitz said lots of Orthodox Jews live out in their booths all week—what?"

Ben was eyeing Yo-Yo from beneath scraggly white eyebrows. "Do I look like a Boy Scout, Yo-Yo? And can't you just see the Queen Elizabeth here"—he jerked a thumb in Ruth's direction—"docking up in a deck chair?"

Ruth rolled her eyes and passed the last of the schnitzel right past Ben, dumping it on Denny's plate. "Eat, eat, Denny. You're skin and bones." To which Denny laughed and gave her a big smackeroo right on the cheek.

It was good to see Ruth and Ben having fun. "Here's to Indian summer!" I lifted my glass of iced-tea-from-instant-powder (good thing she didn't invite Florida!) and clicked Yo-Yo's glass.

Ben lifted his bottle of beer and waggled his eyebrows. "Cheers."

Ruth pushed back her chair. "Hot weather we don't need. Hot apple crisp we do. No, no, don't get up. I can bring it." No one had moved a muscle to get up, but we did break into mutual chuckles as she waddled herself and her "cargo" through the back door.

Yo-Yo, slouched on a deck chair in the inevitable denim overalls, was chatty tonight; she seemed pleased to be invited to a grownup function and to be sitting with the adults. "Yeah, Becky's doin' good at the Bakery. Real good. For some reason she hit it off with Mr. Hurwitz, 'specially after Stu brought Little Andy by the Bakery one Sunday when she was takin' him home. Man! The fuss they made over that kid. Now Becky can do no wrong. She's Lil' Andy's mama, and that's that! . . ."

We kept talking, but it seemed to me that Ruth was taking a long time bringing out that apple crisp. "'Scuse me," I said, getting up from the deck table. "I'm going to see if Ruth needs any help."

But when I'd picked my way through the mudroom—full of

coats and old shoes, shelves of canned goods, and gardening tools—and peeked into the kitchen, Ruth wasn't there. "Ruth?" I called, heading through the narrow kitchen into the dining room. "Ruth?"

She was sitting on a straight-backed chair in the dining room, one elbow on the table, her hand supporting the weight of her head. The other hand clutched her side.

*"Ruth!"* I was at her side in two strides. "What's wrong?"

She turned and looked at me, eyes glittering with pain. "Pain . . . my side . . . my head . . ."

*"Ben!"* I screamed, running back through the kitchen. "Dial 911! It's Ruth!"

# 36

*J*rode in the ambulance with Ruth and Ben while Denny took Yo-Yo and the kids to her place, promising to pick up Amanda and José later. When Denny found us in the emergency waiting room of Rush North Shore Medical Center half an hour later, he looked anxiously at Ben slumped in a chair in the corner and then shot a questioning glance at me. I beckoned my husband into the hallway.

"They're still examining her, have her hooked up to fluids. All they've said so far is that her blood pressure is high, something about preeclampsia."

"What does that mean?"

"I don't *know*, Denny." I saw him wince. I took a deep breath. "I'm sorry. I'm just worried. Ben's a wreck. Doesn't want to talk. Went over there to sit by himself." I peeked around the corner. Ben hadn't moved.

"OK, we won't talk then." Denny moved back into the waiting room and eased himself into a chair two seats over from Ben. Didn't say anything. Just sat.

I sat, too, and we waited. I must have nodded off at some point because I jumped when I heard someone say, "Mr. Garfield?" *Sheesh*. Couldn't I even stay awake one hour to "watch and pray" with Ben and Ruth?

A thirty-something doctor in shirt and tie—no white coat, sleeves rolled up, tie loosened—was talking to Ben. Both Denny and I moved closer. "—elevated blood pressure, some protein in her urine," the doctor was saying. "That and the headache and pain in her side all point to preeclampsia, which can be a serious complication. Left untreated, it can—"

"Treat it then," Ben growled. "What's the cure for pre—whatever?"

The doctor stood relaxed, professional, arms crossed. The brown-haired poster boy of doctors. "There is no 'cure' for preeclampsia except ending the pregnancy. I would recommend—"

"Ending the pregnancy?!" I blurted. "What do you mean?"

"I'm sorry. A poor choice of words. I simply mean that the only cure for preeclampsia is delivery of the baby—or babies in this case."

Delivery?! Oh God, no, not yet! Ruth's babies couldn't be more than two pounds at this point—maybe even less since there were two of them. "But she's not due for another two months—Christmas, she said!" My heart was racing. I knew the doctor was talking to Ben, but I couldn't help it. Would Ben stick up for Ruth carrying the babies to term?

"Exactly. Mrs. . . . ?" The doctor lifted his eyebrows at me.

"Baxter," Ben filled in. "Mr. and Mrs. Baxter, friends of my—of ours."

The doctor nodded. "Mrs. Baxter has a point. If the twins were even a month older, I'd recommend taking them now by C-section—

and we'd do it anyway if Mrs. Garfield's condition got to a high danger point. But while there's no cure for preeclampsia except delivery, it can be managed in many cases, at least until the babies are more fit to thrive on their own. It's a bit touch and go, given your wife's age and the fact that's she carrying twins."

Ben suddenly wobbled. Denny caught him and lowered him into a chair. "Jodi! Get Ben some water." I flew.

When I got back with a paper cup of water, Denny had loosened Ben's shirt collar and had one arm around him in a tight grip. The doctor had disappeared. Ben took the water in a shaky hand and drank, his Adam's apple bobbing slowly like a plastic ball on the end of a fishing line.

Denny blew out a breath. "The doctor said they're going to admit Ruth for observation, told Ben to go home, get some rest. They'd like to do some tests—"

Ben snorted. "But you know what Ruth's gonna say. No tests! Stubborn old . . ." He let it go and sank once more into a bitter, pressed-down silence.

Denny left to get the car. Even in our Caravan on the way home, Ben simply stared out the window, a silent hulk in the darkness. As we pulled up to the Garfields' brick bungalow, Ben muttered, "You guys go on. Don't mind me. I'll be all right." He struggled with his seat belt.

Denny was out of the car and had the side door open in seconds. "Come on. We're going in." Ben didn't protest.

I'd forgotten about the Sukkot celebration. Dirty dishes and cold food sat out on the deck, just as we'd left them hours earlier. The white minilights sparkled cheerfully, as if waiting for the party to simply pick up where it had left off. I turned to Ben, who was staring stupidly at the remains of the Feast of Booths. "Ben, go sit down. I'll clean up these dishes. It won't take long." Again Ben didn't protest, just let Denny take his jacket and cap and sank into an overstuffed chair in the living room. I followed the menfolk, still talking, wanting to encourage, wanting to speak words of faith and hope. "It's going to be all right, Ben. Even if they had to take the twins now, it's amazing the care they can give preemies! Why—"

"No, it's not going to be all right!" Ben's voice was suddenly so loud, so sharp, that it felt like a slap to the cheek.

"What . . . what do you mean? I don't understand."

"That's right! You don't understand!" Ben was suddenly on his feet, yelling, as if a surge of anger had strengthened all his bones. "We're Jewish, don't you get it? And I'm a carrier! I've got the gene! If Ruth's got the gene, one or both of those babies got a high chance of dying by age five—a horrible, debilitating death! But she won't get tested, will she! *Will she!*" Ben's fists clenched in utter frustration.

Even Denny's face had paled, his summer tan gone, the blood rushing downward. He grabbed Ben's shoulders. "What gene? Ben! What are you talking about?"

Ben stared at him, eyes wide. Long seconds hung in the air. "Tay-Sachs," he finally croaked. "Tay-Sachs disease. I saw my cousin's kid die . . . it was . . ." He suddenly crumpled backward into the chair and began to weep, his head in his hands—huge, gasping sobs, as if speaking the words haunting him since Ruth first announced she was pregnant had pulled the finger out of the dam.

BY THE TIME WE CLEANED UP THE SUPPER REMAINS at the Garfields', picked up Amanda and José at Yo-Yo's apartment where they were all watching a video, drove José home to Little Village, and finally dragged into our house, it was going on one a.m. Josh wasn't home either. I was too wound up to sleep, so while Denny steered a sleepy Amanda into her bedroom, I turned on the computer and called up the Internet. "T-A-Y S-A-C-H-S," I typed into the search engine.

Instant list of Web sites.

Article after article, much like the ones I read before.

None of them encouraging.

*"A genetic disorder . . . prevalent among Eastern European Jews . . . if both parents carry the gene, a one-in-four chance that their children will have the disease . . . a seemingly healthy baby ceases to smile, crawl, turn over . . . ultimately becomes blind and paralyzed . . . kidney failure, mental retardation, skeletal deformities . . . shutdown of the entire nervous system . . . death by age five."*

Willie Wonka, awakened from his sound slumber by all the strange nighttime activity, pushed his nose into my lap. Forehead wrinkled. Dark eyes worried. "Oh, Wonka," I moaned, and suddenly I was on the floor, cradling the dog's head in my arms, crying, shaking. *Ruth . . . Ruth . . . Oh God, not Ruth's babies . . . don't let it end like this, please God . . .*

Denny came in, turned off the computer, picked me off the floor, and held me until I'd cried it all out. Somehow we got to bed, slept a few hours, woke exhausted. I briefly considered staying home from church that morning, then decided the second Sunday of the merger wasn't a good morning to skip. People would wonder. (Did I care?)

But I did get on the phone and call Yada Yada, especially the sisters who didn't attend "Uptown–New Morning" or whatever we were going to call it, since I'd see them in a few hours. I didn't say anything about Tay-Sachs disease to anyone. Ben had kept it to himself all these months, hadn't even told Ruth—especially not Ruth. But I did tell Delores Enriques about the preeclampsia, wasn't sure if it was "for sure" or "possible," but I knew she'd be able to figure it out.

"Jodi," Delores said before she hung up, "Yada Yada meets tonight, supposedly at Ruth's. Ironic, no?" She slipped in a little laugh. "But if Ruth's still in the hospital, why don't we meet there? To pray for our sister. For God's mercy."

*God's mercy.* I wrapped those words around my heart as we automatically got ready and drove to church. I don't know if I went to meet God—I was too numb at the danger hanging over my dear friend and her babies, too burdened by carrying Ben's secret—but God met me there. Showed up when Peter Douglass sang a solo— Avis's Peter, shy but steady at the front of the church, accompanied only by the keyboard and a sweet, mournful sax.

"Precious Lord, take my hand, lead me on, let me stand! . . ." Peter's voice was surprisingly deep, slow, rich. I didn't know he could sing! I remembered the story of the famous gospel singer, Thomas A. Dorsey, who wrote this song, grief-stricken after his wife and child had died in childbirth.

"I am tired, I am weak, I am worn . . ."

*Oh Jesus! That's Ben Garfield! He's living in fear, and it has worn him out.*

"Through the storm, through the night, lead me on to the light . . ."

*Yes, Lord! Ben and Ruth are in the middle of a storm, raging around them, a storm others can't see.*

319

"Take my hand, precious Lord, lead me home!"

Tears poured down my cheeks; Denny handed me his handkerchief and laid a comforting arm across the back of my chair. *Yes, Lord, yes! Lead Ben home—home to You, Jesus.*

I don't remember much about the rest of the worship service. Didn't even notice that it was the second Sunday and we *didn't* have a potluck afterward—though Stu told me later, as she and Becky and I drove to the hospital that evening, that some disgruntled Uptown members decided to go out and eat together, grumbling about Uptown's traditions getting walked on in this merger.

"Aw, y'all gonna get that kinda stuff worked out," Becky said encouragingly. "After all, we had that big spread *last* Sunday after church. Don't seem like a big deal to me."

I wanted to laugh. A pitiful laugh. Sometimes we church-born Christians were our own biggest enemies. *Oh God, give us all a new-born heart like Becky's.*

Adele, Chanda, and Yo-Yo were already in the maternity waiting room when we arrived at Rush North Shore. I was surprised to see Chanda, parked in a padded chair, still moving gingerly and waving off any hugs. "Nah, nah. No bumpin' an' grindin' for mi yet."

"Hey, Stu. Hey, Becky." Yo-Yo gave *me* a punch on the shoulder and a grin. "Didn't I see you this mornin' already, 'bout midnight?" I just rolled my eyes.

Delores and Edesa were already in Ruth's hospital room, no doubt trying to find out "what's what" and praying the blood of Jesus over every inch of that room. *If they only knew the real deal,* I started to think—and caught myself.

They didn't have to. Jesus knew.

As the other Yada Yadas straggled in, we all slipped into Ruth's room in twos and threes, stayed for about five minutes, and gathered back in the waiting room. Ruth, bless her, pooh-poohed all the concern, saying there wasn't anything ailing her that couldn't be fixed with some bed rest and some hot blintzes. My heart squeezed. Ben obviously hadn't spilled his guts to Ruth about the Tay-Sachs gene yet. But back in the waiting room, we held hands and fervently prayed for Ruth and Ben and the babies.

"Oh God!" Nony prayed. "Your Word says that You knit us together while we were still in our mother's wombs. So you know these babies! You even know their names! Thank You, Lord God of heaven! You know them by *name!*"

A chorus of "Glory!" and "Hallelujah!" followed *that* prayer.

But no "Thank ya, *Je*sus!" That's when I realized Florida wasn't there. Hadn't seen her at church this morning either.

Others asked about Flo. "Don't worry. She's where she should be," Avis said. "Resting at home with the kids and Carl. She's been working double shifts."

Everyone nodded and seemed satisfied. Except Chanda. "Sista Jodee!" she hissed at me as we were giving goodnight hugs and heading for the elevator. "Why Sista Flo working double shifts, when dat girl got t'ree kids at home an' a working mon in she bed!" She shook her head. "What be going on dere?"

Straight question. Deserved a straight answer. "Chris was caught tagging. Not sure what's going on, but my guess is they've put two and two together and got him for two or three other walls they have to blast clean. The city sent them a big bill. Guess who pays."

I expected Chanda to roll her eyes, give a short, impassioned discourse about the city soaking its citizens out of their money left and right. But she just hung back with me as others crowded into the elevator and headed down to the first floor. She seemed to be thinking. Hard.

"How much?"

The question startled me. "I don't know. Blasting two or three walls, three or four hundred per wall—really, I don't know Chanda. Enough to make her work double shifts."

Again the thoughtful look on Chanda's round face. Her chin came up. "I will pay it. Dat's what God's bin saying to mi dis week, Sista Jodee. Maybe mi been spending me money in all de wrong places."

# 37

*W*e totally forgot Yo-Yo's birthday. "Ack!" I screeched, staring at the kitchen calendar a few days later. Denny and I had had Monday off—Columbus Day—so I'd gone back to the hospital to see Ruth. Josh couldn't believe *he* had to work when his parents and sister were on holiday, a fact Amanda had rubbed in with a few phone calls to Software Symphony's shipping department: *"Yeah, sunny and breezy, think we just hit seventy-something, no humidity though . . . slept in till ten . . . Dad and I went for a bike ride along the lake, lots of windsurfers out there . . . Oooo, big brother, you better talk nice to me or I'll tell Willie Wonka on you."*

Later that day, Denny and I had taken advantage of the holiday and actually gone out for supper—on a Monday! Over a big Greek salad with gyros slices and fat Greek fries sprinkled with vinegar at Cross-Rhodes, a wonderful little restaurant we'd found in Evanston, I'd told Denny about Chanda's offer to pay off Chris's wall-cleaning bill. He'd frowned. "Hm. Don't know if they'll take it. The Hickmans have their pride, especially Carl. They don't want 'charity.' Not sure it's a good thing for Chris either. Hope they're taking this out of *his* hide some way, not just Florida's."

I hadn't thought about it that way—had just been amazed at Chanda's response to my little suggestion that she "listen to God." I shrugged. "Guess it's between Chanda and the Hickmans to figure it out."

That was Monday. Now it was midweek, all systems were back on schedule, and I had taken a quick glance at the calendar just to see what was coming up on the weekend. And there was Yo-Yo's name: "Birthday, 24."

I called Yo-Yo that afternoon when I got home from school but only got her voicemail. "Yo-Yo!" I said when I heard the beep. "I can't believe we forgot your birthday! Please call me back. We still want to celebrate."

She called me back the next day. "Yo, Jodi. Whaddya mean, forget? You called me on my birthday. Thought that was cool. By the way, tried to call you back last night, but no one answered."

"Sorry about that. Amanda's a phone hog; she doesn't answer the other line sometimes. I just mean we forgot to wish you happy birthday at Yada Yada last Sunday night. Should've remembered, even if we were at the hospital."

"Aw, that's OK. You guys gave me a cake an' everything last year."

"Well, we can still celebrate. Sorry you have to wait a couple of weeks."

"Nah, that's OK. But if you really wanna do somethin' . . . aw, I shouldn't ask."

"Yes, you should! Ask away." I hoped it was within reason.

"Well, um, ya know that violet thing—that flowerpot you guys gave me last year for my birthday, because of my name, ya know."

I grinned. "Yep. Yolanda, 'lavender flower.'" That had been a hoot, giving a pot of purple violets to Yo-Yo of the perpetual overalls.

"Well, I really liked those flowers, made me feel kinda special every time I looked at 'em. But, well, I kinda killed 'em about ten months ago, an' I was wonderin', if it's not too much trouble, could you find me another one?"

I sat looking at the phone after we hung up. *Dear, sweet Yo-Yo. Jesus, thank You for dropping her into my life. She always goes for the simple, not the complicated. Reminds me to find joy in the down-to-earth things of life—*

"Mo-om! Are you off the phone?" Amanda's head poked into the kitchen, then she yelled over her shoulder. "Dad! Mom's off the phone! *Pleeease* call and ask him!"

I followed Amanda and the phone back to the living room, where Denny had his feet up in the recliner, papers in his lap, briefcase open on the floor. Those weren't game plans, I'd bet—not as athletic director. Probably tons of administrative mumbo jumbo. My heart gave a tug. I wondered if he missed coaching, regretted taking the AD job.

"Please, Dad?" Amanda said, holding out the phone. "Just ask him again."

Denny looked up at our sixteen-year-old girl-woman with thinly disguised patience. "Amanda. I've already asked Mr. Enriques *twice* to come to the men's breakfast. Both times he said no. Get the drift?"

"Da-ad! José says the guys his dad hangs out with aren't, you know, they drink and gamble a lot, stuff like that. He doesn't go to church either. Just ask him!"

Denny sighed. "I feel like I'm bugging him. We don't know each other that well."

"But you should! I mean, like, José's my *boyfriend*, and Mom and Mrs. Enriques are good friends. Shouldn't you, like, get to know the father better?"

I raised an eyebrow at Denny. *Boyfriend?* We'd have to discuss that later. But for now, I tried not to laugh at Amanda, lecturing her father on getting to know the boyfriend's parents. *That* was rich.

Denny did laugh. "All right, all right. I'll ask him." He held out his hand for the phone. "But just one more time, OK, Mandy? If he says no, that's it."

RICARDO ENRIQUES said yes. Had hesitated, Denny said, but when Denny offered to pick him up and give him a ride back home, he'd relented. "*Gracias,*" he'd said. "You are kind. And your daughter is *una muchacha especial*—a special girl. I'm glad she is José's friend. Yes, *gracias*, I will come this time."

"Don't think he really wants to," Denny muttered to me out of Amanda's hearing. "But he's polite, you know. Probably thought it'd be rude to refuse three times."

"Are you still having men's breakfast now that we've merged? I mean, we didn't have Second Sunday Potluck. Maybe everything's up for grabs till the dust settles."

"Yeah, it's on. Guess both Pastor Cobbs and Pastor Clark heard from Peter Douglass and some of the other guys—maybe after the potluck got passed over last Sunday—that they really want to continue the men's breakfast. I was thinking about picking up Mark Smith, but maybe Peter can do that since I'm going after Ricardo."

Which gave me an idea. "Denny, can I ride along? I'd like to spend some time with Delores and the kids; haven't seen the munchkins in a long time. Then you could pick me up when you bring Ricardo back."

Which is how I found myself at the Enriques' home Saturday morning, along with Amanda, who saw an opportunity to hang out with José. "José!" Ricardo had said sharply before he left with Denny. "Walk the dog. Give him some exercise in the park. And I want it done before I get back."

"*Sí, Papa,*" José had mumbled. It was only eight o'clock, he was still barefoot and in sweats, and he hadn't had breakfast yet. Seemed to me he took his sweet time too. But I couldn't blame the boy. Not after what I'd heard about this pit bull.

Delores, whose shift didn't start until three, made breakfast burritos for all of us—rolled flour tortillas stuffed with scrambled eggs, crumbled chorizo, chopped tomatoes, and bunches of other stuff with homemade salsa for garnish. The Enriques' five sleepy-eyed children gave us shy hugs and picked at their burritos, their appetites not yet awake.

Emerald, thirteen-going-on-fourteen, the next oldest after José, babbled away in Spanish to Amanda, who babbled back. Delores winked at me. "Amanda is getting good with the Spanish, *sí*?"

I nodded, a little taken aback. Very good. Very leaving-Mom-in-the-dust good.

Ricky Jr., maybe eleven, made off with his burrito to play video games. The two youngest girls, nine-year-old Luisa and six-year-old Rosa, kept looking at me shyly with big black eyes and dimpled grins, their straight black hair hanging long and silky down their backs.

José finally got himself dressed, took the leash and a leather muzzle, and headed out the back door of the six-flat apartment building, Amanda right on his heels, shrugging into her jacket. I started to cry out, *"Wait!"* but Delores touched my arm and gave me a reassuring smile. When the door closed behind them, she said in a lowered voice, "It will be all right. José always uses the muzzle, and the dog knows Amanda."

I wasn't convinced. "But what about that bite on your arm last summer?" Not sure I was going to relax until Amanda and José were both safely back in the house and the dog back in its pen.

Delores shooed the other kids out of the kitchen and poured me a second cup of strong coffee. She smiled, but her eyes filled with tears. "Jodi, how do I say . . .? My heart is so grateful that Denny asked Ricardo to the men's breakfast this morning. Saturday is always tense. Ricardo says he is taking the dog out for exercise, but he doesn't come home for two hours! What kind of exercise is that?"

"Didn't you give him an ultimatum? Give up the dogfighting or you'll call the police?"

She sighed and looked down at her cup. "It's complicated." She lifted her eyes, bright with unshed tears. "I love him, Jodi. He is a good man. But losing his job, not being able to provide for his family, it's like . . ." She balled up her fist and punched the air a couple of times near her stomach. "I want to give him a chance to figure this out. Calling the police . . ." She shook her head. "I could not do it. And the mariachi band, he loves it so. It's the one thing that pulls all that is good from inside."

Delores shook herself as if shaking off our conversation. "Enough. Tell me, Jodi, how is Josh? Working, *sí*, at Avis's husband's place of business?" She chuckled. "Does he talk about Edesa all the time like she talks about him?"

I stared at her. "Edesa talks about *Josh* all the time? I thought . . . he thinks . . . oh, dear. He's been going out, dating, doing stuff with—I don't know *what* to call it!—a girl named Sue at work. Don't know *anything* about her."

Delores laughed again. "Leave it alone, Jodi! All will work out. Edesa enjoys working with Josh very much at Manna House. They think alike, have the same heart. Maybe that's all it will be." But the motherly twinkle in her eye said something else.

The front door buzzer made me jump. She rolled her eyes. "Excuse me *un momento*. I will send whoever it is—"

"Mama! Mama!" Luisa and Rosa came screeching into the kitchen, their tousled hair and nightgowns flying. "*El policía! El policía!*"

Delores's lips tightened. She headed with quick steps to the front of the first-floor apartment. Eyes wide, I scurried right behind her, coffee cup in hand.

All four kids were crowded at the front window. Revolving blue police lights sliced again and again through the sunshine streaming through the windows. Delores peeked out the front door of the apartment; over her shoulder, sure enough, I could see two uniformed police officers standing in the foyer.

She turned to me and closed her eyes for a brief moment, as if saying, *Pray, Jodi, pray.* Then she crossed the hall to the foyer door and opened it. "*Sí?* Can I help you?"

"Mrs. Enriques?" The police officer's voice verged on demanding but was still polite. Delores gave a slight nod. "Is your husband home?"

My heart pounded. Delores shook her head. "No. He is not home."

"Where is he?" Less polite, more demanding.

Words flew to my mouth. "He and my husband are at church."

The police officers glanced at each other. I could read their looks: *Yeah, right.*

The first police officer narrowed his eyes. "Mrs. Enriques, where is the dog your husband fights?"

"D-dog?" Delores seemed taken aback. "We have a dog. But it is not here. My son took it out, is walking it."

Again the *Yeah, right* glances. I wanted to screech, *"But it's true!"* And then my heart pounded. *Oh stay away, José and Amanda. Stay away.*

"Emilio, check around back." The second police officer trundled back outside and disappeared around the side of the building.

"*Madre del Dios!* What's going on here?" Ricardo's voice startled all of us. He and Denny came in the outside door into the foyer. Was it eleven o'clock already? I was so glad to see Denny, wanted to run into his arms. But like Delores, I stood immobile. Ricardo's eyes darted between his wife and the police, his expression a mixture of indignation and . . . fear?

"Ricardo Enriques?" The officer nailed Delores's husband with a piercing glance. "Where were you between eight and ten o'clock this morning?"

"With me." Denny's tone was curt. "Uptown–New Morning Church men's breakfast. Two pastors and twenty men present." *As witnesses,* was left unsaid.

The officer named Emilio returned, looked Ricardo and Denny up and down, then shrugged at his partner. "Garage is empty. Dog pen recently used, though."

"What did I say?" Delores's eyes flashed. "We have a dog; our son is walking it."

The first officer—his name pin said Blackstock—ignored her. "Mr. Enriques, you have been seen with a dog in the vicinity of . . ." The officer checked his notebook and rattled off an address. "This is a known site of illegal dogfights. Have you—?"

Denny interrupted. "Officer, are you charging Mr. Enriques with anything? Arresting him?"

The officer glared at Denny. "No, sir. But we'd like his cooperation."

Denny gripped Ricardo's shoulder. "Ricardo, don't say anything."

The air in the foyer seemed to crackle with heated thoughts and unspoken words. Officer Blackstock twitched an eyebrow, then tipped his hat with exaggerated politeness. "Mr. and Mrs. Enriques. Have a good day." The two officers sauntered out the doorway.

A phone was ringing in the background. A moment later Emerald appeared in the foyer. "Mama! It's Mrs. Cordova! She's crying!" She held out the cordless phone. Delores took the phone and walked back into the apartment, phone pressed to her ear. The rest of us followed, strain moving our joints like puppet strings.

Delores listened. "*Sí . . . sí . . . no . . . no . . .*" She finally clicked the phone off and turned slowly around to face us. "That was Elana Cordova." Her voice barely rose above a whisper. "The police raided a dogfight in a garage in their alley this morning." She swallowed. "All the men were arrested, including her husband, and the dogs impounded."

All of us stood frozen in the middle of the Enriques' living room, with its sparse furniture and bare floor, surely thinking the same thought. *If Ricardo hadn't gone with Denny this morning . . .*

The color drained from Ricardo's face. He fumbled for a chair, breathing heavily, as if the weight of the situation pressed him down, down. And then his head sank into his hands. *"El Dios, El Dios,* I'm sorry . . . so sorry!"

# 38

Denny and Ricardo already had the dog pen in the back of our Dodge Caravan when José and Amanda showed up with the dog thirty minutes later. With only a few terse words, Ricardo shut the tawny pit bull into the pen and the men drove away.

José scratched his head. "Where are they taking it?"

"Anti-Cruelty Society." Delores's voice quavered.

"Ha." José all but rolled his eyes. "That's a joke. Wait till they see the scars."

His mother winced. "José, my son, come." She put an arm around his waist, and they walked into the house together.

"Mom!" Amanda hissed at me. "What made Mr. Enriques—?"

I held up a finger that meant *later* and sent Amanda and Emerald to help dress the two younger girls—who no doubt told their own wide-eyed version of the police showing up—while I cleaned up the breakfast dishes. Even from the kitchen, I could hear the rise and fall of passionate voices in the front room as mother and son talked, even the occasional, "Praise You, *Jesús!*" and "*El Dios* is merciful, José."

No dishwasher. I filled up the sink with hot, sudsy water and slid the breakfast dishes under the suds. The soapy water soothed my rattled spirit.

*Oh Jesus, I'm not sure exactly what You did here this morning, but You are an awesome God! Thank You for honoring Delores's prayers!* I lined up the clean plates and cups in the dish drainer on one side of the double kitchen sink.

*Thank You for Amanda's persistence, bugging her dad to call Ricardo. Talk about "a little child shall lead them"!* Never had been sure exactly what that meant, but I did now. Even if she was a "big child."

I pulled out the spray hose and rinsed the dishes in the drainer. *And thank You for opening Ricardo's eyes to see the lie that almost destroyed this family . . .*

I thought about that while I dried the dishes and searched the neatly arranged cupboards for where to put them. *What lie?* The lie that God wasn't sufficient, that Ricardo had to resort to illegal means to make money for his family. The lie that he had to be macho and do it himself, rather than lean on God and the church family at *Iglesia del Espírito Santo.*

But, I thought, hunting for a cupboard holding pots and pans, how different was that from the rest of us, doing things our way, getting distracted from God's way, not listening, going off on tangents—maybe not *illegal* tangents, but still, trying to fix things on our own steam, by our own blueprint. And then we get all tangled up in our own mess. Sometimes God lets us flounder there a while, all tied up until we yell, "Uncle!" And sometimes . . .

I stood in the middle of Delores's spotless kitchen, holding the frying pan, as the miracle of that morning washed over me again. *Sometimes,* I thought, God snatches His children out of the quicksand we waded into ourselves and says, *There. I'm giving you another chance to trust Me.*

Another chance for Ricardo. Thank You, Jesus!

Another chance—like He'd given to me after the car accident that killed Jamal Wilkins.

"*Gracias,* Jodi." Delores stood in the kitchen doorway, short, loose dark hair framing a gentle smile on her round face. "Will I be able to find anything after you're done doing my dishes?" I turned, only then realizing my eyes and nose were running and my face was probably all blotchy.

"I . . . I was just thinking about God's mercy."

We just looked at each other for a long moment. And then we were in each other's arms, crying and holding and praying and thanking Jesus for all that mercy, all that grace God willingly squandered on us.

Never did find where to put the frying pan. I left it on the counter.

NO ARGUMENT WITH THE WEATHER THAT WEEKEND: temperatures securely in the sixties, October skies beaming with sunshine, and playful winds rattling elm trees until the leaves fell in little golden showers. The ushers propped open the double doors of our shopping center sanctuary on Sunday, letting the last of the good weather in—not to mention letting some of our good, rollicking praise music *out.*

I was so glad to see Florida on Sunday morning. Gave her a big hug, but she didn't seem her usual self. Tired, she said. I wanted to ask if Chanda had called about paying the bill from the city, but knew I'd be sticking my big foot in it if she hadn't. "Just pray for us, Jodi," she said. "Know what I'm sayin'?"

*Oh God, so many things to pray for!* I felt like I was falling down on the job. Should be praying for our church, which didn't even have a proper name yet. (Couldn't call it Uptown–New Morning forever.) Should be praying for Mark Smith's full healing, sitting over there beside his beautiful Nony, his wings clipped, the first quarter of Northwestern University's academic year in full swing without him. There was Becky with Little Andy on her lap, but at the end of the day Andy had to go back to his grandmother. Should be praying for *something* to move, the earth to shake, walls to come down so Little Andy could come home to his mother. And Stu, her heart enlarged with concern for others—but still estranged from her own parents. Avis and Peter, looking perfect and calm and compatible up there on the first row, but a wound in their blended family tore at Avis's heart. *Oh God, don't let it tear them apart!*

*And it's been a while since you've prayed for "that girl," Jodi,* nudged the still, small Voice in my spirit. *Pray, Jodi, pray!*

I felt so pressed in my spirit—not depressed, just urgent—that I went outside to sit on the porch swing later that afternoon just to pray. *Intercessory prayer,* Avis called it. Praying for others. Had a few thanksgivings too. Top of the list was the Enriques family. Still could hardly believe how God had put a hedge of protection around Ricardo yesterday!—for Delores's sake, I was sure. And I sure was thankful that Pastor Cobb had announced a church business meeting that morning for the second Sunday in November, encouraging all the members to be praying for God's wisdom how best to merge the leadership, activities, and ministries of both churches. *Thank You, Lord!* Knowing there would be a time to raise concerns and seek solutions would go a long way to calming fears and gossip. Get it all out on the table—

"Hey, Jodi. You busy?"

My eyes flew open. Becky Wallace was peering down at me over the railing of the outside stairs. "Not really. I mean, I was just praying. But that's OK. What's up?"

Becky scurried down the stairs and plopped herself on the bottom step, dressed in her favorite getup: skinny jeans, tank top, and jean jacket. "Talked ta my parole officer yesterday. Monitor comes off first week in November." She stuck out her left leg, the ankle monitor wedged between her gym shoes and the hem of her jeans.

"Oh! My goodness, Becky! That's wonderful!" Had it been six months *already*?!

"Yeah. Thought I'd go crazy sometimes, but the job really helps." She frowned. "Thing is, I been thinkin'—I want ta get a place of my own so I can work at makin' a home for Andy. Talked ta Flo 'bout renting that little apartment on their second floor. 'Bout all I can afford on part-time pay. She an' Carl real excited 'bout it, though. They didn't want just anybody livin' there, bein' so close to the boys' bedrooms an' stuff."

I kept a straight face. *But an ex-heroin addict and convicted felon of an armed robbery would be all right, as long as she's a Yada Yada sister. You've got a strange sense of humor, God!*

"But I'm kinda nervous 'bout tellin' Stu, after all she's done for me. Don't want her ta think I'm ungrateful. It's just . . ." Becky wasn't even looking at me, just leaning on her elbows and staring at the warped floorboards of the old, weathered porch.

I leaned forward too. "You can't worry about that, Becky. Living with Stu was just the first step. Of *course* you need to get your own place." *Might even be a relief to Stu,* I thought. But I didn't say it.

"So could you help me pray about it, Jodi? I'm still not so good at talkin' ta God. I just know I wanna get Andy back real soon. But . . ." Worry lines between her eyebrows puckered. "I wanna be strong, not get tempted ta slip back into the old ways. Know what I mean?"

Oh wow. That was a biggie. Living on her own, no supervision, no roommate, maybe months still to go before she got through all the red tape of getting Andy back. She'd only been clean one year, counting her time in prison.

I left the swing and joined her on the bottom step, taking her hands in mine. Long, thin fingers, nails cut short, skin rough from digging in our flowerbeds. Could use some hand cream. "You pray just fine, Becky. But thanks for asking me. I feel honored to pray with you about this."

I did too. Honored to be part of the miracle that was Becky Wallace.

TEMPERATURES ZOOMED INTO THE EIGHTIES the third week of October before nose-diving into the forties on the last Sunday. A nippy reminder that summer was over and winter was just around the corner. The time changed, too, from daylight savings to central standard. "Spring forward, fall back"—gotta turn all the clocks back one hour.

At least this year I remembered. Last year we did the Baxter hurry-scurry to get to church on time—and the door was locked, the street empty. Thought my kids might disown me forever for getting them up an hour *early*, but as it turned out, the Hickmans forgot, too, so we all went out for breakfast. All the Baxter and Hickman kids had so much fun, they said we should "forget" next year too.

Well, here it was next year. Why not? I called Florida and asked if they wanted to meet somewhere for breakfast on Sunday to celebrate the time change. "Nah, don't think so, Jodi. Thanks for thinking of us, though."

*Nah, don't think so? That's it?* "Oh, come on, Flo! We had fun last year, and you could use a little fun."

"Could use a little more sleep is more like it. Look, Jodi, I 'preciate the thought, but that was a whole year ago. Things was different. Now I'm doin' good to get Carl an' me an' the kids to church *period*. But I'll try to make it to Yada Yada this time. Where we meetin'?"

So we didn't have breakfast out—couldn't talk my kids into it, either, especially if no one else was coming—but we did have a good turnout at Yada Yada later that day. Chanda begged us to meet at her new house, now that she had a nanny-housekeeper to finally get the house in shape, to have a "house blessing" like we did at the Hickmans.

Florida sounded a lot spunkier when she showed up at Chanda's than she had yesterday on the phone. "Girl," she said, looking Chanda up and down, "you lookin' good for somebody who's gettin' all them radiation treatments. How often ya have to do that thang? Ain't your hair s'posed to fall out or somethin'?"

Chanda was making the most of being queen bee, seated in her plush recliner, feet up, while the rest of us milled around, admiring the new house and sampling the dry roasted peanuts, chocolate candies, and dried fruit from little bowls placed around the room. "Sundays are mi best days. Two days rest since mi last treatment! But Monday tru' Friday? Ever day, go to de hospital, ever day after feel lak de truck run mi over. An' t'ree weeks to go!" She shook her head and waved a grateful hand in the air. "But praise Jesus! Still got mi hair! It's dat chemo make de hair fall out. T'ank You, Jesus!"

As long as Chanda was praising, we decided to go ahead and do the house blessing while we waited for the last few Yadas to arrive— Ruth and Yo-Yo, specifically. "*Sí*, might as well." Delores agreed wryly. "There's no way Ruth is going up those stairs anyway."

We clumped up to the second floor, sounding like a herd of hef-falumps. The house was a four bedroom, two and a half bath. Cheree and Dia each had a separate room, as well as Thomas and Chanda. No guestroom. The housekeeper—Chanda introduced her as Yohanna Popescu—must not live in. But all the rooms were spotless. A sense of order pervaded the house.

"Lord, thank You for Yohanna!" I prayed as we came out of Chanda's bedroom with its new bedroom suite, all scrolls and flour-ishes. (Nony had prayed for the Holy Spirit to speak to Chanda in the midnight hour; Delores had prayed for sweet rest. I wasn't sure if those prayers negated each other or not! Well, let God sort it out.) "Thank You for the gift Yohanna is to this family, especially as Chanda goes through radiation treatment and regains her strength. Bless Yohanna and the Popescu household as well."

The Romanian housekeeper must have heard her name, because she stood at the bottom of the stairs as we came down. "Thank you," she said to me in a heavy accent. "She appreciate it very much," pointing to herself and giving me a shy smile.

I wanted to hug her but decided not to push my cultural igno-
rance.

Ruth finally made it, huffing and waving off our chorus of
"How are you?" "What, you want details? I'm here, that's as good as
it gets," she said, taking over the queen bee's recliner. Chanda lifted
an eyebrow when she came into the room but said not a word, taking up residence on the cushy couch.

Avis kept the rest of the meeting fairly short, given the thor-
ough "house blessing" we'd done. (We'd even prayed over the
garage and the Lexus.) We made a lot of noise rejoicing over
Delores's answered prayer for her husband and God's mighty inter-
vention last weekend. Also did some whooping and praising when
Becky, hardly able to contain herself, said that next time Yada Yada
met, she'd finally be a free woman.

"Oh, my sister!" Nony bestowed one of her megawatt smiles on
BW. "Yes, God wants you free. But write this scripture on your
heart." She flipped open her heavily underlined Bible. "This is what
Jesus said about freedom: 'If you abide in My Word, you are My
disciples indeed. And you shall know the truth, and the truth shall
make you free!'"

"That's in the *Bible*?" Yo-Yo blurted. "Man, I hear that all the
time. 'The truth will make you free, dude.' But if ya ask me, everybody has their own idea what truth is."

"Exactly," Nony said gently. "We pick and choose pieces of
God's Word, and it sounds good even to the world." She held up
her Bible. "But Jesus said, 'If you *abide in My Word*,' that's the truth
that will make you free."

There was suddenly a lot of page turning as we all looked up
what Jesus said in John 8, in our various translations.

"Speaking of someone who needs to be free . . ." Hoshi's careful Japanese accent stilled the page turning. "I would like to invite my friend Sara to visit Yada Yada, the girl I met in my history class. She—I do not know how to say this exactly—needs friends so much, but she doesn't let anyone close to her. More than that, she needs Jesus. But . . ." She shrugged. "Since we are meeting at our house next time"—she pointed to herself and Nony—"it's close to campus, and I thought maybe she would come."

We looked at each other. A few gave a shrug. For myself, I thought thirteen Yada Yadas was plenty! Could hardly keep up with each other as it was. But how did we say no to someone who needed Jesus?

We didn't. We all said, well, OK. Next time.

# 39

November blew in cold and nasty—and so did Stu, showing up at our kitchen door one evening while I was writing reports for parent-teacher conferences. I took one look at her scowl and put on the tea water. "You need chamomile—or valerian," I said, taking two hot mugs out of the dishwasher, which was on the Dry cycle.

Stu plopped herself on the kitchen stool and glared at me. "Not valerian. Hate that stuff. So, did you know that Becky's been talking to Florida about renting their apartment?"

I could pretend innocence. Or I could 'fess up. Better get it over with. "Um, yeah. She asked me to pray about it with her." I found the box of assorted herbal teas; no chamomile. "Peppermint? Out of chamomile."

"Oh, great. So I'm the last to know, is that it?" She ignored the box of tea bags I was holding out to her. "How ungrateful can that sorry excuse for a druggie mother be? And what a dumb idea! Does she have *any* concept of how hard it's going to be to get Andy back?

She couldn't even keep her nose clean living *here*! Should've reported her that night we caught her smoking weed on the front porch—"

The teakettle screeched. I poured hot water over two peppermint tea bags.

Stu got off the stool and began to pace up and down our boxcar kitchen. "What's going to happen when all the restraints are taken off, huh? Tell me that. When her old druggie friends start coming around again, like the loud-mouthed jerk I found in my living room that night, eating all my food. When she's free to go wherever. When no one's looking over her shoulder. She's going to mess up her chances to get Andy back big-time."

"Here. Drink your tea." I held out a mug of peppermint tea laced with honey. The minty aroma spiked the air.

Stu stopped pacing. "Did I say I wanted some tea? That's the trouble with you, Jodi Baxter; you think everything in the world can be fixed with a pasta dish or a mug of hot tea! Why *didn't* you tell me about Becky planning to move out? Don't you think *I* had a right to know? Some Yada Yada friend *you* are."

"Whoa, whoa, whoa!" Was I shouting? I took a big breath and dialed it down, then put the mugs of tea back on the counter with a *thump*, sloshing tea everywhere. "Look here, Leslie Stuart. Don't make this personal between *us*. I didn't think it was my place to be telling you what Becky was thinking. She needed time to think. She asked me to pray with her about it. And just because she wants her own place doesn't mean she's ungrateful. Good grief! She *told* me she appreciated everything you've done for her. But that ankle monitor came off this past week. *Off!* Can you imagine the freedom she feels? Probably so giddy she feels like she could fly—could do anything."

Stu just looked at me. I took a chance and laid a hand on her arm. "Believe me, Stu, I know this affects you too. I don't know anyone who would've done what you did, taking Becky in. But honestly, I thought this might be good news. You've been taking care of Becky's mess in one way or another for a whole year. Maybe it's time to get your own life back—your apartment, anyway. And it's her decision." I grinned. "At least you're not having to kick her out."

Stu absently grabbed a dishrag, mopped up the spilled tea, and picked up a mug. She blew on the tea and took a sip. I let out my breath slowly. Guess she wasn't going to go off on me. "Yeah," she mumbled. "But we'd worked out most of the kinks. And I'd kinda gotten used to having someone around. Especially Little Andy on Sunday."

A renegade tear slid down her cheek. "Guess she won't need me to pick him up any more. And he—he started calling me Auntie Stu. But now . . ." Her eyes met mine, stricken. "Oh, Jodi."

I plucked the shaking mug of tea out of her hand and wrapped Stu into my arms. "Oh, Stu, I know, I know . . ." I should have known, anyway. Should have known that Andy had wiggled his hot-chocolate-with-whipped-cream self right into the empty, aching spot left behind by Stu's own missing child. Heaven's angel named David.


WHILE I WAS BAGGING UP THE INGREDIENTS for a taco salad the next Sunday before church, I saw Becky and Stu heading for the garage. Probably going to pick up Andy. *Huh.* We'd have a woman president in the White House before Becky Wallace got a car. I had an idea she'd welcome "Auntie Stu" still doing pick-ups for the weekly visits.

The church business meeting that had been announced for that Sunday had somehow morphed into a potluck meal. Somebody was smart. People would probably be more mellow and friendly after eating together. The fact that it was falling on the second Sunday might also ease some of the grumbling from Uptown folks, who'd felt overlooked last month. Today, at least, we'd have a chance to make a decision together about stuff like a monthly potluck.

Or not. It got put on the agenda, along with "New chairs!"— Stu's impassioned plea—but it became apparent others had more critical things to talk about. Like what, exactly, was our leadership structure? Would former elders and deacons from both churches simply double up, or would new ones be chosen? Who had input into our music and worship style? Would we have age-graded Sunday school classes for the kids, or a children's ministry with the kids younger than teens all together?

The discussion got pretty intense, in spite of tons of cold fried chicken (we didn't yet have a functioning kitchen), potato salad, lukewarm baked beans, taco salad, chips and more chips, fruit platters, and veggie trays. One grievance that got a lot of "amens" was that some of these things should have been decided before we actually merged—leadership structure, for one.

Pastor Cobbs, who was moderating the meeting, leaned aside and conferred with Pastor Clark who sat nearby. *Mutt and Jeff, bless 'em.* Pastor Clark hunched over, all arms and legs in that wobbly chair, nodded, made some murmured comments, and then sat back. Pastor Cobbs took the mike again. "As your pastors, Pastor Clark and I agree that in many ways the 'urgent' has crowded out the 'important.' We apologize for failure on our part to chart a systematic path toward merging Uptown and New Morning."

I poked Denny. Pastors who could apologize were a good sign.

Pastor Cobbs cleared his throat. "Admittedly, we are sailing in uncharted waters. We have no maps. That's why the list of concerns raised today is vital, and we thank everyone for your input. But one thing is clear: there is no way we can reach agreement today on all the issues we've put on our agenda. We need to prioritize, and we need to be patient—"

"Pastor?" Sherman Meeks raised his hand, then stood stiffly to his feet. Beside him, his wife tugged on his jacket sleeve, but he ignored her. "I move that the two pastors *and* the present elders and deacons of both churches function as a Merger Committee, do the prioritizing, and bring the rest of us some proposals. It's more important for this here church to get things movin' than it is for all of us to have a say."

"I second that motion!" someone called out.

The two pastors exchanged glances. "All right. We have a motion and a second. Everyone in favor—"

There was a chorus of "ayes" all over the room.

"Opposed?" There were a few "nays" as well.

Pastor Cobbs looked pleased. "Well, then, maybe we should adjourn—"

"Pastor?" This time it was Debra Meeks who raised her hand. "I know things like the potluck we enjoyed today aren't exactly at the top of that priority list. But fellowship should be. We are two churches who've jumped into the same pot, and we need to get to know each other while all the structures and programs are getting hammered out. What better way to fellowship than around the table? So I move that we continue Uptown's tradition of Second Sunday Potluck. Make it temporary if you'd like."

"I second that motion!" Florida called out.

"I third it!" Becky Wallace said.

Laughter and a groundswell of clapping broke out around the room. Pastor Cobbs smiled and raised both hands. "I take it that's an 'aye'?"

Well, well. Bully good for Sherman and Debra Meeks. I caught Debra's eye and gave her a thumbs-up and my biggest grin.

"Pastors?" Avis Johnson-Douglass stood to her feet. Her hair was swept into a French twist in back, with soft tendrils falling on one side. She wore an elegant shawl with rosy flowers on a dusky background. I felt a pang. Avis's loveliness always shone from the inside out, almost breathtaking. Did she know how beautiful she was?

"—our first priority should be prayer," she was saying. Obviously, she wasn't thinking about her loveliness. "Prayer for our pastors, prayer for the current leaders as they tackle the things on that agenda. Prayer for the Holy Spirit to make this merger a light and a witness to the world. Not programs and structures first. Prayer first." She sat down.

"I second that too!" Florida sang out.

By the time the first business meeting of Uptown-New Morning broke up, it was three o'clock in the afternoon, the sun was already sinking westward, and we had four "temporary" decisions: an acting leadership group, two fellowship times (the men's breakfast got thrown in as a rider), and a weekly prayer meeting.

We'd done some good praying too. Now I couldn't wait to get home, get out of my nylons and heels, maybe soak in the tub, and get in my jammies early.

*That* little bubble burst when I saw Florida, Stu, Becky, and

Avis clustered around Nony by the front door, talking, shaking heads. All Yada Yada sisters. I smacked my forehead. "Oh, no," I groaned.

"What?" Denny was collecting our salad bowl and tongs.

"Yada Yada is supposed to meet at Nony's house tonight! But maybe Nony's canceling," I added hastily and headed in that direction. Who could blame her? It'd already been a long day. I'd go over and cast my vote for calling it off.

"YOU'RE *STILL* GOING TO YADA YADA TONIGHT?" Denny looked at me as if I'd just announced a trip to the moon.

"Not if it was up to *me*," I grumbled. "I think everybody wanted to cancel, even Nony, but Hoshi invited somebody from school and I guess she's coming. Nony didn't want to disappoint Hoshi or her guest." I sighed. "And then there's Delores and Edesa and Ruth and Yo-Yo and Adele and Chanda. It was Adele's birthday last week too. If we skip tonight, that means a whole month not seeing half the group or praying together."

Denny frowned. "Where was Hoshi? I saw her earlier, but not during the business meeting."

"She took Nony's boys home. Nony said she was preparing a special treat to have tonight since we were having a guest."

"Yeah, well ..." Denny sighed. "Guess I see why you can't cancel. But something's gotta budge, Jodi. You can't do church, potluck, business meeting, and Yada Yada all on the same Sunday."

I rolled my eyes and booted up the computer. "Tell me about it."

"What are you doing now?"

"Making a birthday card for Adele. 'Noble, kind'—remember?"

A wry smile slipped on his face. "Oh, right. Last year. When she wasn't speaking to anybody. Especially me."

I winced. "Oh, Denny. I'm sorry. I didn't mean to bring that up."

He waved me off. "Nah, it's OK. That was then. This is now." He left me to the computer. A moment later, he was back. "What's Mark going to do while you women 'yada yada'? Maybe I'll go along. It's been a while since we got to just hang out."

"WHAT? JUST ONE CARD? NO MONEY?" Adele's hoop earrings jangled as she shook the card several of us had managed to sign right under her nose that evening. "Last year y'all sent me a whole bunch of cards."

"Yeah, well, we were trying to kill you with kindness back then," I tossed back. "This year, one card, but you get twelve hugs. Well, maybe ten. Or eight." Not everyone had shown up. And those of us who had were stalling until Hoshi arrived with her guest.

Nonyameko swept in with Hoshi's special treat and set it on the coffee table of the family room as Adele read the inside of her card aloud: "'Adele. From the German *Adelheid'* . . . Adelheid!" she snorted. "Lord, have *mercy*. MaDear had no idea!"

I snatched the card. "Here, I'll read the rest. 'A combination of *athala*, meaning 'nobility,' and *heid*, 'quality,' meaning 'from noble ways.'" I simpered at her, and continued reading. "'Adele, you reign like a queen, lofty and serene, your words are few, but they always ring true. Happy birthday, our Noble Adele, from all the Yada Yadas!'"

Yo-Yo, Stu, and Becky clapped and whistled. Delores and Edesa laughed. "*Feliz cumpleaños*, Adele!"

But Adele just lifted an eyebrow at me. "Don't quit your day job, Jodi."

Yo-Yo eyed the little squares of flat cake. "Hey, Nony. Can we eat? What is it?"

"Hoshi said sweet rice-flour and coconut cake, or something like that," Nony said absently. "I wonder where she is? It's starting to get dark out there." She headed for the front door, her at-home caftan flowing with her.

I zipped after her. "Feel free to send Denny to pick them up if you want. He won't mind." By this time Nony had the door open. "Oh," I said. "Then again, maybe not."

Denny and Mark were standing in front of the Sisulu-Smiths' Audi sedan out by the curb, their heads under the hood with a trouble light.

Nony stood at the top of the stoop and peered down the street. The sun was gone, but streaks of pink and gold tipped the tops of the almost bare trees along the parkway, creating a blue and lavender twilight. "Oh, there they are." Relief almost giggled in her voice. She waved. "Hello Hoshi! Hello, Sara! Welcome!"

The two men pulled their heads out from under the car hood in casual curiosity as Hoshi and her friend approached the house. My insides smiled. Definitely a study in contrasts. Hoshi's willowy height and dark, swinging ponytail flowed along the sidewalk like a gentle stream. Her friend—shorter, pale eyes, yellow hair—scurried alongside with nervous rabbit steps. And somehow . . . familiar.

Suddenly the young woman with Hoshi stopped dead in her tracks. She stared at the two men, her pale eyes rounding in fright. Her head jerked and she looked toward us on the steps—but not at us. Looking at the house. But I had a full view of her face.

My heart tightened in my chest. I could hardly breathe.

"What is it, Sara?" Hoshi asked kindly, taking her arm.

The young woman's eyes locked on mine for half a second; then she took another frightened glance toward Mark and Denny. She jerked her arm out of Hoshi's grasp. "You—you *tricked* me! You brought me *here?*" Her voice was almost a screech. "How *could* you, Hoshi?!" And the pale young woman spun around and ran—*fled!*—back the way they had come.

Hoshi's hands flew to her mouth in total bewilderment as she watched her new friend disappear.

"Lord Jesus, have mercy on us! What was *that* about?" Nony hurried down the short walk to Hoshi's side. "Hoshi, are you all right?" Her arm encircled Hoshi's shoulders, pulling her close.

I looked at Denny. I looked at Mark. Neither man had said a word. Both men seemed in shock. They knew. *I* knew.

The young woman fleeing down the street had been to this house before. Had been at the racist rally with the White Pride people. Had probably been the one who'd bravely tipped off the police, leading to the arrests of the monsters who had beaten up Mark Smith and left him for dead.

The girl with no name I'd been praying for, for months.

"That girl."

Sara.

# 40

ark Smith muttered something sharp under his breath, shattering the frozen tableau. Throwing down the greasy rag he'd been holding, he strode quickly toward the house, stumbling on the bottom step. "Mark!" Nony ran after him. "Mark, be careful! What's wrong? Denny, come, please!"

My husband ran to Mark's side. Mark brushed off Nony's and Denny's help and stumbled inside on his own steam; the three disappeared inside.

Hoshi's eyes were wide with confusion. "Jodi? What is happening? I do not understand."

I took her hand. "Come on. Let's get inside out of this damp air." How did I tell her about this? She couldn't have known. She hadn't been to the rally. Had no reason to make a connection. Nony, either, for that matter.

In the family room, the waiting Yada Yadas started to babble welcomes as Hoshi entered, then faded when they saw she was alone. "Where's your friend?" Yo-Yo asked bluntly. "Thought she was comin' tonight."

I glared them all into silence with a shake of my head. I wished Nony would come back in. But minutes passed, and she didn't return. Avis hadn't made it tonight; too tired after the church marathon that day. Neither had Flo. So I held Hoshi's hand and told them that this girl, Sara, had been at the rally last spring with the White Pride people, that Mark had recognized her then as one of the pair passing out hate literature in this neighborhood. "And when she saw Mark outside this house tonight . . ."

Hoshi began to weep. "Oh. I have hurt Dr. Smith and Nonyameko. I have brought their enemy to this beloved house. They have given me a family, trusted me with their children—and look what I have done!" She buried her face in her hands, her dark hair spilling over her shoulder.

"Hoshi, baby." Adele's strong voice and massive presence moved to Hoshi's side. "Why you makin' this your fault? You didn't know who she was. Mark and Nony aren't going to blame you. They're bigger than that. Fact is, *God* is bigger. God knew who she was. God sent you to reach out to her, baby, to be her friend—"

"Yeah." Becky butted in. "An' ain't she the one who ratted on the guys who beat up Nony's husband? Doesn't that make her one of the good guys?"

"Well, we *think* she is. The papers never named her," I said.

Hoshi slowly raised her head and looked at Adele. "God sent me?"

"God sent you, honey." Adele laid a hand on Hoshi's silky head and began to pray. We all gathered around Hoshi, touching her, holding her hands, giving her tissues, praying words of comfort and hope and blessing for listening to God, for reaching out to that hurting girl in her class, for making her a friend. We prayed for Mark, who'd been through so much, who'd had a shock tonight. We prayed for Nony, who only tonight had learned the identity of Hoshi's friend.

And we prayed for Sara. *I* prayed for her. Prayed that she would know that Hoshi only wanted to be her friend, that what happened tonight wasn't a trick or a conspiracy. Just a holy coincidence. Prayed that she would be free of her connections to that hate group. Free to discover her real identity. And I thanked God—oh, how I thanked Him, hallelujah! And glory to Jesus!—that He had put a burden on my heart to pray for "that girl," and now God had given her a name: Sara.

"PRINCESS."

"What?" Denny was already in the bed, weary after sitting with Mark Smith for over an hour, listening to the feelings, the anger, the fear that seeing "that White Pride girl" had pulled from the deep place they'd been buried during his convalescence.

"That's what Sara means: 'Princess.'" I'd looked it up in my name book as soon as we got home.

Denny groaned. "Give it a rest, Jodi. Not everybody lives up to the meaning of their name. I'd say this one is a stretch." He buried his head under his pillow and groaned. "Turn off that light, will ya?"

BUT IT STUCK IN MY MIND all that week. *Sara. "Princess."*

It was a strange week, schoolwise. Veterans Day was a Monday holiday. (No school for the kids; slaving on midterm student reports for me.) Then two and a half days of school (mostly useless). Then a day and a half of parent-teacher conferences. Why the powers that be planned it that way, I'll never know. They never ask me, anyway.

*Oh God!* I prayed, as I trudged to school Tuesday morning, lugging my tote bag full of student reports, hunkering inside my fall jacket against the early morning nip. *Adele said none of this was an accident. You must have a plan for Sara! Is that how You see her? As a princess? Royalty. Beautiful. Graceful . . .*

It was a little hard to do—see her as a princess, that is. She was so plain! So pale. Even for a white girl. No healthy color. *Huh.* I'd love to see what miracles Adele could do with her. Not likely to happen, though. She wasn't likely to trust *any* of Hoshi's friends at this point.

I stopped in the school office to see Avis before heading to my classroom, but her office door was closed. Avis had missed out on the whole Hoshi-Sara fiasco Sunday night, and I hadn't talked to her since. Well, somebody else would have to fill her in; I had my hands full with thirty-one miscreants. Even my "good" kids were pushing on my last nerve. I did everything but bang on my desk with my shoe, trying to keep order.

*Good grief,* I thought, using the time-out chair for the third time that day. How did the school district expect us to teach anything with so many days out in one week? Another day like this, and I'd end up snarling at all the parents during conferences too.

But I kept sending up prayers—the old *"Help, Lord!"* kind. Help came when I remembered Amanda's flip advice last year: *"They're third graders, Mom. Play games. They all like to play games."* So I came to school on Wednesday with a large bag of assorted candies, a yardstick, and a book of Aesop's fables. We did fractions with the different colored candies and gobbled up the results. Measured their height in inches on a long sheet of butcher paper I'd taped to the door; then they had to figure out how tall they were in feet and inches. We ended the day acting out two of Aesop's fables in the Reading Corner. Carla Hickman's interpretation of the squeaky Mouse in "The Lion and the Mouse" had us all giggling.

They were squirrelly and loud all day—but fun squirrelly. Fun loud.

I felt good. I felt ready for parent-teacher conferences.


BUT I WAS DRAGGING by late Friday afternoon. I looked at my list of conferences still to go. Parents had signed up using the student's name: *5:30 Caleb Levy . . . 5:45 Mercedes LaLuz . . . 6:00 Carla Hickman . . . 6:15 Adam Turner.*

The end. Home. Dinner. Long bubble bath. Could hardly wait.

Couldn't blame Carl and Florida for signing up late in the day, if Carl was going to come after work. Well, good for him. He was working hard to be the provider and father, making up for lost time. Just hoped I was still coherent by the time they got here. I really did want to talk about Carla's progress and behavior issues in a professional situation. Teacher to parent. Hear their concerns too. I could tell them about her starring role in "The Lion and the Mouse," start off on a good foot, go over some of her reading progress, then discuss her short attention span and quick temper. Maybe come up with a school-and-home plan. Parents and teacher hand in hand, so to speak.

*So to speak.* Six o'clock came and went. Neither Florida nor Carl showed. I would have called in the next set of parents, but Adam Turner's mother arrived promptly at six fifteen, not a minute before. A gushy woman. Probably sold real estate. Bragged about Adam for ten minutes, how bright he was, maybe they should put him in a class for advanced students, didn't I agree? I let her gush. When she finally took a breath, I agreed Adam was bright. But he was also lazy. Did as little as possible to get by. He often lost his homework papers or didn't even take them home. Maybe we could work on that before we pushed him into a class for advanced students, didn't she agree?

OK, so I was a little snippy. Ms. Real Estate got off easy, because, truth be told, I was mad. Mad at Carl and Florida. The nerve! They stuck their daughter in *my* class and then didn't show for the first parent-teacher conference? I'd tried my best to limit discussions at church or Yada Yada of how Carla was doing in school, because I knew—yeah, *right*—I knew we'd have a chance to discuss stuff at the appropriate time.

Didn't figure on them just blowing off conference time. They'd signed up, hadn't they? How could I expect a third grader to follow through on tasks and be responsible if her parents didn't even show up for appointments? So what was *that* about?

I gathered up my things and headed toward the office to leave the conference sign-up list. Well, the Hickmans were going to get a call from me tonight. No nicey-nice teacher-talk either. I was going to give Florida a piece of my mind.

Avis's office door opened just as I came into the school office. She looked flustered. "Oh! Jodi. Just the person I want to see. I need—" She stopped, as if changing her mind. "Come in my office a minute, can you?"

I dropped my conference list in the tray and followed Avis into the door marked Principal. As she shut the door behind me, I was startled to see Rochelle slumped in a chair, arms wrapped protectively around Conny, who was playing with some sticky notes. She turned her face away, but I could see her eyes were puffy, red with crying.

"Jodi, is Edesa still volunteering at that women's shelter on the North Side?"

"Manna House?" I nodded. "Josh too. Most weekends. Friday night, all day Saturday."

"Do you know the add—"

"I don't *want* to go to a shelter, Mama!" Rochelle's eyes flashed, in spite of the puffiness. "I came to you for help, and you're going to send me to a *shelter*?" She stood up, hauling Conny up onto her hip. "Fine. It was a waste of time coming here."

"Sit *down*, Rochelle." The firmness in Avis's voice took me by surprise. "But you did come here. And I'm glad." Her voice softened. "What did you expect me to do at school? You can't stay here."

Rochelle rolled her eyes, still standing. "Oh. Well. I came *here* because if I showed up at your apartment, just Conny and me, Big Boss Man Peter would throw me out. But I thought my *mother* might take me home with her. Yours and daddy's home, Mama. Where we were always welcome until . . ." She pressed her beautiful mouth into a tight line and slumped back into the chair. Conny whimpered. She put the toddler over her shoulder and rubbed his back.

Avis closed her eyes a moment, steadied herself on the corner of the desk. Then she motioned me outside, shutting the door behind us. The office had cleared, though there were still a few stray parents and teachers out in the hallway. I closed the main office door, locked it, and turned the wands on the Venetian blinds covering the office windows between office and hallway. Diffused light filtering through the blinds bathed the office in a tranquil hush, as if the sound had been turned off.

I leaned against the door. I had never seen my friend look so stressed. "Avis," I whispered, "can't you just take Rochelle and Conny home with you tonight and decide what to do tomorrow? Peter isn't that mean; he wouldn't just kick them out, would he?"

She sank into an office chair and shook her head. "No . . . yes. I mean, if Rochelle would come just for one night, long enough to decide what to do, yes, that would be fine. Peter and I have even talked about that. But I'm afraid she's stubborn enough to do a standoff, and he'd literally have to throw her out to make her leave. We . . . I don't want that." Avis pressed her fingertips to her temples. "It's not like we haven't taken them in several times in the past few months. And I have to agree with Peter: *we* aren't the solution to this mess she's in. But . . ."

Tears slid down her face. Had I ever seen Avis cry? I could hardly imagine having to choose between my husband and my child—even if she was grown. And then Avis was weeping silently, shoulders shaking.

I grabbed some tissues from the box on the counter, pressed them into Avis's hand, and just held her and let her cry. Then, as her weeping calmed, I found the telephone and punched in my home number. "Josh? Hi, it's Mom. I need the address to Manna House. Are you or Edesa going there tonight? . . . Good! Avis is bringing her daughter and grandson there tonight; she's going to need a friend . . . What? What about Carl Hickman?"

I pressed the phone to my ear. Josh kept talking, but his words didn't compute. My mouth went dry. My heart seemed to hang, suspended, in my chest.

*No, noooo . . . this can't be happening!*

"What about Carl Hickman?" I heard Avis echo my own question. She blew her nose and looked at me as I hung up the phone.

I turned slowly to face her. "Carl and Florida didn't show for Carla's conference tonight. I was really mad too." *Oh God, forgive me!* "But Josh said Carl got a call at work this afternoon, around five o'clock. Chris was picked up by police along with some other guys, something about"—I tried to push the words out—"an armed robbery."

# 41

I don't believe it!" I told Denny. I paced back and forth in our kitchen while he opened a couple of cans of tomato soup and made grilled cheese sandwiches. "Chris is mixed up, doesn't always make the right choices—but he wouldn't take a *gun* and point it at somebody—no, no, no, I don't believe it." I grabbed the phone. "I'm going to try Florida again."

Still no answer. *Oh God! What is happening? Where are they? If they're at the police station, who's taking care of Carla and Cedric?*

"Jodi, sit down and eat. You're a wreck. You're making me a wreck." Denny balanced two small plates with the grilled sandwiches on top of two mugs of hot soup and carried them into the dining room. But I wasn't thinking about food.

"Some friend I am," I muttered. "Carl and Florida didn't show up for conference, but was I worried something might be wrong? Oh, no. I think they're blowing it off. That they don't care." I stared morosely at the steam rising from the soup mug.

Denny ate his soup and sandwich in silence. I resented the fact that he could eat. Didn't *he* care? Two of our best couple friends were in agony tonight over their children! Avis was probably still down at Manna House, not wanting to leave her daughter and precious grandson at a *shelter*, for heaven's sake! . . . Carl Hickman was probably at the police station; Florida too—unless she was still working two jobs. Why didn't I think of *that* possibility when she didn't show for Carla's conference?

The phone rang. I jumped, looked at the caller ID. *Hickmans.* "Hello?"

"Hey, Jodi."

Not Florida. Sounded like . . . "Becky?"

"Yeah. Just wanted to let you guys know that Stu and I are over here at the Hickmans—just got here actually—with Carla and Cedric. Florida called, asked us to come pick them up at the police station. Guess you probably heard about Chris."

Florida called Stu and Becky? Why didn't she call *us*?

I squeezed my eyes shut. *Oh Jesus, forgive me for making this about me.*

"I'm . . . I'm glad you and Stu are with Carla and Cedric, Becky. I was worried about them. And we only heard the bare bones about Chris from Josh—that he got picked up by the police." I couldn't bring myself to say *armed robbery.* "What do you know?"

"Only what Carl and Flo told us. Guess he hooked a ride home from school with some guys in a car; they stopped at a gas station. One of the guys ran in, pulled a gun, robbed the cash. Chris swears he didn't know anything about it! Guy ran back to the car, laughing . . . next thing Chris knows, police are all over the car, got all the kids spread-eagled, found the gun, cuffed 'em all."

Relief flooded my spirit. "But if Chris just happened to be in the

363

car, they can't keep him, can they? I mean, sounds like only one guy
went in the store."

"Huh. They still gonna book him. They got that Accountability
Law now. If you didn't do it but you're with the perp who did, they
gonna charge everybody with the same thing."

I licked my lips and looked at Denny, who was trying to piece
together this one-sided conversation. "Which is . . .?"

An entire two seconds of silence went by. "Armed robbery.
They're takin' him ta juvie."

*"JUVIE."* The Cook County Juvenile Detention Center.

I couldn't sleep. Were Carl and Florida still at the police station?
Florida must be going crazy. What was "juvie" like? As bad as the
stories we'd heard about Cook County Jail? The adult prisons?
Young man makes a mistake, gets incarcerated, comes out a bona
fide criminal. *Oh Jesus! Don't let this be the beginning of the end for
Chris.*

But maybe it didn't have to be. Both Becky and Yo-Yo had survived prison, and look at them now!

I heard Josh come in about midnight. I padded out into the
hallway in my robe and slippers. "Hey," he said. "You didn't have to
wait up."

"Didn't. Couldn't sleep. How are Rochelle and Conny?"

His grin slipped a little. "Not very happy campers. Mrs.
Douglass looked on the edge too. But . . . guess they're OK. Edesa
is spending the night with Rochelle, helping her get settled. She
didn't bring much—just one bag for her and the little guy. When I
left, they were trying to figure out how to go back to her house, get

her things without creating a big scene with Rochelle's husband."
He yawned, stretching. "You should go to bed, too, Mom. 'Night."

*Yeah, right.* How could I go blissfully to sleep if Avis was still
down at the shelter, hating to leave her precious daughter there
alone? How could I crawl into my comfy bed when Florida was
probably lumped in some uncomfortable plastic chair at the police
station, worried sick what was going to happen to her boy?

I made some hot milk with honey and curled up in the recliner
in the dark living room. Willie Wonka, confused by all this nighttime wandering around, heaved a sigh and stretched out on the
floor beside me. The tree branches outside our bay windows were
bare. Occasional car lights lit them up, like skinny arms lifted
toward heaven . . .

I should pray. I used to pray in the nighttime for Hakim Porter
last year. Everyone said God had put the brother of the boy I'd
killed in my classroom for a reason. Why hadn't I been praying like
that for Carla and Chris? Maybe my prayers for Hakim had been
selfish, because I wanted—needed—him to succeed and learn and
be healthy to exonerate *me*. Had God put Carla in my classroom for
a reason? Brought our families together for a reason?

To stand with each other. To pray, if nothing else.

*Oh God, I'm trying to pray, to learn what it means to use "spiritual
weapons," but I still fail so often. Forget to pray until things fall apart.
Forgive me, Lord! But I'm praying now, for my hurting friends and
their hurting children . . .*

"HONEY? JODI?"
Denny's voice swam somewhere above my head. I opened my

eyes. He was leaning over me, hands resting on the arms of the recliner. "I'm going to pick up Ricardo for the men's breakfast. Invited Ben, too, but he's coming on his own. If Carl's not there—my guess is he won't be—I'm going to stop by the Hickmans to see him before I come home. Hey, Jodi! Wake up. I'm leaving."

I blinked at him and smacked my dry lips. "Mm, yeah, OK. Got it."

My neck ached from lolling at a strange angle in the recliner. I briefly considered crawling into my bed and going back to sleep, but I finally lowered the footrest with a *whump* and meandered into the kitchen, wrapped in the afghan my grandmother had crocheted. The coffeepot was half-full of hot coffee . . . the swing on the back porch danced in a stiff November breeze . . . the birds pecked hopefully at the empty birdfeeder.

Saturday was up and running. I might as well be too.

I was lugging laundry down to the basement when I heard clumping feet on the back stairs and knocking at our kitchen door. I ran up the stairs and pulled open the door. "Becky! What's up? You guys just getting back from the Hickmans? What's happening to Chris?"

"Uh . . ." Becky looked as if she was sorting through my questions, then she shrugged them off. "Just wanted to tell ya I'm movin' today into that little apartment above the Hickmans."

"Becky! I thought you weren't gonna move till the end of the month—Thanksgiving weekend or something." I pulled her inside and shut the door. November was flexing its muscles today.

"Yeah, but we talked this morning when she an' Carl finally got back from the police station—hey, can I have some of that coffee?" She poured herself a cup. "They booked all the boys, took 'em to juvie. It's gonna be a long haul till Chris gets a hearing; they gotta get a lawyer, all that stuff. We decided it'd be helpful if I moved in early—ya know, another adult in the house for Carla and Cedric when they gotta be gone."

*Whew.* My head was spinning. Chris had been charged and taken to the detention center, the Hickman family probably felt like that game of Fruit Basket Upset, and Becky was moving out. In. At the Hickmans.

I found my voice. "Wow. Yeah, guess it makes sense to move now. But I'm sure gonna miss you, Becky."

"Yeah. Me too." She suddenly stooped down and scratched the dog's ears. "'Specially Willie Wonka. Gonna miss me, Wonka? Huh? Huh?"

OK, I wasn't going to take that personally. "Uh, do you need some help moving or anything? The minivan's not here this morning, but maybe this afternoon . . ."

Becky stood up. "Nah. I don't have that much stuff. Stu said she'd try to fix me up with some of the basics. Maybe go to a few garage sales, get dishes, pots and pans, stuff like that."

"I've got a better idea." I laughed. I *really* laughed. That's what Stu always used to say when I tried out one of my ideas on Yada Yada. Well, this time, *I* had a better idea. "What you need, Becky Wallace, is a housewarming party. We're going to make it happen! But you need to register at Target and Linens 'n Things—places like that."

Becky's face was blank. "Register?"

I laughed again and gave her a hug. *Oh God, it feels good to laugh even when our hearts are full of pain!*

DENNY STILL WASN'T HOME BY ONE O'CLOCK, so Stu and I took Becky to register at Target in the Celica. It was like shopping with a new bride. She was starting from scratch. We'd need more people than just Yada Yada to get all the basic stuff she needed— and we did have to explain that these were just *suggestions* of what folks could get for her, that she probably wasn't going to get it all.

Denny was home when I got back, making himself a late lunch. He'd been over at the Hickmans, said Carl seemed to appreciate that he'd stopped by. "They believe Chris, that he didn't have anything to do with the robbery, but he's going to need a good lawyer. Right now, he's been assigned a public defender. But it's going to be tough. Some of the guys in the car were known gang members, probably pulled the stunt to prove their stuff. It's a tough lesson for Chris about who you hang around with."

He swigged a glass of milk as he leaned against the kitchen counter, then waggled his eyebrows at me. "Hey. Ben Garfield showed up at the men's breakfast. All the Uptown guys were glad to see him again; we introduced him to Pastor Cobbs, Sherman Meeks, some of the New Morning men. At the end, when it was time to pray, Ben asked us to pray for his babies. That's what he said: 'Pray for my babies.'"

I stared at Denny. That was *huge*. Ben Garfield had asked prayer for *his babies*?

I finally had a chance to talk to Florida on the phone later that day. "Florida, I'm so sorry about Chris. You must be going out of your mind! But we want to stand with you through this, whatever it takes. The rest of Yada Yada too."

Did I know what I was saying? What *would* it take?

She was quiet a long time. "Yeah. I guess. I'm just . . . tired of talkin' 'bout Chris, worryin' 'bout Chris, everybody askin' 'bout Chris, prayin' for Chris. People get all holier than thou, poor Florida, sure glad *my* kid's not in some mess—know what I'm sayin'? Don't really want to talk about it right now."

*Whoa.* I heard *"back off"* and *"don't want you and your perfect little family to feel sorry for me."* But if I hung up that phone—no. I got stubborn. "Don't do that, Florida. Don't bottle it all up and try to carry this on your own. Isn't that what we've learned in Yada Yada? That Scripture tells us to carry each other's burdens?"

"Know what, Jodi? I'm not bottling it up or goin' out of my mind, like you said. Not feelin' all upset. I'm really OK. Fact is, you really want to know what I'm feelin'?"

"Well . . . sure."

"Relieved."

# 42

*elieved?* Didn't understand it at first. But I shut up and listened. Flo said she'd been sick with worry for months, dreading that Chris would get caught up in a gang, end up in jail, or get shot in a drive-by like so many other young black men.

"But I been prayin' for that boy, Jodi. Askin' God to do whatever it takes to turn him around. An' while I was sittin' there at the police station, bein' ignored by the officers, waitin' ta find out what was happenin' . . . I suddenly felt the peace of God come all over me. Like God was sayin', *Well, you said, 'Do whatever it takes.'* An' this mornin', when I woke up after gettin' a few hours' sleep, I realized I wasn't worried for the first time in months. Felt big relief, in fact. I knew where Chris was. He wasn't out on the street. He wasn't dead. He wasn't skippin' school. Did you know they got a decent school at juvie? Kids can keep up with their schoolin', even get their GED while they waitin' for the system to bring up their case." She snorted. "Course, can't promise you I ain't gonna be mad again on Monday. *Mm!* Jesus, help us!"

# The y a d a y a d a Prayer Group Gets Caught

I SAW FLORIDA TALKING TO AVIS the next morning at church. Made me realize a *lot* had happened since Yada Yada met a week ago at the Sisulu-Smiths, stuff that couldn't wait until our next meeting to pray about. And then there was Hoshi—had anyone called her to find out if she'd talked to Sara since the fiasco last Sunday night? I knew I hadn't—not with everything else that had happened this week.

But I saw her come in with the Sisulu-Smith family, so I pulled her aside before the service started. "Hoshi, I'm so sorry I didn't call you this week. I've been praying for you and Sara, though. Did you get a chance . . .?" I stopped as her almond eyes lowered. "Hoshi? Are you OK?"

She nodded. "But Sara didn't come back to class all week. I am so worried. Now that I know her background, I realize entering university was a big step for her. I wish I knew where she lived or had a telephone number for her. But . . ." Her eyes lowered again. "I don't know if she will talk with me again."

"We'll keep praying, Hoshi. I don't believe God is finished here yet, like Adele said. God chose you to be her friend."

I was going to ask if she was at peace with Mark and Nony over what happened last Sunday—but just then the sax player and praise team launched the worship service with "Let everything that hath breath praise Him!" Hoshi quickly slipped into the row next to Nony, who gave her a sweet smile. Guess that answered my question.

The gospel song was new to me, but Denny and I sat next to Debra and Sherman Meeks, which helped. "Lift up those hands and praise Him . . . Clap those hands all ye lands . . ." Out of the corner of my eye, I saw Little Andy Wallace in the aisle clapping his hands happily, then jumping up and down when the praise team sang, "Move those feet, get out of your seat, It's time to praise Him!"

*Oh God, thank You for bringing Becky into Your kingdom! Lord, for Little Andy's sake, we want to take back all that Satan stole from her.*

To my surprise, the praise team wound up the worship with a hymn: "On Christ the solid rock I stand, all other ground is sinking sand . . ." Everyone seemed to know the words; the singing was deep and soulful. As we sang the third verse—"When all around my soul gives way, He then is all my hope and stay"—I heard Florida shout, "*Thank* ya, Jesus! Thank ya! Oh, thank ya." And on the other side of the room, I heard Avis cry, "Glory! Glory to You, Jesus!"

The hymn stuck in my throat. I couldn't imagine being in their shoes—my daughter and grandson in a shelter? My son arrested for an armed robbery he didn't do?—and yet there they were, shouting, "Thank You!" and "Glory!"

*Oh God! Give me that kind of faith! Faith in You, no matter what.*


I SENT OUT AN E-MAIL to Yada Yada that afternoon with new prayer requests, tried to keep it brief and not say more than necessary about Avis's daughter or Chris Hickman. Also included the news that Becky had moved over to the Hickmans, needed a lot of household stuff, and could we give her a housewarming party?

Chanda was the first one to respond—by phone. "Sista Jodee! What you tinking 'bout where to have dat party? Mi tinking me house would be good."

"Really? That'd be great, Chanda. Except . . . aren't you still getting those radiation treatments? You said fatigue was a big problem."

"Oh, girl. Dat be true. Mi boobs draggin' like a cow wit short legs. But dis week be de last. I'm tinking if we can wait till Tanksgiving weekend, mi have one whole week ta be mi self."

I laughed so hard over the "cow with short legs" that I forgot to tell her that one week to recover from six weeks of radiation didn't sound realistic to me. But I let it go. If Chanda thought she could, maybe it was good therapy.

That third week of November passed in a blur. At school, Carla came with her hair uncombed and took it out on the other kids. But this time I saw the scared little girl, afraid her family was falling apart again. At lunchtime, I asked if she'd like to eat in the classroom with me. "S'posed ta get a hot lunch," she said warily. "But Mama forgot ta give me money."

"My treat," I said, though how anyone could call a slice of cold cardboard pizza and canned fruit cocktail a "treat" is beyond me. I added chocolate milk. As we munched, I told her I knew about her brother being in jail, how sorry I was, and anyone would be upset. I gambled: "Would you like to move your desk close to mine this week?"

Her eyes narrowed. "You givin' me a punishment?"

Bright little girl. But I shook my head. "Nope. A treat. You could be my special helper, pass out papers, pick them up, stuff like that."

She frowned.

"And," I added, "having your desk close to mine would remind me to pray for you and your mom and dad and Chris."

"An' Cedric?"

I smiled. "And Cedric."

"An' Becky? She livin' in our house now."

I smiled bigger. "And Becky."

BY THE TIME THE WEEKEND ROLLED AROUND, the temperature had moved back up into the sixties and it felt like Indian summer again. Half my class had sniffles from the up-and-down temperatures, and I didn't feel so hot myself. But Yada Yada was meeting at my house that Sunday, so I bucked up, sucked on my zinc lozenges, and downed copious amounts of orange juice. I really didn't want to get sick with Thanksgiving right around the corner. Who wanted to spend a four-day weekend in bed?

Thanksgiving . . . hadn't given it much thought. But the bowl of candy corn I put out for Yada Yada Sunday night got me thinking. Last year—*oh Lord, was it only a year ago?*—Nony and the boys had been in South Africa, so we invited Mark Smith and Hoshi Takahashi to be our guests. On the way to our house, Mark and Hoshi had been pulled over by police for no reason except "driving black" in a white neighborhood, and maybe to check out why a black guy was driving with a "light" girl. *Sheesh.*

But it gave me an idea. Maybe we should do a reprise and invite *all* the Sisulu-Smiths for Thanksgiving this year, and Hoshi too. Might be good for Mark to get out of his housebound state.

The doorbell started ringing; Yada Yadas started arriving. Well, I didn't have time to ask Denny about it, but maybe I could check it out with Nony tonight, see if they had any other plans.

We had a good turnout that night—even Ruth showed up with her inexplicable knitting, every part of her rounder and plumper than the last time I'd seen her. "You are looking *good*, girl!" I laughed, giving her a big hug.

"*Humph*," she snorted. "Mashed-potatoes-slathered-in-gravy good? Or a one-humped-camel good? Water I'm storing like one."

She sank onto the couch like a sinking ship settling underwater. I did wonder how many of us it would take to get her up again.

I thought maybe we'd skip worship and spend more time in prayer, given the number of critical situations that needed prayer this week. But Avis took us to Isaiah 61, reading the first three verses in her New King James Bible. "The Great Exchange," she called it: "Beauty for ashes! . . . the oil of joy for mourning! . . . garments of praise for a spirit of heaviness!"

"Here. Let me read that in my Bible," Florida insisted. We ended up reading it four or five times in different versions, each one driving the words deeper and deeper into our spirits. I heard sniffles all around the room.

"That is so beautiful," Hoshi said, her voice almost a whisper. "'Beauty for ashes' . . . That is what I want to pray for Sara." Seeing the questions about to pop, she held up a slim hand. "Yes, I have a little good news. Sara came back to class this week. She avoided me the first day, but on the second day, we talked a little."

"Uh-huh. All right, now!" said Adele.

"She was nervous but finally told me she had hoped to be anonymous on this campus, just go to school and put all that White Pride stuff behind her. So when I brought her to Yada Yada, and she saw Dr. Smith and recognized the house—recognized you, too, Jodi, from the rally—she was afraid her past had caught up with her. That's why she didn't come to school the next week. I tried to tell her the Smiths were grateful for what she did, telling the authorities who was responsible for the attack on Dr. Smith, but she didn't want to talk about it. But"—Hoshi smiled at Adele—"if God chose me to be her friend, I won't stop now."

"Oh, thank You, precious Lord, for those promises!" Nony cried out. And there we were, pouring out our hearts in thanksgiving—*thanksgiving!*—that God was bigger than all the trouble in our lives. Bigger than Mark's long road back to health . . . bigger than the shock of discovering Hoshi's friend Sara had been in the White Pride group . . . bigger than Chris Hickman ending up in the juvenile detention center for an armed robbery he hadn't committed . . . bigger than Rochelle's flight from her desperate marriage, with nowhere to go . . . bigger than Ruth (oh dear, I snickered at that, couldn't help it) getting pregnant "late in life."

But my private smile quickly faded and I added my own P.S. to the prayers for Ruth: *Oh God, Ben is still scared about the possibility of Tay-Sachs. Thank You, God, that You are bigger than Tay-Sachs! Bigger than Ben's worry! Bigger than—*

The prayers had quieted. A rustling filled the room as heads lifted, noses were blown, people helped themselves to another cup of tea from the carafe I'd set out on our beat-up old coffee table. Stu cleared her throat and broke the silence. "Well, if I say it, then I have to do it, right?"

"Say what?" Yo-Yo said.

Stu took a deep breath. "OK. I've been thinking maybe I should go home for Thanksgiving—you know, visit my mom and dad."

*"Gracias, Jesús!"* Delores lifted a hand in the air.

Stu tucked a stray wisp of blonde hair behind her ear. "The family reunion didn't work out last summer—probably wouldn't have been the best way to, you know, get our relationship back on track even if my parents had come. But . . ." She blew out a breath. "Becky's moved on, and Jodi's been telling me it's time to take care of my own mess."

I hid a grin. Stu was quoting *me?*

"Well, my biggest mess right now is that I'm not speaking to my parents, or maybe vice versa. But . . ." Tears slid down her face. "I'm the one who pulled away when I got pregnant. I was too ashamed. Then I got, you know, the abortion, and that terrified me even more, what they'd think of me. But God's been telling me the only way to untangle the mess I'm in is to tell them the truth. You know, that verse we read a couple of weeks back: 'You shall know the truth, and the truth shall set you free.'"

"If you abide in My *Word*," Nony corrected gently, "*then* you will know the truth that can set you free.'"

"Abide?" Yo-Yo piped up. "What the heck does *abide* mean?"

We laughed. Hoshi, of all people, screwed up her face as if searching her English lessons. "*Abide*, I think, means to dwell in it, live in it, comply with it."

Stu smiled through the tears dripping off her chin. "All right. I got it. But please pray I'll have the courage to ask my parents to forgive me. Not just for the abortion, but for—for cutting them out of my life. But I know if I don't invest anything in my relationship with my parents, it's going to die. Maybe already has. But . . ."

"No, no, no. With God, *nothing* is impossible," Delores said emphatically. "Lord God of heaven! We come to You with our sister, Stu . . ."

Delores moved into an impassioned prayer for Stu. Others reached out and held her hands, murmuring assent. But Stu's words kept replaying in my mind: *"If I don't invest anything in my relationship with my parents, it's going to die."* What had I invested in my relationship with *my* parents recently? How long had it been since I'd seen them? When they came for my birthday a year ago? *A whole year ago?* They couldn't come for Josh's graduation because my mom's health kept them from traveling. So why hadn't we taken the time, made the effort to go see *them?*

I peeked at Ruth, sitting there so very pregnant, so eager for her babies to be born, willing to take all the risks to bring them to term. Had my parents felt like that when I was born? Duh! Of course they had! Hadn't Denny and I cried for joy when Josh had been born? Then again when Amanda came squalling into the world?

But would Denny and I one day spend Thanksgiving alone, because our kids were too busy with *their* lives, *their* friends, *their* activities? . . . Like us?

I could hardly wait for my Yada Yada sisters to leave. I had a phone call to make, a Thanksgiving invitation to propose. And it wasn't to the Sisulu-Smiths.

I CORNERED DENNY AND THE KIDS that night for an emergency family meeting. "I know it's last minute, but we haven't seen my folks for a long time. I'd really like to spend this Thanksgiving with them. In Des Moines."

Amanda pulled a pout. "Mo-om! I won't get to see my friends all vacation!"

"You see José every day at school," I tossed back. "You'll live."

Josh shrugged. "Sorry, Mom. I promised to help with the Thanksgiving dinner at Manna House. Why don't you just invite the GPs here?"

But the Voice in my spirit said strongly, *Make the effort to go see them. Invest, Jodi, invest.* "This is important to me, Josh. I'm sure there are other volunteers who can help at Manna House." *Avis and*

*Peter Douglass, for instance,* I thought wryly. "But no one can take your place visiting your grandparents. We need to do this."

I looked hopefully at Denny. Nothing happened if Dad wasn't on board. He rubbed his chin. "What about the dog? Becky moved out, and Stu's going to *her* folks."

OK. He almost had me there. "Details," I said. "We'll take Wonka with us if we have to."

When we got my parents on the phone, my mother was so happy she started to cry. Even my dad's voice got husky. "That's great, honey. We'll be so happy to see you. But I don't know about a big dinner. Your mom has arthritis in her hands now, can't cook like she used to."

"Dad, don't worry about dinner! We'll bring it—or cook it there, or whatever. Just stock up on a lot of popcorn and dust off the Scrabble. Your fireplace still work?"

To tell the truth, I was excited. I'd missed the family trip to New York last spring, when Denny took the kids to see the Baxter grandparents and do the Big Apple during spring break. The SARS scare had been rampant, and me without a spleen. But all I had now was a minor sniffle. And Des Moines was only a five-hour drive.

Well, I hadn't counted on the extra hour and a half it took just trying to get out of Chicago on Wednesday afternoon—after delivering Willie Wonka to the Hickmans for Becky to take care of. It was nearly seven o'clock by the time we got on I-80 heading west. I'd packed the usual bagel sandwiches with shaved chicken and cream cheese, so we didn't have to stop to eat. But by the time we got to the Iowa state line, Denny said he needed a nap. Josh took over the wheel, and I stayed up front to ride shotgun and navigate while Denny crawled into the third seat and zonked out.

Josh drove silently into the night for another half hour, broken only by bits of small talk as we left the Quad Cities behind and sailed smoothly along the interstate toward . . . home. I glanced into the second seat. Amanda was plugged into her CD player and curled up in her big yellow-and-black comforter from her bed at home. I glanced at Josh in the driver's seat, looking more and more like his dad, except for his scraggy hair, which hung around his ears in casual indifference. Couldn't wait to see how long it took my dad to comment *this* time. But mostly I wondered, what was going on in Josh's head? We didn't seem to talk much anymore. Why was that?

I decided to risk it.

"So when are we going to meet this Sue you've been dating?"

Josh shrugged, kept his eyes on the road. "Not really dating her. Just doing stuff. You know, a friend from work."

"Well, still. Dad and I like to meet your friends."

He cast a sideways glance at me. "I don't *want* you to 'meet' Sue, Mom. That would definitely send Sue the wrong message. She is *just* a friend."

"Oh. I just thought . . . I mean, maybe you had a new love interest, and we should—"

"Mom!" Josh hissed. He glanced in the rearview mirror, seemed satisfied that his father and sister weren't eavesdropping. "Look, Mom. I only have one 'love interest,' as you so delicately put it. That's right. *I . . . love . . . Edesa.* But she's not giving me two cents right now. So, I go out with friends, even hang out with some other girls. I'm just . . ." My stoic, six-foot son's voice caught, and he had to clear his throat. "I'm waiting."

His voice trailed off. I think I forgot to breathe. I kept my eyes fixed on the yellow dotted lines racing through the pool of light from our headlights. Finally, Josh spoke again, his voice barely a whisper, full of pain.

"I love her so much, Mom. But I don't know what to do."

# 43

*I* got out my travel pack of tissues and blew my nose. Wished God had travel packs of wisdom I could pull out. My son had just bared his heart to me, and like the doctor's creed—"First do no harm"—I didn't want to bungle this moment. Delores's words echoed in my head: *"Edesa talks about Josh all the time."* I'd brushed it off at the time. We all knew they were *friends.* But—did Josh mean something else to Edesa?

Finally I screwed up my courage. "Josh, does Edesa know how you feel? I mean, have you *told* her?"

In the glow of the panel lights, I saw the slight shake of his head. Well, who could blame him? He'd asked her to his prom and she'd said no. His mother and probably everyone else had pointed out the obvious: he was just out of high school and she was a third-year college student. To his credit, he'd pursued the relationship on a casual—but maybe deeper—level, asking her to come along with Uptown youth to Great America and as a chaperone for the girls at Cornerstone Music Fest. And now volunteering together at Manna House. The prom was then; what was Edesa feeling now?

I couldn't believe I was saying this. But I reached over and laid a hand on my son's knee poking through his ripped jeans. "I think you need to tell her. And then—leave it to God to work out His purpose."

THANKSGIVING WAS, WELL, DIFFERENT. Josh got my brothers' old room—the site of many sibling battles and Girls Stay Out signs posted on the door. Amanda slept in my old room up under the eaves of the two-story house, which still looked pretty much as I'd left it twenty-plus years ago. My ceramic collection of dogs and cats. The broken music box with the ballerina on top. The faded, flowered bedspread. The bookshelves were empty, though. I'd confiscated all my favorites and read them to my own kids.

Denny and I got the foldout couch in the living room, a backbreaker if there ever was one. We pulled the mattress off and actually slept quite comfortably on the floor. But it meant I heard every trip to the bathroom my parents took during the night. Four or five times between the two of them.

Still, Thanksgiving Day was fun in a visiting-the-grandparents sort of way. My dad cooked sausage and scrambled eggs and pancakes for breakfast, making a Mickey Mouse pancake for Amanda, just like he used to do when she was little. Denny and I got out of doing the dishes with a shopping run to a Hy-Vee Food Store that—hallelujah!—was open on Thanksgiving Day. From the deli, we loaded up on smoked turkey breast, Hawaiian salad (the kind with mandarin oranges, pineapple chunks, and marshmallows in a sweet, fluffy dressing; not *my* cup of tea, but Josh and Amanda—and my dad—loved it), ready-to-heat dinner rolls, and two bakery pies: pumpkin and apple. But Denny balked at the two cans of chicken gravy I'd put in the basket. "*Canned* gravy?"

"And just how are you going to make homemade gravy with no turkey drippings?" I shot back. But I had second thoughts when they charged us a buck-fifty per can. *Sheesh.* I could make gravy at home for pennies—maybe less.

If my dad ever said anything to Josh about his transformation from bald-with-a-single-topknot a year ago to hair now only inches away from the hippie look, I never heard about it. In fact, when we got back from the store, Josh and Amanda had my dad shouting with a noisy game of Dutch Blitz, while my mother suckered Denny and me into a game of Scrabble—then kept putting down five-letter words on triple-word-scores. *Sheesh.* When did my parents get so competitive?

But I knew what I was thankful for this Thanksgiving. Time to just hang out with my parents. For that matter, just hanging out with Amanda and Josh, which hardly happened anymore. *Thank You, Jesus! Thank You for Stu reminding me not to take my family for granted. And speaking of Stu—oh God! Cover her with Your grace as she goes back home. Help her parents run to her, just like the father of the prodigal son—*

"What?" Denny was adding up the scores. "Mom Jennings, are you sure you *only* got 235 points?! I'm shocked!" My mother giggled like a schoolgirl.

Later, as my dad prayed over our store-bought meal—a rather lengthy prayer that included my two brothers who were spending the holiday with their in-laws, a smattering of missionaries "in foreign lands far from home," and "all those in our own country without the comforts and blessings we enjoy"—I peeked at my parents holding hands with Josh and Amanda on either side of them. My dad's voice was still commanding, even if his hair had lost the battle. My mom's finger joints, however, looked swollen and misshapen with arthritis. How painful was it? All the ads on TV made it sound like arthritis relief was just a pill or a cream away. Her hair was almost completely gray now, worn short in a nondescript style. *Hm.*

My mind began to plot. I could take her to a beauty shop tomorrow and get her hair done. Then we'd pick up Amanda and go to lunch, "just us girls." Though maybe it would be too expensive to do both.

*Invest in your relationship, Jodi. What's money for?*

"CLOSE YOUR EYES, GRANDPA!" Amanda hollered into the house the next day, after our Girls Day Out. "Oh, no, I don't trust you . . . here." She waltzed to her grandfather's recliner and put her hands over his eyes as I steered Mom into the living room and stood her in the middle of the room. Then we yelled together, *"Ta-da!"*

My dad stared. Mom was as nervous as a Jack Russell terrier, but she turned around obediently, her cheeks pink. "Well," he said. "Well. It's a change, isn't it?"

*"Grandpa!"* Amanda rolled her eyes.

"Dad!" I echoed. "She's beautiful, and you know it!" A bit of a sassy cut, a rinse that lightened and brightened the gray, and a set and blow-dry had taken five years off my mom. I laughed and pecked her on the cheek. "Don't mind him. He's just afraid all the young bucks are going to start calling."

That's when I saw Denny crook his finger at me from the doorway. I followed him into the kitchen, grinning. "You like it?" I jerked my thumb back toward the living room.

Denny nodded absently and held up our cell phone. "Ben Garfield called. Ruth's water broke this morning."

"Ruth's—what? Her water broke?" My heart skipped a couple of beats. "But she's not due till Christmas! Is she . . .?"

Denny shook his head. "I don't know. Ben was scared; he called an ambulance. They've taken her to the hospital. He wasn't exactly coherent. Just kept saying, 'Pray, buddy. You gotta pray for my baby.'"

*Baby.* Singular. Probably meant Ruth. Was she in danger?

We stood in my parents' kitchen, nursing our thoughts. Mine tumbled through my head like kittens on catnip. *Ruth's water broke! This is it, then. Either she'll go into labor, or they'll have to induce it. How long will it take? Are the babies big enough? What if there are complications with the birth? Is anybody with Ben and Ruth? Has Ben called anyone else? We should be praying. They need us to be praying! Not just praying. Praying* with *them, being there for them—*

Denny and I said it aloud almost in the same instant. "We need to go home."

MY PARENTS TOOK IT PRETTY WELL, CONSIDERING. The kids didn't complain about going home so suddenly either. "In fact," I told Denny as we pulled onto the interstate an hour later, "maybe it all worked out for the best. We had a couple of days with my folks, not too long, and we'll have a couple of days at home too."

"Yeah. Except . . ." Denny's face puckered into his lost puppy look. "No turkey leftovers at home. No apple stuffing. No leftover cranberry-and-orange relish—"

"Oh, stop." I whacked his shoulder. "Feel free to roast a turkey. Make all the trimmings. Knock yourself out, kiddo."

We didn't get back to Chicago until almost eight o'clock that night. My heart was pounding as the four of us took the elevator to the second floor of the medical center. Had the babies already been born? Was everything all right? *Oh Jesus, please . . .*

To my surprise, we found Edesa Reyes curled up in a chair in the waiting room outside the maternity wing. "Jodi!" She jumped up, her delight genuine. "I am so glad you are here!" The young Honduran gave all four of us hugs, even pinched Josh's midriff and teased, "You don't look one bit fatter after your Thanksgiving dinner, *amigo.*"

Josh snorted. "You don't really want to know about our Thanksgiving dinner."

Easy. Playful. Friendly. But in my heart, I heard my son's tortured whisper: *"I love her so much, and I don't know what to do."*

I blew out a breath. Hoo boy, I needed to focus. "Is Ruth all right? Where's Ben?"

"Ben's with Ruth. Delores is too." The corners of Edesa's mouth tipped a little smile. "Good thing. Ben's kind of a wreck. The doctors waited several hours to see if contractions would start on their own, but they finally started a pitocin drip this afternoon. Couldn't risk waiting any longer. But . . ." Edesa's dark eyes clouded. "Delores says they're worried about Ruth's blood pressure. Way up. If they can't get it down, they may need to do an emergency C-section."

We settled down to wait. And pray. Yo-Yo showed up in her overalls and flopped into a chair, complaining that she'd had to wait until Pete came home to stay with his brother. "It's a blankety-blank Friday night an' ya want me ta *babysit?*" Yo-Yo mimicked Pete's rant. "'Cept he didn't say *blankety-blank*—oh, hey, Josh. Hey, Amanda."

After we'd chatted a bit, Edesa decided she'd go home since several of us were on hand now. "Ricardo has a gig tonight; José's with the kids. If Delores has to stay all night, she'd probably feel better if I stayed with them too."

"I'll take you," Josh said. "Maybe I should take Amanda home too. It could be a long night. Whaddya think—Mom? Dad? Want me to pick up Willie Wonka?"

Oh, that was smooth. But it was a good idea.

The kids left. The big, round clock ticked slowly toward ten. I'd called most of Yada Yada from the car when we finally got a good cell phone signal to make sure everyone knew the situation. Had to leave a message for Avis and Peter. Chanda was still worn out from the radiation, even had to cancel Becky's housewarming party, but told us to call her soon as we had news. Florida said she'd come soon as she could, but they were supposed to visit Chris at juvie in the morning. Stu was out of town; I decided not to leave a message. Only got Adele's answering machine. Same at the Sisulu-Smiths.

What had I expected? It was a holiday weekend.

Ben showed up in the doorway of the waiting room around eleven o'clock. The man looked like he'd been roughed up by thugs. His shirt collar was open, his silver hair hung lank and damp, his face strained. But he managed a weak smile. "What, you guys just happened to be in the neighborhood?" He pumped Denny's hand.

"How's Ruth?" we all said at once.

He sighed. "Worn out. Contractions coming hard, but not making much headway. That Delores, though, she's the best.

Blowing with Ruth, telling her what to do. Me, *ha*. Might as well be that big purple Barney. Just in the way in there."

Denny jabbed a finger at him. "Tell you what, man. Let's go grab a cup of coffee. Jodi, you'll come get us in the cafeteria if he's needed, won't you?"

So Yo-Yo and I weren't invited. Man talk. Maybe that was best. Was Ben still worried about Tay-Sachs? Had he *ever* talked to Ruth about it?

I remember looking at the clock as it pushed midnight. But I must have fallen asleep then, because the next thing I knew Delores was shaking me. "Sister Jodi! Yo-Yo! Where is Ben? We need him—quickly."

"What?" Adrenaline pumped all my systems awake. "He and Denny went to the cafeteria. What's wrong? Is Ruth OK?"

"The babies—one is vertex, but the other is breech. Ruth wants to birth them both vaginally, but the doctors don't want to risk it. Her blood pressure is high, too high. They want to do a C-section—now."


THE NEXT FEW HOURS passed in a blur. After Ben disappeared into the inner sanctum, I finally got hold of Avis, Florida, and Nony. All three showed up around two a.m., wearing sweats and no makeup. Avis pulled us all into a circle and we held hands and prayed and cried a little from sheer tiredness and frustration and—OK, I admit it—not a little fear on my part. This had been such a long, hard road for Ben and Ruth. I didn't have any fancy prayers. Just, "Oh God! Don't let anything happen to Ruth! And please bring those babies into the world safely."

And then we waited some more. "The imbecile who invented these waiting room chairs ought to spend the night in one," Florida grumbled.

At one point Yo-Yo said, "No news is good news, right?" No one answered.

I dozed again, didn't realize daylight had invaded the waiting room until I heard, "*Buenos dias!*" Delores stood in the doorway, a square, white mask hanging loosely around her neck. She was smiling. A weary smile—but a smile, reading the questions on our faces. "*Sí, sí,* Ruth is fine. She's awake. She insisted on a spinal so she could be alert during the C-section. The babies are small—barely four pounds each. But doing good. A boy!" She grinned wider. "And a girl!"

For two seconds the words hung in the air. *A boy. And a girl.*

"Praise Jesus!" Nony cried. And for half a minute, the room rang with all sorts of giddy praise as we hugged each other.

Delores cleared her throat. "Actually, I came to get the Baxters and Yo-Yo for a quick peek. We didn't know anyone else was here. But I had to grovel like a *mendigo* to get even three in."

"Wait up, now." Florida held up a hand like a crossing guard. "You gonna tell us what they named these babies?"

"Um, maybe Ruth and Ben should tell you themselves."

"Delores Enriques! If we was in high school, I'd say, girl, you better not let me catch you in the hallway or you never gonna make it to your next class!"

We were all so tired and giddy, I'm not sure if we laughed or choked. But Delores was already heading out the door, so we privileged three hustled after her. "Here." She handed us three square masks with flapping strings. "Put these on."

We tiptoed into a recovery room with a lot of machines and a partially closed curtain. We heard, "But why didn't you tell me, *bubelah?*" Ben's usual growl was muffled by a loud snort as he blew his nose. "You let me be worried sick."

"I *let* you? *Oy!* Did you ever *ask* me if my family was a Tay-Sachs carrier?—Oh, look, she's sucking her thumb. Careful, you big *nebbish.*"

I poked Denny. Did that mean Ruth *didn't* have the Tay-Sachs gene? That if those two had just *talked* about it, it would have saved Ben all that grief? Denny shrugged and rolled his eyes. I made a fist and shook it in the air. Wasn't sure if it was a pumped-up *"Yes!"* to God—or an urge to sock two stubborn old goats.

I calmed down and peeked around the curtain. Ruth, hooked up to an IV and a couple of monitors, looked up and winced. *"Ay ay ay,* look who's here. Our favorite *goyim.*" Her hair was a damp mess, her skin pale. But resting on her chest, skin to skin, were two waif-like creatures, a blue knit hat on one, pink on the other, tiny oxygen tubes taped to their red, elfin faces. I caught my breath.

*Ben and Ruth's babies.*

Yo-Yo stuck her hands in the pockets of her overalls and hunched her shoulders, as if she didn't know what to do with herself. "Hey. Guess you two are OK, since you're fussin' an' all that." Denny and I laughed.

A nurse bustled in and fiddled with the monitors, frowning. "Mrs. Garfield needs to rest."

"Rest, shmest." Ruth rolled her eyes. "They wanted to knock me out during the C-section too. What, miss my own babies' births? *Oy!* What kind of *shmegege* do they think I am?"

Ben crooked his finger at us to come closer. Ruth's eyes got soft as he reached out a leathery finger and tenderly stroked a tiny cheek under the little pink cap.

"Havah," he said softly. "My daughter. That's her name. *Havah*. It means 'life' in Hebrew." Then he chuckled. "In Yiddish it means 'little bird.'"

*Havah*. It had a hushed, musical quality to it. *How perfect*, I thought.

A tiny fist poked into the air beside the blue cap, as if not wanting to be left out. Ben touched it and the miniature fingers curled around his own. "Yitzak," he whispered. "Isaac. My son." He looked up, his eyes shining with unshed tears. "It means *laughter*."

And Ben threw back his silvery head and began to laugh.

# 44

The hospital discharged Ruth four days later but kept the babies for another three weeks until they reached a going-home weight of five pounds and had developed good sucking reflexes. I could just imagine the fuss Ruth put up. What, leave her babies?! C-section or no C-section, she was determined to breastfeed the twins, so she pumped and froze bags of breast milk and made Ben drive her to the hospital every day, where she spent ten to twelve hours holding, feeding, stroking, and singing to her babies.

"We don't have a life," Ben complained.

We just laughed at him. The man was a little crazy himself, buying two of everything. "Ben!" I told him. "You don't need two changing tables! Besides, you don't have that much room."

"Sure we need two," he said stubbornly. "What if they poop at the same time?"

The hospital must have wondered about the large "extended family" that came to see the twins. We even had our first Yada Yada meeting of December in the maternity waiting room at the hospital again—didn't actually ask permission, just showed up.

"What can they do? Ask us to leave?" Adele believed in asserting yourself; by the time the powers that be figured out what to do, you'd had your time in the sun.

So we did, and they did—ask us to leave, that is—but not before we had a chance to catch up with each other and do some quiet praising.

I'd already heard about Stu's visit to her parents, but she shared again with the other Yadas. "Thank you so much for praying, everybody. I was so nervous driving to Indianapolis that I threw up in a gas station toilet and they didn't have any soap or paper towels, so I ended up smelling like—well, you know. So I was kind of a mess when I got to my parents' house, but I told myself that's the first thing I'd do, clean myself up, calm myself down, have a sit-down talk with my parents. Then, when they opened the front door, my mom just said my name. 'Leslie!' . . ." Stu stopped, her lip quivering. Someone handed her a tissue. She pressed it against her eyes a moment, then blew her nose.

After a few moments, she tried again. "Anyway, we all just ended up crying and hugging, and they didn't even know yet how much I'd messed up."

"Don't think that daddy of the prodigal son did either," Becky said. She grinned. "See? I've been reading my Bible."

As Stu talked, I saw healing in her posture, in her voice. Her parents had cried when she told them about the abortion—the grandchild they would never have—and cried again when she told them the baby's name was David, and he was waiting for them in heaven. "I invited them to come have Christmas with me. Now that

Becky has new digs"—she grinned at her former housemate—"I've got my guestroom back."

"Speaking of Becky's digs," Yo-Yo drawled, "what happened to that housewarming we was s'posed to have? Whatchu been eatin' on, girl? Paper plates?"

Becky didn't immediately respond but looked at Chanda, who was picking at her nail polish. "Aw, Chanda, I know you didn't want me ta say anything, but . . ." Becky's face turned pink. "Last week-end, Chanda took me shopping. We bought half the stuff on my list at Target—dishes, pots an' pans, silverware—"

"Stainless flatware," Chanda sniffed. "Not'ing special."

"Special ta *me*. And she bought me a shower curtain an' towels an' sheets—all that kinda stuff. But the best thing of all was goin' ta Wickes Furniture and gettin' a real bed for Little Andy, so he don' have ta sleep on the floor when he comes on the weekend." Becky threw her hands wide. "Y'all have ta come see my place! Not all at one time, though. Ain't *that* big."

I felt humbled. God was so patient. He could use a little boy's lunch *or* a lottery windfall, as long as we let Him. *Bless Chanda, Jesus.* I wanted to hug her. Maybe later.

All the time Becky was talking, Florida had had her eyes closed and was murmuring, "Thank ya, thank ya, Jesus, yes, I thank ya . . ."

"Flo?" I ventured. "What's happening with Chris's case?" She'd better not give me that "relieved" business either. Even if God was at work, she had to be dying with her son in the detention center.

Florida just shook her head. "Jesus, Jesus, that boy sure do need some kind of miracle." Her eyes were still closed, so I wasn't sure if she was talking to us or praying. "Public defender say they wanna put *all* those boys away for maximum sentence 'cause the perp used a gun. But he didn't fire at anybody, an' he was the only one went into the station. But they sayin' Chris was in the getaway car, so he's just as guilty." Tears squeezed out of her eyes and ran unhindered down her cheeks, wetting the scar that lined the side of her face. "I jus' gotta thank Jesus for what He's gonna do, because Carl an' me, we feel like we buttin' our heads against a brick wall." She reached out and grabbed Becky Wallace's hand. "An' I thank God for Becky movin' in. Cedric an' Carla takin' to her real good—which helps a lot, frees us up to deal with this, go see Chris."

"Flo, the rest of us can help too," Adele said. "But before we pray for Florida, how 'bout you, Avis? Your girl still in the shelter?"

Avis nodded, her face a shade of sadness I hadn't seen before this whole mess with Rochelle and Dexter. "She's trying to get an order of protection. And working with a lawyer to get Dexter out of the house again so she and Conny can move back in. But . . ." She shrugged. "It's always harder if you're the one who left."

"And you and Peter?" I asked. *Yeah, right, Jodi, just barge on in where angels fear to tread.* "How's all this affecting you guys?"

Avis turned her head away, looking somewhere beyond the walls of the boxy waiting room. "We're . . . working on it. We did agree to invite Rochelle and Conny to come stay a week at Christmas." She shuddered. "Just couldn't let my babies stay in a shelter over Christmas."

So we gathered up a few more prayer requests, laid hands on Florida and Avis, and began to pray. Nony's prayer came straight out of Isaiah 61, the same scripture that meant so much at our last meeting: "Oh God, You came to free the captives and the prisoners, and bring good news to the poor. You have promised to all of us who grieve and mourn that there will be a time of the Lord's favor!"

"Yes, *yes*, Jesus!" Florida cried.

"You have promised a crown of beauty to replace the ashes of our lives! To give us joy instead of mourning, and garments of praise instead of a spirit of heaviness! Oh, thank You! Thank You, gracious God!" A chorus of ragged praise joined Nony's prayer. Nony herself seemed overcome by the scripture she'd just prayed and couldn't speak.

The door of the waiting room opened, then shut. "So quiet you are," Ruth said dryly. "They can't hear you on the first floor yet."

She still looked pregnant, though nowhere near as big as she'd been before the twins were born. But she was beaming. "As long as you're thanking the Big Guy Upstairs?—see, Yo-Yo, you've got me saying it now; irreverent she is—might as well add one more. If all goes well this week? We might be able to bring the babies home next weekend."

Ruth's eyes sparkled like the Christmas lights that decorated the nurse's station down the hallway. *If this were a movie*, I thought, *this is where the background music would swell and take over the scene.* But Ruth wasn't done.

"Home," she said again. "Home in time for Hanukkah."


THE FIRST DAY OF HANUKKAH, the Jewish Festival of Lights, was the last day of school before winter vacation. I had a couple of Jewish children in my classroom, so I asked Jessica Cohen and Caleb Levy to tell us about Hanukkah. They stood in front of the class and fidgeted.

"Um, we light a candle for eight nights—" Jessica began.

"No, first tell 'em how it got started," Caleb hissed.

"No, *you.*"

"OK." Caleb lifted his chin. "We celebrate Hanukkah to remember the rededication of the holy temple in Jerusalem back in—well, I forget the date, but a man named Judas Maccabee and his little army defeated the big Greek army that had ruined the temple. My dad says the victorious Jews wanted to light the menorah candlestick as a sign that God was back in His temple, but they could only find a little bit of oil, enough for one day. But by a miracle, the oil kept the menorah burning for eight whole days! That's why we—"

"That's why we light a new candle each night for eight days," Jessica finished. "And eat latkes and play games and get little presents. It's fun. I like Hanukkah."

Ruth seemed to think it was special that the twins were coming home on Hanukkah. Well, we should make it special. And Caleb's little report gave me an idea . . .

WE STILL HADN'T HAD ANY SNOW TO SPEAK OF—an inch one day, gone the next—but the temperature was consistently below freezing now. Denny picked up Ben and Ruth and took them to the hospital to bring the twins home Saturday afternoon. That gave us Yada Yadas time to arrive at the Garfields' home with our baby presents and Welcome Home signs and rehearse our parts.

We set the Garfields' menorah on a little table so it would shine out the front window when lit. Then we waited . . . and waited. Yo-Yo peeked through the drapes in front of the living room window. "It's already dark. How long does it take to—oh, I think I see 'em. Yep, it's your car, Jodi."

"Turn out the lights! And open the drapes. OK, now light the *Shamash*—that middle candle. Who's got the matches—Stu?" I felt a little smug about my newfound knowledge. The *Shamash* was the ninth candle in the middle of the menorah, the one that lit all the other candles.

But as Stu lit that single candle, my throat caught with a sudden revelation: the *Shamash* was like Jesus. Jesus, the Light of the World!—the One who lights up our lives and brings us out of that subtle darkness where we so easily fall prey to Satan's deceptions. *Oh Jesus!* I almost felt like crying. *Thank You for Your light! For the truth that sets us free!*

"Shh, shh," Yo-Yo hissed. We waited in the darkness. Car doors slammed. Footsteps. Then we heard Ruth say, "Ben Garfield! You left the *Shamash* burning! What, you want to burn the house down and leave us homeless?"

Stifled giggles rippled through the living room. A key turned in the lock. The door opened. Yo-Yo waited two seconds, then flipped on the light.

"Surprise!" we yelled. "Welcome home!"

Ruth, eyes big, fanned herself. "You want I should have a heart attack?"

"Keep it down, keep it down, will ya?" Ben, carrying a baby carrier with one of the twins swaddled in blankets, shook his head, but I caught a little grin as he shrugged off his coat and helped Ruth off with hers.

"We've come to light the Hanukkah candles with you," I said. "This is the second night, so we get to light two candles—one for each twin. Who was born first?"

"Ladies first!" Ruth passed the bundle in her arms to me. "Here.

You want to hold Havah, the *oldest*?" She tossed a teasing grin at Ben. "Then I can light the candle."

Did I want to hold her! I was so mesmerized by that pink little face I almost forgot what we had planned to do until I heard my Yada Yada sisters begin reciting the prayer I'd found on the Internet to accompany the lighting of the first candle:

"Blessed are You, oh Lord, our God, King of the universe, who has sanctified us with His commandments and has commanded us to kindle the Hanukkah light." Faces in all shades of skin color grinned as Ruth lit the first candle with the *Shamash*. "Blessed are You, oh Lord, our God, King of the universe, who wrought miracles for our forefathers, in those days at this season. Blessed are You, oh Lord, our God, King of the universe, who has kept us alive, sustained us, and brought us to this season!"

"And we thank You, Father God, for precious Havah," I added, pulling the blanket down so all could see the little face, her mouth making sucking motions in her sleep, "who is another miracle You have given to Ruth and Ben in this special season." I looked at Ben. "You want to light the second candle?"

Ben handed little Isaac to Denny, who looked startled and then bewildered, as if he couldn't remember how to hold a baby. Then his face lit up with an *aha*. Tucking Isaac's feet under his arm, he held the baby's head in his right hand, like a football. He looked at me and grinned.

The group again repeated the Hanukkah prayer. Denny took his cue and added, "And thank You, Lord God, for Isaac, this second miracle, healthy and whole—"

"Yes! Thank ya, Jesus!" Florida said.

"I thank You, too, Jesus," said a growly voice. Ben suddenly had to blow his nose.

I looked up, startled. Had Ben Garfield actually said, *"Thank You, Jesus"?*

"—and we thank You for the light they have brought into our lives," Denny finished. "Bless them! And make these children a blessing to all who know them."

Someone—I think it was Adele—started to sing, "This little light of mine! I'm gonna let it shine! . . ."

Probably not a traditional Hanukkah song, but it seemed appropriate right then. I looked at the faces of my Yada Yada sisters perched everywhere in the compact living room. *Oh yes, Lord Jesus, we need Your light to shine in some very dark places.*

As if reading my mind, Florida added her own verse. "Let it shine at the juvie jail—"

The rest of us jumped in lustily. "We're gonna let it shine!"

"Let it shine at Manna House—" Edesa gave Avis a squeeze.

"We're gonna let it shine!"

"Let it shine for Becky and Andy—" Yo-Yo put in.

"We're gonna let it shine!"

"Let it shine for Uptown–New Morning Church—"

"We're gonna let it shine!"

The tiny girl in my arms squirmed and made a mewing sound as more verses were added—for Mark and Nony, Hoshi's friend Sara, all our children . . . My heart filled with thanksgiving. *Thank You, Lord, for precious Havah and Isaac, Your sign of hope, of Life and Laughter.* And then the final words filled the house . . .

"Let it shine! . . . let it shine! . . . let it shine!"

# *Book Club Questions*

1. **Chanda George** is caught up in the glitter of her sudden wealth. (OK, 'fess up! Most of us have fantasized about Publishers Clearing House showing up on our doorstep with TV cameras and a big check—or a rich uncle naming us sole heir.) What would *you* do with the money if you had such a windfall? Why do you think sudden wealth is not God's usual way of meeting our needs?

2. Is **Chanda** the only Yada Yada who struggles with money issues? Who else does, and why? What money issues loom largest for you?

3. How do you react to **Peter Douglass** (Avis's new husband) telling **Rochelle** (Avis's married daughter) that she can't keep running home? If you were Avis, what would *you* do in that situation? How would you feel?

4. The issue of domestic abuse is large in our society. Why do you think women like **Rochelle** keep returning to abusive spouses? In what way might some Christian teachings create confusion about how to respond? What Christian teachings would be most helpful?

5. Do you know a kid like **Chris Hickman**—talented and has lots of potential, but making poor choices, lacking vision, and heading down a path from which there might be no return? Is

this kid on your daily prayer list? How might praying for him or her change *you*?

6. If you've put up with **Jodi** through all five books, in what ways do you see her growing from "good girl" to a real Christian woman? In what areas does she still get caught in Old Jodi responses? What "old responses" catch up with you?

7. Discuss the **lemonade stand** incident. How could something that seemed so positive have an ugly downside? What was the trap Jodi fell into? Have you ever felt "shut out" (like Denny did) in a relationship? If you are married, in what ways does this common trap play out in your own marriage?

8. What lies did **Ricardo Enriques** believe that caught him up in illegal dog fighting? Who are the people God used in his life, and how did each one contribute to Ricardo's redemption? Has God ever saved *you* "by the skin of your teeth" from the consequences of a huge mistake? (If so, take time to do some serious praising!)

9. What presumptions did both **Ruth** and **Ben Garfield** bring to their surprise, late-in-life pregnancy? How did these presumptions create misunderstanding and miscommunication? What common presumptions lead to misunderstanding and miscommunication in your own family? What can you do about it?

10. **Uptown Community Church** and **New Morning Christian Church** have taken the plunge and merged their congregations. What do you think the benefits of such a merger could be? What might be the pitfalls, in spite of good intentions? Does this fictional merger seem too idealistic? Just plain foolish? Wouldn't be interested? Give you hope? Challenge you?

11. Read John **8:31–32** in several translations. What are the conditions for "knowing the truth"? How does God's truth make us free? What does this scripture mean to you? What is one way you can apply this scripture to your own life situation?

12. When **Becky** is offered a job at Bagel Bakery but would have to work Sundays (Little Andy's visitation day), she struggles with "half-answered prayers." What about you? Has God answered some of *your* prayers only "halfway"? Share some prayer journeys and what God has shown you (or not!) along the way.

13. The Yada Yadas had a **"house blessing"** for both Florida's and Chanda's new homes. Have you ever experienced a house blessing? In what way might it be significant for you and your home—or the home of someone else in your book club?

14. When **Stu** finally decided to suck up the courage to visit her parents at Thanksgiving, in spite of years of no contact, she said, *"If I don't invest anything in my relationship with my parents, it's going to die."* Are there relationships in your family that

are withering and about to die from neglect? What are the obstacles to investing in these relationships? Can you pray together about this?

For more information about *The Yada Yada Prayer Group* novels or to contact author Neta Jackson, go to www.daveneta.com.

# *Find out how the*
# *Yada Yada Story begins . . .*

I almost didn't go to the Chicago Women's Conference—after all, being thrown together with 500 strangers wasn't exactly my "comfort zone." But I would be rooming with my boss, Avis, and I hoped that I might make a friend or two.

When Avis and I were assigned to a prayer group of 12 women, I wasn't sure what to think. There was Flo, an outspoken ex-drug addict; Ruth, a Messianic Jew who could smother-mother you to death; and Yo-Yo, who wasn't even a Christian! Not to mention women from Jamaica, Honduras, South Africa—practically a mini-United Nations. We certainly didn't have much in common.

But something happened that weekend to make us realize we had to hang together. So "the Yada Yada Prayer Group" decided to keep praying for each other via e-mail. Our personal struggles and requests soon got too intense for cyberspace, so we decided to meet together every other Sunday night.

Talk about a rock tumbler!—knocking off each other's rough edges, learning to laugh and cry along the way. But when I faced the biggest crisis of my life, God used my newfound girlfriends to help teach me—Jodi Baxter, longtime Christian "good girl"—what it means to be just a sinner saved by grace.

**THE YADA YADA PRAYER GROUP**

ISBN 1-59145-074-8

# BOOK 2

# When they get shaken up, The Yada Yada Prayer Group Gets Down

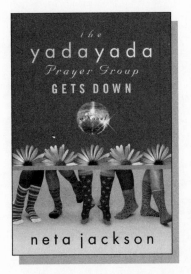

I had never felt so violated! The Yada Yada Prayer Group was "gettin' down" with God in prayer and praise one night when a heroin-crazed woman barged into my house, demanded our valuables and threatened us with a 10-inch knife—a knife that drew blood.

We wondered if we'd ever get back to normal after this terrifying experience. I assumed we would (although "normal" doesn't usually describe the 12 of us mismatched women anyway). After all, we'd been through a lot already as spiritual sisters. This was just one more hurdle to conquer, right?

But then a well-meaning gesture suddenly incited a backlash of anger in the group, forcing us to confront generations of racial division, pain and distrust—and stretching our friendships to the limit. Initially I thought, Surely I, Jodi "Good Girl" Baxter, am not responsible for other people's sins—am I? But a shocking confrontation in my third-grade classroom forced me to face my own accountability, and God used the Yada Yada Prayer Group (and my own husband, of all people) to show me what true forgiveness really is.

**THE YADA YADA PRAYER GROUP GETS DOWN**
ISBN 1-59145-151-5

AVAILABLE WHEREVER BOOKS ARE SOLD

# BOOK 3

# God gives the Yada Yadas a crash-course in forgiveness

After all that we Yadas have been through in the past eight months, I told God I could sure use a little "dull and boring" in the new year! That was before Ms. Perfect herself—Leslie "Stu" Stewart—moved upstairs in the same two-flat as us Baxters. And before Delores Enriques' son wanted to throw my Amanda a party for her 15th birthday, Mexican style. And before Avis—*our* Avis—started being courted by a man we don't even know!

I guess I should have realized that with 11 Yada sisters as diverse as a bag of Jelly Bellies, life would always be unpredictable. At least Bandana Woman, who held up our Yada Yada Prayer Group at knifepoint last fall, was safely locked up in prison . . . or so I thought. We visited her, like the Bible says; even sent her something for Christmas. But then she ends up back in our face. I mean, how far is forgiveness supposed to go?

All I know is that the longer we Yadas pray together, the more real things are getting, not only with each other but with God. Dull and boring? Not a chance.

**THE YADA YADA PRAYER GROUP GETS REAL**

ISBN 1-59145-152-3

AVAILABLE WHEREVER BOOKS ARE SOLD

*The Yada Yadas got tight in the past year, but they're about to learn the real meaning of togetherness*

We'd done it: we'd taken a mismatched, diverse group of women and cobbled together a prayer group that really worked for all of us. Now that spring was here, we were celebrating our one-year anniversary—and a wedding, an early parole and two baptisms in the lake! Everything was feeling pretty great.

But it's when we're in our comfort zone that we're most likely to let our guard down. Without warning, lots of little things seemed to become big problems. With a white supremacy hate group targeting a local university, our very diversity almost became a liability. It took a vicious attack on Nony's husband to make us see that we had to get tough—and fight back together.

Oh, there are still plenty of loose ends flapping in our faces; there always will be! But now those verses about the different parts of the Body needing each other—Paul's letter to the Corinthians, I think—really mean something to the Yada Yada prayer warriors.

**THE YADA YADA PRAYER GROUP GETS TOUGH**
ISBN 1-59145-358-5

AVAILABLE WHEREVER BOOKS ARE SOLD

# *Your chance to "yada yada" with God*

A prayer journal to go with a series of fiction novels? Whoever heard of such a thing! Yet the Yada Yada Prayer Group novels have impacted thousands of lives as these rollicking prayer sisters have inspired a heart-hunger in readers to "yada" (know and be known intimately by) God and each other, and to "yadah" (give praise to) our Lord.

Now you can join author Neta Jackson on a journey that will take you even further into the three books' themes of grace, forgiveness and redemption. Each of these 60 daily devotions include an excerpt from one of the novels, Neta's personal reflections from her heart to yours, thought-provoking questions with relevant scripture and prayer guides . . . and space to respond with your own thoughts, prayers and praise.

Using this journal will not only change you, but may even ready you for the next step: your own prayer group of "Yada Yada" sisters. For Jesus said: "Where two or three are gathered together in My name, there I am in the midst of them" . . . and where Jesus is, something glorious happens!